NOW
WE HAVE
SECRETS

SECOND EDITION

OTHER WORKS BY THE AUTHOR

Poetry
Above the Mountain
Passage Through the Rockies

Digital Media
Three Gardens of Japan

NOW WE HAVE SECRETS

A novel by
W. David Smith

Through the study of secrecy,
we encounter what human beings want above all
to protect: the sacred, the intimate, the fragile, the
dangerous, and the forbidden.

—Sissela Bok, *Secrets: On the Ethics of
Concealment and Revelation*

*I am the silence of mysteries
Amongst the secret I am silent*

—*Bhagavadgita x. 38*

BRISTLECONE PEAK BOOKS
Interlaken Town, Utah

Published by Bristlecone Peak Books
bristleconepeak.org

Printed in the United States of America
following Council on Library Resources guidelines for paper.

This is a work of fiction.
Any resemblances to persons living or dead are coincidental.

ISBN 978-0-9893753-3-7
Library of Congress Control Number: 2014947797

E-EDITION ISBN 978-0-9893753-4-4

Book design by the author

Cover art: From right, 1. Sandro Botticelli, *Birth of Venus,* c.1485
Detail: Zephyr and a nymph. Galleria degli Uffizi
2. W. David Smith, *Carmel-by-the-Sea, Sunset*
3. Charles Levy, *Nagasakibomb* 4. W. David Smith, *Sawtooth Range,
North* 5. Steve Jurvetson, *Milky Way Night Sky* Detail 6. W. David
Smith, *American Lotus*
For more complete acknowledgments, see p. 389.

For Jerilyn

Her curiosity and wit, courage, companionship,
gifts of language, generosity, patience and love have made this
work possible.

Contents

I. STARTING OUT IN THE '60s

Chapter 1

BOTH ENGINES were cut to abrupt silence. The phantom vibrations buzzed on in Jim Burgess from the DC3 like a recently awakened foot. The plane itself was still, the passengers around him beginning to stir. Through the porthole window to his left where the sun reflected through a nest of scratches was a flat field of sagebrush and grass lush after rain. The charcoal stripe of runway through it led to an airport, which from the air had looked like a toy country store a child had left behind on a springtime green carpet.

This was Pasco's airstrip, over an hour's drive to the fenced edge of the Hanford nuclear reservation, southeast Washington State. Jim was to pick up his life's continuance in two suitcases his father had passed down to accompany him to his first job: "Engineer, Chemical." He was now J.A. Burgess, the next new name in the company phonebook. His pulse sounded in his ears. He had survived Berkeley's rigors, womanless, on a thin social life of quick fraternal outbursts ending in homework, with the Free Speech Movement somehow going on elsewhere. *This is life—right now, where I've ended up.* His future awaited—his to be made, opportunity at the growing point of the Atomic Age.

A small group of men in dark slacks, short-sleeved dress shirts and dark ties had gathered for the plane's emptying at the edge of the tarmac. One of them, Roy Ziegler, his first boss, was there to greet him. No one had ever done anything like that for him before. Why now? There were arrangements, a situation, a real future. He was needed here. They were willing to pay him a big salary, complete with this kind of attention.

A rusting out-of-service stairway on wheels reached behind the group upward into nowhere. It was 1967, an unusually hot day on this way to oblivion.

This is really just a trick. Something I've pulled on myself. Is it? Faked myself out so my life would start, so I could get started, is what. So here it is. So where the hell am I now?

Mr. Hansen, his high school guidance counselor, had met with him back then alone in the office next to a baking empty classroom and hallway smelling of old wood, school floor polish and teenage sweat. *Five years ago was this morning.* Seated behind the tiny polished desk of red oak, Mr. Hansen lifted up his artificial right hand, the fingers curved to touch the tip of the opposing thumb, and rested it on the top of the desk, then smoothed his tie and shirtfront with his real hand. The sun came through the tall window that opened south behind him, lighting up trapezoids on the rough plaster walls. Mr. Hansen leaned forward, his graying hair combed back and set with water like a student's, his face in a perpetual slight smile mellowing to seriousness as he talked.

"The Russian satellite is up there and beeping its challenge to the youth of America, Jim Burgess. You can be an engineer, you know. It'll be hard work, but you can do it. That's where the future is. It's easy to see that."

Burgess thus had put himself together as an engineer, guided prof-by-prof through the costly books, the problems with set solutions, step-by-step hypotheticals, his future perpetually almost here, yet perhaps never. Cal Commencement was a strange sleep with a hangover, half remembered, half daydreamed. From the five companies to which he had been recruited to work, no frat brothers knew this choice. He had tried only once to explain. The recruiter with the genteel Virginia voice never mentioned killing folks. Burgess' friends wouldn't understand. He didn't, himself. *They'll all end up in similar spots, or 'Nam,* he told himself, aghast in a soon-forgotten flash. *Because that's what there is.*

Truth was once 2 a.m. talk with the beer almost gone, but this was his life. For a moment, leaving the chapter house forever was a cut thumb with work to be done. Brothers had already crossed the Pacific. Other worlds persisted, somewhere else where they all would go someday. *Anyway, I'm not getting my ass shot off.*

Everything's right with this, Mr. Hansen would have said, himself war wounded, proud of his advice. Work would be Burgess' own entry into the new age, the door now open, the discipline mastered. "Atoms for Peace," at the core, one way or another. At least now he wouldn't be broke or drafted. *There'll be more to it than I could have seen.*

He stood up quickly to leave the plane but was forced back down, the stained seat belt still fastened across his lap. He clicked it open, his face heating up, and hustled for his new brief case from under the seat in front of him, one ear clearing as he bent toward the aisle. The plane was less than half full now and slowly emptying, men rumpled in business suits, every age of being older, standing hunched in the aisle, waiting to get out. No one had travelled beside him. He would be almost the last person to leave.

At the foot of the stairs, Roy Ziegler stepped forward from the group of men like a quarterback to call a coin flip, his hand out for shaking: "Welcome aboard, Burgess. Glad you decided to join us at Hanford."

The men were standing around each other, as if the representatives of ascending school years. Roy was 1956 grown just older, his hair the color of dark chocolate combed in a flattop with both sides longer and smoothed back, duck-tailed, barbered close over the ears, and with clothes matching—white shirt, Sunset Strip thin tie, charcoal pleated slacks and tan welted pebble-grain wingtips, almost as if off to the Senior Stomp. Class president in college two years running plus Caltech graduate school for starters, Roy was a manager with climbing room, destined for it, yet not much beyond Burgess in years.

"Those DC3s are maybe the most reliable planes ever built, however old they are," Roy said as they entered through the glass doors of the building. "That's why they're still in use. There's a lot can happen on milk runs like this."

They waited with others inside the worn terminal at the baggage claim, a sloping metal platform for receiving suitcases and shipped packages, loaded and unloaded by hand. The two didn't wait long. Burgess lifted his bags as they were delivered with others through the wall from a cart outside. He put the last momentarily on the floor to reposition his briefcase for carrying. Roy grabbed it and would have the other had Burgess not been holding it. New to the sudden attention and sense of being

13

hurried along, Burgess wondered how much indebtedness he was building up, how long the hospitality would last.

"Thanks for the help, Roy."

"The car's out in the parking lot here, second row back, and I'll get you to your apartment. Movers are bringing your household goods in soon, right? They're usually quick, considering."

"I don't have much. They could deliver it in a pickup."

Immediately outside the exit was an immaculate black 1927 Rolls-Royce Phantom I parked headlong to the curb, its high vertical chrome grille and sculpted hood ornament of a silvery stooped goddess, the 'Spirit of Ecstasy' perpetually about to fly, reflecting the sun in the hot atmosphere, as if spirited from an old British movie. Ecstasy. The car's back door was opened, a red-faced animated man in his early 40s guiding in another wearing a glossy black continental suit with a greenish cast, wind-mussed hair in patches, first off the plane. He seemed new, raw and eager, his eyes grabbing at the sights, cat nervous. Burgess breathed in, immediately trying to be relaxed.

"That's not our car. Jack Sparling's the man holding the door," Roy said, hushed but talking louder as they continued to walk away, Burgess not sure where. "That car's his baby. Brought it up here from Southern California. I can't imagine why . . . but it's his money. He's a director at one of the research labs. I don't know who he's delivering to the Project this time. It's his thing to do with dignitaries. You've got to find a way to keep it together here after hours without hanging out in bars and gradually falling apart. In addition to the car, he's black-belt judo and sometimes publishes, though everyone wonders how, security being what it is. Resourceful. Lives with his mother. She's enjoyed her maladies for years. Shares a few."

"I'm a big Corvette fan," Burgess said. "Also a family man. I'm here to get a chance to raise one. That and of course the company. I mean the company's mission is why I'm here."

"Sting Ray? Well, this is a good place to raise kids, like I said. But the work comes first when the nation's at stake. You're young, just starting out. You gotta know that now, and watch for mistakes. Don't make any yourself. Total dedication is what it takes to do well here. Long hours of it."

"As you said, without the Project, there might not be an America as we know it."

"I see it more every day. The Russians've got thousands of nuclear warheads aimed at American cities, and you can damn well bet some are aimed at us. We're building deterrence. The idea is 'massive retaliation,' and it's a serious strategy. 'Mutually assured destruction.' Unless we're called upon to strike first, of course. There is ample reason to."

'You're such a lovely audience,' Burgess thought, the latest tune suddenly in his head. *'We'd like to take you home with us . . .'*

He glanced back over his shoulder at the Rolls as they walked through the parking lot. No Spirit now, just lots of paved space and a score of parked vehicles, most beyond their warranty dates.

'. . . we'd love to take you home.'

"Here's our pool car," Roy said. "New, but I can't say yet how good it is. We get what we get here on government bids. Smells new, anyway. Better than the American Motors beasts we used to have. Ramblers. Dank cigars."

The glossy battleship-gray four-door Plymouth was missing the fantasy fins of earlier models though looked even more swept back, streamlined, with sculpted almost square tail lamps. It was new. After putting the bags in the trunk, Roy opened the driver's door, and with a single engineer's sweep bounded in and flipped open wide the passenger's side for Burgess.

"I'm a Buick man myself. Crank down your window," he said. "It's hot. I'll take time to show you some more of the town. The idea here is that lives are supposed to be as normal as possible, so the houses are as normal as possible. Laid out with a use plan, however, since the town could be built from scratch, more or less, but only with the essential materials. There's no 'other side of the tracks' here. Your apartments came later and are different from the town itself, as you saw—sets of rectangles, more modern looking. They won an architecture prize, but the pipes all froze the first year they were built anyway. Designers thought they were in San Diego. So the owners packed insulation around the pipes in the carports and framed them in. The places're okay now, but for what the metal windows let in during the dust storms. You'll want to buy a house when you can. The government just sold the last of what it had built and owned, so there's an open market these days. People call the units where you are staying the 'rabbit hutches.'"

WITHIN the hour the car pulled into a central driveway along which flat-roofed two-level apartments were arranged end-to-end like sets of stacked shoeboxes, "hutches," one unit in each cluster placed perpendicular to the others and on stilts to form carports, for five units in all. Dozens of pastel clusters lined the the driveways off the highway at parking-stall angles, each top unit trimmed with a central dark redwood painted panel.

"I'm at the hutch farthest in," Burgess said. "It's farthest from the highway and the nearest I could get to the shopping center."

"The bus to the Project stops out front as well. I guess you know the drill. I'll see you at the plant sometime before 8."

BURGESS was to give up the core of his waking life, but this time with no end in sight. He was to remain throughout the day in a vast windowless plant. PUREX was a concrete canyon building more than three football fields long. Most chemical separation processes the plant made possible went on beneath the canyon floor, in cells covered with heavy concrete "lids."

The two thick canyon walls were of heavily reinforced concrete topped by an immense crane used to transport equipment and materials the length of the canyon. All visible was concrete, metal containers for chemicals, pipe-work, processing equipment, protective enclosures, and walking space. Most operations were controlled remotely by people in protective clothing, protected again with a multitude of radiation detection devices, from whole body counters to dosimeter identification badges. Some of the action went on behind thick glass viewports with the aid of robotic arms. Mostly the processes went on unseen, behind thick concrete walls, where it was deadly radioactive.

Burgess worked in a small engineer's office up a flight of stairs and along a hallway with walls of painted concrete—white above to the ceiling, pale green below to the floor. He must do what was given him to do in a long progression of days, out of which the rest of his life might be grown, fruits of his personal Atomic Age.

Soon the first day that seemed without end shaped into a routine in which pieces of his education came together in the practical work of extracting heavy metals from the spent fuel rods of nuclear reactors in a process of many steps and enormous scale. Because he lacked a top-secret security clearance just starting out, he could only imagine the complete chain of chemical processes in detail to their end: product, byproducts, and nuclear waste. *Boom for the Bomb, molecules for research.*

Days became months of work, well back from the edge of technological discovery and the place he had once pictured for himself. He set his routine of measurements and calculations against the disorder of the world. He grew slowly more lonely, away from the university and the people he knew. He waited for the security clearance, anxious to do what needed to be done— or perhaps to be sent away. At times, he forgot to be lonely.

*   *   *

A WOMAN was obscured in the dusk outside, a silhouette beyond the screen door of his top-floor mostly empty apartment. She hesitated, a dark presence, then reached to ring the bell. Television had been noise and blurry patches of color he clicked on and off ten minutes before her arrival. Here was someone actually to talk to, maybe. Or to turn away to be alone again.

"Sorry, I don't have a wife to come to let you in," he proclaimed through the screen door. "Please come in anyway if that doesn't frighten you. I'm Jim Burgess. Now I am just 'Burgess' because I work at Hanford. Please. Who are you?"

17

"Your happiest day."

"Not much is going on in here, as usual, and you're very welcome, Happiest Day. You're selling petrochemicals for the face and body, or you can't find someone, or you want to clean my house for some coin for your rent, right?"

Then, to the silence, "I said something wrong. Sorry."

"Hello?"

In the midst of his life of concrete walls, controls, pipes, valves, gauges, formulae, slide rule calculations and invisible waste to make you jump, here was this first visit from heaven, and he had botched it. Yes? Try again.

"Please, I'm sorry."

And this could have been his new life! He had longed for a woman in his loneliness and all through college, a condition he had throttled with schoolwork until now, a continuous now, when a life might at last be possible. Starting out, no prospects.

Someone out of the vast emptiness had stepped through his doorway, guiding a black leather carrying case before her into the white room. She stood there as if in stone, looking at him. He directed her awkwardly to a daybed of big blocks of floral colors and shapes surrounded with broad black chiaroscuro lines, passable as a sofa.

She was his height, tall and tanned, with sun-streaked honey blonde hair pulled back into a thick back-braid reaching to her waist, dressed in royal blue wide-wale cord bellbottoms, light sandals, a white cotton blouse and off-white linen dress jacket. Her eyebrows were darker, as were her lips, her nose almost Grecian, sculpted and ending in a slight ball, her eyes hazel, though perhaps only in that light. She was without makeup save the shine of lipstick, and without jewelry. The scent of her was a mountain meadow after a spring shower, not perfume, for she had been walking outside and brought springtime in with her. She sat erect, on the edge of the daybed. All of Burgess' hopes suddenly thrilled him.

His vision of her filled him to the soul, for she looked like him, at him. Perhaps it was he who looked like her, were he a woman. He felt undone, unable to take his eyes off her. He broke his attention to pull out a chrome chair from the kitchen table near the doorway beneath a window, and sat on it backward, a leg on each side of and arms on the chair back, intent. Then he looked away, not wanting her to think he was staring.

Where he looked, Venetian blinds opened on a cloud-darkening sky, grass courtyard, and apartment the mirror image of his own, set at 90 degrees to the left over the carports. This is where he was, looking toward the vast empty landscape, as if toward his future. He was far from the person he had meant himself to be. That person at the moment was impossible for him to act out. He saw it in her eyes.

"I'm Kristi Miles. How did you know why I was here? I do represent ExCel products," she said, opening her case. "They are 'petrochemicals' mostly for women, but we have a line of excellent stuff for men, too. I'll show you."

Amazed at her presence, Burgess stared despite himself, listening to her talk this way until she paused, his face a blank wall.

"You must be bored senseless," he said, "having to repeat that pitch time after time."

"I'm . . . look, you do what you can. Let me finish, then we can talk."

"I'll buy some aftershave, so can we talk please now? Will you please tell me your name again? I was too surprised by your sudden arrival to catch it."

"Take the deodorant," she said. "The aftershave's too potent and the smell turns into something else in time. Some other smell. My name's just Kristi."

"I'll take the deodorant, 'Just Kristi.' The aftershave changes chemical composition with oxygen and body heat. Your word's good with me."

"Well, as I said, I'm Kristi, and I'm back from college for a few months, visiting my mother and trying to decide what to do with my life. It seems there's not much I can do. I was a psych major at the UW. My father's school. I didn't want to be a teacher, now I wish I had gone through the necessary training. I'm not the secretary type, either, and don't have the stomach for nursing. At least with this job I have someone to talk to besides Mother, and people to meet. My friends from high school are married and consumed with children or gone to live elsewhere, all of them. Do you work at one of the reactors or somewhere else?"

"Somewhere else. In the 200 Area. I'm a chemical engineer. Just graduated from Cal."

"You must be smart, then. My father was an engineer, too. Like everybody else, he couldn't ever talk about his work. At least, he didn't. I really never knew what he did, exactly. Even when finally he could talk after things had eased up, he wouldn't."

"Enforced silence becomes a habit, I guess. 'Loose lips sink ships' goes a long way, even when there are no ships around to sink. I can't say much, either. We had to sign an oath. We die if we talk, eternal damnation and all. I work at an extraction plant, PUREX, it's called. Not the bleach. The plant separates, recovers, and purifies heavy elements like plutonium and uranium from nuclear fuel from the reactors—also neptunium and thorium. Acid dissolution, solvent extraction. What we do gets delivered elsewhere, and the finished products are sent offsite eventually to make bombs or other stuff. Mostly bombs. PUREX is third generation. The first were triplets, called B, T and U. The second was REDOX. Do you know anything about this stuff?"

"No. Some. Do you want to tell me more?"

"That part's unclassified, but even what's secret is secret, how's that? Maybe that's secret, too, and I've screwed up royally. What I've said so far isn't secret, I think, since it's in the recruiting publications. What's to say? I didn't mention the big kablooey once. Hanford is huge. But if you live here, you already know that. From town it seems to occupy the entire western half of the continent. I haven't seen it all because my security clearance hasn't come through yet. It takes too long to get it—the clearance, that is. I won't see all of the Project even when I do, it seems. There's too much tied up in secrecy. Too many secrets really must impede production. Maybe that's why they loosened the rules from the old days. There have to be too many levels of management otherwise. Secrets have their own advantages, though. I can't imagine how many bomb parts this place can pop out in a year, for example, or how many it actually does. Somebody must know. Maybe the president or his secretary."

"My father really can't talk now. He's dead."

"What?"

"Sorry."

"I don't understand. I mean, did I say something wrong?"

"Just an obsession of mine to step through. Sorry. Everyone's at cross-purposes at first when they meet, if they're saying anything, aren't they? At any rate, I'm the one to be sorry. It was cancer that took him. Cancer. Working here's not worth it just to stay out of Viet Nam if that's . . ." she said to him, to his eyes, and looked downward, fast. "Maybe it is."

"I'm not . . . I'm just doing my job. American dream, food on the table, you know? People hang on to what they've got here, hard. Since you were born here, you might not have noticed. Maybe that's true everywhere, though."

"In high school we were the Bombers," she said, and then silence in silence. "Try that for hard assed."

"Sorry. I know the public lore here, but probably not much of it, and none of the private."

"My father was bright and kind," she continued. "He came back here to work at the Project during the War and met my mother. She was here almost from the start, too, but they never knew each other then. Nobody knew what was going on. First B reactor was built, and it was the saving grace of the nation. Nagasaki, August 9, 1945. The war stopped in a hurry, along with everything here, then things started again with H reactor and DR, and then C, and KE and KW jumbo reactors, mostly when I was just little. Some shut down because of warped cores and new technology. And now we have N, which produces electricity as well as plutonium. I don't know what else we have, but there's a lot of it. I've seen what N looks like. There's a model of it up town at the Science Center."

"You must know a lot more than you've begun with," Burgess said.

"No, I don't, not really. I used to want to, until a professor told me I shouldn't be an engineer. I believed him. I don't regret having studied psychology, but now I think he was maybe a liar."

"My father never pushed me at anything," she said. "Mother the realist did that. But he was always there whenever I had questions—except about what he did at the Project. All my friends were in the same situation, I'm sure. Maybe just because it was something not talked about, I always wanted to scratch at it to learn something. Like an itch. Only, maybe not now."

"Why not?"

"Look, I have to go. Let me write up your order, and I'll be back next week, when my stuff comes in for delivery."

ON THE following Tuesday Kristi delivered the stick of deodorant in a small white paper sack folded over and creased neatly with the order form stapled through the fold.

"I can't stop now," she replied to his invitation to come in, passing the sack over the threshold with a peddler's smile. "I have to deliver my orders before dark."

"That comes late here—like an extra hour."

"Only in summertime," she said, turning to go. "The shadows are getting longer. Wait 'til winter. This isn't Cal. You need a cat's eyes to see sometimes."

"Don't go yet," he said. "Let's do something together Saturday. I have a new Corvette Stingray, and I want to try it out. It has a 427, four-on-the-floor, and air conditioning. You'll like it."

"I don't know what those things are. Where shall we go?"

"I've never seen the Blue Mountains. They're close by, aren't they?"

"They only look close on maps, but they are a good place to go. Peaceful."

"Where shall I pick you up?"

"I'll come here. My mother will be too curious to have to deal with right now. See you Saturday morning?"

"How's 9 o'clock? I can't wait."

"Please wait," she replied, turning around, smiling at him, and then the door she shut between them was silent.

ON SATURDAY Kristi parked her white Toyota Corona 'college car' in Burgess' carport, out of the sun. Then they were down Jadwin Avenue south through town in the Corvette Stingray, the convertible top up and the air conditioning blowing in the vermillion-red car shaped to suggest its name, and soon were into open territory with no houses, only sagebrush and riverfront and dry farms of cut wheat. Then they were into the desert, sagebrush and sparse dry grass. And then through desert for a long time, with hills and wheat land and hay shaped to the roll and flatness of the terrain and up hillsides as high as a tractor can plant, the highway winding and stretching along.

They crossed over the Columbia River's translucent blue-gray waves on a high narrow bridge, rumbling for long seconds into Oregon. Then on southward through Pendleton's outskirts in a deep valley, and again into farmland. Not ten miles farther along they saw on the horizon before them a ridge of mountains, haze blue, and seeming almost flat on top with an undulating wash of foothills, the frontmost in colors of sun-bleached straw.

The roadway ran straight, getting a start up a hill, then turned sharply to the right upward and disappeared a third of the way along behind a foothill once barely visible in the distance. Soon the car began to pull them upward through turns, switchbacks and basalt road-cuts five, six miles. The car tested his senses, the steering wheel alive with the road and new again because he wasn't driving alone. This being was alongside him, at last not just a wish or dream but alive. He was new to himself somehow, tight throated. He was silent with the hope she didn't notice this strangeness. He looked at her in glances, but had to watch the road. She was so new. Now she was out driving with him. What could he make happen? He felt too self-aware, awkward. Here he was, suddenly on the edge of his own destiny, his to choose, with only a slight dull ache at the rest of his world.

Because of the wind, the engine and air conditioning noise, and his hapless state, they had difficulty talking. He couldn't hear all she was saying, and the sun and wind interfered, the car over-heating. At the top of a steep hill after several switchbacks, he pulled over at a view cutout alongside the empty bleached asphalt roadway.

He was surprised at how high they had climbed. He saw green fields in broad perspective, set in fields of mown straw way off to the horizon with a tip of distant hill showing over the gently curved landscape as if it were asleep there like a stretched-out cat, everything much smaller than he knew it was, against the long flat stretch of valley floor nearest them and mostly pale yellow. The farms were big, some having hay fields watered by giant sprinklers mounted on long sections of elevated and mobile irrigation pipes, too distant now to be seen.

Kristi and Burgess couldn't see the peaks of the Blue Mountains because of the steepness of the foothills and climb of the road. The top of the hills just started happening past the signs for Poverty Flat Road, Old Emigrant Hill Road, then on past the Deadman Pass exit. The mix of pines emerged scattered through the grass alongside the roadway first small, then much larger and more rugged, until a dense forest surrounded them—ponderosa, lodge-pole pine, Douglas and grand fir, Engelmann spruce and western larch.

"We'll be exploring," Burgess said. "Something new."

"I came here once with my family. I'll show you where to go, if I can remember."

"Let's find somewhere where we won't run into anybody. "

"That's a pretty safe bet, up here. The city this isn't. We probably won't see a soul, no matter where we go."

"Have you noticed that we look alike? I mean, our physical appearance?"

"I noticed. I wondered if you had. We're probably nothing at all alike, as such things happen. There's no destiny thing for anybody, so far as I can tell. It will be fun to discover how we are different, even if we don't have much in common. Don't you think? The ways we are alike will be a bonus. But you're from California and I'm from atom country, and we might not be like each other at all. Luck of the draw, you know?"

"Yeh. I keep hoping you like lunchbag engineers."

In the deepest part of the forest, past Emigrant Springs, a half-hour without a sighting through thick trees, Kristi inhaled quickly and said, "I can't find the place I'm looking for. Nothing's the way I remember it except for the quantity of trees. We're probably over the summit and starting down the other side. Why don't we just pull off on a road into the pines, only don't go very far in. This is embarrassing. No civilization, and I have to go, if you know what I mean. Coffee and the long drive. I don't want us to get lost. We can become lost out here, you know."

"We'll find separate bushes to duck behind. Or I'll be the lookout, better yet. The car's overheating some. We should give it a chance to cool down. We have arrived."

Well along an unpaved fire road, Burgess pulled into a small clearing to his right, and, with some back-and-forth maneuvering, turned the car around so that it was facing the exit onto the roadbed leading to the highway. Thick evergreens and deciduous shrubs created a barrier and wall of privacy, save for the roadway that got them there.

AT THE clearing's edge, their conversation came easier: family, university, work, books. They were leaning against almost barkless ponderosa logs that had blown down long ago and bleached gray, one log crossed atop two others. A great stand of black huckleberry bushes seemed to disappear behind ponderosa clustered down a slope southward, framing a bed of kinnikinnick and pine needles at their feet.

The two shared a wedge of sunlight, facing the side of the car not 15 feet away. A loud vehicle approached out of the quiet day and grew louder, though they couldn't see it through the trees. Then a powdery white '53 Ford pickup truck with a bull nose and down-turned spotlights cracked suddenly from the right through the trees along the roadway followed by billowing dust. The truck stopped short in front of Burgess' car, within kicking distance. The dust that followed reached over both vehicles and hung around them. Kristi's left hand slapped down hard on his right and held on.

"It's okay, just somebody lost," he told her. "Getting back's easy from here."

"You watch him," she whispered.

The driver's side door of the truck opened with a rusty squawk, and a man dressed in camouflage green fatigues and shirt stepped over the running board to the ground. His shoes were not army issue, but like cowboy boots that lace up, bleached and dusted to an almost uniform beige above the sole.

"He's got a gun," Kristi said, squeezing the top of Burgess' hand.

Burgess glanced at the man's outstretched arm and the hand-gun pointed at him.

"Stop where you are," the man said in a tinny cracking voice, and then he took a few steps toward them ending in a slight gunslinger's stance, pelvis thrust forward. He stared at them and spit in the dust quick, returning to his staring. They raised their hands shoulder high, a movie holdup.

"What you want?" Burgess said, fearing his car was soon to be gone, leaving them stranded. Or his wallet. He looked around, trying to find some way of defending himself.

"Don't you never mind what I want; you're going to find out soon enough," the man said. He walked around the Corvette counter-clockwise, glancing in quickly as if looking for something. He scanned around them, down the roadway and into un-caring trees.

"What you fuckin' hippies doing out here in the woods all alone with a Stingray?" he said.

"We're not ... "

"Shut up," he said, then paused a moment, as if thinking.

"Don't have one of those. Well, you folks happened by at just the right time. I was thinking about something. Did all morning. You two are going to get me off. Now ... take ... your ... clothes ... off, slow."

"What? Just a ...." Burgess began, but an explosion, a bullet smashed into the branches of trees behind him.

"Do what he says," Kristi whispered. "Get him to go."

"Quiet. Just do it," the man said. "Both of you. You, lady girl. Especially you. I want to see what you got, you being rich folks."

They finish undressing at the same time, their summer clothes draped apart over the fallen trees, their useless underwear last. She only glanced at Burgess, both embarrassed and scared, shaking, looking at the ground at his bare feet. Burgess looked down at her naked body, shaded, marked amber and white by spots of sun through the almost motionless trees, then glanced at the man, who had managed with one hand to get himself unzipped and exposed.

"Ut! Don't look at me again or I'll kill you. I need your listening-only attention here, pilgrims," he said, clearing his throat. "Are you listening? Don't look, now. That's what I do. Both of you get down on your knees, close together. You're going to screw each other that way, just like kneeling down to pray.

"Do it or I'll shoot her in the head and blow your balls off just for fun. You will have killed each other as sure as if you pulled the trigger yourselves, which I'll make it look like you done. Now I want to see some serious fuckin' goin' on. I know you been practicin' for this. Show it goin' in. Then do it kinda' fast-like. Now!"

They paused, and then seemed to fall awkwardly together, their hands reaching the ground to kneel down, bodies at angles, then kneeling up, into each other's arms, foreign, as if in a strange dream.

27

"Havin' trouble git'n it up? Don't, not now. I ain't."

"Do it to me, please. He'll kill us," Kristi said, touching him on the side, her shaking fingers ice.

They fumbled, awkward. She whispered, "Closer." She took hold of him, thrust her hips forward, and gasped. They seemed to drift back and forth together, moving for a moment like trees whirling in the sun, kneeling in a twisted reverie, their hearts fast, throats and mouths dry, in flashes unaware of the man sharing this strange act.

"Faster," the man shouted.

And then all too aware. *How long has my life been to end this way?*

EYES AVERTED, they heard another bullet, this time against metal and a blown tire, and a racing motor and tires throwing dirt, almost all at once, and turned to see the truck speeding backward in the dusty air out of sight down the lane, then stop and speed off, leaving them alone. They pushed apart, gently, then got up, knees imprinted with pine needles and dirt. They brushed themselves off and dressed in silence, unwilling, unable to speak. There was blood, but they were scarcely aware of it.

Silence. Then Burgess:

"Did you see the license number?"

"No."

"I've hurt you. I'm sorry.

"I don't know what to do about it. I'll have to put on the spare tire in order for us to get home. It hurt me, a little, but I'm okay now.

Silence.

"Please you be okay, too, if that's possible."

"Please don't talk."

IN THEIR EARS there was the hushed breeze and the beating of their hearts—then only the sound of the car, driving back through contorted time. When they were at his apartment and away from the sounds of the car and the town, so quiet all the way back, neither of them knew what to say or how to say it, until Kristi whispered, "I'm going home now.

"Please don't tell anyone about this, ever.

"I don't know if I can see you again.

"Please don't call me."

Chapter 2

CHEATGRASS GETS its growing done early, comes to seed, then dies, a bleached yellow windswept in the desert sun, spreading its seed while other plants are still young. Kristi remembered that from her father. Thus the bunch grass all but vanished. It had fed the black-tailed and mule deer, prong-horned antelope, big-horned sheep, elk, and the horses of the Wanapum in the river valleys. Domestic sheep brought cheatgrass seed in their wool as they overgrazed where the Wanapum, sharing and trading with other tribes, once could seek their food. And there were cous and skolkol, Indian carrot and Indian potatoes, flowers, huckleberries, sweet currants, chokecherries, and serviceberries, with black pine lichen and more. There were salmon.

General William Jackson Palmer said, "Why do we offer so much? Because our Great Father told us to take care of his red people," with a treaty of 1858 to set up a reservation after three years of Great Father's war on the tribes. The Wanapum did not sign, but what did it count? The land that should not be given away was taken, parcel by parcel. White Bluffs, the rivers, and miles of plateau would soon be open to homesteads, irrigation companies, and the raiload, all gotten, relinquished, and gotten again with struggle. You could take the desolation or the desolation could take you. To fail was to leave or to die.

In 1868, Isaiah Miles took a wife after the cattle drives to British Columbia played out with the mining claims, leaving him stranded in White Bluffs to try homesteading. They were young, he two years on the trail, she watching the drives from afar. She danced with her people, but her being wondered after new ways. She fell in love in late summer during the salmon-fishing months. Isaiah found her by the water. She ran away to him after a season, suddenly, and claimed her will. They made it through a bitter cold first winter, fumbling to trade language in the long nights in a small homestead cabin, and she saved him in spring with what she could gather from the earth. She was Kristi's great grandmother. This is the way Kristi imagined that it happened, dreamed from what was passed down or made up, explanations against the vast unknown. It wasn't much to go by. Kristi could never visit where they had lived, but it is nearby, behind fences.

This story may be to you like a Wanapum tale: First there was Shuwapsa, back before the waves of white people, over 200 years ago, who had the power of dreams and reverenced the old ways and cared for Mother Earth, like the Sahaptian speakers before him, and in a time of legendary abundance told what was to come. Then Smohalla the Dreamer was born when the awful vision was being fulfilled, and in his young man's vision quest on a sacred mountain Smohalla saw that his people had lost the shape of their lives as they lost the old ways, and the white man had violated life and would violate it, with sickness and war and slashing the land. Smohalla foretold the great quake of 1872 as Mother Earth's anger, and that his people should keep to the old ways, and prepare to meet the dead, alive again in the heart of the Mother Earth. The ghosts speak through the sounds of the river.

IN 1943 the Great Father needed abundant clear water on a big land of 560 square miles with rail access and electric power and a geology to sustain and withstand another vision, with a device that would put an end to the dying of the next generation in an all-consuming war. That was the thought, though at first it was a race with the Germans for the Bomb. For the U.S. government, the land would be bargained for, purchased, and, when all else failed, condemned: towns, open range, homesteads, all and the river. For the Wanapum came relocation, willingly but with a revelation new people would not understand, near the ancient settlement of Pna.

*　　　*　　　*

"PLEASE SEE me again," Burgess said for the first time not a week after their first encounter when he was overcome with concern and loneliness for her. She waited a silent moment on the phone, and then quietly hung up.

A wave of loss passed through him, then retreated but remained, part of a persistent anxiety. It was with him at work and in his moments of thought when alone. She would never know his drive through the Blue Mountain territory, looking for an old white Ford truck, first with rage and an absurd souvenir Colt .44 handgun, then with anxiety and dread that he would never be able to face himself again, regardless of what he did.

He did see her again because the town was small and they couldn't help but run into one another. She avoided him, though, whenever she saw his car or caught a glimpse of him. But there were times she couldn't help it. The library was a wood frame structure of a single story, government issue but with an odd trapezoidal roof over the front door, flat horizontally over the walkway, after the style of the '50s proclaiming modernity, retrofitted from a military building.

The tall checkout desk, varnished so many times it had darkened to amber, was to the left inside the double entry doors. Two librarians, both women, were behind the desk. The heavier in a gray floral cotton dress and almost-white hair worked at an old Underwood behind an old oak desk; the other, slender and pale with black curly hair and thin though slightly puffy chapped lips, stood at the counter. Kristi handed a half-open copy of Joyce the color of the sea to her to be stamped, when Burgess came in. Kristi glanced at him; their eyes caught, and she turned away suddenly.

"Hello, Kristi," he said to her, coming too close.

"You stay away from me," she replied so only he could hear, turning back to her task, head down. In a harsh whisper: "I'll cut your nuts."

He paused, shocked, and hurried past the circular desks of a dozen or so readers and into the stacks.

"Did something happen between you two?" the librarian whispered later, her face inquisitive, concerned.

"I scarcely know him, so no, Jane," Kristi said.

"Okay, Kristi. But your faces say differently. He seemed like a nice guy to me. He comes in here, sometimes. His name is Jim Burgess. He's new," the librarian said, handing Kristi her book. "Also, available. You *startled* him."

32

I WILL not cry, Kristi remembered thinking. She had told herself that, coming back from the Blue Mountains and their first time out together, but neither could she talk. She had no control of her voice, so she sat silent while Burgess tried to say something, polite conversation to reestablish their world, then he, too, fell silent. She thought she wanted to talk, but emotion choked her.

"Nothing has happened," she said to herself. "Dissociate." She tried to give him a muffled good-bye inside the car as it pulled up in the parking lot near her Toyota that day, and then she began to drive home alone. That was her intention, but she couldn't let her mother see her like that. So she drove until her composure came back, and she could go home and shower and clean up, the water as hot as she could stand, then cold.

"T HAT BURGESS person called again," her mother said. "He seemed anxious about something. He asked if you were all right. Are you?"

"Yes, Mother, I'm fine," Kristi said. "We just went for a drive. It was too long and hot. Flat tire. That's what happened Saturday. If he calls again, please, I don't want to talk to him. Okay?"

"Yes. Is everything really okay?"

"I'm a big girl now. Everything has to be okay."

That, too, was her memory, there in a heartbeat. She remembered it for weeks. She remembered swirling there, knees gritted in the dirt, naked, penetrated. She had tried to have more than memories in her life, better ones. This memory hurt her, recurring, and more, because she had tried to be someone else to herself in a lie. The visit to the Blue Mountains didn't happen, really, and the more she told herself that, the deeper the act possessed her. She was enraged.

I have to be rid of this obsession, she told herself, and busied about the house. She had to be honest. That's what she had decided about herself. *What if things had been normal, I had known Burgess a long time, and we were alone? Why couldn't it be like, as if we were lovers? Things started well with us. I was beginning to feel for him, discover him. Did I like it 'no.' I keep feeling, enough of this.*

She vacuumed the living room carpet, fast. She found a galvanized bucket on the back porch closet and began to scrub the kitchen floor on her hands and knees with a bristle brush, at first with both hands pressing down, then she lingered in thought, immobile until she caught herself again.

I can scarcely think his name. Jim Burgess. Millions of Jims. Then Burgess. Could he possibly know that other creature? He said he didn't. Said he would get even with him. Who's him? Which? How can he ever? Violence, do I? From me? Who, the air . . . .

What can he be thinking? Now. It's always this time . . . .

Whatever happens, it's always this. What can he possibly think of me? What can anybody possibly think? About anything now.

"IT'S TIME you repainted the upstairs bathroom," she told her mother, who saw herself since her husband's death a strong, take-charge spirit, still secretary to a manager at a reactor—a prized job, 55 and straight-backed, tall and with hair like Kristi's but streaked with gray, thick strands which she refused to color and wore up.

"I'll be the one to do it if you help me carry in the ladder from the garage," Kristi said. "You get to choose the color of the paint, so long as it's cheery."

"Then you should choose it. You're the one who needs cheering up. That room's too small for two to work in. And I know you will clean up after you, please."

"Don't complain, and I may roller the living room as well. The heat vents are growing dark wings from the furnace."

"Don't you complain then, or you'll have the job whether you want it or not."

34

"Since you trust me with the color, I'll go get the paint for the bathroom right now. There are left-over tiles in the garage I can use to match things up."

"Make it lighter than the tile. The tile's too dark. I wish you could change that instead."

"You must have changed your mind about it. Dad did such a good job putting it in, I couldn't possibly get it off the wall."

"Just thinking out loud. If I could change it, I wouldn't. Pick whatever color you like. How's about a pale, pale yellow?"

KRISTI SCANNED the parking lot for Burgess' car at Miller's Hardware and Garden, a low building with a ranch-style porch having deep green support posts and crowded with hanging plants. She pulled in, thinking, "How do I hide this car?" She would just have to take a risk. She wasn't giving up her life. She would go look over the outside plants first.

Jason Miller was watering trays of crimson and white bachelor button starts with a light green garden hose equipped with a brass sprayer the circumference of a baseball, dribbling the water methodically along the rows, a two-year-old attached to the left leg of his worn tan canvas overalls, to his, "Careful, son, I don't want to knock you over."

She was looking through a sloped tray of light pastel paint sample cards along an aisle, a piece of coffee-with-cream ceramic tile in her left hand aligned with some samples.

From behind her right ear, Burgess' voice: "Hi, Kristi. I thought I saw your car in the parking lot. It looks as if you've got a project going."

She jumped, nearly dropping the tile.

"Hi," she said back with a forced 'nothing's happened' smile.

"Why isn't this just normal? I'm painting a bathroom, as you can probably guess."

"What color are you going to paint it?" he asked, breathlessly. "I'm pretty good with a paint brush."

"I'm sorry, Burgess. I guess I'm not ready for this yet," and she started to walk away, her hands empty.

"Don't leave then. I will," Burgess said. "You still have to pick your paint. I didn't mean to upset you. Just think about seeing me sometime when we can be alone, maybe for my sake, if not yours. But for yours, too. I know you won't attack me, really. I don't want you to hurt, and you obviously do. I don't want to be the source of your hurting. You don't have to answer now. Sometime. Please."

THE PAINTING went by too quickly, though her shoulders ached and her right hand cramped from striping along the masking tape around the edge of the tile wainscot, the tub, and the mirror, the vanity sink. She had been meticulous, even with shaking hands, in stretching and smoothing the tape, meticulous in painting, and was finally cleaning up, her mother away at bridge.

I have to talk to somebody about this, and I don't want to wound Mother with it. Can I talk to Burgess? Can I talk to him? Have I misjudged him? Am I hurting us both by not talking? If only he weren't so damn: what? A jerk. And how else can he reach me if he's sincere? An engineer. I've tried to avoid him, and I can't. He doesn't really know me. Then I should at least talk. It doesn't have to go beyond that. Perhaps he'll at least understand a little. I have to talk to somebody. Who else? Nobody, is who.

The lights were on, but Kristi thought she would have to give the paint a touch-up coat, as daylight was sure to reveal. She was alone again the next afternoon, the project cleaned up, she looking for something more to read in the empty house, when a call:

"Please see me," Burgess said into the black handset, standing in stripes of sunlight in his white kitchen . . . . "You're not being fair to me."

36

"You can't . . . ." She paused. She couldn't believe she was doing this.

She almost whispered, "You can't ever mention what happened in the Blue Mountains. Then I will see you."

"Please just talk to me. I'm really not so much different from you. Will you see me now?" he asked.

"Now?" she replied. "Oh, now, I can't right now. My mother, I have one, you know?"

"I tried to be as polite to her as I could. She doesn't know, does she?"

"Know? Oh, no, I could never . . . not to anyone. Are you kidding? Well, do you want to see me on Saturday, maybe? Just remember. Nothing happened, okay? We're like starting over."

"Whatever you say. Maybe we can drive along the river, if you'd like? You'll know it much better than someone still a new-comer does."

Chapter 3

"YOUR SECURITY clearance came in today," Roy Ziegler had told Burgess over the noise of the plant, Roy standing before Burgess' government-issue desk in shirt sleeves, his back to the doorway. Burgess tipped back his chair and took a breath.

"Now you can contribute more to what goes on around here. Part of your job is to know a lot and to keep me informed. We're running with a skinnier budget than we had a few years ago. Look for cost-savers when you can. No mistakes. Keep your file drawers locked now that you'll be seeing classified documents."

Burgess' colleagues were a mix of managers and engineers, fewer than a dozen, all older, all male. All knew him well before he knew them. Some had been at the Project since the first days. They shared lunchtime stories about the characters the Project had brought in and what had happened to them. ("Old Johnny got burnt out in Reclamation spraying down a used piece of equipment that looked like a green flamingo. Someone warned him but he wouldn't listen. His dosimeter badge refused to lie for him.") When he heard a woman's voice on the telephone, it would be the secretary of some manager who increasingly wanted information and wasn't always particularly friendly about the request, with the same authoritative tone of voice to which he was slowly becoming accustomed.

This is the way things get done around here, he thought. Occasionally a blue-uniformed security officer stopped by with a "Hiya" to pass the day, not always the same person, never on a predictable schedule, and always seeming to be just in the building for something else that had to be taken care of.

The operation fascinated: enormous technical accomplishment, first built with no trials to know if anything would work. It hadn't been done before it was done here. Few had even dreamed any of this possible until one day everyone read about its results in the newspapers. Results beyond comprehension. All else secret except for what it did in Japan. He saw devastation in a collection of photographs from *Life* magazine when he was 12, a woman trying to wash a paralyzed child who had a locked upward gaze, the blown up buildings and the dead, and had tried to forget them, but couldn't.

The Project went on in the mist of history, almost totally isolated from the world, cut off from what others might think. Life centered in glory—the days before War's end, then sudden victory. Burgess couldn't find himself one of them. He wasn't fully there. Perhaps when Viet Nam was over he would leave, maybe go back to graduate school. Maybe before then. It was not like the old days here: not much new being done within his purview. The Cold War preserved the plant, the jobs. Others now had the Bomb. "We are in a great battle for the souls of men," Ron had echoed. "When you go in there to fight a war, you don't hold back. Unchecked, the godless enemy doesn't. You let 'em have it. So that's what we're up to, when we're needed."

Burgess still lived the Project, what security and his age permitted, immersed in his engineering. He was not at times the person "who needs to know," he discovered. The best spot for finding things out was as an industrial engineer, who had the task of wrenching the most possible productivity out of workers. "The problem is, nobody likes you then, not even managers," someone told him. People got "burned out" from periodic overdosages of radiation, as their individual badge dosimeters revealed, and had to be reassigned to other work. It was not what he had expected, even though work was work.

It WAS in the midst of the first rush of information when Burgess had worked late into the night that he discovered the Blue Mountains and Kristi. Afterward, he needed to see her, obsessed, rehearsed what he would say to her, until the thoughts wound into a loop. He rehearsed calling her in a long chain of thoughts. He drove by her house on a curved street, a small two-story frame house identical to many others in the neighborhood, but for personal touches to say "this house is ours"— shutters or an extra porch or a recomposition of windows and a picket fence and new paint—until he became embarrassed, the houses looking back at him. He thought the neighbors recognized him, or worse, that Kristi would. The car he once had loved now blared his presence. He felt pathetic.

He worked harder, until once again he found himself thinking of her. Her mother had seemed patient and understanding over the lone phone call, and he tried to win her attention even as she was steering him away, until, long hushed, he called again. He was perhaps harassing Kristi after all. Then he could help himself no longer. She was the first time for him with a woman, for all the college talk. She led him through the insanity of what happened in a moment, then she vanished. Time was lost. He worked onward.

WHEN AT last they were together the wind was blowing hard, in gusts. It pulled at the screen door as they were leaving her house and nearly blew the car door out of his hand helping her in. The car seemed to rock and jerk as the wind shook the canvas convertible top. The trees roared. Dust gritted in their teeth.

"I've never been in anything like this," Burgess nearly shouted. "Look at the dust on the dash. It blows through everything."

"This isn't the worst I've seen. Bad enough. Want to call it a day?"

He drove without a reply through the band of bushes and trees encompassing the neighborhood as a windbreak. They could see to the northwest an immense sienna cloud half illuminated by sun. The desert seemed to have climbed into the sky. It slanted upward there and reached to the east.

"I waited too long for this. Let's see what the Columbia is doing."

THE EMPTY park was a long, thin strip of sand grass through which a narrow blacktop roadway ran parallel to the river. The grass was pale green with dust, water-starved, curved

40

and blowing in waves. Stark young locust trees rattled and bent along the water. Whitecaps rose and disappeared quickly into others on the speeding river, the water ripping to the right and southward, wide as a lake and darker than the darkest thunderhead. The car stopped perpendicular to the water on a small gravel strip.

"No boats today," Kristi said. "Just look!"

"At least we're alone here," Burgess replied, turning in his seat to face her, his right knee up and leaning against the transmission housing. "Nobody out in wind like this. All ours."

"Really—shouldn't we go back?"

"Stay a while, anyway. I worked too hard to get here. Thanks for seeing me. I keep saying that. I was worried."

"What's to worry? We got busy. "

"How is your life?"

"You know. Sell a few, sell a few. I should be doing something different."

"Like what?"

"Good question. I've been repainting Mother's house inside, bit by bit. You forget how long it takes to do something like that. No wonder craftsmen can make a living."

"Would you like to be a painter?"

"No way. It needed to be done and I needed to do something physical. I helped Dad once or twice. Long ago. The house needed a change. Wouldn't it be great to be a real painter, like Georgia O'Keefe, to see life that way?"

"Never thought of it. The closest I've gotten to a paintbrush except in elementary school is a Rapidograph."

"It's a little late for me to start painting canvases. I was pretty good with crayons and could draw my friends' faces. Sometimes they liked them."

"Where are they, now?"

"Could you talk louder? Mostly married or moved away, or both. One or two are in Seattle, where I went to college. I had a friend who died a couple of years ago. She had leukemia. I tried to do what I could to be a friend to her. She would go along, looking fine, then start having trouble. She recovered, then suddenly she was gone."

"I'm sorry to hear that."

"What about you? Where are your friends?"

"I never had anyone die. Not yet, at least so far as I know, but it's bound to happen. They're spread all over, my fraternity brothers. Blew away like dust, it seems. Some are in 'Nam. One works for a college in Idaho. Graduate school got some; others are with companies on deferments. Some are still at Cal, finishing up. One went with IBM and gets looked after as if he were family, but he's required to wear a dark suit and tie. I got a call from some bros at the house on Founders Day. I called one of them earlier, Skip Harper. I was thinking about being there instead of out here alone and working."

"You'd go back there for Founders Day?"

"No, I'm too busy really, and I couldn't spend the money on an airline ticket. I'm saving for a patch of property, maybe. I just thought about being there, you know? Basic nostalgia, but I'm really not regressive that way."

"I guess so. I never joined a sorority. Too expensive. Besides, I wanted to make my own friends, not be stuck with someone I didn't really like. It worked out."

"It seems like a long time ago for me already."

"Once I was doing something important, being a student, studying about people. I liked social psychology better than metrics and rats. Now I'm doing what I could have done if I'd never gone to college. Maybe I'll go back to graduate school and become a counselor. Women don't have a lot of options, you know. But my mother needs me right now. At least she seems to like my being here. For now, as I say. She's all I have, besides."

"Please don't be put off by this, okay? Because except for

work, thoughts of you are all I seem to have. We were such strangers. Caught in an insane moment . . . . I like your being here, too, even if I haven't seen much of you. I hope you won't go back. Not right away."

"I'm here, mostly. Shh."

"I missed seeing you and getting to know you."

"There's something we weren't going to talk about just yet, please. We're getting too close to that subject."

"It happened. It wasn't our fault."

"Nothing happened."

"Why did you refuse to see me, then?"

"Look. I wanted things to be different. The first time is supposed to be . . . something other than what it was. And there we were. I feel so awful about it. Don't you understand? I won't talk about it. It never happened. It's more than bad memories."

"Was I so awful? I mean, I hadn't done that before either. Obviously. I did try to be careful."

"That's not it. Be quiet."

"Sorry."

IN A LONG pause Kristi looked at the deep blue Columbia rushing past through her side window. The words to speak stuck together, feelings like branches broken and adrift and caught, then adrift and gone. She thought, *I must talk about this.* Along the road back, their eyes had changed in the small brief life that was all there was.

"Don't you see how it hurt? Hurt all of me. So please be quiet. Please. Not now."

"Okay. But do I love you, you see?"

"No. You don't. Can't. I'm nothing. You heard a song somewhere. I didn't sing it."

"I said that. I do love you. Why else would I be so persistent? At such a risk to my future, not to mention my ego. I never want to hurt you again. You are my obsession."

"There is no love. You don't even know me, not even in the slightest, not in the way life should mean, 'know' or 'love.'"

"I do love you. Whatever happens."

"Some people save themselves for just one person," she said. "Old fashioned of me. That possibility's gone, now. It won't come back."

"You are like my best dreams. I mean, like the 'to-cherish' dreams. Truth, no matter what."

"Shhh."

"We won't talk about it, then. I'll wait, 'til you're ready. I'm here when you want me."

THEY TRIED to talk, escape into trading lives, each concentrating to hear over the wind. They slowed and repeated themselves aloud, missing words yet sharing each other's presence. When the talking stopped after a long time, he leaned, only to brush lips.

"We should be getting back. This wind is blowing the paint off your car."

"It was a long time making it to this point. Let the paint vanish in the sand. We just got here."

She paused. Inhaled, coughed.

"We can come back, then. You've never seen the thunder boat races, have you?"

"Only heard about them. They're fast and loud."

"They're next week. The wind will have died down by then, and this place will be back to its peaceful self. If you can call crowds and boat noise peaceful. The races are about the only thing that goes on around here that isn't home grown."

THE WEEK that passed before the races was not Burgess' favorite time. Chemical samples came back from the lab wrong, by his calculation. After refiguring, he was sure of it.

"What do you mean, 'They're wrong,'" the lab manager shouted at him. "You were wrong in the first place. How long you been doing that job? You just start?"

"Come on. I can't use numbers like that. Can't you run another batch? That one's been dumped. Were the containers contaminated?"

"Not likely."

"Can you make an adjustment?"

"How?"

"You tell me. You're the lab manager."

"It isn't done. Should I call Roy Ziegler?"

"I'll call him first. I'm trying to ask you if there is a way of running the test again."

Things were not happy. Then Burgess had his first run-in with the union, an experience that sat in the pit of his stomach like a sea urchin. Wasn't he on their side? He swallowed, thought how green he still was. What else was bound to happen in a place so complex and beyond him?

"GIVE ME peace," he told Kristi on the way to the races. "Did your father ever come home angry? How did he ever put up with the bullshit?"

"I don't remember him ever showing anger about work," Kristi said. "I knew he was angry when I messed up, but he was usually . . . well, reasonable about things. He was gruff sometimes, but we always thought he was just being macho. Mostly."

"I guess that's what I've got to be. Reasonable. Gruff. The latter comes natural to me in certain situations. I'm not the one that's the problem. I'm good at what I do."

"I didn't say that you weren't."

HE MUSED through the race heats, the rooster-tail spray of the distant boats shooting high into the air, the prows of the boats knifing fast and bouncing through the wakes. He shouted with the pitched swarming noise as if he had a thousand dollars on a boat, and it felt good to shout.

During a break in the action, the two went to see the leading boat up close at dock. They walked along the crowded strip where people were standing, some starting back toward their places along the shoreline, some waiting for something to happen. The spot where they had parked on their first outing had been transformed into hot-dog stands with bluish cotton candy and chasing kids, wet, dirty and laughing, dodging through groups of people. The boat was beer-can red and big close up—far bigger than a car—with a broad bow and a cockpit like a jet fighter.

Then the races were over, except for a blaring loud speaker. Miss Budweiser had won, once again in a close race, the time, sponsors, 'drive safely,' and then the announcer stopped. Only crowd noise lingered above the sound of the river.

"We're not getting out of here anytime soon with this mob," Burgess said. "The parking lot looks to be a mess. We might as well take it easy leaving."

Kristi felt sticky, the top of her head hot, and her eyes dry and itchy behind her sunglasses. Jim's ears ached from too much noise and sun, his lips greasy. The dust from the parking lot billowed and hung in the air above the cars exiting up an embankment south to the roadway—many cars and pickups, more than would fill the town. Groups of people walked between them. Cars pulled out toward the crowd, then U-turned to the right, each in order, as if to a preordained plan that everybody seemed to know.

He watched the crowds and looked protectively toward his Corvette, covered in sandy dust, keeping it watched. He saw a white Ford truck make the turn out, a familiar face looking blankly at the crowd from the open window, then move slowly with the traffic toward the highway.

"Jeez, it's that bastard!" Burgess yelled, and started pushing his way through people toward the truck.

Kristi grabbed him by the back of his shirt collar, pulling backward until he felt the neck stretch taught against his throat. He turned back to her, bewildered.

"Stop it, Burgess! You're a damn teenager!"

He stopped, facing her, gape-jawed. She let go of the twisted shirt and began to shake, grasping her face, the people around them staring, then pushing on, some looking backward at them.

"It doesn't matter any more!" she shouted, with an astonished gasp through tears. "You can't do that here. They'll get rid of you! Of me!"

IT DID MATTER, everything mattered, as they started back home through the same aching silence as the return from the Blue Mountains. It seemed even worse.

"Please see me again," he said when he could take no more of it, his voice seeming far away.

She was slow, and articulated each word: "Don't ever do anything like that again."

"I overreacted. I just wanted to see justice."

"It's not something for you to do anything about. You'll spoil everything. I'm strong now. I can deal with it. I have lost no face that I care anything about."

"I wanted to help you. I want to help you now."

"There can be no revenge. This place has no tolerance for such things."

"I wasn't going to . . . I don't know what I was going to do."

"It isn't worth it to even try. Everything will end."

Chapter 4

AFTER MANY thoughts about being free of Burgess but also alone with scant hope for her silent self, Kristi found him at the doorway of her mother's house. It was a calm Sunday afternoon in the high 70s, and he was over for dinner by invitation, early. The house smelled of oven-steamed roast beef and vegetables, and the air was damp.

Burgess looked from the small hallway and staircase into the off-white living room, to his left, while his eyes adjusted to being inside. The thin oak staircase, in front of the door and to the right, had a simple banister that ran straight up to the second level. A small formal dining room was to the right, the table set for three with inherited silver and diamond-pattern crystal stemware, a large and small for each setting.

"Come in and sit down in the living room for just a minute while I help Mother load the table," Kristi said, gesturing toward the living room.

He sat in a deep rose wing chair to the left of the fireplace opposite the hallway so he could see when things were ready. The glossy white Italianate fireplace mantle, with a Carrara marble surround and hearth, was added after the house was built, and was the focal point of the room. A newly varnished oil painting of the Cutty Sark hung above the fireplace in a broad gold frame with a buff woven matting. A walnut spinet piano with a cross-hatched music stand, manufactured by Jesse French and bought on time, was opposite the fireplace, beneath a grouping of three family photo portraits—Kristi's father in the center, her mother to her father's right, and then Kristi, the smiling high school senior in cap and gown. A tufted sofa with high curved arms and sculpted floral patterns was at the far end of the room, and in front of it a coffee table with Duncan Pfyfe legs, all a study in respectability in the midst of a wartime nuclear town.

"This is my mother, Eileen Miles," Kristi said as they entered the doorway, mother and daughter, each dressed as if for an autumn church service. "This is Jim Burgess, the person you talked to on the phone. He says people call him Burgess at Hanford."

"Please call me Eileen. I feel I'm already getting to know you from the telephone," Eileen said. "You're a persistent young man, Jim. Burgess. Come have a seat at the table. You'll be at the head."

"Excuse me for making myself a nuisance. It was the only thing I could think of to get Kristi's attention. You both look great today."

"Isn't she a stunner? There's no one else like Kristi."

"Stop it. You're both embarrassing me. Homely people aren't stunning. Let's eat before it gets cold."

Burgess sat on the wide side of the table facing a shallow bay window, Eileen to his left. Sheer curtains framed in stiff cream-colored satin draperies diffused the southern light. He could just make out the movement of the occasional car on the street. The dinner was his first home-cooked meal in months. Even so, he was on edge, with a secret wishing itself known.

"Thanks for having me over to dinner, Mrs. Miles. By the great smell, you are a really good cook."

"It was a joint project with Kristi. She has told me about you, but I'm sure you will say something for yourself. You're from Berkeley?"

"That's where I went to school. It's been a while since I left, but I still wake up thinking I'm in the frat house back there and have to get up quick to study. I'm actually from the L.A. area. A mountain town to the northeast, near Pasadena. My father practiced law in the big city."

"Miles used to wake up with a sudden urgency about things. He always had people call him by his last name, too, but actually starting out here in his school years. I always called him that. Kristi only ever called him 'Dad.' He was just finishing up his engineering degree when he was recruited to the Project, and I met him here. This is where Uncle Sam wanted him, too, I guess, since we stuck during the war and after, up until the day he passed on. Why did you want to be an engineer? It's so much work and not much thanks."

"A guidance counselor in high school got to me," Burgess said. "Engineering seemed like important work. The time I put in has been worth it, mostly. I had to come a long way from home to get here, but now I am an engineer. This is a good first place to be. I get to work in a big company with Atomic Age promise, but I also live in a small town on the Columbia."

"I hope you like it well enough that you will call this town your home," Eileen said. "It's been ours for so long. I can't imagine living anywhere else. I'd feel swallowed up in a city. Do you have family back in Los Angeles?"

"Thanks. I actually grew up in Sierra Madre. It's in the foothills east of L.A., where *Invasion of the Body Snatchers* was filmed. The center of town was filled with pods of aliens. My father takes the Pasadena Freeway to the city every morning and said he has to dodge the aliens on the road. Then he's back late at night, with more "billable hours" as an attorney. Normal life. I never wanted to do that, myself, even if I could. I didn't want to have to defend someone just because they could pay for it, and everybody who has a lawyer wants something that demands delivery.

"I prefer knowing how stuff works and how to make something of it. People baffle me. But I'm probably not being fair to my father. We get along fine. I just never saw him much. My mother studied home economics and sort of ran the house, including us, as if to prove it. I think my parents are just glad I went to college, but they did expect it. Never 'if,' always 'when,' and with a warning. I have a brother, busy being a flower child one week and a beach boy the next. He'll be something, though, some day. I'm talking too much."

"YOU'RE FINE. Tell Mother about your car. He has a Corvette."

"It's my joy toy. I like taking care of it. Of things in general. Having things last a long time and keeping them in great condition, that's me. What I want to do, anyway. So far it's been a good car, mostly."

50

"He ordered it from Justin's Chevrolet just after he got here and had money for a down payment. Now he's saving for some property."

"For a house?" Eileen asked. "Maybe you can help me look for a car. Our old thing is starting to rattle, and the neighbors are beginning to stare."

"She's exaggerating. It's only a few years old."

"Do you two have the same car?"

"No," Eileen said. "I wouldn't have a foreign car, even if Kristi did only pay $1,200 for it."

"Really? Only that? I thought it was new."

"It might as well be," Kristi said. "It's a fun car to drive, and I like that it's little. Dad bought it for me so I could come home from college more often than I had been. Are you going to build a house on the land you are buying? You never told me."

"Yes, though frankly, I've never thought of the options. Options. A pasture. A garden nursery. A car dealership. An airplane hangar. Patch of beans."

"You're teasing," Kristi said. "What kind of house do you want to build? Something different, I hope."

"The rabbit hutches are different."

"You know what I mean. Not like the houses in town—all alike. More like the houses out along the river."

"Where some of the managers live. That's what I have my eye on, though I don't know what they cost. Probably plenty."

"I like our little house here," Eileen said. "We worked so hard for it. Did you know that Kristi painted this dining room?"

"I saw her picking out paint. Nice job."

"All things considered," Kristi said. "I did a couple of other rooms as well."

"What things considered?" Eileen asked.

"Oh, you know, just things, Mother."

"You've seemed distracted, dear. I do hope you will tell me why sometime."

"You don't want to know about it," Kristi said. "And you've tried this before. Often."

"Nonsense. I'm your mother. I deserve to know everything."

THE TALK stopped short. Burgess noticed his hands had begun to sweat.

"Don't I have that right?" Eileen asked.

"Excuse me," Kristi said, and left the table.

"I'll be. I said something wrong again. Do you know what's been eating her? Oh, you wouldn't know. I must seem to be croaking in desperation."

"She seems fine."

"Well, you don't know her yet. I've never seen her leave the table that way. Except as a child."

"Perhaps she just felt the urge."

"And that's certainly something that would not have been said in my day," she tells him. "Are you the problem? No. I just don't know what to expect of anyone these days. Look what's happening in San Francisco. It's just me, perhaps, getting old."

"You're not, Eileen. I'm sure everything will be just fine."

Eileen paused to think. She examined the table settings, rearranging the salt and pepper, then putting them back where they had been.

"I hope so. It's good to have a man at the table once again. I hope I haven't spoiled things. I just still miss Miles."

"Kristi misses him, too. He must have been quite the man."

"Yes, he was. Reliable. We could count on him. I know

people think that dead people close to them are better than anybody else. In Miles' case, he was."

KRISTI RETURNED to the table and put her napkin back on her lap. *She's smiling some, but for her eyes,* Burgess thought.

"You must still miss your father a lot."

"What? Yes, but I've missed you a lot, too. Haven't we, Mother?"

"I was just telling Burgess that it was good to have a man at the Sunday table once again. You two do look alike, have you noticed? Like brother and sister."

"I was just in the kitchen. I'm glad I could rely on Burgess at another time, too, or I would be doing the daisies with Dad right now."

"Whatever happened?"

"We met this funny man out in the woods who threatened us. But Burgess, that's him. Came to the rescue, and the nasty man ran away. No secrets from you."

"The woods are dangerous. You should stay out of them. And that's not a good answer. Where did you go?"

"Just the Blue Mountains. Where else? I was looking for a place where we went when I was younger . . . .

"I remember one place—really beautiful. We were both younger. Panoramas and thickets of trees. You couldn't stop exploring."

"I couldn't find it this time, that's all. I couldn't find it. We found the wrong thickets, instead."

"I hope you had a good time anyway, but I doubt that you did. You never answered me the first time I asked. I assumed you didn't want to talk, so I dropped the subject."

Kristi looked blank momentarily, then looked toward Burgess for words that wouldn't come.

"A time to remember. I'll never forget it."

"I won't forget it, either. Let's go in the living room. It's too hot in here."

"May I help with dishes?" Burgess asked.

"Why not play the piano for us instead? You said you did a little. We can do them later."

Burgess played three lines of Grieg's *Piano Concerto in A Minor,* an old melody in his head to render order from stress. He stumbled at midline, and again, then stopped.

"I've gotten rusty. The music's not right for now, anyway. I haven't had access to an instrument for a while. Let's talk instead. Or you really should let me help with dishes."

WHEN LATER the couple escaped for a Sunday drive, going slowly through the neighborhood streets, just to be driving, Kristi said, "This is a really bizarre beginning, isn't it?"

"Nobody else's, that's for sure. What if something like that happens all the time in some form or another, and people just didn't know how to start talking about it, so don't?"

"If we hadn't been forced, would I have been bad for you, too, that day? I just need to talk about some things, and don't know where to start. I shouldn't . . . sorry. I mean, you didn't think I was that kind of woman?"

"Can I say this? No, but forgive me, please. I would like loving you, under any circumstance. I realize it was a life-or-death situation, probably. You grabbed me and thrust me in while I was fumbling and bumbling. The experience wasn't anything I'd expected, ever in my life. I recognize we were maybe just trying to stay alive. But it was my life as well as yours. I mean, I have you to thank. I try to think it was a loving act, because perhaps it saved my life, too."

"I wondered what I would say to you if you had asked me that question," she replied. "If I ever could talk about it. Here's half an echo. I thought you were after me because that's all you would want now, if you ever really wanted me at all. The real me? I stopped existing in a way. You kept calling. Please don't be insulted. For a moment I didn't care, and then I did, all at once. Like we told Mother the truth and didn't. It was ambivalence and ambiguity loose in my brain and emotions. Like sheep moving with a sheepdog somewhere behind my eyes. Two dogs, different directions. Tired sheep, staying alive in the unknown. It's the worst. So now I can't and I can't not talk about it. I know what I said. But I needed to talk about it, thank you."

"I just wanted us together somehow."

SHE BEGAN to rub her left thigh back and forth with the palm of her open hand, fingers up, her eyes affixed to the dashboard of the car, a minute, two. She turned to catch Burgess' eyes and took a deep breath, to speak.

"I did what I did to save our lives. I didn't think of love, or feel love. You couldn't make love to me, at least at that flash of moment, and I had to act fast because of that guy. I don't want to want you. Or to have you. I think it's too late now for anything normal between us. Perhaps it was so from that very beginning for me. But later I felt I owed you something for keeping us alive, I needed someone to talk to, and I didn't know how to respond. I had no one at that point. Understand?"

HE SAT shocked, wordless, their eyes locked.

"I'm trying to respond," he said. "How shall I?"

"I tried understanding it as if it were somehow just in the nature of things. Something to work out for the best, the way things seem to in a thousand books. But how can it? I'm trying to ignore it. Or just not let it matter, to not let it get the better of me and destroy whatever might have been possible in my life."

"I understand. I'm trying to understand, without being you. Do you see? I can't tell, only I'll keep on trying, if you'll let me. What can I do?"

55

"I have to tell you this, so please let me. Most of the time, I feel so totally ambivalent. I'm saying I want a relationship with you, to get to really know you, and feel I owe it to you, if you have feelings like mine. Everything. But then, I also really don't, no relationship with anyone, ever. Things have never been this way before with me. Life was so ordinary. Now there's so much tension between us, even when you are not around. Don't you feel it, too? Sexual tension, but more than that. What should I do? What can I?"

"I'm . . . . Was I okay this afternoon? I mean, I tried not to say anything you would object to. Or that would make matters worse. I still fumble like that. I'm good with chemicals. Maybe I always will fumble. But I am trying to reach you. I can be strong for you. For us both."

"I was the one that nearly messed things up," she replied, "out of the clouds. I didn't mean to. Do you know how it is when you try too hard not to do something, and it becomes the very thing you do next? I couldn't ever keep a secret, now I'm vulnerable, and I don't want Mother to know. It would hurt her so much. And then it would be all over town, because she's truly the worst person ever at keeping personal secrets."

"I want you to know I didn't say anything. Not that there's anyone I could have told and not made a mess of it."

"Sometimes I go around thinking everyone knows about this. Then I feel naked all over again, on the edge of it all, right in front of them. It's not something I think I can be able to deal with always. But I have to."

BURGESS PUT his hands to his face a moment, removed them and exhaled. He slid his hands left to right along the steering wheel and asked:

"Should you see a counselor or something?"

"I have a degree in psychology. I shouldn't have to do that, right? At any rate, there's no one around here to help that way. I don't want to 'tell it all,' especially to a stranger."

"There is me. 'The fool on the hill.'"

"Burgess, you went through it with me, so yes. You were the instrument, so no. But you were also the victim, and I was the instrument. I don't think of you as being a fool. And I am talking to you now."

"I don't feel like a victim quite the way you must. But I still feel as if we were forced to star in someone's personal porn show."

"For some sick voyeur. I'm that way, too, the way you are. Together in something. I don't know what."

"What can we do now? You know I want to keep on seeing you. We can work things out if you give me a chance."

"Sometimes talk helps, everybody says. I had thought that that old bromide was wrong, at least for me. What are the alternatives? A glaring blank stage or shivering in the darkness."

"Or just a whole lot of anxious emptiness. That was me. So thanks. For this much. You've made me feel much less of a misfit."

"Please take me back home. I need to be alone now. Back to that point. That's how I adapted for a while. Maybe not the right way, but now I need some continuity from there. And I still have Mother to be on stage for. Perhaps in the ring with. She's not through.

"Sorry, but now you're in this with me, and I do need you. You can still get out of it, if you want. Before it's too late for us."

Chapter 5

FOR GETTING to his days at Hanford, Burgess had two options, and both took 30 miles worth of time. He could drive—across what in time cycles eons long had been the bottom of a lake that ice dams had created and destroyed repeatedly with geologic patience. Now it was sagebrush flatlands, with a narrow mountain range to the southwest and the great river reaching around chalky white bluffs in an elongated arc of 62 miles. Driving left his car hot and dusty and put miles on it, but was the only way to travel if he worked late. Since much of his work was classified, it didn't come home with him. He could also take the bus and have time to read—something he could only do before in the summers. Books were a possibility of something to share with Kristi. He couldn't keep up with her, however, as she moved beyond him in a long silent communion with the creations of the ages.

"Where do you get all those books," a bald and roundish with short arms in shirtsleeves seated next to him asked one bus ride morning. "What are you always reading so intently?"

"Mostly books from the library," Burgess replied, closing *Man's Fate* on his left index finger. "That's where they sleep on the shelves. Mostly my girlfriend comes up with them for me. It's something we can talk about with each other. They expand her world and give her new ideas, she says, but to me she really has her own bright world and ideas to live in. With. I don't have time to keep up with it all. It's interesting to try."

"I wish I could do that. After college my wife and I just sort of shut up, you know? Except for the kids. I never read much anyway outside of textbooks, which took all my waking time in college, except for labs and a part-time job."

"I never had time either, except in the summer. Some of Kristi's books are what she wanted to read in college but somehow didn't. She also does rereads. You'd never know some of that stuff exists. I can't master it all with work to be done."

"Is Kristi your wife?"

"Girlfriend. Kristi Miles? Maybe you knew her father."

"Miles? Only one around here, so far as I know, besides his missus. He's been gone a couple of years."

"He was before my time."

"I know a story about him. Probably no big secret."

"Tell me."

"He was of Indian ancestry, you know. Not all of him. Real interested in wildlife, and not just for hunting. Nature. So an old mother coyote started coming around to the plant when the lunch whistle would go off, and it became a regular thing. The coyote would wait until it got tossed a sandwich, then it would pick it up off the ground in its mouth and lope off with it, kind of sideways. She probably had pups hidden somewhere. Miles got disturbed about it and told folks not to feed her. She'd be thought a hazard because she could dig up and spread around radioactive material, and so would be shot. They didn't listen. Sure enough, two or three days later the coyote disappeared. So Miles tells somebody this story, if I can remember it right.

"COYOTE WAS hungry, as usual, so he thought he would go off gambling with Stink Bug and Eagle for something to eat. Stink Bug always had a way of never being hungry, and Eagle could find food from wherever he was, then drop in and grab it. Coyote always had to keep his wits about him to stay fed, and sometimes made his own luck at gambling.

'Jackrabbit came by. He had been out hunting, and had his bow and arrows with him.

"Come gamble with us," Coyote said to him.

"I always win," Jackrabbit said. "It wouldn't be much sport."

"Then let's have a race," Coyote said. "Put down your bow and arrows."

Jackrabbit put down his bow and arrows to get ready to race. But before the race could begin, Coyote jumped on him and ate him.

"I must have won this race," Coyote said to Stink Bug and Eagle. "You must give me your food now."

"You have already eaten my food," Eagle said, and he flew off.

"Let's have a race," Stink Bug said.

"MAYBE THAT was just something Miles made up," the man said. "I heard the real stories are secret."

"Some things happen in the human world according to the way Coyote did things. Kristi told me. The whole trick. What do you think is supposed to be secret?"

"I don't know. Same way with Hanford, don't you think? Like who knows what? Or why?"

"Built by the world's most curious people. Had to find out if they could to do it. Then why—yet to be answered, except to beat someone else at it. Maybe an open question that's never to become a real open question. 'What' seems to have worked so far."

"Strange kind of curiosity, coyotes."

ROY ZEIGLER ignited Burgess' day at work: "There's something you should know. A new leaky tank on the Tank Farms."

"Leaky tanks? Where?"

"Waste Management gets the buck again, and everyone has more to worry about. There are scores of single-wall tanks built out here starting during the war, and they've got faulty leak detectors under them—something the engineers didn't know what for. Never been done and had to be. Now we're building tanks with double steel and concrete walls to transfer and hold the radioactive waste from the leakers. Maybe a million gallons have already leaked into the ground. Nasty stuff. Makes everything ultimately temporary. Our geologist is watching it. Silence on the subject."

"What do you do about it?" Burgess asked.

"There's nothing right now except pump what's left into another tank. When you can pump it. It's just part of the huge price of things. Someday maybe we can turn the stuff into glass, if they could ever prove it would work and wouldn't break the bank. Could be decades from now. Recover what's useful of the other elements. Feasibility studies on recycling fuel rods are ongoing. This can't get to be an issue, of course. We've had to slow down production since 1964 because of politics. D.C.'s like hammered mercury on the subject."

"Waste makes that much difference?"

"If the wrong people find out, it could really curtail things. We live and die by legislative appropriations. Jackson and Magnussen have to be in action constantly. The Atomic Energy Commission's our only buffer."

"So those are the risks."

"Risks? Actually, they're only part of the paradox. If there's an incident, a single breath and you could be pushing up tumbleweeds right out here, too hot for a normal burial. Even a drop on someone's shoe could create a terrible situation. Imagine what your own shoes touch and can transfer in the course of a day. This is one of the most dangerous places on earth. With care, the safest. But there are scientists we can't convince even to come near the place. It never says that in the brochures."

"This is the most orderly place I've ever been," Burgess said. "By far."

"You'll change your mind when you're up close. One day there could be nothing but radioactive waste out here. If production stops, it could be disastrous for this part of the country. For the entire free world. We're in a unique position. So eyes always open. Think."

Burgess SQUIRMED. Roy's mouth was spit foam and white lips. Roy was his boss, and all the other layers of bosses were like him. The time when Burgess could question what he was doing had vanished with college days, replaced with work and a growing sense of doom, inevitability, enveloping even Kristi in their strange divided affair. Yet he continued to yearn for her, and the idealization of her eased his own ruminations.

She accepted this work part of his life, even when he didn't himself. He found himself drifting in music: Dylan, Beatles, Baez, the stereo turned down low in the mornings before work, in the evenings just after—slice-of-time albums from college, with nothing much new to be had that wasn't purchased somewhere too far away. He worried after his security clearance for playing them, worried about the neighbors. He hid his doubts and tried in Kristi's presence to live what a real life would be like.

"Burge, I've got deliveries tonight, and I need your help," Kristi said into the phone.

"Anything you like."

"I've got this customer I'm worried about. A single guy who stares and drools. Would you mind coming along partway on a delivery, just to make sure things stay okay?"

She guided him in his car to a parking area six apartment units farther along the street from his place and told him where to park.

"I don't need you to go in with me, just stay down here and look up at me so he can see you. Okay?"

She disappeared into the stairwell, then emerged on the second floor stairway and entry to an apartment, her legs and arms tan in a flared aqua summer dress. She rang the doorbell. The door opened just slightly. Burgess could only see hands in the dark crack of doorway accept a white sack, disappear, come back a moment later with a check, then the door closed. She smiled, waving the check to him over the railing before descending the stairs back to his car.

"I did it. Scratch him. Nothing can get rid of that smell."

She slid into the passenger seat, reached over and patted his bare arm.

"What would I do without you. Let's go back to your place."

*　　*　　*

"GLAD THAT guy wasn't me," he said, unlocking the door to let her into his apartment.

"You're not like that."

"How often do you run into guys like that?"

"Their wives are usually home."

"When did you start noticing them?"

"Men aren't all alike to me, if that's what you mean. Blue Mountain isn't any more. I keep saying. Behind us both, yes?"

"Yes."

"Well. I met someone else you might like—a couple. Just to prove I'm doing okay with this. They have a baby who is just walking. Want to go see them?"

"Now?"

"They said just to drop by. They're only two buildings down. We can return to normal for a while."

TOM HENDERSON opened the door for them into a space much like Burgess' own apartment, but furnished with an old tan overstuffed set with fat rounded arms and cushions that looked often slept on. A door at the rear of the living room opened as a walkout to an expanse of lawn reaching to another set of apartments. Tom was as thin as a marathon runner, his face somewhat pale and angular, sporting a short black beard and a front tooth that tilted slightly outward, rimmed in gold. He projected high seriousness, but with contact through pale blue eyes and a smile as if he were about to give you a humorous perspective on your mutual presence there. Jill, his wife, in a seafoam bathrobe, was just heavier with dark hair pulled back over her ears. She finished up the evening's dishes, dried her hands on a dishtowel, and walked up with a damp handshake.

"You'll have to excuse my appearance. Angie got me with her spinach. Didn't you, Little Bit?"

She leaned over to pick up the child and sat down with her on the sofa, inviting Kristi and Burgess to sit as well. Tom moved an opened book out of the overstuffed chair and sat. Angie commanded Jill's attention, finally wriggling free to the carpet.

"Tom works at the Project as a computer specialist," Kristi told Burgess.

"How do you get away with wearing a beard?' Burgess said.

"I just do it. They need me. Computer people are scarce."

"Doesn't anybody say anything?"

"Somebody always says something about everything. I'm not one to care that way. That's life since the early Greeks, and probably before that. The First Emperor of China buried its scholars alive, and I imagine them still talking, anyway. I haven't been here long, but I am still me and still here."

"How do you like it here?" Kristi asked, like a nervous host to a tourist.

"*Anicca, anatta, dukkha.* 'It's a living,' in other words. I've been reading some of the stuff Oppie read. The library here actually had that and lots more. I admire Woody Guthrie's river. There's nothing like it on Earth for character and clarity. A life model, no? I have my books and the library, which is quick to get to. There's a lot to like here."

"I wish I could swim that river," Burgess said. "But it's too fast to be much fun. You'd have a long way to walk back if the current got you. And there's nowhere that I can see where there isn't current."

"Yes, there is," Kristi replied. "It's out near the confluence, where the Columbia gets wide joining the Yakima and the Snake."

"It's there for us," Tom said. "Let's try it."

Burgess tried backing away from the idea. "Not in the day-light. I still have to work here. Apparently it's much different work from yours."

"Then let's go at night," Tom countered.

"When the moon is full," Kristi said.

"No, thanks," Jill replied. "Angie says I'll be busy."

"When the moon is full, then."

EIGHT NIGHTS later the three, minus Jill and Angie, drove off the highway down onto a sandy road in Tom's elderly Jaguar sedan, the color itself of dry sand, blending in, winding through cattails and willows on a fisherman's trail a long way, and coming to a stop with only the sound of crickets and the river. Tom turned off the headlights. They slowly began to see where they were. They took off their clothes down to swimwear and quietly got out of the car. The night was full of the moon, with deep indigo shadows and willows, ghostlike and scarcely moving, on both sides of the road. The night smelled of river, of wet sandy soil, of water grasses and fish.

They inched their way along on bare feet, Kristi first, to the sparse, flattened grass along the bank, the black water glistening with moonlight and stars, and put their rolled towels near the water's edge.

The first to be in the water, Kristi said, "It's cold, but you can handle it," crouching down, neck deep, with Burgess entering close behind her. "Don't dive, please."

"It gets deep quick," Burgess said from the water, soon out beyond her, turning shoulder-deep with his hands to face the shore. "Don't come in gradually. It's too cold and you might never make it."

Tom was still on the bank, watching.

"I'll come all at once, then," and he dove headlong into the darkness.

Burgess and Kristi turned away quickly to avoid the form overhead suddenly between them, and they were engulfed in a splash of water. Burgess slipped on the mossy boulders beneath him, struggling to stay standing but going under momentarily.

"Hey, I said no diving," Kristi shouted.

They turned back to wait for Tom to come up. He didn't. Then he did, bobbing up face down all of the sudden, moonlit, buoyant in the water, but motionless.

"Are you okay, Tom? Burge, is he okay?"

"I don't know. You okay, Tom?"

"Something's wrong. Grab him, quick!"

"Help me get him to shore. Careful he doesn't grasp on to you if he comes to. Sometimes they panic."

BURGESS ROLLED Tom face up, struggling just out of foothold with the shore until he could get Tom's unconscious head out of the water, Kristi moving out to meet him. They pulled him to the embankment, one on each arm, Burgess lifting his head to keep it out of the water.

"He'll be heavy getting out," Kristi said. "I can barely see because of the clouds all of the sudden. Be careful."

They pulled him over the bank and onto the grass.

"He's still breathing some. He didn't drown," Burgess said, trying to think out the next action quickly—artificial respiration, mouth-to-mouth, hand on stomach to make sure air went into the lungs.

"He must have hit his head on something. We're lucky we caught him when we did. What can we do?"

"Find a flashlight in the car," Burge said between breaths. "One of us goes for help."

Kristi ran, stumbling in the cloud-blotched moonlight, then ran back.

Tom's face showed yellow in the wavering beam of the flashlight, his beard and hair soaked and muddy. Then his eyes squinted and he began to cough violently, rolling away from the light, his knees bent upward. Slowly he sat up, still coughing.

"He'll be all right, now," Burgess said.

"Look at that cut above his eyebrow. It's bleeding."

"Hold the corner of a towel against it. It doesn't look too bad, but who knows. He was out cold. Let's try to get him home."

"Am I okay? I am, yes." Tom pushed away the towel, still coughing.

"You hurt your head," Kristi said, attempting to stop the bleeding. "You dived in the water and hit something. People throw stuff in the water. Is your head okay?"

"Yes, I'm sure, yes. Take me home—no hospitals."

"You have a big cut on your forehead."

"I can feel what's there. My head's okay."

"You really should see a doctor about your head. What if you have a concussion?"

"I'll see one tomorrow. I'll get patched up at home."

"We'll have to drive you there. I'm not riding with you if you drive. Where are your keys?"

No response.

"Do you remember where you put your keys?"

"Try the pocket of my pants. I don't remember."

Tom BLACKED out attempting to get up, dropping to the ground on the side of his face and shoulder. He had patches of mud and sand where he was in contact with the ground. He be-

67

came conscious within seconds, and made another attempt to stand, slower this time, up from hands and knees.

"You're covered in dirt," Kristi said. "Hold still and I'll try to clean you up. You'll track stuff into your car, and so will we."

"Never mind. It's just an old car."

They drove back shivering, their clothes wet where their swimming suits had soaked through, and they were filthy. They walked Tom shambling to the door, three dark wraiths, Tom holding a dirty towel to his head. A neighbor's door opened and closed in silence, as if a cat had been let out.

"*Dukkha*," Tom said. "'Suffering.' Never mind, I'll be fine in the morning."

"You TWO have done quite enough to help him," Jill huffed upon seeing Tom, and hurried Kristi and Burgess back outside, attempting to hide her anger. "My turn. Goodnight."

Kristi AND Burgess walked over the moonlit lawns and through the parking lots back to his apartment in silence, socks tucked in their pockets and their shoes full of dirt. They opened the door and closed it, softly.

It had been a long wait.

Chapter 6

KRISTI KEPT her self-discipline starting with a small ivory plastic wind-up alarm clock set at 6. This morning she stopped the buzzer, turned on the lamp sitting on the dark cherry Early American desk to the left of her bed, and looked at her mud-caked khaki shorts folded on a captain's chair. They'd have to be washed, along with her swimsuit, which was rinsed and on a hanger in the bathroom. She imagined arising with Burgess, making breakfast. She wandered momentarily after her imagination and got up lost in wisps of daydreams that were anything but breakfast.

Her mother was waiting for her with scrambled eggs, peppered and buttered, with toast. Kristi thought herself trapped in a replay, hungry, irresponsible, there by luck, duration unknown, but safe. *Burgess the man from destiny.* 'Well, I guess he is,' her mother would say. *Is that what she would say? She'll say something. What other future is there, I wonder?*

"Good morning. And excuse me. Are you taking precautions?" her mother said. "I saw your wet swimsuit in the bathroom. It wasn't there when you left last night, and you haven't been playing in the sprinklers."

"At least you know we didn't go skinny dipping."

"The river is dangerous, even in the daytime. You know how fast it is."

"I always try to be safe, Mother. You know that. It was just a small adventure. God knows I needed something."

"I've been young, too. No Miles, and I'm just me. Have mercy. You scare me."

"I do look after myself. You do too much for me. It ties me down, you know?"

She CALLED Jill, four, five rings.

"This is Kristi, Jill. I thought I should call in case I should maybe apologize? How's Tom?"

The line was quiet. Kristi heard a stifled sob.

"What's the matter, Jill? Is Tom okay?"

"It's nothing. Tom had a little headache this morning, and he's patched up with a bandage. I'm still being emotional about nothing."

"Is he seeing a doctor?"

"No. Of course not. Unless he concludes he wants to. I can't make him."

"Well, you're the judge. I hoped I could help."

"No, I'm not the judge. He is. And the jury. Maybe I'll hang. Maybe I'll go free. He'll do whatever he dreams up. You see, he's free. The only person I know who is."

"Look, it's none of my business. You're having troubles, and I'm of doubtful help right now. I'll call later. Or I can come over, if I can do anything."

"No troubles. Honest. None to share. Or even to make out much."

"Are you sure? Talking helps, you know? Talking about most anything."

"Nothing, and no. Do come over, though. I miss adult conversation. I'll make you coffee."

After FISHING the last damp white sock from the washing machine in the garage and tossing it into the dryer, Kristi set the timer and started the dry cycle. Seemingly as quickly she was driving northward through the neighborhood where Burgess lived as well, then she was with Jill. They stood in the doorway to the back lawn of the almost empty apartment. They sat in the morning's light breeze with the coffee poured and the baby set to exploring the thick sunny grass before them, just outside the apartment.

THEY SAT on the edge of a cement slab outside the doorway, their feet, in sandals, impressed in the edge of the lawn.

Jill said, "You and I have scarcely met, yet I seem to have known you for a long time. Maybe that's a 'should have' or 'wish I had' known you, so at least, let's pretend. I was angry last night, I know. I was worried about Tom. I always seem to be."

"He was on the bank of the river," Kristi said, "then suddenly he was a wraith overhead and in the water before we could stop him. I tried to warn him, I really did."

"I should have warned *you*, that you can't warn him. But how could I? You just have to give him his way."

"Is he happy being that way?"

"Well, usually, no. He doesn't like being directed, and that would do it. Don't bend his freedom, in other words. I'm not a lens, and I'm not a light, either."

"Jill, did you fight because of us?"

"Please, I can't say. Who knows why. Just me."

"Sorry. I didn't mean to pry. My mother's bad habit. I just thought maybe I could help. I don't know why I thought I could do that. Just a human obligation, you know? I felt responsible for having suggested we take the swim."

"Let's just say, we had an exchange. I was the mother, and he was the orphan. Which he really is, you know. Though I'm not much the mother."

"Orphan? No, I didn't know."

"Not all orphans are like him, I'm sure. Probably none, in fact. I've only met a few, ever. Neither is anybody else on the planet like him, for that matter. The orphans I've met tell you they are orphans almost as soon as they tell you their names. He

71

would never do that. He had a hard time being alive early on, I suspect, though he rarely talks about his first life, even when you ask. When he did once or twice, there was this big catharsis. When we have disagreements, sometimes it comes down to his being an orphan, but only in private. That's the illusion he creates, one of them. He's someone who knows things, and there's actually no coming down to anything in his conversation. I guess I can tell you. We live in a strange sort of cloud, the two of us. Maybe we are the cloud."

"Friends keep confidences. Cross my heart."

"There's no one else to tell, so forgive me. He was so eager to be a father, I wish I could say. Not really. He just leaves me to look after Angie. She occupies all my time. I never knew babies did that. Their clocks of consciousness are much faster than ours. She makes me feel like a tree sloth most of the time."

"Like the long-suffering wife?"

"Me suffer? No. Tom suffered. That's one way he sees things other people don't see."

"Sees like what?"

"Things about the world. For starters, like computers. What are they? Like having a job here, just because he knew how to get it and didn't hesitate. He can do anything. He just decides to do it and reads up on it. He fixes his own car. Nobody ever showed him how. He just figured it out. Sometimes he just knows something, no telling how he learned it. Like intuition. Like he has talent that figures things through in a flash. Who knows anything about computers? He does, and a lot. But he also distrusts people, all of them. What they are capable of. He distrusts situations. Sometimes he gets crazy if he sees or hears the wrong thing. So please be careful. He's more at home here than back home. Still, that's not saying much. Structure? Non-structure?"

"Sure. How did you two get together, anyway?"

KRISTI SAW an instantaneous flash of fear in Jill's eyes. In the poplar trees outside the open window three crows argued and

flew, and an old oak wave-swell mantle-piece clock on a book-
shelf chimed the three-quarter hour through the open door. Jill
waited, and so did Kristi.

"We met in Palo Alto," Jill said, "when my parents brought
him to dinner for the first time to see if I would like him. That's
what they said, but they already knew I would. I was an only
child and lonely. He was fourteen and I was thirteen, barely, and
nobody would adopt him. He was too old and too skinny and
too foreign-looking. He became my soulmate, instantly, even
through my goose-bumps unconfessed fear of him. He was so
much himself. He came with an old cardboard suitcase, which
my parents threw away despite his protest. He was home. They
said it would be unfair to put him on trial to be turned down
again for a family. As if he were a convict or a pound dog. So
adoption was right for us all."

"You are sister and brother?"

"Not now. Adoptive, you know? Used to be. We ran away
together when I became pregnant, okay? I came of age early that
way. So did he, though I always thought he'd been of age since
birth."

"But you grew up together. Attractions like that don't usually
happen."

JILL UNDID her sandals. She lifted herself closer to the
lawn and ran her bare toes through the grass, then brought her
legs back to rest her chin, her arms around her knees, and sighed.

"That's how I came to know him so well, you see?" she said.
"We did grow up together, but I loved him that very first night.
He came to my bed in the dark, when my parents were asleep,
and he touched me and touched me. It was our secret. It was beyond my words to tell, anyway. So we've been loving each other
that way since the moment I knew how it was done. He taught
me. Everything.

"We lived through the experience. It happened so fast
because he thought he would be gone the next day, so he had to
seize love . . . or anyway, seize me, that night or it would never

happen. For me, it was love like in the movies, suddenly there in my very bed. Bacall and Bogart. For my very own, a Bogart, and I was lost in the mystery of him without end. Even of I could feel his ribs when I touched him. So now you know, and I don't care anymore about secrets. Don't tell anybody this, please, or I won't like you anymore.

"We're from different countries at times, he and I. Like everybody else sometimes, I imagine. But he is so inside of me and a part of me. So now, are you still my friend? And you really won't tell anybody this, will you?"

"Yes, of course I am, and I won't, and thank you. You have helped me understand me, as well as you. "

"Me? I don't know how I did that."

"I have my own secrets, which you will know in time, I'm sure, when I can muster the courage. Do you mind if I ask you about your parents?"

"They couldn't have understood us, our secrets, our life, obviously. So we were quiet about it. He said not to tell or they would take him away again, and I'd never see him. Simple as that. Like everything else, mostly, you get used to waiting to be yourself.

"Tom never would have given up our baby for adoption, anyway, and certainly I wouldn't. They would have sent me off to Aunt LaLa for nine months. I would be forever empty armed, and Tom would be gone, probably to some place awful. He wanted to be free for both of us, the three of us. All we could do is find a new world to live in. It seemed that was all we could do. Could it ever have been nothing of the sort? So here we are."

"He could have done something much worse about your situation. Some men just disappear, you know. Do your parents know where you are?"

"They must. Tom's security clearance interviews would have made sure of it. But somehow they perhaps don't. They've left us alone, whether they know or not. I miss them, but that's the way it is. I think they've disowned us. Part of my life has vanished for the sake of the rest. Crazy, huh?"

SHE STRAIGHTENED her legs beneath a pastel blue cotton summer dress and crossed them at the ankles. She was content to be silent, having said much more than Kristi had anticipated hearing.

"What do I say now, Jill?"

"What?"

"Forgive me, my friend Jill. May I ask what was he like when you were growing up? I really can't imagine him. I have no brothers, myself. Or sisters, for that matter. Like you, in your early years."

"He came into my life just when I had left childhood for adolescence, and he always seemed to be ahead of me, helping me through what he just went through, after all our differences. I followed him in school, taking the same classes he had taken. The same teachers, the same thoughts about them."

"Did he look out for you?"

"He never had to, just because he's who he is. I think he would have, though, if he'd been challenged. I stuck up for him at times. Maybe he did me, too, and I just didn't know about it."

"Against bullies?"

"No, just the usual big talkers. He probably got teased. You know how kids are when someone's different."

"He doesn't seem so different, now, except for the beard. And in some places on the Earth there are more beards around."

"We are different. I don't have any illusions about that. I can't smooth us into normal, and probably wouldn't if I could. Everything seemed so natural and inevitable in our lives. We were paired from the day he put his suitcase on our floor."

"Didn't you ever fight, the way real siblings do?"

"It never seemed to matter to him who won. Sometimes we would play fight, just because that's what we were supposed to do, then break out laughing. He was always living in the future, when nothing then around us would matter—you know, above it all? It got him into trouble sometimes. I was forever stuck in the present. Am. One of our differences. Just call me Sancho. There are, of course, other ways we're not alike."

"Because he seemed superior or because he didn't care?"

"Both. Whichever was worse for the circumstance, it seems. When the other boys wanted to go on a camping trip, he wanted to stay at home with an important book, even when he had suggested the trip in the first place. He loved tools and anything that led him to think.

"Then he got into his computer thing. By way of number systems in math. He says he likes it because everything boils down to just zero and one, which can be the whole world, depending on how you arrange them. He took every class relating to computing, and read everything he could find, and then left school without a degree. Didn't need it.

"I loved being with him in his *Eureka!* moments. He seemed to become the core of my being even moreso, but he scarcely noticed it. He looked surprised if ever I could win his attention face to face in some silence or other. I was the zero, and he the one.

"He found this tremendous job just because he could talk himself and the company into it. He could do the work when nobody else knew how or could even guess, so here we are. The degree didn't matter to the company. It was Tom they needed. What he knew and could do. Quietly, on his own. That's the way he wanted it, and perhaps the only way there was."

"Then you do love him."

"I don't even know to say it anymore, he is so much of who I am.

"—Angie, spit that out! Excuse me, she's got something off the lawn in her mouth. I'll have to fish it out. Angie!"

IN A SWEEP she stood, bent down to Angie, stuck her finger into the child's mouth, and fished something off her tongue, then repeated the process, Angie gagging, grimacing.

"Firebugs," Jill said. "She's so fast I can't catch her. Can you imagine eating one of those things?"

"She doesn't know any better."

Jill sat back down, gathering her skirt behind her knees as she sat. She straightened it over her extended legs. A lone yellow Piper Cub plane droned on overhead, along the river to the east.

"She's his, alright. Has to sense everything, try everything. Right now, taste seems to be her favorite sense. Some bugs apparently don't taste that great."

"She's so brand new, just starting out."

"Sometimes she seems like a totally alien being, and other times I can see with her eyes, as if seeing the world for the first time. Tom gave her to me. She split me down the middle and came out of me. It's so incredible!"

"Isn't it supposed to be the other way around—the woman gives the man children?"

"She's mine. Tom said he'd look after us. He didn't have to say that."

"She's a beautiful little girl. She makes me wish for children. My mother would absolutely adore that, I think. Does your mother know about her?"

"No, I really don't think so. She never knew what was going on for a long time right under her nose. I actually left her a note that we were going away together. Didn't tell Tom about the note, no. I don't even know if she read it, or if she erased it from her mind if she did. No evidence, no world echoing back. She probably tore it up. Don't you think she could have figured things out and made it a little easier?"

"My mother would have figured it out. Before it happened.

God knows what then. Wasn't it hard, having the baby without her?"

"It was something I wanted to do myself. Perhaps I was a little bit ashamed to have her know, I don't know. Societal norms and all. I couldn't play out a pretended past any more, anyway. It was something I'd gotten myself into, liked it, and had to live it through until after the baby came. Now I don't know. Sometimes I just wish I had a mother again."

"What happens if you try to see things through her eyes? Wouldn't you want to know about your own grandchild if you were she?"

"What would she tell the neighbors? That her daughter and son did what? I don't think so yet. She always cared too much that way. Other people. I cared that they made me feel sneaky, that's all. I hated it."

"But you and Tom don't have the same genetic material. It's not an issue."

"We might as well have. Such things just aren't done in this strange world, you know? But we had our needs. Ourselves. Us! We had to live!"

"Okay. You found each other and are making your own lives."

"Our own lives. That's it. What business is it of anybody else?"

"I don't want to talk you into doing something you don't want to do. I just wondered."

"I'll think about it. We've adjusted. I don't think Tom will ever want to."

"It isn't any of my business, either."

"Tom and I have been alone together for well over a year. Living this stigma that nobody else has, or even knows about. It's nice to have someone else to talk to. Other people around here wouldn't understand such a situation."

"Sometimes it's just hard to get to know people in a place if you're new. Especially so if you're old and locked in those confines."

"Yes, and also if you're weird."

"Don't think you are weird. You risk making yourself that way if you think it. I don't think you are."

"I wish, Kristi."

"Excuse me for prying, but why would Tom object to your communicating with your mother?

"Oh, he would never say anything. He would just turn into hushed marble. Then I would know."

"Know what?"

"Know that I had hurt him. I don't need to be hurt that way."

"I don't understand why it would hurt him. Isn't that a risk you should take?"

"He takes care of me. I can't ask for more than that. I don't need him to be hurt. The world has done too much to him already without my joining them."

"What do you mean?"

"He's a very private person, Kristi. Only I can enter. And I won't say more."

KRISTI STARTED her car, backed a quarter circle, and drove toward the street from the parking area, the southern sun hot on her arm. She was bewildered, feeling both needed and rejected. She thought: *Jill needs her mother, even having passed through her time of greatest need without her. Jill is so reliant on Tom, and her own needs are not something she will even admit to having.*

Why does she think Tom would object to something so natural as a mother's love? He has no mother, save for hers. It should be a matter of convenient mother-in-law, one set of flowers on Mother's

Day, right? More? She will have to find out from Tom? How?

"My NEW friend Jill is married to her adopted orphan brother," she told her mother. "Please, do not tell anyone. I'm serious. Her mother's screwy about it. I think they're having a hard time, but she doesn't say so. They have a beautiful year-old little girl who puts everything into her mouth. Did I have to be watched all the time?"

"All the time. Her what?"

"Adopted. I know. It's hard to imagine yourself there. But that's where she is."

"Whatever were her parents thinking when they allowed that?"

"Jill and Tom ran away, sort of. Their parents don't know about Angie."

"Why ever not? She should tell them. The damage is done."

"She thinks that Tom—that's her husband—doesn't want them to know."

"Or they would have done so by now."

"I couldn't convince her that she should tell them. She didn't want me to even try."

"You only just met. There's time. I need to get my hair done. Are you serious about Burgess?"

"Mother!"

"Well, I like to know these things. Everything about you. You're my life, too."

"We're doing fine, and you like him, too, don't you?"

"I like him if you like him. You didn't answer my question."

"We've never discussed marriage, if that's what you mean. Too early. You want to have grandbabies, don't you?"

80

"Of course. Don't you want to have children? Life is so transient without them."

"Sometimes yes, sometimes no."

"You'll change your mind, once you have them."

"That's what I'm afraid of. You can't ever give them back if you find yourself wrong about having them."

"Does your friend feel that way about her child?"

"What would happen if the Bomb were ever dropped here? More likely here than anywhere else, except maybe D.C. No more children, right?"

"Where did that come from? Are you really worried about something like that?"

"It did happen somewhere, you know, and not very long ago. There was a war, and now there's a cold one. I'm sure we're sitting in the middle of a big target for the USSR, and not too far away for them to reach us, either. Anyway, what if something has already happened to us, just from living here?"

"You know how careful they are at the Project."

"What if careful doesn't count? What if everything really isn't okay out there?"

"You can't shape your life on that. Why did you come back here if you feel that way?"

"I wanted to be with you for a while, Mother, since Dad had passed on. This is home. Seattle's too far away right now."

"Are you telling me everything?" Eileen asked. "You aren't."

"That should be enough."

"What else? I can tell when you're holding something back."

"Hmm. I've been wondering a lot about that myself, you know? Just a buried feeling, maybe. I don't know how to say this. It was as if something happened here that was a piece of me I'd left behind, but I didn't know what it was. It isn't just that this is home. I was ready to move on with my life and become success-ful, as you are supposed to do after college.

"There was something pulling me here through a core of ba-sic old melancholy. Not nostalgia. As if for some reason or some thing I had to go back to, hiding here like a lost secret. Why? Something nameless was here for me somewhere. Just mine, like the end of a vision quest. I didn't know where to look for it, other than here. Like finding my future, or at least my present, and not just my fortune, either. A mystery lost in the mundane plot everybody plays out here on the surface of things."

"Well, you obviously don't mean like a husband."

"It's more like what will happen to the very deepest me and why, no matter whatever else happens. Sort of like loving some-one you don't even like, or sickness of heart, or looking back at my own death, but none of those purely. I had to be here to face it. I couldn't just dread it and let it alone, out there and always there.

"I don't know why I'm so obsessed. I try not to make it show. Like a mirror I keep trying to see into when nobody's looking. Like my own face as I've never seen it, how it really is. I don't mean to upset you, but you said you wanted to know everything.

"I can't imagine you ever feeling this way, or anybody else, for that matter. Has it ever crossed your mind? Maybe children shouldn't talk to their parents this way. What if something has already happened to me and I don't even know it, like I'm about to die or I'm already dead?"

"Please don't blame us for whatever it is you feel. We did what we thought was the right thing. Anyway, we had to make a living, and this is what fed and housed you all your life long."

"I don't blame you for anything. It's just how things are with me right now. I'm afraid to have children. I really am. What if I'm damaged because I grew up here? Chromosomes or something?

EILEEN STOOD up from the dining room table where they had been talking. She leaned forward on her hands, as if to see or hear Kristi more clearly, looking at her, eye to eye. She looked at the table between her hands and sat back down, looking away.

"Have you discussed this with Burgess, Kristi? Because if you haven't, don't. He may drop you on the spot."

"We're a different generation, you know? I'd feel close to him without having to have children. Maybe we'll be closer, because of the way children consume time. Anyway, the subject just plain hasn't come up."

"You sure know how to depress a person. You need to think kinder thoughts."

"I'm sorry. You asked."

"I don't even remember what I asked. But lots of women are afraid to have children, until they do. I was, a little. But then the decision gets made for you. You're pregnant, and there you are."

"I fear for what the children will be or will die from, not for bearing them. Horribly damaged, and I'm to blame, punished every time they look at me. But that's only part of it. Let's do talk about something else."

"Let's just say you came home for a rest after graduation and keep it simple. Maybe you are really an initiate on a vision quest."

"Some vision. You and Dad have always been the best part of being here, so let's think about that. Sorry if I suggested otherwise."

"You didn't seem damaged to me. Don't you seem that way. And now you have Burgess."

"Keep that thought."

"I have to get my hair done."

Chapter 7

BURGESS AWOKE to a loud phone ring: *it must be seri-ous—something's happened at work? His mother.* He was a front sleeper struggling to get untwisted from the sheets, trying to moisten his mouth and clear his head, the bedside phone awkward plastic in his damp stiff hand.

"Jim? This is Steve—Steve Bourne. You sleepin' this time 'night or can you talk to an old friend? You never go to bed, right? You alone?"

"Yeah, Steve, sleeping alone. Was. It's the thing to do here at 2 a.m."

"I'm just sitting here, down here in Idaho with my friend Jacky Daniel, remembering the good times. I miss 'em. Thought I'd call."

"It's a little late, Steve. Can't this wait until tomorrow? Give me your number. And call me Burgess. Burge. I'll explain."

"Remember the swamp party? Sheet plastic on the frat house floor to make a swamp, with rocks on top for walking. Leaked through the floorboards and down . . . down where the goats live, and we had to clean it up but couldn't. Too shit-faced to shine. What happened to us? You still like that, right, bro? You changed? Where in hell are you, anyway?"

"Me? Oh, I'm not doing anything. Sitting here in the rack, talking to a drunk."

"The best times were the all nighters, right? I mean there's no one around here. I'm going nuts. So I was thinking, so why not pay you a visit?"

"Are you in trouble, Steve?"

"I need to talk to someone from reality, is all. Remember 'escape into reality?' You're the only Rho Alpha within hundreds of miles. You got time for an old friend who knows the secrets?"

"I'm busy, Steve. I can't do late nights anymore. I have responsibilities like you have shadows. I can't talk long. You want to drive over here sometime when I can get free, let's do that."

"How 'bout this weekend? I'll get there around—hmm—2 on Saturday and make it back here the next day. Work sucks."

ALL ACROSS America this could be happening, Burgess thought, but not here, in the house of the ultimate death. He thought of his high school classmates who never went to college but who went to work and got married instead, or to war, who grew up too soon and not enough. Nobody ever grows up enough. The long black disorderly line at Commencement headed off to unknown places to start life. Life. Beneath the platform party were those he knew but mostly didn't, in classrooms and labs now over with, faces going away, to statehouses or companies, to the draft or more classrooms, to marry for the sake of what was done. Most just to disappear, their best years become oblivion with the toss of a mortarboard. Or they transform into the vast unknown—maybe every one of them.

Burgess' new life had gradually crowded his old from his consciousness. What had once counted for so much was simply odd and gone, something none of his coworkers had been through, to which he was sure they couldn't relate, and that he would be embarrassed to reveal.

STEVE'S LIVING-ROOM presence made Burgess feel nostalgic and at once sated, on the edge of forgetting. Brotherhood was of a time grown dim, when the sudden freedom from high school days and the new worlds of college exploded his being with pure possibility, with ready-made friendships and a life shaped with the rigors of mastering chemical engineering. He remembered his first chapter meeting when a hundred 'elite' brothers included a folk-song group back from Europe and student government leaders, athletes, scholarship winners, the "best of the university," dressed in "We are the best" coats, button-down shirts and ties for a pinning at a sorority house, the serenades, all the wondrous new life, and then homework.

He had been determined to grow himself into the brother-hood. It was expected, and he wanted to compete that way. There was a clear pathway, and he was standing on it. So here is Steve, president of the fraternity pledge class. Mr. Student Government, success without effort. Ran for a student body office, vice president, on the promise of doing nothing, and won.

"I found this job at a college in Idaho," Steve said, leaning back on the day bed, his left leg crossed at the ankle, his arms opened wide, gesturing with an open hand, fingers turned up. He wore a navy polo shirt bearing a small embroidered alligator, suntans with sockless Bass cordovan loafers—a fine-featured "golden boy" with a ready smile, a trim Ivy League haircut, tennis forearms, and slightly sun-damaged skin. "The job doesn't pay much. Beautiful country full of Martians."

"You start to miss the old days you took for granted, right?"

"Imagine me, advising students. I'm tempted to tell them, 'get out, while you still can.' Or 'get laid a lot, because you won't later on.'"

"'Tune in, turn on, and that.'"

"Not like that. Drugs haven't hit there yet, surprisingly, except among the few furry folk. The law just comes in and whisks them off unseen, and you don't ever see them again. Booze, though. Runs in the gutters."

"Tune in, throw up. It's hard to imagine you being a papa-cop, but I guess you're as good at it as anybody. Do you have to do a lot of that?"

"Only to answer complaints. Booze has been big time since the days of sepia photos. It's a part of calling yourself educated."

"'The quality of your education is directly proportional to the amount of beer consumed.' Who said that?"

"Not me. I'm just a simple practitioner," Steve protested, "not an actual philosopher. Whatever you think the world is, that ain't the case."

"Not every place can be Berkeley."

"There's no money where I am. My boss the Dean of Students is a retired army colonel, affordable because he's on pension. They're raising tuition again next year, which means more students in my office with emotional problems. I wanted to be their friend, the kindly old adviser, you know? Instead I'm the blank-stare authority figure justifying the cause. Boss Hog. The Enforcer. So I'll play the role until something happens to get me promoted or thrown out. Probably thrown out. What are you doing?"

"I can't tell you exactly. Making stuff to put into thermonuclear bombs."

"Jesus. What stuff?"

"Plutonium-239. Mme. Curie's third great find was plutonium. Mother Nature never made any that's still around on earth much, so we're helping her out."

"Jimmy, I hardly knew ya. What are you doing here? How many times over can we wipe out humanity already?"

"I'm agnostic on that subject, mostly."

"Why?"

"All I know is, we've got plutonium and there's a whole lot of inertia behind producing more. If we can destroy more upon retaliation than they can with a first strike, it keeps the Soviets from attempting it. And everything we do could stop on a dime if D.C. wants it that way. That won't happen."

"Big-time checkmate."

"I'll leave sometime, but I am starting to like it here. Scary. There's more to the Atomic Age than the Big Boom."

"Like it here? Why?"

"I keep asking myself that question. It's important for me to do things well, right? I'm a good engineer. The pay's good and I have Kristi, at least right now. The Atomic Age was born here. Whatever is likely in the future with atomic energy could happen here first. I have a chance to get in on that—maybe to lead out. Besides, Livermore didn't need me."

Steve leaned on his left elbow, then his right, uncomfortable on the day bed. He slid to the floor, new green and blue short shag carpet, his legs out, both elbows resting back on the bed, supporting him from behind. He tilted a nearly empty gold Miller's beer can side to side from the top, thinking.

"Man, you're locked in here. Why don't you do something to get thrown out?"

"Who wants to go to jail? And there are punishments worse than that."

"You need a caper, then. Think of the rush."

"You mean you need a caper so you can feel young again. It's amazing how old you can get in a year."

"You mean how old we can get."

"We, then. I feel as if I were sixty years old, except that I'm on the bottom of the management ladder, still the new guy, and the only way up is to work my ass off, play the office politics game, and stick around until I get there."

"You do need a caper. Why don't you take an atom bomb and blow up a dam or something? Like, fish gotta swim."

"You have no idea how unlikely and impossible that is. The bombs are put together somewhere else. Probably in the center of Iowa, in an ordinary corn burg impossible to find called "Middletown." What happens here always happens slowly, so far as I have evidence of, unless the politicos in the other Washington do something with the budget. Then it happens all at once."

"You could smuggle out some plutonium, then smuggle it back in, just for kicks?"

"It's been tried, at least the smuggling out part. Some guy put some in his lunch bucket and set off every alarm in the county."

"Maybe not that, then. Why don't you just leave?"

"Several reasons, most of them lame. I met this woman. That's the reason that sticks. She's coming over later on. You'll like her."

"So what about her?"

"She's got everything I need. Looks, brains, talent . . . ."

"Money."

"No money, just a lot of life. Moreover, I found her here."

"My kind of woman, if she could pay her way. What's she doing here? Sane people would have left long ago."

"She has family here—her mother. Her father died of cancer last year. Kristi's just out of college a year, too. Lone child. Going back to graduate school's her option, but who knows? She said she had to come back for a while to get some things straight with herself. You know?"

"That's why I wanted to *leave* home."

"Pretend it's like her personal journey of the soul."

"Are you part of that, too? You'd better watch out."

"I gloomified things some. I'll let her tell you herself. Her father worked here, so the place put food on her table."

"Hanford giveth, Hanford taketh. Long live Hanford," Steve said.

"I thought you'd come over here and try to convince me to leave. Instead, you seem to think my being here is okay?"

"Your life. I've given up on value judgments. Do you want me to convince you to leave? Then there'd really be none of our crowd around but me. So you just got here."

"I might never leave if I stay now. If I do go, what happens to Kristi? But she may be the one to leave."

"You don't . . . ."

Four quick rings of the doorbell: Kristi brought in the sunny out-of-doors on her face. She gave Burgess a quick kiss and met Steve. A bit breathless, she found a place on the floor near the rumpled-flower daybed.

"We were just talking about here and you," Burgess said.

"I hope not in the same breath," Kristi laughed.

"We should exchange pleasantries," Steve said. "May you have many of them."

"I was singing your wonders, Kristi. You're my salvation."

"You don't need to be saved, and you could get along quite well without me," Kristi said. "But don't try just yet. I still like you."

"Are you going to stay here?" Steve asked.

"I'm being non-directive. Non-directed. Who knows what life will bring?"

"I hope you'll stay," Burgess said. "You're good company."

"So's a dog. I'm okay here for right now. So how do you like our little town, Steve? Strange, huh?"

"I like it fine," Steve said, "though it sure is in the middle of nowhere. It's worse than Idaho."

"I love that state. Have you gone to Sun Valley and Sawtooth country?"

"Sun Valley the first chance I had. I'm in student affairs at a little college. Maybe Burgess told you."

"He said you were going stir-crazy there. I guess it's okay to repeat what he said."

"No secret. I confess."

"We were talking about having one last caper," Burgess said. "Hypothetical, purely."

"Who said so?" Steve replied.

"What's a caper?" Kristi asked.

"It's an assault on the absurd for the sake of a laugh," Burgess said. "What fraternity brothers do in the dead of night, when they're not sleeping or blowing lunch."

"But you're not in a fraternity any more. Are you?"

"Once a Rho, always a Rho," Steve said.

"An active Rho no mo," Burgess replied. "Nothing can be done by way of a caper."

But a challenge was out, an idea to be stretched until broken. What would happen if a model reactor were to disappear from the visitors' center? What if the model were to stay and experience a meltdown? Or start to play like a calliope? What if some nuclear waste were to escape, like, into the river? Already happening. What if everyone suddenly knew everything about the plant? Least likely of all: mass panic. Write graffiti in Russian. No, in Chinese; they've got the H bomb now. In both. In Arabic. Plant welcome signs in all three. 'Occupied' signs. Mail nuclear arms treaties to the staff on pink slips.

"Here's something different," Steve went on. "Let's open a ski lift on that mountain named in the honor of rattlesnakes. I saw it on a map. Or start a winery there."

"That's not a caper," Kristi said. "You want to tweek the beak of Mr. Death, don't you? Isn't that what you want? That's just an escape."

"How do you laugh," said Burgess, "when you're at the most humorless place on earth? The thing that's funny is that they've spent huge amounts of everybody's money on something sane people hope will never be used, just to have it so that someone else who's doing the same thing will stay in the same position.

"Only we want to be able to destroy them more times than they can destroy us. That's what drives us. Then if anything actually happens, we eat our own fallout and freeze in forever winter, on the odd chance we survive. Some race. And we have a good-for-10,000-years legacy of nuclear waste to prove it, regardless. Then when both sides realize what they have given up in life so they'll have the Bomb, who's going to like us then? But we go on because we have to. 'I am become death.' One of the guys who started this all said that. Called him 'Oppie.' So that's my job."

"What's the alternative?" Kristi asked. "There's no defense against an ICBM except its own degree of reliability, and the

Russians are just as fearful of us as we are of them. Right? Maybe more fearful. Paranoia isn't a very logical guidance system, no matter who owns it.

"Build defenses, assuming you can, and there will be more missiles to overcome to 'maintain deterrent strike capability.' So then the arms race becomes a race of economic systems and who has the best engineers. Maybe it has been that all along, and that's what kept my father here. Maybe the results killed him. Who knows? "

"Sometimes it seems we're in the 'spare no expense' mode," Burgess said, "and other times things get downright stingy. Then there's safety. I'll shut up, now. Fluid dynamics."

"So how do you caper around that?" Steve asked.

"You don't," Kristi said, "even if you want to. You'd be boiled alive in a waste tank. People feel threatened. No one has even tried."

"I don't know what I am anymore, except when I'm being an engineer. I need a good caper, but not these."

"This place has history, but it's all set in the future," Kristi said. "Frozen there in time when Fat Man—that's our bomb—blew up Nagasaki. I can feel it every time I come back here. It isn't just because it's home or historic or gothic or a place befitting of purgatory or worse. It's as if it were the end of the Earth insisting that this is not the end, that all will be okay, despite whatever has happened or will. Just a minute."

KRISTI STEPPED a few feet into the kitchen for a can of beer. She opened a drawer for a can opener, opened the can by punching two triangular holes on either side of the top, and returned to the chrome dinette chair on which she had been sitting. She drank a slow draft, and continued:

"This is a place that just is. Set by an invisible hand. It's where we work out the inevitability of our own deaths. Maybe that will be sooner than would otherwise be the case, just because we were here. I don't love that, but it is part of my experience that I have had to come to terms with. I'm not all the way there yet, but I'm some of the way, and maybe the path doesn't reach to the end or even have one. Perhaps the path is just chicken scratchings in the yard. Here I am. Here you are."

"So when does Jim get to leave here?" Steve asked. "Do you call him 'Burge' or 'Burgess?' You're the reason he's staying."

"Am I?" she asked Burgess. "Why leave? And who are you, 'Burge' or 'Burgess?'"

"Yes, I am both of those names. The latter is my company monaker. So why leave?"

"I don't know. For me, that's still an open question."

"It seems to have been that way from the beginning. It's as if we both are seeing what will happen. Whatever it is, trying it together beats snaking along alone."

"We're seeing what we can make of all this," Kristi replied. "Call him 'Burge.' 'Burgess' has become his company name, it's true. Did you mean anything more?"

"We should leave whenever you are ready to."

"That's enough for right now. No 'bad faith.' You can leave whenever you want. You don't owe me anything. Only, please don't leave just yet."

BURGESS HAD left the top down on his car to give Steve the ride around the block. Rain was threatening. Kristi volunteered to move the car into the carport. She needed some air anyway, and vanished down the stairs with Burgess' keys. In a moment there was a loud whistling from the parking area, then an explosion.

"Sounds serious," Steve said, grinning. "Your car?"

Chapter 8

THE LANE of roadway leading back through the sagebrush from the plant to the town darkened, brindled in the autumn evening. Burgess drove work-tired but with fewer worries, the long stretch of buses having disappeared, hours into the silence. The northern days were shorter, the low sun lighting the tops of the sagebrush, amber above the deepening stretch of shadows. Soon he would drive home in darkness.

Kristi had delayed graduate school for him, for her reading and for her own obsessive tangle of thoughts. She wished to stop the progress of her life to avoid losing the years, but it went on. The new season would change everything. Or would it just change Burgess, or perhaps her own being? *Whatever's different, now?*

In the moments she was not herself she became what she read or wished; Emma or Emma Bovary, Jake Donaghue and the Secret Sharer. She tried to lose herself in the love act; she explored each different nuance to its end and searched for something new or 'here is this, again,' in moments a disinterested act, then something merely endured, and again really loved. Sometimes it was nothing but pure sensation, thoughtless rapture. She felt a mood into being, a half-wish, like stepping out of a car to the smell of sagebrush or a sudden shower on hot pavement.

THERE WAS no rain. The Blue Mountains came back, a stilled memory at a time. And in one moment was the thought of her death, or something deeper, she thought, wordless. No salvation, but love, nonetheless. And in another, something was gone.

"Do you ever feel moody, sometimes, Burgess?" she asked when they were together on that evening, the cold breeze locked outside and the apartment room's forced-air heat running for the first time of the season and smelling of burnt dust. "Melancholic. The first glimpse of autumn. You don't seem to feel moody. You must. Everyone does sometimes, don't they?"

"Why? When did I act moody?"

"Do you feel that way?"

"I suppose so. Work. The weather. You know. Nothing worth displaying."

"Do you ever think about . . . you know . . . death?"

"What's this? That again? I'd have to think. The adrenalin jolt might have made lies of what I do remember. Stuck images with slow recovery, stuff from the margins of sleep. Whatever happened, happened. I don't dig death—just don't think about it. No point. It's not going to be poking around me for a while. Do you? You must, if you brought it up."

"Far away, the Blue Mountains are, and yet they are too close. I should have thought things still bothered you a little. I once thought only of my experience, and couldn't get into yours. I told myself, I should try. I tried. All I found was me. Selfish old me, and I wanted more. Some things people shut up about. I should."

THE BRIGHTNESS of the overhead bedroom light seemed to have washed out the time of day. She sat down on the white sheets of the bed, not tired, but it was the usual time for her to go. Burgess' book closed, and he placed it on his nightstand.

"Blue Mountains," Burgess continued from her conversation. "It's the only time I've ever had my life threatened, except maybe on the playground. It was really our lives threatened, that's the killer. Who likes being out of control that way? Or any way? Maybe somebody does, I don't know who. I do feel moody about that, sometimes, if that's what you're leading to. It didn't come to any resolution in my mind. How is it that when we think 'moody,' we never think of it in the sense of being in a good mood?"

"You're either in a good mood or you are put in a good mood or you put one on, and the same with a bad mood. When you're moody, you're not quite in a bad way but you seem to be in stasis, and you're temperamental about things at the same time. Several shades of gloom. Old Mr. Melancholy, baby."

"How much do you think about such things? A lot?"

"I never did, ever, until when I found myself away after Dad's death, and thought about home. Please forgive me. I do become obsessed occasionally with it now. Not often. It's a small black kitten that sits at my feet, waiting for me to pick it up. I always do. It scratches and writhes to be put down, and sits there again."

"Do you still feel that way, Kristi? You don't seem to."

"When I am alone, I do. Sometimes when things are quiet and there's nothing else that has my attention, those feelings creep up on me. I do have you now, so I do think about it less often. It's not a death-wish or anything like that. I don't want to say anything more about it."

S HE LIFTED her legs onto the bed, fluffed the pillow behind her, then opened a thin burnt-umber leather book from the nightstand.

"I didn't mean to be morbid, Burge. Something got it started, so I'll read it to you. *I play the tune of negation: when you die death will disclose the mystery . . . . I am drunken with desire for Non-existence, not for the existent, because the Beloved of the world of Non-existence is more faithful.* That's Rumi for you. I just wondered if everyone might be as obsessive as I am. Was. I guess not. Rumi just had some words for it."

"You don't want to be like that around Hanford. They get rid of people who are depressed. There's mystery to uncover sometimes in sorry logic, but it's still sorry logic."

"Except for that, you're my echo. You seem to be, anyway. I'm really not depressed now. At any rate, I don't work at the Project, so I'm free of having to worry about it. I guess I seem to be trying to depress you, though, so I'll shut up."

"I didn't mean to cut you off. Please discuss anything you want to with me."

"That was just how I felt then. I change a lot, I've discovered. So let's find a new subject."

"You're still not over your Dad's death, are you? That it?"

"It's not that, no. I've come to terms with Dad. The fact of death is so much bigger than any individual death, it seems at times, including mine. Maybe Death with a capitol D is really only your own, square on, times all living things. When you face it, somehow you are also forced to face life for the first time, or the fact you're walking around in a shades of gray cut-out version of it. Accept it or accept what you've made up of it?

"To live is to die." Or maybe that's reversed, and we're in the mirror, framed with our being or train of actions. That's wrenching an old thought, I know. Take where we are, for example, if Death equals more than all the specifics of death. What I wonder is, how can it?"

"Kristi, if that's how you define it."

"Or maybe you just find it somewhere, whatever it is. What if it's more than a matter of words? Like what's left when you take the words away."

"You mean like nothing. Or maybe there's a Platonic death, sort of ideal form of it? Why?"

"Okay, what if something like that's true? It seems true to me, sometimes. A transcendent death for each living thing. The energy in the universe, in contrast to bundles of minute control systems programmed to wear out and be replaced in a flash of Earth time just to keep the systems running until they don't. To be alive in our own blip of time is the most important thing, it seems. So along comes someone with a fistful of universe with some hellish contents, then someone else, and now China, then who else?"

"Hey, I'm part of that," Burgess said. "And you are, too. Just try to escape it."

"So, we all are. America, the Soviet Union—whoever's got the Big Boom. And we're so glad to have the deterrent, our very own Boomer, because life is unthinkable now without it. Less than a half-hour's delivery to any place on earth on an ICBM. Tried and tested. What's to stop it?"

"Politics? Diplomacy, maybe."

"So that's what I think about. Over 250,000 dead in Japan. I jump out of my skin and can't get back. Now, just one bomb goes off and it sets off a chain reaction of bombs. In moments, everyone's lost."

"I hope not. Imagine evolution in startup mode on a radio-active Earth. Everything's too tired, anyway, to start over."

"A '60s couple, us? Inside out, mirror backward."

"Who escapes whatever destiny is? I never thought I was so unique. Just seizing the day, getting a fistful of night dust."

"Do I think too much about death?" Kristi asked. "Tell me yes, kindly."

"I still don't know how much you think about death. I'm the Lone Ranger with no Tonto. If I think about it at all, then that's too much for me. It's just not something I mess with. 'Get 'um up, Scout.'"

"I'll keep my thoughts to myself, then. I hope you don't mind my . . . you know, just getting things out. You said that was important."

"I know I did."

"Look. I can't sleep now. So let's go down to the Zero for suds and pastrami. You don't have to work tomorrow."

*   *   *

THE GROUND Zero bar and grille was done up west-ern-style with a recycled barn wood interior, the splintered saw marks of its construction in the silver-brown wood looking like new pine. Red and chrome stools surrounded a carved mahog-any bar gotten from some lost decade and the first thing visible through the door, with a tangerine and lime lighted-but-silent Wurlitzer jukebox standing to the right on a tiled floor shining through the darkness. Pine booths with high backs stained wal-nut and edged in red paint lined the other walls. A lone road couple were hunched in a distant booth in drowsy conversation, eating shelled peanuts from small cellophane packages and drinking beer. A black and butterscotch newly clipped airedale stood up with a stretch near the jukebox, shook, ticked stiff-legged half-way across the floor toward Kristi and Jim, then returned to his place and folded himself down.

"It's my turn for visitation rights." the bartender said. "Don't mind Zachary."

"Bring us a couple of drafts, will you please, Nat?" Burgess headed for a booth centered along the right wall but away from the couple. "Miller. And a couple of pastrami sandwiches with chips."

"You got it," Nat said. "You want 'em hot? I can stick 'em in the oven for a minute."

"Yes, with mustard," Kristi said. "Burgess, too. Right?"

"Yep."

N AT BROUGHT the sandwiches steaming in oval wicker baskets, one in each hand, the chips standing upright in white and royal blue packages with red lettering. His eyes smiled, his mouth covered with a large mustache so you could scarcely see him talk. He had full dark-brown curly hair and a slight limp through a new pair of Levi's button-fly denims. Zachary came up and nosed his head under Nat's hand.

"Never mind, I know what you want," Nat said to the dog. "Go lie down, Zach. He wants your sandwiches. Don't feed him; he won't eat his dog food. I won't either, so I'll have to throw it out."

Zach sat down next to Nat, waiting intently for pastrami.

"So you have visitation rights," Burgess said.

"Yes. One of those things you can't agree on when you get divorced. The judge worked it out this way, being the standard model for kids. Good until one of us decides to move away or something."

"You thinking of moving, Nat?"

"No time soon. I like living on a target. Adds extra excitement to life. Annie may move. Annie's my ex. You probably know her. Whatever she does is beyond me now, so I figure she might move."

"Was she a Sharp?" Kristi asked.

"Yeah, Sharp. You know her then."

"From school, a year ahead of me. She's the only Annie I knew. I didn't know her well. Saw her in the hall sometimes between classes."

"She works out in the Project?" Burgess asked.

"Yeah, well I have a few I can tell on her. Go ahead and eat. It'll ice over if you wait 'til I stop talking."

NAT ROCKED, balanced on both boots and shoved his thumbs under a canvas carpenter's apron and into his jeans pockets. He continued to stand parallel to the open end of the booth, trapping them in.

"Annie was always busy doing something to establish family unity, making a show of it the way her mother did. Myself, I would rather go steelhead fishing like a good husband, but she felt cramped in a boat, even with lots of river and the whole sky over her. She would rather have a reunion party and sit around playing games she half made up or heard they played somewhere important. She had one of those on the back lawn before we separated. I had to be there to make sure the folding chairs and stuff got set out, and she hollered everything else into order. Something to keep me there. I also did the hamburgers.

"Zach did overly like such fare—still does. So Annie shut him out of the back yard, and then started loading the table so it would be ready when folks arrived, and we could just sit down. Anyway, when she came out of the house, she saw Zach standing with all four paws in the center of the picnic table, munching potato salad out of a big yellow glass bowl, just as if table rules only applied in the house and this outside spread had been set just for him. We don't have any idea of how he got there, and he wasn't talking. Dogs usually just gobble and git, hard to catch in the act."

"He's a good Zach, isn't he?" Kristi said to the dog, her hands full of sandwich.

Zᴀᴄʜ STOOD up, his stub of a tail wagging stiff.

"Can I get you anything else?" Nat asked.

"No, we're doing great," Burgess said. "Say, how come you two broke up, anyway?"

"Don't pry," Kristi said. "Sorry, Nat. Engineer's manners. Same as Zach's."

"Zach's manners are usually pretty good when someone's around," said Nat. "Good company. It's quiet in here early on, you know. Not that your manners are bad."

"Sorry," Burgess said. "None of my business."

"That's okay. Anyway, I don't know what happened. First 'Nam. Then I have to work late to make a go of this place, and I guess Annie didn't like sitting home alone. Didn't want to help out here, none. I guess I see why, now. She doesn't sit home alone any more. She's keeping my competitors in business with my alimony money.

"Does she have to do that? I mean, why does she have to? She just sort of went wild, like an escaped house dog."

"Maybe work, Nat." Burgess said. "It must get to everybody some time."

"She could have quit. I thought she would after we started to have kids. But we didn't have any. She had to have something to do, that's why she worked, that and the money. Not any more. C'mon, Zachary."

NAT TURNED to walk away, Zach trotting ahead. Nat turned back after a few steps, Zach moving on, settling down by the juke box again.

"I don't see her ever," Nat said, "except to deposit the dog. Used to be that's all there was for me. If you see her, maybe you can tell her 'thanks a lot' and ask her why she's so crazy. It's not that she's getting back at me, or anything, because she can't rock salt me any more than she already did. I see what happens to people when they screw up. They look at me over the bar. She's screwed up. No secret. You can tell for yourself, if you can find her."

HE WALKED to the bar, turned on the water full blast, washed his hands and dried them on a well-splashed bar towel, then disappeared into the back room behind the bar.

"Why does he still love her?" Kristi whispered. "Fool."

"Better stay out. Let Zach help."

"Maybe that's why she agreed to joint custody. Or maybe just letting him down easy, or enjoying the time."

"Who knows? All three. Maybe something else, too."

"They can't even talk to each other. Not us, Burgess. If that happens, it's your fault."

A GRIZZLED-HAIR woman dressed in sad khaki shirt and pants and a worn pair of Red Wing boots walked from the end booth to the bar and yelled 'Hey.' She waited.

She yelled 'Hey' again.

Nat stuck his head through the door and yelled back, "More beer?"

"Bar tab."

Nat scribbled on a pad with a strawberry lumber-yard pencil stub from his apron and handed it to the customer, who paid from a crushed wad of bills.

"I don't like the name of this place," she replied. "Why'd anybody wanna come here, anyway?"

Chapter 9

When KRISTI, Jill, Angie, and Mrs. Miles met for coffee at the Miles' house, it was well past winter, and little seemed changed for Jill. Kristi was her only friend. As Angie began to grow into toddlerhood, she still did not know her lone set of grandparents. It bothered Kristi, close to both of her grandmothers before their deaths, and moreso it bothered Kristi's mother. Kristi had been afraid of her mother's forthrightness, and hence this delayed first meeting, but Mrs. Miles was insistent about meeting Jill. It was time for them to meet, Jill having been cautioned, and then perhaps Eileen would understand.

"Your house is so friendly, Mrs. Miles," Jill said. "You must enjoy living here."

"Please call me Eileen. New paint aside, I've had these walls to look at a long time. They are filled with what Miles and I found to build a nest of over the years. Sometimes I think I'd like something totally new, but then I don't want to put up with the disruption. Perhaps I'm too used to things."

"The disruption's over quickly," Kristi said. "I'll help when you want to change anything. Not everything at once, though."

"You did such a good job with the painting. That's enough. Perhaps I mean disruption in a broader sense."

"I hope our house will be like this," Jill said. "Full of good memories."

"Kristi said you live over by Burgess."

"Someday we'll have a house. Only right now Tom says he doesn't want to be owned by a yard. He thinks hiring someone to mow the grass is beyond our . . . whatever. So we'll wait."

"Do you let him make all the choices? You should tell him that your daughter needs a yard. She also needs a grandmother."

JILL SAT shocked into silence. She flushed. Scarcely had she ventured out in almost two years, and the worst of her fears had suddenly come to pass. She was attacked, criticized. It had all played out in her imagination again and again. She was unfit, a misfit. She had broken rules. She had a child. One to be scorned. There was no forgiveness; she can never get back. She had nothing now without Tom, she thought. She gave him Angie. Her life was following theirs. She shouldn't have wanted anything else, like having a friend.

"I . . . I should really go now."

SHE BEGAN to gather Angie's things, a wooden block with the first six letters, a small pink blanket.

"Oh . . . please don't be so sensitive. I didn't mean anything by that, Jill. I'm just an oaf, okay? Only, you shouldn't close the world off around you. It's much more forgiving than you might think. Mostly, it just doesn't care about such things, and it has a bad memory anyway. You shouldn't let it get in the way of a life for your daughter."

"Kristi, you told," Jill said. "I trusted you, and now it's spoiled. I'll go now."

"Please, no, it isn't. Mother, that's not like you. I'm shocked. Why?"

"I'm not like that," Eileen said. "It slipped out. Jill, I needed to say something. I put myself in your poor mother's place, and there's so much of Angie's life that she'll be missing if you go on not seeing her. You owe it to her; she gave you life, and there are some things stronger than 'what people think.'"

"She's not like you, Mrs. Miles. You put her in your shoes. You didn't see through her eyes, or think with her brain, or feel with her heart. You can't. She will disown me . . . us. She possibly already has. That's more than I can face right now. She is so vulnerable to the thoughts of others, even to what she thinks them to be, unspoken. She never does anything wrong or socially disagreeable. I can only make problems for myself now, even when my eyes are wide open. Really, I should go away now. Limbo is best. Not seeing her at least leaves me with hope. Now please excuse me."

"Please, Jill, not until we have resolved this. I want to help you, honest. I could be your intermediary. I could call your mother and talk to her, at least. Or should I talk to your father?"

"Neither. I mean, no. This really disturbs me, can't you understand? I don't know what's the right thing to do now, and I don't like other people making up my mind for me. Tom's not that way."

"Please stay and have a cup with us, okay? You have my apology for forcing a violation of confidence. Let me get you something."

Jill was lost in thought, Angie tugging at her.

"Just coffee, then, please, Mrs. Miles, if it's already made. Black."

"Let's go into the dining room then. Thank you so much for bringing Angie with you. She is such a sweet, innocent little thing, and I do miss children."

"You'd think that, wouldn't you?" Jill replied. "Can I talk with Tom? Do I want to talk with Tom? I should? I can't talk with my parents until he feels good about my doing so. This situation is half his."

"Maybe he's changed his mind," Kristi said, shamefaced.

"I'll see."

WEEKS LATER, Jill told Kristi over the telephone that Tom would think about it.

"I called them yesterday," Jill said, "on a strong impulse, with Tom just sitting there with a book, as usual. I got Dad when I called and told him he had a granddaughter. He started to cry and couldn't talk any more, so he gave the phone to Mom. Her voice wasn't so shaky, but mine was then. I dropped the handset in Tom's opened book rather than hang up on her."

"What did he do?"

"He looked wiped-out confused when I told him who it was, but he talked anyway in a burst, and everything seemed suddenly okay. My parents are coming to see us, can you imagine? Our parents. Strange, everyone would say. We should be going to see them, if there are any 'shoulds,' but they couldn't wait until our vacation time, and Tom can't be done without at work just now."

"Are you ready for them?" Kristi asked.

"That's the problem. Here we are in Richland, in a small apartment, which is going to get really cramped with both us and them. They're used to a big house."

"Our apartment is the same size as yours, so no help there."

"I was thinking, maybe we all could go to the Riverside Inn for dinner? That would mean more people to talk to than just us, and I *would* like you to meet them. Also, having friends makes us seem normal. You know? Riverside has a private room, so we wouldn't be bothered with the usual restaurant noise and can have some privacy. What do you think?

*   *   *

THE PRIVATE dining room was narrow on the eastern end of the Riverside Inn, which opened on the Columbia River flowing to the south. The room also gave people a sensation of drifting northward. The worn maple captain's chairs and lone high chair surrounded two smaller rectangular tables pushed together. Maroon tablecloths, white embossed paper napkins, stainless steel service and squat amber water glasses with ice graced the table, at which Jill seated her guests.

"Thank you for inviting us to dinner," Eileen Miles said, from next to Burgess. "I've enjoyed getting to know Jill and Angie, and now Tom and both of you."

"We've enjoyed meeting you," Mr. Henderson said. "We've enjoyed meeting you. A week ago our children were lost, and now they are all ours, once again, thanks to you, they say. We are suddenly grandparents."

"We're glad you are all here," Jill said. "Our place is a little too small to serve you all, so here we are."

"Thanks for coming," Tom said.

A BRIEF but uncomfortable pause followed, until Kristi said, "Our pleasure, and thanks for being our friends."

"Don't you find the circumstances just a little odd," Rebecca — Mrs. Henderson — said. "I mean, who besides us here is going to accept them, once all the facts are known? They just ran away and did it, without much care for us. Don't you agree? And Angie."

"Now Mother, you've been very good so far. Don't get started," Mr. Henderson said. "We're here to celebrate, family and friends. We've been through this before. It's like the prodigal son returning, only much better."

"Well, that's easy for you to say," she replied. "You haven't a care in the world, not even for yourself. But what about me? For a woman it is different."

Mr. Henderson spoke. "I care about our children and grandchild, and I care about you, too. I think you should be more accepting of this. For your sake and theirs, too."

"I might have known," Tom said. "I did know. Please let's just try to enjoy dinner and not make soap opera."

"And you, Tom, after all we have done for you," Rebecca said.

"Why is this all coming out now?" Tom said. "No audience! Let me call somebody!"

"Oh, you—how could you? After all we've done for you."

"We love each other, Tom and I," Jill said. "We always have, even when we were just children. Couldn't you see that?"

"Let's face the future with a smile," Mr. Henderson said. "Can't do anything now about things in the past."

"You could get a divorce, Jill. Come back home and marry somebody proper."

"We do have Angie to think about now," Jill said.

"I am proper, despite what you have always thought about me, Rebecca," Tom said. "I'm not a dirty stray cat. I get to be happy like anyone else."

"Call me Mother. If you still can. And that's the point, isn't it? You were raised together, adopted or not. We never showed the slightest favoritism. You are brother and sister. That's how I've always thought of you. And now you've done this, thing. What will be said of you?"

"Mother, it's you we're concerned about," Jill said.

"And then you disappear and don't speak to us for almost two years. And we find you up here in the middle of nowhere, with child, doing God-knows-what."

"Tom's a computer programmer, Mother. It's a reputable job, I mean a really good one."

"I still don't know what you do, Tom. Never mind. Don't bother. It doesn't matter, anyway."

"Computers are used mostly by military contractors now, but in the future everyone will have them. You'll see."

"You might have inherited your father's jewelry store. You're a man. But not now."

"Jewelry's not for me. Let's not lay this burden on our guests any more. Everything's fine with our situation. Really."

"And you have such a beautiful granddaughter," Eileen said to Rebecca.

"What's to become of her?" Rebecca replied. "When people know. There are no secrets anymore in this world."

"Now there aren't," Tom said. "Now there aren't. Maybe we should go, Jill, and not bother these people any more."

A lone waitress, dressed in black skirt and apron with a ruffled white blouse and too much to do opened the dining room door with a "Ready to order?"

"We need menus first," Tom said. "Then give us a few, okay?"

The waitress looked embarrassed but said nothing, then started a quick head count.

"Be right back."

She RETURNED, split the stack of stiff paper single-sheet menus, and handed a resulting stack to the person on either side of her. She waited long enough to see that the two understood what she expected them to do, then quickly left the room.

"Tom, maybe we should get a divorce. You know, for Angie."

"Don't say that, please. I'm insecure enough right now."

"The best thing for Angie is for you two to tough it out as parents yourselves," Eileen said. "With your parents' help."

"Isn't it for a mother to say what's best for them?" Rebecca replied. "But I don't feel much like a mother today. Only astonished by this."

"You don't feel much like being *my* mother, don't you mean?" Jill said. "What shall I do? Shall I give everything up? There's nothing else for me, ever again. How can I?"

"It's your father. This might not have happened. You just accept everything. You're gullible. That's how Tom seduced you. You're so naive. To your bones."

"It wasn't like that," Tom said. "We love each other. What's wrong with that?"

"Tom, and you must have no conscience" Rebecca said. "You didn't let on that you were doing that to her. For how long? Always had to have your own way, and we gave it to you, I guess. I thought you were casting off orphanhood to become the assertive male. I see now we spoiled you beyond what we could possibly comprehend."

"We get to have our happiness, too," Tom said. "We get to do what makes us happy."

"I'm not very happy right now," Jill said.

"What do you mean?" Tom asked.

"I mean, maybe we shouldn't be together right now. Then Mother will feel better, and I will have a mother again."

"How can you say that, after all we've been through?"

"We've been through it, though, Tom. We made it through. You gave me what I have always wanted, and that's a baby. She is my very life, but I need more now. I need my own mother's love, and I need Angie to have it, too."

"So that's it. And so you don't need me any more," Tom said, standing up fast, his chair screeching on the tile floor. "Fine. I'll find my own way in the world. I don't think I can face you again anyway, Rebecca, after this. In front of our friends. How can I ever say I love you? But I have to. And you, too, Dad. Good-bye."

"Wait, I can't believe you are doing this," Eileen told Rebecca, her face suddenly red and deeply solemn. "Please sit down, Tom. Why are you breaking this beautiful couple up, Rebecca? They're not blood relations. I never should have insisted that they call you. I feel terrible. They need you! Kristi and Burgess, don't ever let me get in your way. I don't ever want anything like this to be my fault. You, both of you come to see me, and never say good-bye."

"My son stole my daughter from me," Rebecca replied. "I had only a letter and nowhere to turn. It was from a total stranger, my daughter. It said they'd run off together, with nothing of where they were going. Then nothing from them, not a word, for two years, lost, and nowhere for us to even look! I thought they loved us. Well, I've had two years to think about it, now, and about who we adopted as our own, and what he did to us. How can I ever forgive and forget two years, not to mention what I see before me now? How can I face anybody, with what my daughter and son have done? You wicked . . . wicked children."

"You must forgive them. You'll damage their future," Eileen said.

The waitress entered the room, ashen, and began taking orders on a small pad, her hands shaking. All at the table looked at what could be ordered quickly, for none had decided. The waitress circled the table, where all were hushed with embarrassment to hear what was being ordered. The waitress left the room and closed the door.

"We did this together, Mother," Jill said. "This is what I feared would happen if we saw you again, only I thought you'd disown both of us, without ever coming here to face us. I do need you, as you used to be, and have for two years. Having Angie without you was so hard. But I'm with Tom now, and I want you to accept him, too. He is my soul."

"You mean he *has* your soul," Rebecca said.

"Where's our food?" Mr. Henderson asked. "Tom is our son, doubly, and we are double grandparents. This started out to be a day of perfect sunshine. This river takes a fly downstream fast, doesn't it? What fish are in it?"

KRISTI DROVE Eileen and Burgess back to the Miles' house in her Toyota after solemn good-byes and sandwiches uneaten. The drive in the car was silent, save for the outside traffic noise and the radio down low, playing "Mrs. Robinson" another time while everyone was trying to make sense of what happened.

"I shouldn't say anything, so I won't," Eileen said. "What can anybody say, when things are so difficult?"

"We don't know what to say, either," Kristi said.

"What got resolved?" Burgess asked. "Did anything get resolved?"

"I felt as if it were all my fault," Eileen said. "There is nothing else I could say."

"I don't think it was your fault," Burgess said. "We don't know the minds of other folks much. You maybe saved everything."

"Do you mind if we let you off at the house?" Kristi asked her mother. "We need to go for a little drive alone, I think. Thanks for going with us. Jill wanted someone her parents' age along, and you were ideal. I hope it works out for them."

"I'm sorry about the trouble. Is everything okay between you two?"

"We're okay," Burgess said. "We won't be gone long."

"Don't go just yet. I don't want to be alone with this."

"It really isn't your fault," Kristi said. "You shouldn't dwell on it."

"Whatever could Rebecca have been thinking about to talk that way, when they've been apart for so long?"

"She's the reason they've been apart for so long," Burgess said. "Who knows? Dwelling on things twists them up senseless sometimes."

"I'm concerned about your friends."

"I know," Kristi said. "Let them work it out. It's their lives."

THE DRIVE in Burgess' car took them back to his apartment, though it was Kristi who was behind the wheel. She pulled into the carport, and soon they were seated on the floral day-bed-sofa in the living room, touching one another, not quite knowing what to say.

"Thanks for letting me drive, Burge. After something like that, it helps to have something in your hands you can control, taking you where you want to go."

"Rebecca. Tom's tougher than he acts, I think."

"I don't think Jill's weak, either. Her mother works her, that's all."

"Works her?"

"Some people use a secret shared power language over others to become what they want to be without giving up something they want to keep. Does everybody do that? I don't know. Some mothers and daughters do, obviously. At least I did with my mother. That's my confession."

"Is that what was going on there? A private conversation with other parties present?"

"She was saying, 'Look, Mother, I still love and need you but keep your nose out of our lives.'"

"I didn't hear her say that. Did she really?"

"Look, if it was private, you don't really know, right? But I know closely enough. That's why I think Jill and Tom will stay together and maybe be even stronger for it. I wouldn't tell my mother that, though."

"She probably already knows."

"Probably does. That's why she wanted to stay and talk. But she would never mention it and knows I wouldn't either."

"Does your mother really want us to be together, or was she talking in opposites, too?"

"For all her toughness, she's really afraid of being alone, I think. I'm all she has left. And I'm not so tough."

"But you have a life of your own to live?"

"I do."

"What do you want to do about it?"

"Sometimes I want to put my finger down my throat. Sometimes everything is fine. You make life a lot more pleasant for me than it was ever before. If you wanted to marry me, I would probably say 'yes.' But I have my obsessions and am weird sometimes, so you probably won't ask. Let's not break up yet, though, because between us it is still good."

"Let's not get married now, then," Burgess said.

"Okay, let's don't. Not immediately."

"When do you want to set the date?"

"I don't want a big wedding. I don't have anyone I want to impress, and mother can't afford a big wedding on what she earns, and she'll feel obliged to pay for it. She'd borrow on the house to do it her way, anyway. But I wouldn't feel right about it. Is that okay? So let's not get married for a month or so, unless we can't wait that long. Unimpressed people sometimes leave you alone."

"Want to elope?'

"Let's not have a preacher in the back yard if it rains or there is a wind storm. If the weather is good, let's not go to the living room, in front of the fireplace, unless the mood calls for it. Jill and Tom will be bridesmaid and best man, maybe, if they ever talk to us again. Mom has this preacher friend."

"You have this all thought out, haven't you?"

"It has crossed my mind and made me whole. About the details I'll change my mind several times. Why not? What about you?"

"I've been wondering how to ask without being turned down and thrown out. That's what usually happens when the woman says, 'No.' It wouldn't have mattered, my asking, would it? We might still be getting married sometime if you'd said, 'Maybe.' Whoever does say that?"

"Do you think it's time, sometime soon? Then we won't need to communicate in opposites any more. You'll have my solemn vow."

"I do."

Chapter 10

ON THE LATE October morning of Kristi and Burgess' wedding, Burgess had stayed away from the Miles' house, at Kristi's pleading. He was last to arrive, in a three-piece pinstripe suit, navy club tie, and white button-down shirt, sweating despite the chill, mouth dry and speechless. What he was about to go through was for the rest of his life. What else was there? Was this getting them both stuck?

More leaves had fallen on the grass after yesterday's raking; three cars were parked in front of the house, one of them the Hendersons' old Jaguar sedan, one unknown. He pulled far forward in the driveway. The sun leaned southward.

Pastor Ralph Chalmers let Burgess into the house. The pastor was a tall but slight man near Eileen's age with a ruddy, mildly aquiline nose. His newly barbered black hair, streaked gray, was watered down and combed straight back, with a 'high forehead.' A widower of two years, he seemed sad through a preacher's smile. He was Kristi's childhood minister.

"You brought the sunshine with you, Burgess. Come in and sit. You probably know this place much better than I do. Eileen and Kristi are still getting ready, or Kristi is. Eileen is helping. You're supposed to stay out of sight a bit longer."

THE HENDERSONS stood for Burgess' entry, then sat in unison on the couch, greetings over. They seemed ready for church, uncomfortable, with an attentive, scrubbed look, Jill in a light aqua years-old suit and white satin heels with narrow squared toes, Tom in a newly pressed charcoal gray suit and antique regimental tie. Angie stayed behind with a sitter; they seemed a little lost without her. In the month since the Riverside Inn luncheon, Kristi and Burgess had little sense of what was going on between the couple, absorbed with their own marriage at hand. Jill did call with reassurances. What did 'all right'

116

mean? Jill planned to call her mother regularly, to send pictures and to visit 'next vacation time.' Tom was still feeling estranged, not quite a son-in-law, not quite a son, for however much of the established world Jill's father had tried to reflect on him. Kristi decided to delay requests for wedding help, though she couldn't wait to announce her marriage.

"That should help cheer things up."

After congratulations, Jill told her, "You remind me that I am still married, no matter what. I still don't know what will happen with Tom now that he thinks I might leave him. I never suggested it before. I must have thought it or dreamed it, though. It just popped out when mother said what she did—one of those things you say and you can't call back. It's as if he were trying to behave normally toward me somehow against his will, and then he goes and plays with Angie. And then he leaves her alone and is alone himself with the usual—books. That all makes me try to behave normally toward him, which seems a really artificial act, if you know what I mean. I have to think beforehand what normal is. So I do, and am very kind and attentive, and wonder when is the next time he will jump headlong into the river. I'm out of my mind, hanging on, but bonded. So far, so good."

"I understand you the best I can, Jill," Kristi replied. "You are our good friend, and Burgess and I are both Tom's friend, too. We want both of you to be happy. What can I say? 'Things will be okay if you make them that way' isn't quite right, but we do wish you the best."

EILEEN CAME down the stairs and leaned into the room with a concerned glow.

"Let's everybody take our places. Kristi will start down the stairs in a minute or two, then we can get started. Pastor Chalmers, you stand in front of the fireplace. Do you still think that's right?"

The room settled and Kristi entered through the archway in an off-white double-breasted suit brocaded with twining grapevines, also off-white, a matching felt pillbox hat with lace, and a somewhat frightened countenance, which turned into a stifled laugh. Everyone laughed sympathetically, loudest of all the pastor, who stopped, suddenly self-aware, and smiled, but Kristi kept to her stifled laughter.

"Thanks everybody for coming," she said through welling tears. "We wanted a small wedding, sort of eloping without eloping, and this is it. Burgess?"

THEY STOOD together facing the pastor, the others moving in about them.

"Dearly beloved, we are gathered together."

KRISTI LAUGHED, on throughout the ceremony, quietly, then louder finally after the sealing kiss and through the hugs, handshakes and congratulations, and she couldn't stop—a joyous voice that hushed finally when everyone left and she was alone in her room to change for the honeymoon. When alone, the laughter stopped dead in the pit of her stomach. It was then so quiet. She looked at herself in the full-length mirror her father had mounted on the closet door for her on her twelfth birthday. She began to undress, undoing first the big mother-of-pearl buttons of the jacket, seeing her eyes mirrored, her white clothes coming off, one item at a time, dropping to the floor.

SHE IMAGINED herself, quite without willing it, carved in profile with Burgess, face-to-face on an Etruscan double sarcophagus she'd seen in a book, smiling, white stone sheets outlining their forms. She imagined herself in the long cool darkness inside. She saw her actual self in the mirror, standing nude, an indented ring of red about her waist from elastic, the vanishing suntan markings of a two-piece swimsuit, and all that was once private. She remembered her first sexual encounter with Burgess. She affixed her eyes on her mirrored eyes, hazel on hazel, fixed, drifting. She separated her lips, then let them close. "Anyway, I'm safe now. Alive." Until her mother called from downstairs.

"I'm getting dressed," Kristi shouted through the door. "Just a minute and I'll be down."

SHE PUT ON newly purchased and washed underwear—printed with painterly blue grapes and green vines on a white background—and shook out and hung her clothes on a clear plastic hanger destined for the closet, as if to be worn again. She put on camel wool pants, a white blouse, white stockings and Adidas tennis shoes, all new. She stamped her feet twice to get them in the most comfortable walking position, gave one last mirror check, this time again at her eyes and face, then stepped downstairs to the living room. Eileen was sitting on the sofa looking toward the window, still dressed for the wedding.

"You always think about days like this," Kristi's mother said, "but they're different from what you ever imagined. They're for real, for one thing. I always imagined that Miles would be here, and that we'd be in a church full of people. I do wish Miles could have been here to see his daughter married."

"Did you like the wedding, though? Was it enough? We really didn't want anything big."

"Life has its turns. And I did love seeing you getting married. Pastor Ralph said exactly the right things, didn't he? So what's next? When do you leave for your honeymoon?"

"Burgess is trading the cars around and loading the Toyota so we can drive it to the airport. If it's okay with you, we'll leave his car parked where mine usually goes in the garage. I didn't think to ask; I hope it's okay. The Corvette doesn't hold enough luggage, and Burge thinks it's too risky to leave it in a parking lot on the west side or even in the carport for very long. With my car we can use the back seat for his stuff when we pick it up. We'll leave the Toyota at the airport in Seattle and rent a car in San Francisco to drive down to Carmel. Burgess had something reserved for us just as soon as we knew where we were going. That's him."

"The Corvette will be fine in the garage. I promise not to race it around. Say, are Jill and Tom okay? I mean, is their relationship okay, now? I didn't know how to ask."

"Yes, I think so. Why?"

"They said hardly a word the whole time they were here, Kristi. It was as if they didn't know anybody."

"It's a long story, Mother. Please don't tell anybody this, truly. Jill doesn't know what will happen between them. Does it always get to be that way sometimes when you're married?"

KRISTI STOPPED and looked around for something to do to reestablish the room following the wedding. Burgess had already pushed back the chair by the fireplace, so that the legs fit the carpet indentations. Only two bouquets of mixed flowers in cut glass vases were out of place, one on the piano, the other on the coffee table. There was no regular place for them. She decided to leave things alone, to remember them.

"Are you going to tell me something?" her mother asked. Kristi couldn't think of what to say.

"They had another misunderstanding after Jill's parents' visit," she said. "That's all. She said their relationship was changing and there's nothing she could do about it. She thinks she said things she shouldn't have said when we ate with them. They prey on Tom like coyotes at a dog, and she can't get him to shake them."

"I wish there were something I could do. Let that be a lesson to you."

"So many lessons."

"You have a college degree and all, Kristi, but you still have a lot to learn. You'll see. Especially in the first year."

"Jill seems to have wanted a child for herself. At any rate, that's what she got. Maybe that's part of the whole problem. Not enough pride of ownership on Tom's part."

"I hope you won't wait too long to give me grandchildren, greedy old me. But that's not what I meant. Things happen between people when they are so close for long periods of time. Unless they are really simple people, they don't have a single re-

120

lationship. They have many, and those contradict and conflict. I think sometimes the simple ones are the lucky ones. Something to strive for, even if you can't have it always."

"As in Thoreau or Zen, yes?"

"You have read so much, Kristi."

"Not so much. Is that the kind of relationship you and Miles had? I guess I wasn't in a position to tell. I did know when you'd said enough."

"I don't know those people, Zen and Thoreau. Your father's work enforced a certain simplicity on things. He simply couldn't discuss most of his life. I couldn't discuss my work, either. As if to compensate, he'd tell me everything else. I felt as if I knew all his sins and misfortunes. Some things I'm sure he wished he hadn't told me. At least, I wish he hadn't. War's a funny thing that way. You do things you wouldn't do at any other time, even though the actual fighting is going on elsewhere. Miles. And that made things complicated."

E ILEEN'S HANDS fumbled in her lap, as if trying to speak for her. There was only quiet.

"Are you going to tell me something?" Kristi asked.

"No. Not important. Just be forgiving, even though it's usually hard."

"You can't let it go at that."

The back screen door closed with a bang, followed by the back door itself.

"I guess you can. Tell me later."

Burgess entered by way of the kitchen, his jacket missing and his tie undone.

"The suitcases are all loaded, and the car's ready if you're ready, Kristi."

"Look out, world, here we come," Eileen said for them. What she felt for them were excitement and anxiety and all the past, the emotion of the day in sunlight and tree shadows now made right. Her daughter was going away, as she must let her do. Her family would be coming back to her soon. Her family.

"Good-bye, Mother. We'll call when we get to Carmel. Don't worry about us, okay?"

ALONG CALIFORNIA'S Highway 1 the traffic gradually thinned out until they reached their destination. Carmel-by-the-Sea that late afternoon was still misty, even up the hill from the ocean. Kristi and Burgess' navy Mustang turned west onto Ocean Avenue, past the few blocks of small shops and restaurants the color of dry sand, the roadway curving southward through cypress and pine trees and alongside but well above the crescent of beach, on a rocky ledge.

"You'll have to guide me from the map," Burgess said. "I don't remember the way. No street numbers here."

"It's down near the south end of the beach, just up the roadway before you get to the Frank Lloyd Wright house that looks like the bow of a ship on the point. You have to go up the street a block from there."

"I see the ship house. Tell me the street when we get there."

"Look at these cottages," Kristi said. "From a magical movie, from the English countryside, with roofs looking like thatch, all up the hillside, just when you need it. So different. Look how their windows shine in the sea light. Yellow, like solid fire."

"I knew you would like it. This was my place to visit as a kid because my mother liked it, too. She would tell us that this was where the storybook characters actually lived when they were not in their books. If we were observant and quiet, we could see some working in their flower gardens. I especially looked for Dr. Seuss characters. Maybe I became one myself."

"So that's where your thoughts come from. Maybe you should have been a writer instead of an engineer."

"How would I have met you, then?"

"Maybe I'm just a figment of your imagination, and have to go back to live in a book when I'm not with you."

"If you are just a figment of my imagination, then in my imagination is where I want to be."

"I like us better somehow for being the real thing, though. I would like to live in some of the houses. If only we could spend all our time like this. It's such a long time until retirement."

"And I have to protect us from the commies."

"Sure you do. From the commies. What if that were only the figment of someone's imagination?"

"Quiet. Someone's listening."

"Not the Russians."

"They did steal plans to the bomb, or an employee did who turned out to be a spy. His name was Fuchs. That's how we came to be in the Cold War so soon after the hot one. Our bomb supply is maybe why there hasn't been another really hot one. Who knows? I like to think so. Otherwise, it's been an awful expense."

"And this is now, and the Russians are probably more afraid of us than we are of them."

"And that's what I'm most afraid of. You were the one who said that paranoids can be dangerous."

"What does this have to do with storybooks?"

"I wonder what Russian storybooks are like, if they have any. I'll bet there isn't a Dr. Seuss."

"There's the *Nutcracker Ballet. Peter and the Wolf.* We can't escape where we are, Burge, and especially not when we are. So enjoy."

"We look like we're in America, but it's really another country, also called America. Then there's the United States. Sometimes it's difficult to tell them apart. Sometimes it's altogether too plain. Are we getting near where we turn?"

123

"Just right there, then up a block, Burge. We're in the place on the east corner, on the right. Silver Cove Inn."

"Now I see it. Parking 'round back, probably."

"Maybe being married gives us more freedom to say what we want. That just crossed my mind. So now at last you can. But I can, too."

"Let's get the bags unloaded and check in. I don't have anything of consequence to say right now. Just something I think about sometimes. Later."

BURGESS FOLDED the cream naugahyde driver's seat forward and lifted his father's leather suitcase from the back seat and put it next to the back wheel, then lifted out Kristi's tan, varnished buckram cosmetics case.

"Let's take these in and get signed up. I'll come get the others out of the trunk. I'm getting hungry."

They registered at a small mahogany desk with spindle legs turned on a lathe, set sideways against the wall around the corner from the screened back door. A man in his early seventies, dressed in an old blue blazer and narrow striped tie, and with a worn English accent and rather sleepy manner, asked Burgess to fill out a 5x8 registration card, then handed him a heavy brass key with a hand-painted wooden lighthouse affixed to it on a short brass chain.

Breakfast was to be served beginning at seven. The door was to be locked at nine in the evening, though the key that was also the room key would let them in. There were many good restaurants in town; they could be found in the phone book in the top drawer beside the bed in the room—located upstairs to the front, facing the ocean, and northernmost. "It's our biggest room."

"We're lucky to have it," Kristi replied.

The couple looked into the great room to the left, down two steps, with its gray-beamed cathedral ceiling and big river-rock fireplace with a matched painting of the Yosemite valley. Three informal pillowed floral sofas in autumn colors formed a 'U' around the hearth. A long maple table seating twelve with tall-backed spindle chairs was set with three nearly identical silk floral arrangements in fall colors near the far wall. The front window opened on pine trees and an older neighborhood of houses, not of the storybook variety, set close together on small yards. Kristi and Burgess paused. They turned and, Kristi first, tried the entryway stairs, varnished mahogany with a pale gold runner. They walked through a darkened hallway of white paint past two glossy doorways to their own at the end. The locking mechanism was noisy, and surprised them both through their excitement. This was to be their secret room, the one they always would remember, where they . . . . Burgess stopped himself. *This is a moment, like any other. Everybody is doing something else. Yes.*

Kristi looked at the back of his head, at his reddened ear, nearly at eye-level. She touched the back of his shirt, warm from the drive. He turned to look at her, wrapped his left arm around her.

"Let's go in," she whispered.

HE PUSHED open the door to let her enter, then picked up the bags and placed them inside the room. The carpet changed color at the threshold to deep blue. To their right was a high four-poster bed covered with a white chenille spread, and against the far wall a blue-and-white love seat in a windowpane pattern. A white wicker rocker was with the love seat beneath four roll-out windows, two set in each wall. Striped light cotton café curtains billowed before a window left open. The room was seaside humid, a warmth transforming the scent of sea and pine as complex as rare good wine.

"Listen to the gulls and the surf! It sounds as if they were just under the window," Kristi said. They looked in each other's eyes a long time, with only the sounds of the sea. Their hands, their bodies met.

"I'll be right back," Burgess said in time, closing the door behind him.

125

When he returned with Kristi's suitcases, she was sitting in the rocker, her finger marking a place in the yellow pages of a small phonebook.

"I thought we'd try Italian," Kristi said. "Okay? Ristorante Classico. There are a lot of other restaurants, if you don't like that. It's just off Ocean, and I'm hungry for something different."

"I'm game. Shall we go the way we are?"

"I think we're dressed fine. This place is pretty casual. We can unpack later. I'd better call Mother first, though, to tell her we made it okay."

THE TABLE candles and early evening light in the Ristorante made shadows in the texture of the trowelled walls of pale amber plaster. The two had a table against the wall near the front of the darkening room of eight white tables, each set for four, and were tasting *vin santo* and *biscotti* for the first time, following green salad and veal picatta with chianti.

"You are supposed to dunk the *biscotti* in your wine glass, then eat," Kristi said, following the first bite.

"I thought you were doing that just because you wanted to. You must have had this before," Burgess said.

"Just in Seattle."

"We'll go to Europe someday."

"Someday. I'd love that."

"We'll be out of the apartment before too long. The more we can put down on a down payment, the better off we are. Fun to start looking, maybe?"

"Burgess, do you really want to keep working where you are? I mean, Dad did, but we both seem to grumble so at times."

"We could live here. Or the mountains, maybe in the Sawtooths. Sawteeth? The mountains, in Idaho, where it isn't too dry, and still doesn't rain too much. The trouble is, how do I engineer anything here or there?"

"Maybe you can try something else?"

"I'm just getting settled, and I'm an engineer. I never liked being settled before. I always moved around a lot in college, first to the frat house, then to an apartment, then back. I guess I'll get used to being more in one place. Do you want to leave?"

"It's home. You know. It has its attractions, even bizarre ones that only I can understand because I'm me. But I could live here by the sea, any day."

"I'm not sure I could tend a shop. Some people in the fraternity thought the ideal job would be to be a bartender, if it paid anything. The only guy we know to try that is having trouble. You have to have the gift of gab, and to practice it."

"Whatever you do is okay, so long as you're happy at it."

"Good question. Am I happy at it? The work itself, yes. The point of the work gets a mixed response. I've never said that because I didn't want you to think I was being disrespectful of your family and their work. I've never felt completely right about being there, even if it is necessary and important work that needs to be done. What if it really isn't?"

"Some people would be enraged at your saying it's necessary. At school I was always disinclined to tell anyone even where I was from. Telling them was a quick way to become invisible."

"I had to grow up fast when I went to work. That's all. It's nice to know that I have options you'll accept."

"To be married to you is to grow up fast as well. After all. No more young folks' adventures."

"Is it as bad as all that?"

"It isn't bad. Just me, now. Some doors slammed because I was tired of standing outside them. And then, there you were."

"You can help me keep my own life alive, Kristi, so please. When all I do is work, and things grind dull. Find something new for us. You know that place better than I ever will with so much work. Will you please do that? I mean, keep it in mind?"

THE SUNSET was visible through the dark reach of evergreens as Kristi and Burgess drove slowly westward and south back along Ocean Avenue toward their inn.

"Let's pull over, then, and go down to the beach to see what's happening in the sky."

Along the lampless street, silhouettes of people—it seemed a whole town of them—drifted quickly in silence, along a low rock wall, down the long stairway that led to the ocean, toward the descending sun—Earth, sky slowly changing, the sun like facets of garnet, then disappearing beyond the sea.

Chapter 11

KRISTI AND Burgess finished a breakfast of granola with raisins, coconut, and bananas, coffee and a wedge of cantaloupe, all on a table with a single fresh pink rosebud and a light green gingham tablecloth. The table sat next to a garden window in the tiny library, just off the great room of the Silver Cove Inn. This breakfast was their new discovery: something to have at home, a continuance. *Home. Too soon. But everything has changed for me,* Kristi thought. *For Burge as well to me. No more being utterly alone at each decision, each next moment.*

"Let's go for our walk along the beach," Kristi said. "We're getting really used to this. I could go on forever."

"We'll come again. It's not so far away."

"Burgess, this is the only visit to be quite like this one—the beginning of our one life together."

"Could be we're hitched."

"Could be. Could be worse. Let's go."

THEY PUSHED their chairs in, walked through the great room, and stepped into the morning sea breeze. Six concrete front steps led to the roadway, then to the rock wall and down many steps, down the cliff to the beach. Sitting on the wall next to the stairs, his back to the ocean, was a shirtless college student with reddish skin and a new beard just lighter than his face, one leg crossed, khaki pants rolled up, rubbing sand from his feet. The couple moved to sit by his side on the wall, to his left.

"Peace," he blurted. "You have to get the sand off your feet. Otherwise your sandals will sandpaper you a few blisters."

"Thanks," Burgess said. "We're inlanders. Mind if we sit here to take off our shoes?"

"Help yourself," the student replied. "You newlyweds? You look as if you just got that way."

"Yes," Kristi said. "I'll bet there are lots of us who visit this place. Do you live here?"

"Yes, no. Because my parents live here and I live at school usually when I'm not in beach limbo."

"WHERE'S SCHOOL?"

"Cal. When I can be serious about attending. Otherwise, it's still Cal. I'm usually there. Serious, mostly."

"Burgess did Cal, too—in chemical engineering. Before your time. Did you grow up here?"

"Under Mom's omniscient eye. Now I study French and ethnomusicology, and I don't like Sartre."

"Sartre?" Kristi said. "Why not?"

"He's the college thing. I tried to read *Nausée* and it made me sick. No joke. I don't need a writer to make me sick. I can get there by myself. He chews drugs as if they were Juicy Fruit. I can tell."

"Didn't you learn something from the book?"

"Yea, mainly that I don't like being sick. Everyone supposedly digs Existentialism. Big deal. Not tomorrow. Someone I know said he didn't know what Existentialism was, but it's what he was. Actually, it was Norman Mailer that said it. My version of old Norm. 'Existence before essence.' That's the tagline. You know what that means? Okay, sometimes it might mean something. I'd like to be newly married, like you two. The two words do fit nicely together."

"Marriage is what we're trying out," Burgess said. "The experiment ends when we croak. So far I'd recommend it. I don't know Sartre. Cal students might walk on the same concrete in the course of a day. Munch the same sandwiches. That's about it, though, for being like one another, except for being smart enough to get in."

"What was it like, growing up here? Did you live in a story book?"

"The first thing to recognize is that, the ginger-bread hous-es? Folks don't live in them most of the time. They are too busy flying in jets to somewhere else. I only noticed the houses were different from any others where people might live when I had been away from home and came back. All of the boards in the framing are crooked and the roofs wavy. You smoke?"

"We don't have any cigarettes," Kristi said. "Neither of us smokes. And no grass."

"I meant Mary Jane. The houses are real likeable when you enjoy them with Miss Mary Jane."

"Oh, that. Someone was very happy designing those, but I'm not sure grass did it. Probably just movie cartoons and fairy tales."

"I've none to offer," the student said. "I thought you might have some."

"Not us," Burgess said. "I'd lose my clearance."

"Clearance. What's clearance?"

"I need it to work. Security clearance."

"Woo. Then you're some bad dude. You a nark or do you work in a bomb plant?"

BURGESS GOT up from the low rock wall on which they sat. He shook the stiffness out of each leg. He stretched his arms in front of him, fingers locked, palms out, then turned back to talk, still standing.

"Sort of in a bomb plant."

"What kind of bomb plant?"

"A big one. Atomic."

131

"No. How can I get me one of those?"

"What would anyone want with an atom bomb?" Kristi said.

"Just to have it. Think of the prestige. The first kid on the block with a big boom and puffy tall cloud. Pow-pow power! With that, no draft board after me. You two have to go walk. Watch out for the hippies."

"Thanks for the advice. By the way, I'm Burgess and this is my wife, Kristi."

"Hi, Kristi. I'm Del. Hang ten."

"I guess so. Take care."

SHOES IN hand, they descended wooden stairs level-by-level down the basalt cliff face to the sand. Many footprints, pebbles, bits of wrappers, and three damp metal drum garbage cans long ago painted green lined the base of the cliff. The beach had been washed by countless storms into a wave bank covered with footsteps and sloping out to the Pacific thirty yards away.

"You say that all the time, Burgess, and now I know what it means."

"What what means?"

"'Take care.' It means, 'There's real cause for concern, so be careful.' Right?"

"It's a habit I got into saying, I suppose. It's something everyone else seems to say."

"Well, there's danger about, so you take your own advice."

"Danger of what?"

"Where you work. One of the things everybody knows in all the silence. Just because you can't not know. Miles knew."

"You mean like even the slightest taste of plutonium will kill you, deader than a slab of granite. A whiff will give you lung cancer. Much more danger. Yes, careful. Don't worry."

"See that you do. I worry about Mother, too. I never did before."

"We have to live life as if it were to continue. Yes? Usually it does, almost all the time, with no ill consequences. Everything eventually becomes something else, you know. Even us. Doesn't the damp sand feel great on your bare feet? Like they've been deprived all this time. If you just stand still when a wave comes in, the beach slowly washes away underneath your feet, leaving you standing in a slightly different place than where you started. Just like life, once in a while. Beat you to the water."

THEY WALKED in the surf: rushing and bubbling with foam, then gone, and again rushing, never to quite the same spot. Burgess moved deeper into the ocean gradually during the half-hour walk to the rocks at the tip of the Pebble Beach golf course, and Kristi followed above him. A single sandpiper ran ahead of them, stopped, scudded out across the waves and returned behind them. Then more birds.

"I guess that bird didn't like us," Kristi said.

"She doesn't know what she's missing. And we're missing out on eating some fine beach bugs."

Kristi took his hand as she said, "It seems as you get to know more of the world, you sense what can disappear in an instant."

"What? Oh, what you were saying on the stairs. Sometimes you fly behind me, you see?"

"Do you think so, though? The more you can lose, the more you worry you might."

"So why have more, then, right?"

"That's what I used to think, in my student days when I would hole out and do nothing but read books. As if that's all there were to value in life that couldn't vanish, and even some of that you forget. So I liked Sartre then. He used to give his things away so the things wouldn't own him. He even turned down the Nobel prize a few years ago because to accept it would violate what he thought about things. I mean, things. I have to confess that I never read *Nausée,* though. I started to. It seemed to be just a book he had to write before he could write his other things."

"I'd never heard of Sartre before that guy mentioned him."

"The guy's name is Del. I must have been keeping Sartre a secret without knowing it. My psychology teacher said I should read him if I really wanted to know something about life and people beyond textbooks. You know, to have my own life. She was a French major as an undergraduate. I had to read most of his stuff in translation, though. Strictly after class. He's more pessimistic than I thought you'd like, and you don't need downers."

"I'm not always the most optimistic kid on the block. What does he say?"

"There's nowhere to start explaining him. We create meaning for ourselves as individuals, and there isn't any beyond that. What I read of him makes most sense right while I'm reading him. He becomes sort of dogmatic and obscure at times and a burden to remember, though, as he becomes less relevant. Sometimes I read him as if that's just what I've felt all along but never really put into words. Sometimes, though, I'm really glad I didn't write what he did, and I could have been reading the same thing both times. That's my version of a start."

A FAT yellow lab retriever with a slight catch in his left back leg came walking by fast from the north on the water's edge, a wet stick of driftwood lopsided in its mouth. A man in shorts and an oversized black hooded sweatshirt walked behind the dog and straight for them, a black baseball cap down low over his eyes and with three crosses stitched in white on the front. They separated to let him by, Burgess stepping deeper in water.

"Nice going, pal," Burgess said as they come back together, though only Kristi could hear him.

"Claimed his territory, didn't he, Jim?"

"You can tell me more of your version of Sartre, Kristi."

"You can read him yourself. Believe it or not, the Richland

library has a book or two of his. Who knows who's keeping track of who checks them out, though. I'll lend you my copy of *Being and Nothingness*. I found it in paperback in Seattle. You asked for it."

"Yes? I'll be looking for secrets about you that I never knew before."

"How much of us is ever really discovered by anyone else? Maybe creation is all there is to value in relationships."

"Maybe not so much of us in totality but sometimes enough to fill a few present moments in continuity. Enough to hunt or gather berries or make babies."

"Why do I feel put on edge to talk about Sartre? I don't know. As if I were being tested somehow, or were off the mark with him in somebody else's eyes. Maybe everybody is and that's the way he wants it. He seems so judgmental that I become judgmental in kind. Self-judgmental."

"The reluctant disciple."

"I'm not even that. He just echoes in some voids, you know?"

"Loud echoes?"

"Like feeling anguish at your own sense of being. Like there is no nothingness without being, and no being without nothingness. There are times when I actually felt solace in that."

"No life without the bomb?"

"Why do we both have such a strange attachment to that? All of America and maybe all of the Soviet Union—or enough of the right people to claim enough of the budget to keep it going. It must cost us a lot. Never to be talked about but remembered, by some at least."

"Make more and more bombs, as fast as we can go," Burgess said. "This is 1968. How many more years does it go on? Almost our whole lives so far. Perhaps my whole working life, too, until I'm an old guy? How do we always end up on this, anyway? I wasn't going to talk about such things for our whole honeymoon."

"I didn't ask you to. But you can if you want."

"You make me feel so much freer than I feel when I'm alone. Why is that?"

"You make me feel the same way. Maybe most of life can only be lived well in the presence of certain others. What we think of as life, anyway."

"So without others we're not really free to live our lives. Is that Sartre?"

"It seems very unlike him. More like just me, gum-bumping. Maybe when it comes to the freedom to interact, the anguish at the edge of freedom is Sartre's own personal problem, along with his nations of fans, and doesn't have anything to do with us."

"I really didn't intend to talk about work. Let's talk about something else. Anything."

"We haven't run into any hippies, yet, have we?"

"I've seen some along the way, I think. Up on the beach, on piles of sand. You were too busy looking at the waves."

"I was busy looking at you while you were talking."

"Let's just walk for a while."

"Except people can do terrible things to block the freedom of someone else, too. You give up a lot at work. Any work to a degree, maybe."

"Other options, there are none. I've spotted some hippies."

"Where?"

"Up there. Coming toward us?"

"Those aren't hippies. They're just old and out of work."

"Do you have to be young to be a hippie?"

"Under thirty."

"Who says?"

"Whoever it was who said, 'Don't trust anyone over thirty?' Those we're looking at are beatniks."

A GROUP of three women and two men, wrinkling and losing shape, came trudging up the beach not quite paired and in various stages of sunburn, lips blistered, long hair thick and awry or gone, clothes mostly jeans cut off above the knees and crumpled sweat shirts, and faded one-piece bathing suits. Burgess walked up the beach and got in line behind Kristi as the group began to walk heavily by on the side closest to the water, kicking at the waves.

"Hey, are you guys hippies or beatniks?" Burgess shouted above the surf.

"What? Those guys are beatniks and we're hippies," the nearest woman says, pointing open-handed first to the men, then to the women and seemingly without direction as she spoke, waving at the ocean.

"We're all beatniks," said the man following her.

"No, we're all hippies. Peace," said the first woman.

"What are you? You got'ny money?" the second man asked. "You look like you do, so fess up."

"Wanna buy some grass?" the first woman said.

"Quiet, Phaedra, we don't have enough for ourselves," the second man said. "You ain't narks, are ya?"

"Mind your own business. We aren't bothering anybody," the trailing woman marched up and said to Burgess, walking alongside him. She squinted up at his eyes, her shoulders wrapped in a plaid wool shawl in saturated colors badly bled, her wrinkled hair pulled back in a single thick druid's braid. Except for her clothes and hair, she looked vaguely like Jill—like an older, sadder sister. A sodden dark wavy-haired boy of ten came quickly behind her as she passed the newlyweds, grabbed the woman's right arm, and tugged her toward the ocean.

"What do you think you're doing, Siddhartha? Stop it! I'm not getting wet, now."

"Come and be an otter with me," the boy said. "It won't be wrong."

"That water is freezing. It doesn't even look warm. I'm not going in past my knees, and you stay out, too. I'm not swimming after you again."

"Promise me you will. It won't be wrong."

"You're a roach, kid. That's what made you . . . . " And her voice disappeared in the surf as the group moved on, walking down the beach, at one with Picasso's *Saltimbancs*.

"Didn't you wonder what they would say?" Burgess asked, half startled.

"Nobody likes being packaged that way," Kristi replied.

"Some people do."

"Who?"

"You're the psychologist."

"I guess some lost souls do. Maybe even lots of them, some-where. Bad faith."

"What is?"

"Wanting to be called a hippie or a beatnik."

"Well, that's what they look like. 'If it walks like a duck . . . .'"

"I've heard that before, Burge. Really dumb. You can't tell about people from how they look."

"I'll bet an actor's better at it than a psychologist."

"Think so? Maybe in a 'What's My Line?' sort of way. Maybe the response of those people was just because you intruded on them."

"I got out of their way, Kristi."

138

"Then you verbally got back in when you asked them what they were."

"I was just trying to be friendly. I've never seen a hippie before, except in the old days, bumming on campus. I always thought that's what they wanted most to be."

"Maybe everybody's after them."

"I still want to get to know one," Burgess said. "Just out of curiosity. Maybe it would be like knowing the secret America."

"You mean, like what's new is like what's really going on? The leading edge of becoming? Hippies have been around for a while."

"They're new to me. I still don't know what's going on with them. I used to in college. I feel as if I were missing something bigtime."

"As in 'know what's going on beyond the news?'"

"The news is only the news, Kristi. Half a snippet of anything, delivered in increments. Something else is happening that matters, somewhere. Isn't there? Like the unspoken secrets behind the words that you have to discover on your own. Why have they changed their lives, and what from?"

"Don't ask them that, Burge. Major put-down."

"People at work want them off the planet. Like they're the ones that are screwing things up for everybody."

"Why them?"

"How should I know? That's what I want to find out. I guess because they're different. They don't work, and some of their parents are professionals—doctors, lawyers."

"They must be spending their time doing something more interesting, do you think?"

"I want to find out what it is. Don't you?"

"Have you ever done nothing for a long while? It's a drag.

The more people you do it with, the heavier the drag. Until there's break-through or break up. Then you're somebody else."

"No, I never have," Burgess said. "So I'd be just the same, if that were the only way to change. But imagine that what they do is something that requires discipline—just to do what you really want to do—when, where, why, and how you want to do it on the edge of life. In the depths of your life."

"Which one, edge or depths?"

"You know what I mean, don't you? Like when you could all of a sudden finally read when you were a kid, and then you wanted to read everything to know what you'd been missing? Only it's you yourself that you are reading, and you are creating yourself as you are doing it, because what you can read isn't as clear to anyone else as it is to you."

"So that's what we're supposed to be doing on our honeymoon, right?"

"I never thought of it that way. I guess so. Maybe that's what got me thinking. One of the interesting things about walking to the end of the beach is that you get to turn around and see all the people who have been following you," Burgess said.

"So what do you really want to do?"

"See all the people who are following us."

THE SIDES of their legs ached from walking on the uneven slope of the beach. Jim thought the reverse stretch would straighten things out. They climbed up on the storm-beaten blackish rocks and looked into a tide pool at a tiny crab trying to hide in the torn kelp.

"So is that a self-actualizing act?" Kristi asked.

"Is what?"

"Seeing all the people who are following us."

"I could ask. This crab probably knows something."

"Don't you dare. I mean our honeymoon. What an absurd name, but I've never heard it called anything but a honeymoon. 'Post-nuptual holiday?' It made me not want to think about what it was. Now that we're here, do you feel more actualized or less actualized?"

"More, I guess. Don't you? What does 'actualize' mean, anyway."

"My feelings change from moment to moment here. I don't know what I expected. Immediately after the wedding I felt both relieved and scared. In the midst of it I felt the happiest I've ever felt, but it kept being overcome with heightened self-consciousness and what I should say next. Then my usual anxiety at everything and nothing. One time I felt that the cork had been hammered into the bottle, and the thought rebounded a time or two. I can tell you this, can't I? You knew I couldn't stop laughing."

"You just did tell me. Are we going to be completely honest with each other and tell each other everything?"

"No. Not that. I mean yes, except let's respect each other's privacy sometimes, okay? I'm not ready for mental frontal nudity as a general practice. Physical I can now handle."

"But I don't have any secrets from you, except of the occupational variety," Burgess said.

"I can't think of any I have from you, but I'm sure to have repressed something, or it just hasn't come up yet."

"What have you repressed?"

"Talk lower. Here comes somebody."

"What have you repressed?"

"If I knew that, it wouldn't be repressed."

"Does it have anything to do with, I won't mention it?"

"Is it okay if I don't get over that? It wasn't the greatest event in my life."

"I think sometimes that you still blame me for it somehow."

"I don't blame you. However, it is a turn-off to think about it, especially if I do when we're making love."

"What makes you think about it?" Burgess asked.

"What makes us think about anything? It just happens. I try to think about something else and get into the moment, into a moment I was in rapture. When I can't, we stop. You're very good, you know."

"You're very good yourself. I might have enjoyed the first time, if it weren't for the strange circumstance of being forced into it. I wish you hadn't felt so stomped on by it."

"Like Stoical distance? I'll have to ask myself about that. In the meantime, I can't be something I'm not, right? So first of all I won't lie to myself. Knowingly. And why should I lie to you? Would you feel any better if I did?"

"I'd feel much the worse if I thought you were lying."

"There you have it," Kristi said.

"It seems we've been stopping in the middle of things more frequently. Or not even starting."

"We haven't stopped here in Carmel, though."

"True."

"Only, try not to remind me of it, and then maybe it'll be okay. I'll try some more behavior therapy on myself. You'll be my reward. Ha."

"How will you do that?"

"That's my little secret. By sweet creation, the way the sun opens a lotus flower, just by being the sun."

Chapter 12

"OH, LOOK! there's Del, thumbing. Let's stop," Kristi said, almost an hour along on their drive back to the airport, the California hills pale yellow and dotted with shadows and dark green cedars. The morning sun heating up her bare arm glinted across the dashboard chrome. "The guy we met at the beach? Let's pick him up."

Burgess braked the Mustang and skidded quietly to a stop. He shifted gears and backed up fast, his right arm around the driver's seat, the transmission whining, and came to another stop, the car's trunk five feet from Del standing alongside the road. Burgess turned off the engine and opened his door wide. Del, in faded jeans and an oversize white shirt rolled up at the sleeves to the elbow, walked around the car to meet him.

"We'll juggle some luggage around and fit you in," Burgess said.

DEL SUDDENLY recognized them. He unshouldered his backpack and handed it to Burgess, who folded his seat forward and shuffled luggage in the back seat, one leg still on the ground.

"You're folks I met at the beach. Thanks for stopping. I was getting desperate."

"What are you doing way out here?" Kristi said. "There aren't any turnoffs. Where did your last ride go?"

"He said he forgot something and let me out. Did a 'u-ey.' It happens sometimes. I've been walking a while. Nobody would stop. Someone doesn't like you or wants something you're not giving or gets where he's going and there you are, stranded. Stranded's SOP for all thumbers."

"Are you going back to school?" she asked.

"That's the place I'm headed for. I thumb sometimes to save on gas, and it's not as boring as driving alone. But sometimes it's a dumb idea. I'm really glad you stopped."

"How long have you been here?" Burgess asked.

"I started out early. I got my mother to drive me to the edge of town to a spot where it's easier to catch a ride. She said I was crazy, as usual. As usual, I am crazy, but with more bucks. Someone from town usually does pick me up, then I have my ride most of the way to where I can catch a bus. Not today."

"We'll reintroduce ourselves, in case you have forgotten. I'm Kristi and this is Burgess."

"Pleased to meet you again. I'm Del. Still Del."

"You sound as if you do this often," Kristi said.

"No. Not as often as when I first went away to college. Only maybe three times in all. I got homesick."

"Everybody does," Kristi said. "I did too at the UW. In Seattle."

"I'm not homesick any more. At any rate, there's a lot happening that I'm missing out on."

"Like what?" Burgess asked.

"Every time I go back home, I wonder what I've missed happening in Berkeley. But everything's mostly the same when I return," Del said. "The same mass of fingerprints on the glass doors, the same dirt and grass and trees and old buildings and sullen students reading, and people passing out stuff in front of Sproul Hall. But I feel that I've missed something, and I'm always surprised what it is."

"Missed?"

"I'll find out when I get there. This time I'll pay attention. Maybe it really wasn't anything, and I just had the feeling that I should be moving on down the highway to let it teach me something. The highway blues in my highway shoes."

"What have you learned so far, besides sometimes it's hard to find a ride?"

DEL THOUGHT a moment. He scratched over his right ear and put his hand on the backpack in the sunlight coming in from the opposite window. He thumped his fingers.

"Truckers have the best stories, some of them."

"Come on," Kristi said. "You can tell us."

"I don't know if I can. Everyone imagines being picked up by either Sophia Loren or Bela Lugosi. Once I got picked up by a hot-rodder in a '58 Chevy Impala who did over ninety for miles on end, slowing down only at the small towns where he might get stopped in the interest of the local economy for speeding. All the time he was telling me stories, one after the other, about growing up on the ocean. My life wasn't like that, usually. I got chased a lot—off the golf course, out of the stores and hotels. He charmed his way in like a grownup with a bankroll. That's what he told me, at any rate. He had some fun. That's what he said."

"What did he say?" Kristi asked.

"He was a caddy at Pebble Beach. Nice job to have. Big tippers, sometimes. He said one of them invited him to a party—he actually was invited a few times by various golfers when they'd won—and the guy proceeded to get sloshed since he had had such a good day. He probably would have done the same if he had had a bad day, too. It was a party of maybe sixteen people or so at a place along the Seventeen-Mile Drive, back away from everywhere in the woods. Did you make that trip around the loop when you were there?"

"Yes, we made it," Kristi said. "That's the other place we want to live when we get rich. I'd like to have a spread-out place back in the forest, where the beach would be close, and golf, too. Both worlds. I think we'd like that."

"How will you get rich?" Del asked.

145

"Good question. We're working on that. Burgess is an engineer, but he's doing the wrong thing unless he gets to be president of his company or something big happens. It's a new industry. The idea of something big gets him up stomping in the morning."

"Can you do that?" Del asked. "Get rich?"

BURGESS TALKED at the windshield, loud, his eyes on the road:

"Sure, given time. But I keep being reminded how much time it will take. Maybe Atoms for Peace will diversify into something lucrative. It keeps looking that way. There's so much promise, if only a few hurdles can be hopped."

Del wiped his sweating hands on his lap. He cracked his neck by tilting it to the side.

"Don't throw me out for saying this. How do you make something decent out of a bomb?"

"Not from the bomb itself. From the byproducts of making it. For example, how would you like to have really clean clothes when you get them back from the cleaners? You know how they always come back smelling like chemicals and never really seem clean? All you have to do is irradiate them and kill off the bacteria, and there you are. No more B. O. in the tuxedo."

"You're kidding. Doesn't that make the clothes glow?"

"Nothing even touches the fabric. No kidding. You just float the clothes under the radiation source on a conveyer belt. We can get the source right out of one of the waste storage tanks and reprocess it, ready for use.

"What else can you make? I usually just wash stuff."

"You can also do something similar to hardwood before you put it down in flooring, and you've got a surface that resists scratching and wear-and-tear, and that looks fantastic. You could make small heaters for hot water that don't burn out, or power generators like those in nuclear submarines, except they go in trains and trucks. Nuclear pumps for irrigating crops, and turning more western desert land into productivity. Also there's fuel reprocessing, so that power reactors become more and more efficient. There are radioisotopes for medicine. It's almost limitless what you could do—even create power to explore outer space."

"Why don't you?" Del asked. "I mean, why doesn't someone?"

"Right now? Atoms have a bad press because of the bomb. People worry that stuff could fall into the wrong hands. But the same is true for gasoline or dynamite, you know? It'll take some time, and people keep working on it. That's how the automobile and the telephone went, too. It takes time, and you have to be an insider.

"Keeping up the talk keeps up the talk," Kristi said. "So, what about the party?"

"Party? Oh, I was telling you about that, wasn't I?"

K̲RISTI LAUGHED. "Don't get Burge started talking about the future and getting there. It's the pot of gold, the golden chalice, and Ultimate Reasons all finally known."

"Except it's not gold, it's transuranic," Burgess said. "If you want to get in on all that, you're going to have to be connected to the nuclear industry. It grows the research and capital. That's why I put up with where I am in the middle of it. Tell us about the party."

"The party. This guy's name was Bonzo—the guy I got the ride with, that is. That's what he told me it was. I don't know who nicknamed him that or if it was his real name, first or last. You don't know in California. Maybe his mother started calling him that because of the movie or she was sadistic. You know, 'Bedtime for Bonzo?'

"This guy who invited him to the party got shitfaced and passed out, leaving Bonzo free to roam the house at will. At least that's what he thought. He found the guy's daughter in her bedroom, doing homework, door open. She was a high school senior and very foxy. Excuse me. Maybe I'm not supposed to tell you this in front of your wife."

"More," Kristi said.

"The daughter said, 'What are you doing here?'

"'I'm here at the party and was just looking around,' Bonzo told her.

"'No, you're not,' she said. 'You're here spying on me.'

"'What makes you think that?' he asked.

"'Where did my father find you?'

"'Caddy. I helped him with his golf game,' he said.

"'Help me with mine,' she said back, walked into a closet and pulled out a putter and some golf balls from under a mass of hangerless clothes, and a brown-and-white saddle golf shoe she placed across the carpet sideways on its instep.

"She got in a putting stance and putted the air at the inside of her shoe and moved a golf ball into place with the end of her club, shifting her weight from leg to leg for a bare-footed foothold. Then she said, 'Am I doing this right? Show me.'

"So he got behind her with his arms around her and hands on hers and the putter, helping her to putt. They take a shot at the shoe. Right in. Then she turns around in his arms, grabs him around the waist, and says, 'I knew I could do this if I tried.'

"'Try what?' he says to her.

"'Never you mind try what. I'm Ellen. What's your name?'

"'Call me Bonzo,' he said, still holding on to her.

"'You're joking. Do you think I want to monkey around? Well yes, I do!'

"Bonzo could see trouble ahead, since he had no idea where her mother was or when her father would wake up, not to mention her age and that he was in strange quarters. At the same time, he wanted to see where all this would lead, and he was feeling it, so he said, 'We'll get into trouble here. Let's meet somewhere.'

"'No, here,' she said, and started pulling him toward the bed. 'Just kiss me. You'll see.'

"'We can do that standing up,' he told her.

"So there you have it." Del asked, "The story, too true to be false. What do you think happened?"

"Is this going to be a locker-room story?" Kristi asked.

"HERE'S WHAT happened," Del replied. "In the middle of a long, passionate kiss for starters, her mother walked into the room and said, 'Oh, I came in to get you to meet some of our guests before they leave, but I see you're already busy doing that.' You know how she said it, momlike.

"'Mother, this is Bonzo,' the girl said, turning to face her and be proper, straightening the pleats in her skirt. 'Daddy brought him home to see me. A pro, he is. He's been helping me with my pants. Putts.'

"'That's more help than you should have,' her mother said. 'You're playing the wrong sport.'

"'I like it better this way,' the girl said. 'I'm learning so much.'

"'You come with me, young man. You help me get her father into bed. I can't lift him. That will cool things off for you. It certainly does for me.' So he did, and it did."

"Did that really happen?" Kristi asked.

"That's what Bonzo told me. The thing is, the girl was in my high school, one of those who actually says 'hello' back when you pass on the stairs all the time, but that's all. You know her and you don't. She's in college now. Cal, too. Just think, it could have been me to find her. I might have been Bonzo. I never get any of the girls. Bad hair, I guess."

"Your hair's okay. Long," Kristi said. "What happened after that? Did he tell you any more stories?"

"He wouldn't tell me what happened after that. Usually they brag or lie. I'll never know. He told me her name, which I recognized."

"You guys always lie," Kristi said.

"No, no," Del protested. "Some things are really true."

"So, what else?" she asked.

"Do you really want to hear another one?"

"Yes. Why not?"

DEL LEANED forward again to be heard over the road noise. He wiped at his eyes.

"I went to a party on the beach, about a dozen people. Almost everyone was my age, just back from college or visiting or getting ready to go. This was last year after my freshman year—after Bonzo had given me the ride to Berkeley and I had made my way back. The same girl was there, Ellen, only she's a woman now, and I'm surprised. This wasn't your typical beach-party movie thing, you know, like 'Gidget' and the rest. It was like times at Berkeley—a couple of guitars, people singing 'Ain't Going to Study War No More,' 'Keep Your Eyes on the Prize.' You know, stuff you can sing them by heart, but you've already sung them before and this is a new situation. Nighttime, with fire.

"I thought I'd go and try to talk with this woman, who was sitting with a friend a third of the way around the circle of people facing the flames that frankly were puny so that we wouldn't be found out having a beach fire. So I edged in alongside her, and people scooted over a bit so I could sit down.

"'Hi, I'm Del Carpenter,' I said. 'I remember you from high school.' People were looking at me. So I whispered to her, 'Let's walk the beach.'

"She gave me a double-take. She kept looking, then looked

away and said she wanted to listen to the music. But she turned to her friend to say she'd be back in a minute. We left the circle and headed north, brushing off the sand. She asked me what I wanted. I said I just wanted to get to meet her, since we would have something in common. She said she didn't remember me; what classes did I take? We named teachers and traded thoughts. You know, like, 'Isn't LaVita a great name for a teacher?' And 'Mr. Barclay just wanted people to like him.' Stuff like that.

"She liked being free and on the beach again. It gave her peace."

HE STOPPED talking, cleared his throat and rubbed the palms of his hands along his knees again.

"I'm taking up all the talking time."

"We've already talked each other out," Kristi said. "What did she look like? Never mind, don't tell me. It doesn't matter."

"She wasn't Marilyn Monroe or Anita Ekberg. Her hair was blacker than you can imagine. She was letting it grow, the way everybody was, you know? Her small incisors were slightly crooked. High cheek bones. Her nose and cheeks were slightly freckled, as if she had red hair, but she was pale, as if she had also been inside a lot. Strange, for someone who lived so close to a beach growing up. Her head was large for her frame. Other than that, she could pass for a model, meaning she never smiled and walked . . . you know how."

"I had to ask."

"She wouldn't mind my saying that about her. Nobody has to look the same anymore. Better off if you're different, in fact."

"Except for wide ties, wide lapels, and bellbottoms," Burgess said. "Which nobody wears where we're from. You can't even buy them anywhere in town to wear on the weekends."

"I should have said, 'Nobody wants to look the old way anymore.'"

"Judging from where I am most of the time," Burgess said,

151

"nobody's still a lot of people. So what did you do on the beach?"

"Out of curiosity, I asked her if she knew Bonzo, just to see what I could find out."

"And?" Kristi asked.

"She said Bonzo helped put her father to bed once when her dad was potted. She said her father never even knew about it. The next time Bonzo came around, it was to pick her up, and her father wondered how they had met.

"Her father never liked Bonzo after that, so she would try to get Bonzo to come over as often as she could, and they would make out in the tv room, where her father was sure to see them, or on the sofa if the tv room was occupied. Once in the tv room her mother caught them under a quilt, their jeans in a heap at the foot of the daybed. Her mother turned on the tv and watched it with her arms crossed, with them trapped there like that, until her mother had some mercy and left. So that was the end of Bonzo in her life, she said. I didn't believe her.

"She thought her father would have him fired, but he never lost his job. She just told him not to call anymore because she was afraid of what her father might do. She saw Bonzo once from a distance on the golf course, so she thought everything turned out okay."

"She told you all that after you had just met?"

"She's like that. It keeps you on guard, because you never know what she will say to you or about you. Or do. Kills you with the truth. We became friends and traveled back and forth to school a couple of times together, once riding our thumbs. I never get drunk now. We made love once, but only because we were friends who both needed to have some loving right then."

THEY DROVE along in silence, hearing the wind and the tires on the road and the car's engine in the sun, and watching the landscape change into fields and lush rows of flowers, vegetables, and strawberries past Watsonville.

"Friends," Kristi whispered to the silence. *Burgess and I. Just something between us to ease the upsets of nature, letting us be something of what we were. Something from sometime before, even while really being changed forever. I held him in my hand and pulled him into me and saved his life, even as he was saving mine. From trauma, a blessing to transform the pain. For a long time, pain and blessing and change. That's what we told each other, and then I could laugh again. We were what I needed, after all.*

II: CREATION AND DISCOVERY

Chapter 13

DEL CRAWLED out of the back seat of the Burgess' rented Mustang in Berkeley at a shuttered white clapboard foursquare house containing his upper quadrant, a leased room. Burgess and Kristi rushed to catch their plane home, reversing their early start.

Both slept most of the flight up the coast, waking as the captain announced the descent toward Seattle. The windows of the jetliner were flat gray and streaked with water as Kristi and Burgess descended through the clouds toward the SeaTac Airport, a wet stretch of low buildings and runways on deep green in diffused light.

They left the airport in a downpour, winding northward through the pine-clad landscape toward Seattle. The interstate took them east. Rain decreased and then increased in repeating squalls, the highway curving past Issaquah way out in the country to wind slowly upward into the lush Cascade foothills toward Snoqualmie, North Bend and on higher into the mountains under thick rain-shadow clouds. Burgess and Kristi stopped for gas beneath Mt. Si, there like the core left from a washed-away volcano. Solid rock filled a small flat stretch of wooded landscape, surrounded by drenched misty green hills.

"I never could get used to this," Kristi said as they pushed on. "I guess I'm just a desert woman, heart, mind, and soul. Actually, most days the clouds burn off a little by ten o'clock in the city, and nothing left outside ever has to be watered or washed. It's nice that way."

"I'm still wet from loading the car. Complain if you want to, I hear you."

"If you complain, people will think you're from the east side of the state. Big downer."

"Then I'm in big trouble," Burgess said.

"You're safe with me. I'll even be your partner."

"Good thing, too."

"Think so?"

"Yep. Now it's official, and the honeymoon is almost over."

"Burgess?"

"Yes?"

"Do you think you're a 'bad dude' for working on the bomb, you know, the way Del meant it?"

"The way Del meant it, yeh. But I'm defending us. The whole country. I don't mean any harm. Nothing'll happen, it seems. I tried looking elsewhere, but here I am. Where Uncle Sam won't get me shot, nestled in his arms. You don't like me there?"

"I feel at home there right now. But sometimes, Burgess, I do want to be somewhere else. I don't want to be a nuclear widow. Sometimes I feel really ambivalent about our home. Mostly I hate that certain part of it, even if some folks say it's necessary. It's safe for me to say that, out here. Now that we're married and you can't escape. Some people on the west side think that what we are doing is an insane political boondoggle to stay alive out in the sagebrush."

"You always feel ambivalent until you are attacked. That's the nature of things."

"Do you mean attacked militarily? Who's going to attack us?"

"The Bomb's to make sure nobody does. That's life now. It may already have saved us a few wars and created new resources for the way we live. Time makes up your mind where I work. Day in and day out with the ultimate.

"This helped me, okay? One of my work friends is Bayard Jefferson, a Black guy recruited from a mostly Black college in the South. I heard him humming once at his desk, and I asked him what the song was. I didn't know it. He said, 'Ain't Got Time to Die. Gospel. You Got a Right to Be Alive.' He says soul music helps get him through it all. He's an engineer."

"Do you want to think about looking elsewhere to work? Maybe then I can have a real job or go to graduate school, if we can land in the right spot."

"I'll think about it. I know you'd like grad school. You don't have to work, though, you know. We can still live well on an engineer's salary."

"I keep on being different from what you think, Burgess. I keep turning out that way, don't I? I'm sorry if I disappoint you. I can't just be home and be dead. I need life, to make something of it, to feel needed. It's as if the bad old thoughts, you know, went away and left a vacuum that has to be filled. Do you remember what I told you? I'm married, now, and I love you. But I still have this void, deep in my heart. I feel it, coming home. What we are is just so strange, the more I know about anything."

"It's not strange to me," Burgess said. "It's like any place else."

"But they produce something not found in nature. It goes into devices designed to kill people. By the thousands. Times thousands. There is really no other use for them as they are. Tell me how I can help you look for work elsewhere. I mean, sometime, when you have a chance? I do know how busy you are, and I do want to be your woman, whatever happens to us."

"Don't push me just yet, then. Okay?"

"No shoving. Just talking. Loud, though."

"I do have to make a living, you know. I didn't know you felt quite that way, Kristi. Why did you, I mean, I'm amazed that you married me, or that we even met. You knew what I did for a living, and you stuck with me anyway. It must have been a hard thing to do."

"It's you I love, and not what you do, which is what Daddy did, too, and I don't hate him for it."

"How can you divide the two? I wish I could."

A DAMP WIND from the car's motion worked big drops

159

of water to the corners of the windshield, where they collected and quivered, then broke, disappeared and reappeared, beyond the windshield wiper's range. They listened to the car in the rain, avoiding the next moment, and were silent that way. Then Kristi spoke.

"What you do puts me closer to the doorway of death, or at least I can see the doorway, because you've been there so often, and for so long, where I can't go. I've been thinking about this, wondering how to think about it. Not in words. Deeper, perhaps, where real secrets are hidden and finally discovered, or sometimes perhaps only felt. How can I make you understand this, without hurting you? Shall I say it's nothing to do with you?"

"Death is just one of life's little necessities. No explanation needed. Why should we have to have this explained to us, as if we were children? It just is, or perhaps better said, 'just isn't,' a secret never to be told—only 'experienced,' the doorway at the very end of experience."

DRIVING KEPT Burgess quiet. Kristi listened to the wipers and the rain, until the rained lessened and the wipers began to squawk. He turned them off.

"We go back to being the strange and ordinary stuff of stars," he said. "I'm an engineer. How should I know anything about people? That's what they usually say about engineers, whoever 'they' is. What is there to know about anyone? Behavior variables, a suppose. I just try to get along, and sometimes I don't make it. I try again."

Kristi watched the shadows of trees flicker through the windshield as they drive, the tires splashing through standing water, drumming at the car's floorboards as it passes through puddles, and she became lost, drifting through trees, for how long? Then she said:

"You're not just an engineer. We shouldn't be discussing this while we are driving. I don't know where else, though, and I don't want to distract you. I've never thought to tell you. I'm glad I married you, and I wouldn't hurt you for anything. You are changing my life. Changing, and there's so much ahead of us, for us."

"Really, you can talk to me about anything," he said. "Driving's automatic."

"I mostly do feel I can. Talk. But there should be a time and place for everything."

"You've succeeded in making me very curious. Kindly don't stop now."

"Concentrate on the road. Sorry."

THE CAR made it up surprisingly easily through fog and rain over Snoqualmie Pass, the summit of the Cascade Range, considering both the car, its load and the climb. Still, Burgess felt shaken and far away from their destination. His wet hands gripped the wheel hard and began to cramp. It had grown difficult to find and maintain the right gear in which to drive, then it was down through the curves and stretches of the mountain road.

After the steep straight downward slope of the highway running toward Easton the rain stopped and the wiper blades began to squawk on the windshield again until the wipers, with the car lights, were turned off. Kristi started the radio but got only static mixed with occasional distant voices and fractured music, as if heard through the bellows of an accordion. She flicked it off. She took off her shoes and sat with her heels on the edge of the blue-gray seat trimmed with piping of blue artificial leather, her knees under her chin and arms around her legs.

"The windiest part of the drive is over, and so is the rain," she said. "At last. At least I hope so."

"There are a few kinks in the road to go, but at least we can go faster."

"Not too fast. This isn't your 'Vette."

"This little buggy drives surprisingly well, for a . . . ."

"Foreign car, you say? It has been a good car. I wish America would make little cars like this. I'm going to keep it, Burgess. I need to feel some independence. I don't want to have to drive your car around all the time. Besides, I'm not a Corvette lady."

"It isn't just my car. It's our car."

"It can still be your car, so long as I have my car."

"Can't they both be ours?"

"Maybe you can consider it that way. What I want is to feel independent, free, and not under somebody's thumb. That's the way I want it to be. That's what I want to be."

"I want you to be what you want to be. Can that be mutual?"

"Yes. Maybe. I don't know. What do you want to do?"

"I like being an engineer."

"And you don't need agitation."

THE LONG WAY back across the valleys and farmland and desert ended in the driveway of Eileen Miles' home, back where they were married. It just happened, it seemed to Kristi. *And just now, it's all just happening. But so achingly long ago. She tried to feel something—as she was, how she is. Is this the way it's supposed to be? Then it's probably not for me. I'll find the right way for us to be together. I will.*

There were clothes and gifts to be moved before dark—moved to Burgess' apartment, their home until the down payment on the right house can be secured. Dream house? However here? Perhaps a new start somewhere in America. Not too far from her mother, though.

Maybe. It's his money, after all. What I earn will scarcely cover the cost of clothes and car. Freedom takes a lot of cash.

They climbed heavy-footed up and down the stairs with their arms full of Kristi's clothes, as well as other possessions placed carefully into empty liquor boxes from the state store—Johnny

Walker, Wild Turkey, Southern Comfort—until both cars were full. Then they made another trip as it grew dark and their stomachs rumbled for want of supper.

With the last boxes loaded and delivered and the last bundle hung up in the open closet of the main bedroom, they slipped out in Burgess' car for a hamburger at the drive-in a half-mile away, off George Washington Boulevard. Burgess admired the detailing of the car instrumentation again—the car his own obsession. He rolled up the window quarter-way so the carhop could hook over the edge the tray containing two hamburgers on sesame-seed buns wrapped in white paper, two small fries, and two chocolate malts in wax-paper cups.

"Careful, the hamburger's still sizzling," Burgess said, passing her a malt, then burger, juice beginning to darken the wrapper, and fries in a wax-paper envelope. "Have a napkin."

"Okay," he said, midway through a bite, his right hand holding the burger half wrapped so it won't drip, his malt still on the tray outside the car. "Tomorrow I'll start to look through some want ads in the *Seattle Times* and some other newspapers at the library. Inconspicuously, so I don't rouse suspicion. But I don't know what I'll find, and I haven't said 'yes' to anything. Okay?"

"Yes. That's all I want."

KRISTI WAS sinking, feeling emptied. Into the unknown—will this really be what they need? Has she deceived herself one more time? She has never known Burgess as anything but what he is now, a sort of gatekeeper to her future, her lover. What now will he be? What will she be? Has she been too demanding, too selfish? Was it a mistake that would alter the marriage that is so new? She tried to cheer herself up, for him.

"You're being very understanding," she said.

"No deals just yet. I don't know what's out there."

"Ask yourself, besides Carmel, where would you like to live, ever in the world."

"Ever in the world? How's Sawtooth?"

"Sawtooth? Where's that?"

"It's a little mountain community in Idaho, if it still exists. We went there when I was a kid. I stood in awe. It was different from home, but I felt at home there. Mountains, big ones, lots of them. You could stand on a roadway almost on top of one and see others in a jagged, snowcapped band far off, with unbroken lodgepole forests in between, on the valley floor.

"We were staying in Sun Valley and did some exploring from there over a mountain pass. It was the place to go if you were brave enough and had a vehicle that could get you there. We drove down into a valley filled with pines and perfect grass and streams and wildlife, pristine, surrounded by mountain peaks so plentiful the person who named them thought they resembled the teeth of a saw. I had wished we could live there then.

"Sometimes a mining town, Sawtooth is. But no engineering jobs."

"So I guess that lets that out."

"I like it where I am, despite the problems. I will look, though."

On THE first workday of their married life, Burgess and Kristi awakened in darkness to Burgess' fold-up travel alarm and reveled in the comfort of finding each other there, in their bed of white sheets.

She decided to make breakfast and coffee while he showered, the way her mother used to do for her father. She cut open and squeezed oranges on a glass device she found in a cupboard behind oddly matched drinking glasses. They would buy new tumblers, perhaps from the same super store where they bought their groceries at dark after last night's fast food. She beat eggs and milk, and made French toast from square slices of cracked wheat bread, to go with maple syrup and bacon.

Maybe he just likes cereal, but this is what we bought. She bought. He sort of just watched and stayed out of the way, writing out a check at the end. She should have asked. She did explain it to herself: *It was late and they were tired from the long drive. I was distracted, and he seemed not to want to be bothered. He was thinking of his return to work? I should have been more sharing.*

She waited for him, the splashing in the shower declaring his presence. He entered eventually in a white Gant button-down polyester-blend shirt, dress slacks, and the club tie from his wedding. She felt grungy in her old baby blue terry cotton robe. So much for a trousseau, she thought. It was not her priority. Breakfast sat on the stove to keep warm.

"My timing was off for breakfast," she told him. "I hope you like this. I didn't ask."

"It's fine," he said. "Whatever you make."

"What do you usually eat?"

"Just cold cereal. I never have time. I must seem out-of-it. Some of that granola that we had in Carmel would be good sometime."

"I've never seen it on the shelves. But then I never thought to look for it since I'd never had it before. I think the place where we stayed made it up special, and you can't buy it anywhere. I'll check it out next time I'm at the store, though."

"Whatever you feel like making is fine with me. Except poached or undercooked eggs."

"Got any favorites?"

"I like what you made. Whatever you fix is fine. You can surprise me."

"You don't know what you are saying. I've made some pretty awful meals."

"I trust you, Kristi."

She laughed and caught his eyes.

"Awful burden, Burgess."

"What are you doing today?"

"It's time to brighten this place up," Kristi said. "It needs me. Later on you can help me decide on other things."

"Don't get too fancy with the furnishings. Remember, the goal is to not be here long. We're saving up."

"Nothing fancy. I just need some claim to authorship, you know? Then it will be our apartment."

"Have at it. Whatever you want to do. Within reason."

"I want to work with you to see it done. I'll feel better that way. Also, I'll want to open a joint checking account. You can give me a check when you get home, and I'll do the leg work."

"The bank won't let you. I'll have to sign something. Just tell me what you are thinking, and we'll go from there. I've got to go catch the bus."

THE RIDE to the plant made Burgess feel mostly comfortable and at ease with himself, back in the groove, and momentary thoughts of leaving town seem to enhance the sensation. He'd look, but why should he leave? *I can talk Kristi out of it*, he thought. *She just needs a little more time to settle into the marriage. Get a house. Things will be okay.*

He opened his briefcase and extracted a copy of *Scientific American,* its oversize format crowding the space between him and the seat in front of him. He folded back the covers so they were touching and wrapped the glossy pages around them as he read. He had put aside this May issue from his initial flight to begin work at Hanford, but here turned to the contents page: "A Third Generation of Breeder Reactors" by T.R. Bump. "As more uranium is consumed, fuel-breeding reactors will become more attractive." He found on page 25, "The present plan is to develop a plant that will generate a million kilowatts of electric power."

Straight stuff, metaphors not necessary. Proof yet to be delivered, but read on for the shining "what if" and "what should be next" by way of research and testing.

His WINDOWLESS office was cold. He turned on the light switch to his right. The room was as he had left it, his "home base." First, he saw in the fluorescent light the white block walls with a pale green painted-on wainscoting, then the gray metal desk facing the door. In the right corner was a matching file cabinet with rotary combination lock on the topmost drawer front.

The desk was paperless save for an 18x24 white blotter pad with a small monthly calendar printed in the top corners. His in-basket was full. He unlocked the desk, sat down, and opened its wide drawer in front of him containing last week's incomplete work figures in a closed manila folder. He unloaded his slide rule, a K+E Log Log Duplex Decitrig in a dark green case, along with a bundle of writing instruments from his briefcase by the side of his desk. He shuffled through his in-basket, then opened the folder and scanned to see where he left off.

Roy Ziegler stepped into the doorway from the hall, his manner serious and alert.

"I see California didn't keep you," he said. "Did all go well?"

"All went well. Kristi loved the place."

"That's no place I've seen. Carmel, is it?"

"Carmel it is. Carmel-by-the-Sea. I went there as a kid. I'm glad there are such places on the good Earth and that they are relatively easy to get to."

"Who can dislike a vacation?" Roy said. He asked Burgess to catch him up to date with projects before he, Roy, turned out of the doorway and walked sharply down the hall.

BURGESS WORKED on for ten minutes, twelve. A security officer walked by in the hallway. Burgess did not see who. The new officer stopped and walked back, standing where Roy had been. Burgess looked up. Shock: *the officer's face!*

The Blue Mountain man. Shocked stalk still.

Burgess shouted, "You son of a bitch! What are you doing in

167

that uniform? You belong in jail!"

The man didn't understand at first, then did, grabbing for his sidearm. Burgess jumped up, sending his chair hard against the wall, and made a dive at the man, tackling him around the arms. The gun discharged with a ricochet off the floor and into an asbestos pipe shroud, loud and ringing in the concrete structure, and they landed on the floor, Burgess on top. They struggled for the gun, suddenly three men. Roy had plunged through the doorway and pinned both the officer and Burgess to the floor.

"Look out for the gun," Roy shouted. "Push it away."

The men struggled for the gun, Roy jerking it from the man's hand with a knuckle to the wrist.

"Let me up now, Roy," Burgess said.

"Settle down!" Roy shouted. "Skinner! We won't let you up until you stop fighting. Call Security!"

"I am Security," John Skinner shrieked. "I caught this guy doing it with a girl out in the woods. Under-aged."

"Liar! We caught him jacking off out there."

"Cool it off," Roy said. "You're both considered arrested until we can get to the bottom of this. When Security arrives, you're both off the site. You'll surrender your badges at the gate. Don't venture away, or anywhere near each other. Skinner, you will be detained because of the gun. It was in your possession. Don't either of you plan on coming back here until your case is heard.

"Keep this quiet, if you know what's good for you. We can't have this kind of behavior here, ever. Not even the thought of it. This place is too dangerous."

Chapter 14

THROWN OUT. Burgess left his apartment for an appointment with a lawyer about John Skinner. That's the name. Burgess' sudden freedom sickened him. What will he do? He thought to himself, "I'm not going to waste time."

In time he was still in bed at 7 in the morning, nothing to get up for. He momentarily thought himself free from the great protector of freedom. In the name of freedom he was free. Free to not eat, when even his honeymoon had given him moments of guilt for not being at work.

Kristi saw him look at his watch. Kristi made him breakfast: French toast, bacon, coffee. He showered and dressed as if to be ready for work: Brown herringbone suit, white button-down shirt, and a black club tie. It was only Tuesday. Why dress up? He had nothing to say to himself. He must set things right. Somehow.

"I know why you are being quiet," Kristi told him after breakfast. "I'm on your team. You can talk to me. Please."

"How did this happen? What did happen? I feel as if I let you down big time. I was chop blocked by a snow plow and didn't see it coming. Now I really feel it."

"You were protecting my honor. How could you feel you let me down?"

"I got us out of a job, that's what I did. And now we're benched, waiting for a court date that might not come."

"It doesn't do any good for me to say that I said to forget that guy, so I won't say it."

"Thanks. Radical new situation. We have an appointment to see our attorney at three o'clock. I was preoccupied and didn't think to tell you. His name is Lynn Reynolds."

"You told me. I'll do what you want."

"Do you want that guy running around loose?"

"I said, I'll do what you want."

HE PUT his day in order with an early morning drive to the library to go over the classifieds in the newspapers. He looked over the 'new books' shelf out of habit to see if anything interested him, but with too much on his mind, the book spines he stared at might as well have been corn cobs. He went home, took off his suit coat, and looked over his printed résumé, concluding not to have it redone for his first applications for employment, but to update it in the cover letter instead. The résumé was over three years old. He could have a new one printed down at the newspaper office. He sat at his Olympia portable typewriter set up on a folding card table placed against a blank wall in the small spare bedroom.

Half dazed, he typed up two letters to the best of the prospects he had written down. He stayed away from defense contractors, which left him with surprisingly few companies. He applied to Sun Chemical Corporation, Seattle. Shippington Paint, Portland. Is this what starting over is? Was he wasting his time now doing this? He started to type out a third letter:

"Dear _____:

"This letter is to express my interest in the position you advertise,

_____.

"Degree in chemical engineering, University of California at Berkeley. For the past three years I have made fuel for weapons of mass destruction. I tackled a security guard who twice had pulled a gun on me, so I've had to stop working here. Got 'nything I can do?

"Sincerely."

The typewriter was limestone in color, and felt as useful as limestone for composing. He opened the carriage, whisked out the draft, crumpled it up and tossed it high against the wall so it dropped onto the table and bounced against the back of the typewriter. Paper was expensive now. Everything was expensive. The best ads would be out in the weekend papers. It was hard

170

to tell who wasn't a defense contractor. He would wait until the weekend papers were out.

"1967 Corvette for sale, four-speed 427, air. Red, tan rag top. Low miles. Mint condition."

The open package of old résumés was in the bottom of a moving box filled with school papers and supplies on the floor of the closet. Burgess counted out three sheets. He aligned two with their cover letters and folded them to fit #10 envelopes. The third he updated with a clear plastic Bic pen for the typesetter. He addressed two envelopes on the typewriter, signed and inserted the letters, sealed the envelopes and affixed stamps.

"Kristi, I'm going down to place a classified ad for the car and get some résumés printed. I'll be back in a minute, unless you want to come along."

"See you in a minute. I'm busy with something."

"I need the checkbook."

"It's out here in the kitchen drawer by the telephone."

THE SWEET WAFT of printer's ink hit Burgess in the face as he entered the storefront newspaper office. Four government-surplus oak desks with a dark gray Underwood typewriter centered in a drop-down section of each desk were behind a counter that, except for a narrow gateway, reached the width of the narrow room. Two other desks without typewriters lined the side wall to Burgess' left, the first one empty, dusty, and stacked with newspapers. At he second sat a woman in her mid-thirties with curly coppery hair and wearing a charcoal skirt matched with a dress-stewart-plaid blouse with long sleeves, her head bowed over a tire ad on a full sheet of newsprint. An eager woman five years older holding a metal ruler like an upturned sword greeted him with a quick grin showing perfect white teeth and a slight under-bite, her dark brown eyes affixed on his, unblinking. Her chin tilted briefly.

"Can I help you?"

171

"I want to get some résumés printed up, and I need to run a classified ad. Which do you want first?"

"How's about the ad? When do you want to run it? You can start on Thursday, if you'd like."

"That'll be fine. Let's try for a week, under 'automobiles for sale.'"

"Corvette. That's a nice car to be selling."

"The résumés need to be updated. I've written down the line I'd like to add."

"We'll have to reset the whole thing. We can make it look about the same, if that's what you want. Or we can fancy it up some. Ready Friday, unless you have a big rush for it. Costs extra, but not much."

"Friday's good. Make them look the same. Can I pay in advance?"

"Yes, you may. Just a minute and I'll figure it up. Is a hundred copies okay, or do you want more?"

"I probably don't need that many."

"That many won't cost you much more than ten. The big expense is in the typesetting and setup. Do you . . . . Why are you selling your car and leaving?"

"I need new vistas. We all need new vistas."

"Sorry. Didn't mean to pry. Just a habit. We're a newspaper, you know."

"It must be hard to be always after something."

"Everybody's always after something—the news, that is. Not at all hard. We just have to be there first. Anyway, I'm not a reporter. They're on the other side of the office. This is the business side."

"Well, my news is no news."

"Some people just don't like living here."

She looked at his downturned head, at his hands.

"Sorry," she said, "but I think you're on the police blotter."

"I'm on the what?"

"Must be someone filed a complaint and you're on the police blotter."

"What do you mean? Where?"

"Just kidding. You aren't, are you?"

"You'll print anything."

"Nothing classified or untrue. Untrue. It's twelve fifty for the résumés, ten eighty for the ad. Twenty three thirty in all, plus tax."

Burgess opened the checkbook cover from his inside coat pocket and filled out a single check, the paper damp from his hand. He tore out the check and placed it on top of his résumé. The woman put the check in a chrome embossed cash register, wrote out a billing form, tossed the blue carbon paper away under the counter and handed Burgess the canary yellow copy, the word "paid" written out on the diagonal in big script and underlined with two swirls.

"I guess it's done," Burgess said, wanting to smile. "See you on Friday."

"You're kinda cute. Strong, too, I bet. Too bad you're leaving. I hoped to get to know you. We do hear about things, you know. But I keep secrets. Maybe sometime."

BURGESS TELEPHONED Roy, who said, "I don't want to talk to you right now." He called Burgess back instead at the close of the workday, just after hours, with Burgess fidgeting near the phone. Roy gave a time to meet regarding the "situation."

The time off had made Burgess feel worthless and without hope, save for the promise of a day in court with a tale that might not be believed. Will it? The tale is the truth. What had happened to his wife so soon after they had just met? What had she gone through in her head? It couldn't be helped. Could it? He was the instrument of her having been raped at gunpoint. What did that mean?

It kept coming back to him in the absence of a clearer way of having justice. *What kind of news story would this secret make? When it came out, it had to come out.* For months he had had no path that might have eased Kristi's pain and saved his honor, and only time seemed to advance his life. Then time stopped it. His life in an instant had been corrupted because he had defended himself and his household.

"A strange tale from the annals of the courts," it would be reported. *And this is how it happened. A man's wife, before they were married . . . in the woods . . . in the blue, Blue Mountains of Oregon.*

BURGESS WAITED at home. Time slowed, with no sense of something to go on to. He became more anxious. He wanted to go back to work. *Will the newspaper pick up the story of the Blue Mountains? When will it, when they go to court? Will they ever go to court? Or just quietly forget it, like buried contaminated objects.* Lynn Reynolds advised against seeking redress there if they were to maintain their privacy, with much time having passed since the incident in the mountains, the absolute lack of evidence in their favor, and the perhaps more believable counterclaim from a sworn officer. Moreover, the company wanted it handled internally, and Burgess needed his job. Under such an arrangement, Kristi would be protected from having to testify. The story would be safe. No public relations problems or embarrassment for the company. A meeting date was set to hear the case, a time later than Burgess had hoped for, but at least the hope of closure was before them.

ON THE DAY of the hearing, Burgess put on his winter coat, struggled his damp hands into gloves, and said good-bye to Kristi's show of concern at the front door. He drove out of the carport onto the packed snow of a newly plowed driveway. He turned left toward the building where the company was head-quartered—of only a few stories but the tallest in town, an un-adorned '60s box of glass, metal and glossy panels the color of sandstone. He was greeted with the usual smiles at the security desk and given the red temporary dosimeter identification badge of a visitor. A secretary he didn't know escorted him cheerily up the elevator and into an empty partitioned conference room, asked him to take off his coat and be seated, and brought him coffee, fresh but too hot to drink, in a paper cup with fold-out handles.

Burgess sat at the small artificial oak conference table on the side opposite the door, his back to a blank windowless wall. Roy entered the room quickly, with military precision. Just behind him was Wendell Snow, director of human resources, closing the door behind them. Each gave Burgess an automatic smile, re-moved dark suit coats almost in unison, and sat on the side of the table across from him.

Wendell Snow had the demeanor of the newest Air Force captain who has just befriended you, perhaps his superior. He was the long-term shaper of contract negotiations that had come to be known as 'Wendell's Way.' His cast was more serious today than usual, however, as he opened conversation:

"Thanks for agreeing to meet with us here, Burgess. It's better than having you run all the way out to the 200 Areas, especially on a day like this. You've been involved in an unfortunate inci-dent, about which I really know very little, and would certainly like to get your version of it. Mind starting at its earliest point?"

"Okay. This goes back a ways, to the time just after I joined the company."

"When did you join the company? The spring of 1967?"

"Yes. I had just met Kristi, my wife-to-be, and had purchased a car . . . ."

"Corvette. Stingray," says Roy, as if to correct an error.

"Corvette. Stingray."

"That's a nice car," said Wendell. "Go on."

"We decided to take it on a drive—our first outing, Kristi's and mine—to the Blue Mountains. After we arrived there, we pulled off on a side road, talking while the car cooled down from the drive. John Skinner, a person unknown to us and who we'd never seen before, pulled up behind my car."

"This would have been well before Mr. Skinner joined Security, right? He had had successful time in the military. You say you hadn't met him before?"

"Never."

"Okay?" Wendell said to Roy, who asked Burgess to go on with his story.

"He got out of his truck with a gun, which he shot into the trees behind us. Then he told us to take off our clothes."

"He what?"

"He told us to take off our clothes."

"Did you?"

"Yes. He threatened to kill us. The gun was real, and he had proved it. Yes, we did."

"And?"

"He told us to get down on our knees and . . . screw each other."

"Intercourse. Which you did."

"Yes."

"And?"

"Excuse me. I haven't talked about this with anyone before. He had himself unzipped and jacked off while he had us doing it at gunpoint."

"Masturbated?"

"Yes."

"With you two there."

"Yes. Then we heard another shot, which went into the tire of my car. He drove off fast."

"Did you watch him masturbate?"

"No. He ordered us not to."

"Nothing went on between the three of you."

"No."

"Why didn't you report it to the police?"

"It had a bad effect on Kristi. Now my wife. She wanted us to keep quiet because of what it would mean if it got out. She was greatly disturbed by this. I had to think of her. She made me promise not to tell."

"And you went along with that."

"Yes. She tried to forget about it. It didn't work. Instead, it became an obsession. For both of us. At her bidding, we stayed apart. Eventually, we got back together. Got married.

"Then I saw Skinner when he turned up at the plant as a security officer."

"And assaulted him."

"He tried to draw his gun on me the second he recognized who I was. I tackled him. It went off. He could have killed me."

"He has been dismissed, you know. He disappeared after he was driven off the site. We therefore haven't gotten his full side of the story. We expected a lawsuit. Do you know where he went?"

"No, I haven't seen him."

"He had no family here. And you say you'd never seen him before. Do you have any evidence regarding your story?"

"No. No pictures were available. Just our words."

"Sarcasm's not necessary. The car tire?"

"None intended. The tire's long gone. Traded in for a replacement. You try to forget about such things when that's what someone you love wants you to do. I tried to track it down later on but couldn't. The guy at the garage couldn't remember even seeing it. He scarcely remembered me until I showed him the bill, and I had just been there."

"Mr. Skinner's claim is that he caught you having intercourse. Is that true?"

"No. Not beyond what we were forced to do at gunpoint."

"For your wife's sake we've tried to keep this quiet. We do have some problems, however. Mr. Ziegler?"

"Burgess, your conduct before your marriage has made your life other than beyond suspicion and reproach," Ziegler said. "First, you buy a car that is not acceptable for a man in this community, and commit thousands to it when you are not yet a manager, and spend a salaried man's valuable time driving it around. Then you assault a security officer for whatever reason, even if you feel you had a justification for it. There are the Blue Mountains. You did carry on before your marriage. Your work has been solid enough, but I have been warned to watch you. I shouldn't have been warned. It is questionable that you should come back to work. I question it. I have checked this through with others. Do you understand?"

"No, I don't. I am innocent and the security officer is guilty. He didn't even show up here. He's disappeared. You said so."

"Some things should be beyond the slightest question if you are to work here in a capacity such as yours, or work here at all. Our place is to protect our American society. We need to be beyond reproach for that. You're costing us. I can't have that. You can work elsewhere in our vast economy. I'm sure there's a place. I will give you the references you need. But you are no longer a good fit for us."

After a brief pause, Wendell asked Burgess, "How shall we respond?"

Burgess' EARS began to ring and his eyes blur. He looked hard at the closed door to clear his sight. Failure. He felt as if his life were over. Without cause, without recourse. What can he do now? They'll starve if they have to continue living off Kristi's sales, even if they could stay here. So this is it, what it is like to be fired. Is he fired? Where can he work? All the people he has let down. Not his fault, damn it. Would Roy Zeigler give him a decent reference, really? Can he ever fit in anywhere, now?

"No point in doing anything," Burgess told them. "Don't put yourself out any. I don't want to work here anymore."

Kristi OPENED the door for Jim, having waited by the kitchen window for him to drive up.

"Is it bad news? It is. I can see that it is."

"Bad news."

"What is it?"

"I'm not roadworthy now. I can't go back to work."

"But you're innocent."

"Not to them I'm not. They hate me, as if I'd betrayed them. I had no idea."

"Still that's not sufficient cause to . . . what have they done?"

He walked across the entry carpet, took off his coat and pitched it three feet to an out-turned kitchen chair, where it hung precariously before slipping to the tile floor. He left it there, pulled out another chair, and dropped, propping his elbows on the table top, his hands on his face to rub his tired eyes.

"I'm out, I told you. I had to quit. I'm not beyond the slightest question anymore. I can't believe I ever was. Is anybody? How can they be?"

"You must feel terrible. Don't worry. I'm still with you. We'll get along."

179

She walked up to him, put her hand on his head.

"Get along?" he said, turning to meet her eyes. "How? I don't have a job, now. We'll starve. You think you'll like living on the street?"

"No, but we won't. It just means we'll have to search harder. You'll see. Everything will be okay."

"How can you say that? What's okay about it?"

"I'm glad the cars are paid off and rent here is so cheap. We have some time. Something will turn up."

"We'll have to leave here to find work. That's all."

Kristi was quiet. *There are times when it is better not to talk.* Burgess walked across to the daybed and sat and put his head in his hands. This was no way to be in front of Kristi. He leaned back, exhaled. Time in his long days of isolation had slowed and deepened like dark ocean under clouds. He must do something now; the search has become serious. His life in which there was rarely a loss of any consequence seemed with time full of closing options. He felt worthless and deeply sorry for himself, something he had not felt since he was a boy set upon by bullies.

It had only been a matter of time until he would be back to work, but then everything had changed, and there was no turning back. Kristi seemed far away, even though she was only in the kitchen. *What will happen to us? Will we break up, be alone again?*

SHE ALSO felt as if they might, with Burgess' darkening behavior. He came home from the plant early one day just after they were back from their honeymoon with the story that a newly hired security officer had turned out to be the man from the Blue Mountains, Skinner. A confrontation, something that never . . . . Burgess was without a job, applying elsewhere not home, then that office meeting and suddenly he is without a job at all, quiet as the lost carapace of a beetle. It seemed to her that he must feel totally defeated, and they had scarcely started their life together. She opened the refrigerator door to begin lunch. She closed it.

"You were the one who liked Sawtooth so much," she said. "Why not get a truck and move there?"

He had no response.

"Burgess? Why don't we?"

"And do what?"

"Maybe open someplace like that little hotel in Carmel, only maybe with a western look?"

"Maybe a bar. I tried that idea out down at the Ground Zero. I got an earful of woes. I'm not social enough to keep a bar and entertain the drunks. In the end, you'd be doing all the work. Is that what you want?"

"Nothing is going to be heaven. We'll both have to work hard and expect some disappointments. But we'll be where we want to be."

"You mean, I'll be where I want to be, don't you? You've never even seen the place."

"If you're there, that's where I want to be."

"We have enough saved up for a down payment on something, with the car thrown in. Let's be cautious and have a look. I don't know where we'll find any more savings."

Chapter 15

As KRISTI took a grocery sack full of yesterday's garbage down the stairs, she saw Jill turn in the stairwell and step upward toward her.

"Jill, I've missed you! Please go inside where it's warm while I toss this stuff out. Door's open."

"Angie's over her cold. See you in a minute."

When Kristi returned, Jill had taken off her coat and was attempting to extract Angie from a snowsuit under protest.

"Children must feel so powerless," Kristi said. "I felt that way. Not much makes sense to them."

"Except food when they're hungry and sleep when they're tired. And pleasant distractions, of which there are many."

"Is she still exploring everything?"

"I hope it doesn't ever stop. Most of the time."

She put the little girl on the living room carpet, free of the snowsuit and wanting to experience new surrounds. They stood in the kitchen opening briefly.

"I hope she's never hurt by it. But I guess everybody is, at least once."

"Hot means hot, cold means cold, and some things aren't good to put in your mouth. So far, things are pretty basic, but she's learning."

"She has a great mom and dad. That must help a lot."

"Kristi, how do I ask this? Tom heard at work about Burgess' job and some of your troubles."

"Oh? What did he hear?"

"He didn't say from whom, but that Burgess had a confrontation with a new security officer. You know how security is out there. You never find out the details of anything, if you hear about it in the first place. How could you keep it so secret?"

"But Tom heard what?"

"He said that Burgess had lost his job, and the other fellow isn't there either. It's a friend asking, right? After all you've done for us, the least we could do is offer to help if we can. I felt I had to."

"Thanks, but we're really doing okay. I guess you should know what happened, though. I'm trying to brace for the rumors."

"Only tell if you want to tell."

"I don't, but I will anyway. At first I couldn't even talk about it. But now talking helps, I think. It's supposed to, at any rate. That's what books say."

"I want to help. You know that, Kristi. To be able to. I owe it to you. Please, let's go sit down."

THEY SAT on the daybed, turned toward each other. Angie had found a pillow in a chair and pulled it to the floor.

"Okay. This goes back to just after Burgess and I first met, just a while after he moved here from college and started his job. He wanted to do some exploring since he was new to here, and suggested the Blue Mountains. I hadn't seen them for a while either, but I had been there, so why not?

"We took the Corvette and off we went. We couldn't find the place I had been before, so we did some exploring off a dirt road. We stopped to rest and just to enjoy being there, you know, with each other. We hadn't been stopped for very long when an old white truck pulled up and a man—that security officer—got out.

"He had a gun. He ordered us to take our clothes off, and kneel down. Then he made us have intercourse at gunpoint while he played with himself. He did that. Then he shot out a tire on our car and sped off. We were too shocked even to get his license number until it was too late.

"The whole thing nearly ruined any hope for our getting together. I felt totally powerless and depressed. And dirty. And angry. You see? But Burgess kept trying to see me, even when I refused repeatedly. Life got really screwed up. I wanted to be invisible, it hurt so much when I was in his—when he looked at me. The knife drawer yanked out, and you're the kitchen floor. Then finally, he awakened me sufficiently that we were together.

"And all this meant absolutely nothing to the company. There was nothing they would do about it with no evidence or witnesses. It was as if they blamed us for the very idea, that the crime was committed in the mere telling of it. Skinner had gotten us, then he got us again with a lie. They wanted to believe him, I think. As if an officer's word would restore world order."

"I don't understand. Them, I mean. What happened after that?"

"Burgess saw the guy at work one day in a security guard's uniform. That's what. When he recognized Burgess, the guy started to pull out his gun, and Burgess tackled him to avoid being killed. The man had threatened to do just that. The gun went off in the plant building while they were wrestling, and people came running and broke off the confrontation. Burgess ended up out of work, escorted off the site. Then the hearing, which I can't repeat, and that's the end of our future here. Burgess felt he had to resign."

"What will you do? Can't he appeal it?"

"No. They don't want him anymore. I don't know why not. No more security clearance. It wasn't our fault. Now we're just looking to start our lives over somewhere, if we can. I guess we'll have to do that. There aren't any other options."

"Why not?" Jill asked, and paused. "I guess I know why not. They were embarrassed, and embarrassment shows weakness. It's men, is what."

"So remove the source of embarrassment, remove the weakness. Burgess, the rotten tooth."

"That's why Tom has trouble sometimes, too. I just know it. It seems like every day."

"I didn't know Tom had trouble."

"Oh, he never says so. I just know it."

"Because of your history together?"

"Oh, maybe nobody cares about that except our parents. But their behavior shapes Tom's. You know. 'I'm guilty, so punish me. I don't care about you.' It shapes mine, too. Maybe it's just my imagination. Being home alone does that. Thoughts become more and more knotted. Does it do that to you?"

"No," Kristi said. "I really thought everything was just fine. I didn't know how much things could get messed up around you without you knowing about it. Well, I knew about some of it all right, but not all. Things happen in an instant, sometimes, and the house falls down around you."

THE SUN WAS bright through the still-frosted south windows, lighting up the dinette set and reaching down to the floor. Jill stood, picked up Angie, and put her in the midst of the incoming rays. Angie squinted at her mother and crawled out of the sunlight to return to her pillow. Jill continued:

"Sometimes it happens a shingle or brick at a time and you don't even notice what's happening. Your clothes fall off, and you're in your naked dream again. That's the dream everybody has about being naked in some public place. At least I think they must."

"We're friends, you and I, and I do. I want to understand more about you."

"We're friends. Nobody has ever said that to me before, not even Tom."

"You must make friends easily, Jill. Whatever do you mean?"

"*You* make friends easily. That's why you happened to become my only friend. For me it's all impossible. You just insisted on knowing us, that's all. You came through our doorway. And I'm glad you did."

"You sound like the 'lonely crowd.'"

"I can't help what I sound like. Sometimes I feel like I am a crowd, but there's only one of me.

"Angie's okay, now, by the way. I didn't want to give you her cold. You'll be glad you left Hanford, I think, though I will miss you. It's such a shock, what happened to you. Everything. We're all so vulnerable."

"I'm not sure why I should feel glad to leave. Work like Burgess' troubled me in college. It was my dad's work, and kept me alive in those years when he was still my father. Some of my college friends made me feel guilty. I was living and going to college in exchange for aiding in the possibility of so much death and suffering, that threatened the whole world and I was oblivious to it. That's what someone told me. But we would never use first-strike capability, even if we had it, which I suspect we do. So Dad was working for deterrence, I told myself, and others, too, but I did have this secret attraction to so much power. I had thought that all of America had the same attraction, the making of bombs has gone on so long. Maybe it has forgotten what it is doing, and just keeps on doing it out of habit or automatic response, like breathing or breakfast bacon."

"Sometimes it's just the best option someone has for making a living," Jill said. "Also the only option. It's not something anyone really thinks much about, so far as I can tell. There's nothing mysterious about it, except that you don't want the paycheck to stop, and that helps shape your politics and feelings and sense of community about the place. Then it becomes too late, and you're out of options for working anywhere else. But when computers take off, Tom will have something else to do. I feel safe here, or did. I think he wants something else to do for the future. I'll find out when he acts on it."

"Burgess—I guess he's Jim again. I can't call him that. It's before my time with him and sounds like a demotion. Burge. That's

186

better. We've talked about this before. It all means something different when the work's suddenly gone. What happens when the government says, 'We have enough bombs now. Let's quit making them?' I wish the government had said just that, so there at least would be an excuse for us having to look elsewhere."

"There is so much to be afraid of," Jill said. "So many reasons to be afraid."

"You can't let that control your life. At least we aren't, any more."

"I hope you can escape it. I truly do."

"Life doesn't have an escape clause—not for us."

"Nothing works."

"Nothing does work. When you least expect it to."

"What?"

"Nothing."

"Okay. I didn't mean to offend you. Did I? I mean I didn't mean to."

"You didn't offend me, Jill. You just reminded me of something I read. 'Man is nothing else but what he makes of himself.' 'Hell is other people,' because they make of you what you're not. Like being turned into a pornographic diorama, then slandered, an outlaw when that's not what you are at all."

"We had our existential acts," Jill said, "but they led into the usual blind alleys of convention. So now we're completely normal, out here where you'd better be. Aren't we?"

"I was being presumptuous, wasn't I?"

"I wish we could just lock our doors and go away with you and Burge, Kristi."

"I hope you'll stay in touch with us. But then, we haven't gone just yet. Nothing's quite out there for us yet."

187

"You don't know where you are going and what you are going to do?"

"No."

"Just no?"

"Burgess is applying for non-defense work. It's hard to find. He really wants to move to the mountains. If only there were jobs there. If you don't work at the plant, there's not much to do here, either, so there is no escaping it, even if we wanted to stay. We have to go."

"I know."

"So we could have a lodge in the mountains, don't you think? Where people could come and stay, without having to put up a tent or find a spot for a camper? With good beds and running hot and cold water. Close to nature, where you can smell the pines in fresh air, but you can still have a good night's sleep. Don't you think that's a good idea? That's where we've been, in case you stopped by and we weren't here."

"Where?"

"It's in an old mining town in the Idaho Sawtooth Mountains where tourists have started to come in large enough numbers to support such a place, we think. It was the mine owner's house until the late 1920s, when he sold the mine to a big company and moved away. It was abandoned with everything else during the Depression. Mice and other woodland creatures had the run of it. Then during the War a daughter of the original owner bought it falling down and turned it into a boarding house, mostly for miners, the old ones left behind to work during the wartime metal shortage, when silver was sometimes actually used as a substitute for copper, which was in greater demand.

"Finally it became a mom-and-pop kind of small hotel, which is what it is today. It needs work. Mr. and Mrs. Watterson sort of let it go as old age took over their lives. They want to move some place close to better health services because they're well past retirement, but they have loved it there. They told us all about it, as if it were a member of the family. It won't pay out a fortune, at least for a while, and for certain it will keep us busy in one way or other, season in and season out. But it will be a living, and it will be ours—guilt-free."

"I can't believe you just went off and did that."

"We haven't done anything yet. Still just looking. We have to do something, you know. We went in the snow just to see how it was—chains on the car and everything. There's a ski area that opened up two years ago, so the timing might be right. The ski area is struggling, but probably because people don't know about it yet. The mountain pass to Sawtooth closes when the weather is too bad. We could lose everything, just like most of the people anywhere who open restaurants."

"Please don't tell Tom about this. He'll be there before you are. I'll tell him first, when more is decided. We'll come and be your first customers."

BURGESS WASN'T quiet coming up the stairs. A key jammed into the lock. He opened the door, his briefcase in his free hand, his gray wide-wale corduroy car coat opened on a tie-less white shirt, his hair mussed by the wind. He stopped at the sight of Jill and Angie on the living room sofa.

"Hi, Jill. You gave me a start. I wasn't expecting to see anybody here."

"Hi, Burgess. Jim. Kristi called you 'Burge.' Should I?"

"Burge. I still like it, if that's what Kristi called me."

"Burge. We haven't been ignoring you folks. It's just that I've had a cold, and then Angie got it, so we thought we should stay away and not pass it along."

"I told Jill about our situation, Burge. Tom heard something about it at work, but apparently not much that he passed along."

"You should know that the word is out anyway. Both versions, with a twist. I got it behind my back while I was checking newspaper ads at the library. Two women I couldn't see in the stacks, but I could hear all right."

"What did they say?"

He took off his coat, combed at his hair with his fingers.

"You don't want to know."

"Yes, I do. I don't like not knowing something like that."

"I should probably be going," Jill said. "Come on, Angie. Let's get you bundled up."

"Sorry to have inflicted this on you, Jill," Burgess said. "It's something that shouldn't have happened but did. There's not much we can do about it, except make sure the truth gets told."

"Oh, oh. What did you do, Burgess?" Kristi asked.

"Later."

"Tell me now. Jill will feel better for knowing something than for having it hidden from her when she already knows something's wrong."

HE PICKED up his coat, as if to leave. He stood there in the middle of the living room holding it, a moment lost in thought.

"Why don't you let her speak for herself? Do you want to hear this, Jill?"

"I guess so. I don't know what to say."

"What passes between friends," Kristi responded.

Burgess didn't speak right away. He asked how Tom was. He hadn't seen him for a while; they had taken a quick trip to the mountains.

"You can tell me, Burge. I don't have to be protected."

He paused, put the coat back down.

"How's this: 'Jim and Kristi Burgess were caught out in the Blue Mountains, stark naked, by a security officer, who joined them in having a sex party, can you believe it? And they all got fired as a result of it.' I jumped up and said to them, 'That's not true. We were forced to perform an act at gunpoint while that pervert performed another act on himself. Then he shot out my tire so he could get away and I couldn't follow him.'

"They looked horrified and embarrassed, as if the gates of judgment had suddenly opened and caught them standing there, voyeurs themselves. One shushed me and shook her head when I was talking, looking behind me in quick glances. When I turned around to see what she had been looking at, the whole packed library was sitting there, faces in my direction, listening to me.

"That's what happened to me this morning. I hope something nicer happened to you. Sorry, Kristi. It's out, now. You'd better find some way to tell your mother before she gets it behind her back, too."

The coat was on the floral daybed, alongside Jill, forgotten.

"I will. Just as soon as she is home from work."

"I wish we had told her sooner."

"I wanted to protect her from that."

"I know you did. Who could have known?"

Chapter 16

IT STARTED once again with a phone call, this time from Kristi's mother:

"Oh, my lord, Kristi, my dear lord, Kristi. I heard the most awful thing about you and Burgess at work today. The secretaries . . . ."

Kristi had answered the phone. She had been too late. Whatever could she say?

"Mother, should I come over there?"

"Perhaps you should, dear."

IT WAS obvious to Kristi that her mother had been crying, though she had her stiff-backboned 'I am strong' look about her as she let her daughter in the locked front door. Each looked at the other's eyes in anticipation.

"I guess I should start, since I was the one it all happened to," Kristi said. Her story to her mother is like the story to Jill—the Blue Mountains, the gun, the escape of John Skinner, no longer the nameless one. And she recalled to her mother the months before she and Jim were together, that she couldn't see Jim, that she couldn't forget him, either, that she wished she were dead and that her obsessions and guilt could be gone.

"I knew something was wrong, but I never imagined what it was. I wish you had told me. I am your mother."

"Please excuse me, Mother. I wanted to spare you the pain. I thought everything would just go away and life would continue as normal. It never does, though. Nothing is ever normal again."

"But you didn't tell me. I was so hurt by that. My only daughter. And to have to discover it through a lie that I could only deny because I didn't know what actually happened."

"We didn't want you to be hurt, that's all. I never dreamed this would happen after what I went through. It's as if this were the worst part. Please don't be hurt."

"Never mind me. You are the one I'm concerned about. How did you ever survive all those months with that inside you? How could you have been so silent?

"Burgess really helped me, finally, just by being there. And you helped, too."

"I didn't do anything. And I would have wanted to, had I known."

"But what was to be done? It was in the past, and the past was dragging me down. I wanted to forget it. Just get it out of my mind. But it wouldn't go. So when I made contact with Burgess at last, it was a relief, but sometimes I would shut down emotionally with him until I could get past thinking about things. Certain thoughts, awful, and I had them. But he helped, and more and more. And you helped, too, just by being there. Even if you were unaware of what was going on with me. You gave me perspective."

"Are you okay, now? Can I do anything?"

"I'm okay. There's nothing more to think about except the future. We're going to have to find a living somewhere else, you know. There's nothing else here for us to work at. We can't make it on my sales alone. That's the real reason why we took our trip to Idaho. It was a trip with a purpose. We looked at a little hotel to own and manage, and we like it."

"You'll be so far away."

"Not so far. Sort of like college. We can come back often, and you can come visit us when the weather is good."

"I'll be alone. With the rumors. What'll I ever do?"

"We'll have to come up with something. Do you have any ideas?"

"What'll I ever do?"

Kristi wondered if she could just step away from this situation. How? No. She would have to find some way to counteract the rumors and give her mother some peace. Eileen had always cared so much what people think, even with the thick curtain of security that helped keep her protected from knowing until now about what happened to her daughter. Kristi would let the truth be known somehow. Burgess had taken the first step with his response at the library. How would she ever do it? She'd talk to the newspaper editor. No, both her story and the security officer's would get printed with a 'who's right?' message, Skinner's the more easily believed. The rumor would prevail, she thought, if anything at all were to be printed. A letter to the editor? Same risk? An ad? She would talk to Pastor Ralph Chalmers about her mother. The pastor then at least would know enough to be concerned when he saw Eileen. He would show concern. That would be for her mother, for Eileen.

"We'll just let the truth be known," Kristi said. "That's all we can do. You can tell your friends, and have them tell their friends. This town isn't so big that the word won't get around."

"It's the rumor we have to face. How can we ever, especially with you gone? As if you were guilty!"

"Maybe Ralph Chalmers can say something about bearing false witness."

"Has a sermon ever helped that way?"

"It might help us. It just might."

"I'll ask him. It won't hurt to ask."

"Shall I talk to him?"

"Yes. It happened to you. Perhaps he will have an idea."

"Shall we go together?"

THEY DECIDED to visit the pastor right away, as if doing so would somehow stop the flow of words that could slowly poison them. He was in his office, and suddenly they were there, each lost in thoughts driving into the church parking lot in the Toyota. Kristi and Eileen sat at two square-backed chairs covered with a dusty pale blue looped fabric and looked over a completely empty polished walnut desk in the office of Pastor Chalmers, whose face to Kristi had taken on the strangest look—drawn, like the smile of the musing character in the right panel of Bosch's garden. He had heard, and he was deeply concerned for Kristi and Burgess' souls. Yes, he was duty-bound to help them.

"It's not that at all," Kristi said. "What you heard is not what happened. What really happened, happened before we were married. We were forced into it at gunpoint. And the security officer never touched us—only himself. He shot a hole in our tire and drove off. Disappeared."

"Well, thanks for that. But you should have resisted—even unto death. You did sin—a sin you saw yourself forced into, but a sin still the same."

Kristi was silent a long moment. She started to speak. She was silent.

"That's the purest nonsense," she said. "I came here for the sake of Mother, not because my soul needs purifying. How do we counteract the security officer's lies? My soul doesn't matter, but Eileen deserves peace of mind. And please spare me the story of Job."

PASTOR CHALMERS mused, then took a black Shaeffer fountain pen from the inside pocket of his coat, removed the cap, and poised with the pen in his hand, as if to write on invisible paper on the desk. The pen point hovered a quarter inch from the desk.

"I have the answer, from a different Testament, though you might not like it."

"What's that?"

"Forgiveness, on the part of both of you, and Jim Burgess, too. That's the only sure way to peace of mind. Repentance, forgiveness—answers for eternity."

He screwed the cap back on the pen and aligned it straight on the desk before them, the pen pointing between Kristi and Eileen, the cap toward him.

"And let things go, and have lives ruined by a lie?" Kristi said. "Because everyone in this town will be only too happy to believe things happened the way they are rumored to have happened. What about bearing false witness against thy neighbor? What about that?"

"I don't condone any of that. Sometimes in attempting to counteract the effects of those who have sinned against us, though, we multiply the sin itself in our own hearts. We don't recover from our mistakes the way we should."

"I'm concerned about Mother's having to put up with other people's thinking her daughter's a pervert. That's what. What can you help us do about that?"

"I don't know what I can do. I can give a sermon on truthfulness and on being too willing to believe what isn't true, and on forgiveness. I'll do everything I can. However, you must be willing to embrace the whole answer yourselves, and be willing to do what you should do, which is to recognize your own sinfulness and repent, and then forgive. You should do that, Kristi."

"You know you should do that, Kristi," Eileen said.

"Yes, please do give your sermon. But I've had about enough of guilt, thank you, and don't need to hear any more of this. Let's go, Mother. It was nice to see you again, Ralph."

"Pastor Chalmers," her mother said.

"Pastor Chalmers," Kristi repeated. "I won't have you thinking I have committed a sin, Mother, because of what happened. It just isn't true. That man might have killed us."

"Forgiveness is the greatest gift," the pastor said, tucking the pen into his coat and out of sight.

196

FOLLOWING A SILENT walk from the doorway in the side of the red brick church and out to her car, Kristi said, "I know what you are thinking, Mother, and please don't start."

It had become cold inside but seemed to warm slowly with a blast from the still-warm car heater.

"I owe it to you to express my concern," Eileen said.

"I now know your concern. My concern is the goddam rumor, however. I feel it sifting through the town like the Plague of Egypt."

"You were always so dramatic when you were younger. You shouldn't swear. I'm shocked!"

"I'm not younger any more. I'm serious. Burgess and I are leaving. We have to go now. Our lives won't let us be here. Do you understand? Will you be okay? You have to be okay."

"These times. The Russians give me far more to worry about. You do what you have to do. I'll be fine. I do have the Lord."

"I can't stand leaving like this. Everyone will think the worst of us."

"Kristi, sometimes it helps if you don't care too much about what people think."

"I never thought I'd ever hear you say that. Never."

"Well, you never seemed to care much what people thought yourself. Now you do, and too much."

"You always cared too much, Mother. I felt oppressed by it."

KRISTI BACKED the car in a tight curve across the empty parking lot, shifted into first gear, and then drove to the street and southward toward her mother's home.

"When?" Eileen asked. "Never mind."

"I'm sorry. I didn't mean to say that. I'm unnerved."

THE DICK and Jane Book houses slipped by in the periphery of their sight. Kristi imagined the printed father and mother, the girl and boy and spotted dog standing doll-like before each house, all knowing her secret. Everyone knows now, and what they think happened is worse than what really did, which was bad enough. There is nothing she could do about it. What if she killed herself, took pills, and left a note of denial. Would anybody believe her then? Would anybody?

Probably not, she said to herself.

"What did you say?"

"Oh, nothing, Mother. Just talking to myself."

"You can still talk to me, you know."

"I know. At this point, though, it seems hopeless. The situation, I mean. Things will be all right later on. Won't they? 'Balm of time?'"

"I have faith that all will work out."

"That's what I hoped you would say."

"Don't you? Have faith, I mean?"

"Who knows. What will happen in the future?"

"Just do your best. Then everything will work out."

"Why hasn't it so far?"

"It has, Kristi. You don't know. You have everything in the world."

"Then everything to lose. We may have lost it already, and just don't know it."

"You should look on the brighter side. You'll always have a roof over your head, so long as I'm around."

"Mother, we can't possibly impose on you that way. All three of us would starve. We have to find our own way. Our quest."

"You won't be imposing. It's just if you need to."

"You're my mom."

"I'm your mom."

"Nothing but good things should ever happen to you."

"You're the best thing that ever happened to me. That's one reason why I want the best for you. Do what you must. And remember."

*   *   *

BURGESS WALKED in the dream up the dappled roadway through the trees toward the whitewashed house he was told to stay away from, the strangers said so—with its two floors, flat roof and venetian blinds. He couldn't feel his feet, then he could, and he flew so low to the ground that he pushed his way along with his hands, as if floating in water on a warm shallow beach, crawling along the underwater sand. He was in the back yard garden with its tall white walls, grass and fronds of stubby palm trees. No one else seemed to be there, and he flew up to a landing that was the roof of the first story, and then moved into the open doorway. He had been here before. He kept coming back. His typewriter was there on a desk in the room lit only by the sun through the half-open blinds. He looked out the window to the enclosed yard. This wasn't his place, but he kept coming back. It was his place, wasn't it? Here he was, and he could glide downstairs, and he did. No one was there. The living room was big and new, cylindrical furniture in pale caramel, milk and dark chocolate and a carpet like Chantilly cream. This was his home. He moved from big room to room, floating. He was free.

Behind the sofa people were lying like dropped puppets on a stage, half in shadow, half in sun. They did not move. They were all dressed neatly in office clothes of black, gray and white. They did not move. He knew they had to be here, dead.

Had he done it? In a missing paragraph of consciousness, had he killed someone? Them? This was his home. He heard someone talking outside in front of the house, on the other side of a boxwood hedge. He was lying on the grass in the shadows, listening to them, though they couldn't be seen. He could barely

199

hear them, but he knew what they are saying.

"He hit a kid," a woman's voice said.

"There have been others," said a tenor voice. The voice repeated, in song.

"In his car. He didn't stop."

"There have been others."

"Only the start."

"So many now dead."

"Why did he do it?"

"He can't tell you why."

"It's the way he is."

"Everyone knows."

"Everyone but him."

"He did it. He doesn't know how many."

"He must have felt threatened."

"He always sweats."

"He's dangerous."

"Now we know his thoughts."

"What he is thinking. We always did."

"Time tells all. He is Time."

"He hit a kid."

"That was the start."

"He'll pay with his life."

"He's paying now."

"It never stops."

Burgess' THOUGHTS began to race. What did he do? He must have done something. Like holding his breath, he tried to keep his mind blank so they wouldn't know where he was, as he flew low along the hedge, over the top and down the darkened street. At least he could fly, and they couldn't. Could they? He'd always been able to do things better than others.

He AWAKENED on the side of his face on the living room day bed, his heart pounding, a woman's steps on the stairway approaching the door. He sat upright, tried to clear his eyes and mind by blinking hard. There he was, in his apartment living room, in his current jobless situation. He had been dreaming again. He wished he were then, and could wake up.

"You look like someone smacked you on the face with a fly-swatter," Kristi said, looking down on him a few steps inside the doorway. "You must have fallen asleep."

"There goes my discipline. I get no mercy from you," he replied. "I just had a nightmare."

"What did you dream?"

"I dreamed that everybody thought I killed a bunch of people, and I couldn't remember whether I had or hadn't."

"What happened?"

"Whatever it was, it couldn't be helped. I flew away before I could be caught, but it wasn't over, and then I woke up."

"You fly in dreams?"

"Yes, but that's not the important part. I might have killed people. I might have run over a kid."

"It was only a dream, Burge."

"I've had it before. I always escaped, but only by waking up."

"Dreams don't mean anything, unless you're a mystic or Freudian or Jung or Adler or something. I don't know what anybody would say about that one. It's not wish-fulfillment, except maybe the flying and getting away part. Maybe dreams just play out a little entertainment when you are asleep, and your body is bored with sleep. Internal 3-D color tv with you as the star and the viewer, all at once, with no commercials."

"Dreams must mean something."

"Are you feeling guilty for anything I should know about?"

"Yeah. Falling asleep in the middle of the afternoon."

"There you have it, then."

"What else should I feel guilty about? IDM, folks—It Don't Matter."

"You're putting yourself at ease."

"Someone's got to do it. My dream activator won't."

"We should do something different to get our mind off things. You don't work there any more."

"Maybe dreams get you ready for reality in some way. You have to pee, so you dream about finding a bathroom or a bush. But you can't go right then because you are in bed, so you are interrupted somehow in your dream. Cave people must have dreamed about mammoths and Neanderthals. Cats dream about dogs and mice, and make bird noises when they sleep. Their whiskers wiggle. The script and images mostly come from experience, don't they? What am I trying to tell myself here?"

"What *do* you make of your dream?"

"I don't know. You're the psychologist. I make chemicals go bump in the night. Did."

"Why is it important for you to know what your dream meant, if anything?

"Maybe I'd understand something about my world I don't understand now. Like, its craziness."

"Well, I'm not Joseph and you're not Pharoah. Come on, let's go down to the river and throw rocks at it. Maybe they still skip."

III. BETWEEN FRIENDS

Chapter 17

THE SALE of the Burgess Corvette netted them a 1962 Ford 3/4 ton pickup 4x4 with a wraparound windshield and a set of tire chains in a heap like a corroded brain under the passenger seat, the cab smelling slightly of gasoline and wet rust. The balance of the sale, the Toyota, and their joint life savings and parental signatures went for the down payment on the Sawtooth Inn plus a few months' cash to live on.

Although the least of the three properties they were able to gather information about, it was what they could afford, given what the bank would lend them. It crowded their emotions with anticipation and possibility, as well as with relief, for Burgess could find nothing else for himself then in chemical engineering.

He had grown distrustful of all companies and wanted to be on his own. He couldn't overcome his unexplained feelings of guilt. They hid in his throat, choking his speech.

Sawtooth, in the Idaho Rockies, was over a mountain pass along Highway 75 north of Ketchum and Sun Valley. The place was approached along what appeared to be empty roadway. Viewed from the summit of the Boulder Mountains at 8,700 feet, it linked to a narrow magnesium ribbon of road on a deep-forested mountain valley floor. From a summit vantage point, the ribbon ran in a quarter circle west to the mountains, then from that spot in a quarter circle toward the north, and then out of sight. The land ran uphill southward from near the southern tip of the long Sawtooth Valley. It had a glint of a slightly meandering stream, Beaver Creek, that, miles along to the northwest, became the Salmon, then the Snake, and, eventually, the Columbia River at a point near the home they left behind them.

THE TOWN'S main street, which could not be seen from the pass through the pines, ran from the valley floor north to south up a narrow canyon toward the silver mines that were once the only source of support for the town. The mines operated and didn't operate, depending on the price of silver, the cost of labor, technology, fire, and the individual inclinations of a series of owners, investors, and miners. Now the town mostly ran because people who lived elsewhere wanted to visit for the mountain scenery and the outdoor life, however momentary.

The name of the town and valley came from the westward range of mountains, the peaks of which were carved by glaciers to resemble, for the early explorers as noted, the upturned teeth of a saw. They reach over 10,000 feet along a score of crests that have individual names—McDonald Peak, Parks Peak, Mount Cramer, Mount Heyburn, Thompson Peak, Williams Peak and more. From the summit, only the slight line of roadway in its double curves across the valley of pines and grassland suggested the presence of people anywhere. Wilderness.

The Sawtooth Inn was situated on a canyon's western slope to the south on the street a short block from Main, and was surrounded on three sides with lodge-pole pine forest and light gray granite rock touched with sunrise, on a steep hillside of almost-black damp soil. The Craftsmanlike lodge was made of peeled pine logs, blackened with linseed oil aged in the sun, the eaves and windowsills trimmed in glossy white paint, the inside walls plastered and, over two layers of wallpaper, painted the color of aged scrimshaw.

HERE BURGESS and Kristi brought their worldly goods in two truckloads, pulling a small U-Haul trailer along the two-lane highway, winding upward through the pass, and downward into the valley in second gear, still riding the brakes. Fortunately, the lodge came mostly furnished, though the furniture had become antique through years of use in the seven guest rooms and parlor, and the sheets were thin enough to see through—bright blocks of window light and blurred bits of street when held up to the sun.

"I take that to be a good sign," Kristi said, pulling up the covers and straightening them while making up the tarnished brass guest bed on which they slept their first night as owners. "At least we know they had customers."

The bedrooms in the lodge differed from one another in shape, size, and appearance. Most were outfitted with a bath, situated when possible where a closet once was, sometimes with a pedestal washbasin in the bedroom. At the end of a hallway was a bath with a polished pine wainscot and white ceramic tile floor, the tiles shaped like cells of a beehive and accented with black mortar. The pattern of design was similar in three smaller rooms. The hot-water tap in the hallway bath dripped slowly, the chrome tap polished and scratched down to brass highlights.

"LISTEN," Burgess said. "Someone's banging on the front door."

"That probably means the doorbell doesn't work."

"I'll fix it."

"You should go see who that is, Mr. Manager. They sound upset."

"Door knockers always sound that way."

Burgess walked out of the room, down the darkened staircase, and across the floor of bare wood to open the glass-paneled door, which sounded an electric bell. The woman on the other side had been trying to look in through the glass, her shaded squinting face wrapped in her left hand, the right balancing a foot-square aluminum baking pan to the side, her thumb over the edge. She stepped back into the sun at Burgess' approach and smiled. She looked like a '60s pre-Raphaelite model, though heavier and darker, her features slightly Hellenic. She dressed in faded Oshkosh carpenter's bib overalls—no patches, no embroidery.

"Oh, I expected to see your wife," she said to Burgess. "I don't know why I thought I should just walk in on you on your first day. You're probably not settled in yet."

"You can always just come on in through the doorway, you know. We'll unlock it first thing, and guests are always welcome. Is something wrong?"

"Well, I just came to welcome you since you're new here and would probably appreciate some welcoming. We heard from the Wattersons you were coming. I brought you a pan of brownies. You can bring the pan back whenever you want. I'm Joy Cosgriff and I live in the little yellowish house down on the corner with the swing on the front porch, usually with dogs on it. They'll bark at first, but they love people."

"I'm Jim Burgess. Burge, I'm usually called lately. You probably want to talk to my wife. I'll see if I can find her."

He took the pan of brownies from Joy and, with the other hand lifted an empty moving box off the reception desk and carried it to the foot of the stairs.

"Gotta make things presentable," he said.

He called up the stairs to Kristi. She came to the landing for a look, walked down the stairs, then over to meet Joy.

"Here are these, from Joy," he told Kristi, who took them and invited her back to the kitchen so the cake pan could be emptied and returned.

"Joy says we can bring the pan back whenever we want."

"That will be next year some time with the amount of work we have to do around here."

"Whenever's fine," Joy said. "Really. The pan's actually an excuse to get to talk to you again."

"I appreciate the invitation, but you'll need your pan back, and we can always talk with no excuses needed. Come on, I'll show you the kitchen and we can sample brownies."

"I've already seen it, but thanks. I'll follow you."

THEY WALKED down the hallway with its heavy age-darkened pine woodwork past the staircase toward the kitchen on the right, past the two-rooms-plus-bath Kristi and Burgess lived in, stacked with liquor boxes packed with household goods and belongings. The kitchen table was also covered in boxes, which

Burgess moved one-by-one to a pale yellow tile countertop and the floor, until he found a box marked "dishes." He lifted up the top of the box and lifted out a dish wrapped in newspaper, which he unwrapped and handed to Kristi. He then opened a box marked "silver etc.," recovered a spatula, and handed that along as well.

"This should work," Kristi said. "Just a second and you can have some instant coffee, and Burge and I will have also some brownies for breakfast. Everything else is packed away. Thanks so much for making these for us. We appreciate the extra energy, not to mention the company."

"I don't mean to be an interruption, Kristi. I just thought you'd like some quick pick-me-up while you get moved in. Which, by the way, I volunteered to help you do."

"You are too nice," Kristi replied. "Tell us all about you. Have you been here long?"

"Been here long. Too long. Not long enough. I'm dedicated to my skiing and can never wait for snow, even though it usually comes early. I live with my old man and another couple down the street; you passed it when you came in. That sounds like typical '60s but it isn't. It's just that housing is hard to find here when you need it, and they were friends from college. They've stayed here for a while. There's no new building because the town has water problems. Some other people lived at the Sawtooth Inn, too, until the Wattersons wanted to sell. The Wattersons were having trouble getting the rent money from them sometimes, though. We wanted to buy this place but couldn't get a bank loan. You're real lucky."

"What do you do for a living here?"

"I work in Sutton's part time. Full time during the summer and when things are busy. In case you haven't seen it yet, Sutton's is a combination bookstore and boutique with gifts of various kinds. Souvenirs. Little silver shovel pins with pieces of ore glued to them. I do the gluing. You wouldn't believe what people will buy when they want a souvenir.

"Joe, my old man, has a bar. The Silver King. Everywhere in mountain towns there's a Silver King, but it's not a chain. It used to be a miners' hangout, but some of them moved down the street to Mac's Place because they thought Joe was a hippie. He just has a beard and likes to wear those, you know, clothes. But he keeps the place clean. It's a bar and grille, actually. He's trying to turn it into more of a grille. We thought you could try it out some night and maybe recommend it to your guests. On us, of course—I mean you, not the guests."

"Sure thing," Kristi said. "Where else would we send people?"

"There are actually more places than one. Everybody wants to move to the mountains, not understanding they'll soon be leaving if they're not survivors. We hope you'll stay. There's nothing fancy here yet, like Sun Valley. If we could just get some more water, there'd be more business. There are pass troubles in winter, too. We have the best food that comes off a grille, though. Joe is friends with a rancher, so we get the best meat. I tried to be a vegetarian, but it was hopeless. Where ya' from?"

"Washington State," Kristi said. "The dry part."

"Oh. The Palouse. Spokane?"

"No. Farther south. In atom country."

"Oh. We have some of that in Idaho, too. Can't blame you for moving, then."

"We don't glow in the dark," Burgess said. "At least not yet."

"I don't know anything about that, and don't want to say anything bad about where you came from."

"This is our home now," Kristi said. "We wanted to move to the mountains, too. That or the ocean, but everything's too expensive there. Also crowded. Let's have some brownies. Do you take cream and sugar?"

"I do with instant."

Kristi went to the old Frigidaire, which had a rounded top and more-rounded corners, waves down the middle, and a pull-up handle. She brought out a can with a Borden cow printed on the label.

"It's actually canned milk that we brought with us. Sorry to have to serve you that."

"It's sort of a standard here. Come over for dinner tonight, okay? At the Silver King. You'll be too tired to cook for yourself."

"One more thing about me. I do runs to Ketchum for supplies if you ever need something and can't go get it yourself. I do that for Sutton's and the Silver King from time to time, too. I'm used to driving in snow but still don't like ice."

*   *   *

"How DID we get so much stuff? We haven't been married that long," Burgess told Kristi. They were consolidating the last of their possessions at past five o'clock in the afternoon. The bell signalled that someone had entered the inn once again.

"Maybe it's our first customers," Kristi said. "Let's go check them out. In."

"This must be the right place," said Tom from Richland, who had put down two unmatched nondescript canvasbacked suitcases and a quilted plastic diaper bag, pink and white. He reached down to take Angie from Jill in front of the guest desk as Burgess followed Kristi up the hallway toward them.

"Jill! Tom! What on earth are you doing here?" Kristi said.

"We thought we'd surprise you and become your first customers," Jill said. "It's the least we could do, and be someplace new with friends."

"You drove all the way here for that? You do keep your promises. Burge, you grab the bags while I sign them in. Just for the record. We'll put them in the big room."

"We were kind of looking for something on the less expensive side, you know?"

"For you, you can stay for free as our guests."

211

"No, we insist on paying. We're not poor, and you're in business now."

"Well. Thanks for being so understanding. You still get the big room. We'll cut you a deal."

*   *   *

"This is your first time in a bar, Angie, and don't go getting any ideas, okay?"

"Okay, Daddy."

"We don't usually get children here at the Silver King, so Angie is our special guest," Griff, Joy's husband, said. "Here's the booster seat of honor. Only one and scarcely used. Complete with menus. Sorry, all big people's."

EYES ADJUSTED to the dark bar and the short menus folded in worn laminated plastic covers. The five newcomers sat in oak spindle chairs around an often-scratched and water-bleached circular oak table-for-six away from the bar. There a half-dozen men, in Wrangler's or Levi's jeans and teeshirts, sat on tall stools for happy hour. They hunched over with their backsides to the oak table like calves at a feeding station. Griff wore a gray herringbone Harris tweed jacket with a tie-dyed cotton turtleneck, faded jeans and tan rough-out cowboy boots, his beard full but trimmed on a square face with a front shock of chestnut hair and a somber D.H. Lawrence cast, his eyes friends with your eyes, with half a pencil behind his left ear.

"Can I draw you a round or would you like a pitcher? I've also got bottled beer and soft drinks. The draft is Coors this time of year."

"Drafts around," Tom said, "except Angie takes orange juice. Straight. Just a small glass half full with no ice. She's past letting us help her drink anymore, and doesn't mind wearing the juice."

"Are you Griff?" Kristi asked. "Joy brought us over a pan of brownies and said we should introduce ourselves."

"Then you're the . . . you have the Sawtooth Inn. I'm Griff. What did you say your names were?"

"Burgess. I'm Kristi and this is Jim, call him Burge, and these are our friends, Tom and Jill, from Richland, Washington. You've already met Angie."

"Way out. We have the best food in Sawtooth, so get ready for a treat. Steaks and burgers are our specialty, but we also do a mean Idaho rainbow trout if you like fish. Pan fried, usually boneless. Idaho baked spuds. I'll give you a chance to look at the menu."

IN THE midst of dinner, Kristi spotted a big dirty white and russet steer poke its head into the open doorway over the often tripped-over threshold of the Silver King, then pull it back out again.

"Get in there, you son-of-a-bitch!" someone outside shouted. The steer shot through the doorway, knocking stools, tables and chairs awry, the voice doing the shouting planted on top of the steer, his legs forced wide bareback, his hat as ragged and dirty as what he sat on. The steer bellowed as it turned around in the upset furniture, the man pulling back on the reins. Griff came running from behind the bar and stopped short of being trampled, the steer's crumpled right horn knocking over a quickly vacated bar stool.

"Sam, get that goddam critter out of here or I'll shoot him and you both. Sam! He's hamburger, Sam!"

Sam tried to calm the animal, which insisted on continuing the ride, then stopped still, as if momentarily shocked with an insult.

"Don't have to get huffy about it. Just brought him in here to show him what a hippie looked like."

Sam kicked the steer in the ribs with his heels. The steer responded by cutting loose, green manure and slobber splattering steaming over the floor as Sam propelled him toward the doorway, his head bobbing, the timid hoofs thundering on the plank flooring. Then suddenly it was quiet and starting to smell. Angie caught her breath and screamed in terror, her lips blue.

"Sorry folks. It's just Sam having some fun on too much fuel. He'll be sorry tomorrow and will come in and apologize, so I pass that along to you now. Just a minute and we'll have this place cleaned up."

The couples returned to look at their food, but the beef somehow didn't seem the same.

"I don't think I'll need a doggie bag," Tom said.

"Don't worry, folks. This one's on the house. Please do come back. Excuse us."

Chapter 18

THE FIVE people walked back up the hill to the hotel in the dusk, Burge with a six-pack purchased from the Silver King in each hand. The mountain shadow reached high above the plane of sight and made concentration necessary for maneuvering the unlit sidewalk until the lighted windows of the inn that was once a house emerged from around a darkened corner building south and west.

"Sam raised that steer as a pet," Burgess said. "My guess."

"Some places do a better job of tolerating their eccentrics than others," said Jill. "I guess that's what we saw. An act of tolerance."

"So what's intolerant? To be shot?" Tom asked.

"In intolerant places, no one would dare to do something like that. Try Richland."

"In the first place," Burge said, "you have to be in a place where somebody thinks to raise a steer so it can be ridden. It isn't natural for the steer to want that. That's how rodeos got started. Second, someone has to want the attention enough to risk getting shot. Third, the steer didn't know what his urges would be, so it wasn't his fault. So there was an element of accident in all this, the steer being in the wrong place at the wrong time. Fourth . . ."

"Stop, Burge, you're babbling," Kristi said. "Though it's good to hear it after so much morose silence."

"Just babbling. I'm glad we're here now, you see."

"Well, here we are," Kristi said.

"It's just that I had the thought we might have moved from one bad place to another, looked at in a certain light, even though we were careful to scout things out."

"This is where we are," Kristi insisted. "So turn on some other lights. Unlock the door so we can go inside, please. It gets cold around here fast when the sun goes down."

BURGESS TURNED the key in the door and took the "Back Soon" note down that had been taped to the inside of the window. The others walked in and made their way across the creaking floor to the parlor, the only place with enough seats for them all to sit down. Angie sat, laid down on the side of her face, and slowly fell asleep on the pale yellow patchwork baby's quilt arranged for her on the carpet.

"The food was really tasty there, wasn't it?" said Jill.

"At least it was at first," said Burgess. "I'm glad you liked it. We're not much at home cooking just yet. At least we're in and can get settled now, and there's hope for a future if we get some lodgers and don't share the war."

"That issue seems long ago, being here," said Tom. "What if the cold war were to turn hot? It looks as if it will at any minute to me. It has ever since I can remember, so that you become dull to it, tired, even if it's as real as Cuba. You two are the lucky ones. I still have to be the 'Concerned Scientist.' Until someone else willing to pay me starts using computers."

"It never got to be that bad for me. I guess it might have, had I stuck around any longer. My job was being an engineer. Of what didn't matter much. The mystique wore off. You know. The giants of the atomic age weren't around the site any more. Except you, of course."

"You tell yourself how important the work is if you are to keep at it. If there is ever a nuclear war, at the plant we're toast. Carbonized. Here in the mountains, you can at least pretend to be safe."

"Thanks for all the reassurance," said Burgess. "Bob Dylan's dream. One of them, I think."

"We're keeping war away, it is said."

"Now you're the only one. My term expired."

"Your work becomes your conscience, as well as your consciousness," Kristi said. "And vice versa. Don't you think? But then sometimes we get employees who turn into spies and sabotage things. Explain the world."

"I'm sorry about that, Burge," Tom said, half ignoring her. "You'll have the name of your own choosing here. I guess there's one reason why we came here. To show you that we still care about you two, Jill and I, and we don't think what happened is right. We wanted to wish you the best in your new life."

"*La vita nuova,*" Burge replied. "Maybe it was meant to be this way, though I don't think any longer that we are big enough for nature or the fates or whatever to have meant anything by us. Though 'meant to be this way' assumes something in a universe where we are less than a dot in space can actually bestow meaning that way. Maybe we're just a happy eventuality, and some of us seem determined to snuff that. Happy us, sometimes, at any rate. But nature seems neutral on the subject and doesn't care if we turn ourselves into nano sunspots."

"Nature means a lot by us," Jill replied. "People have their lives to be conscious of, and other lives, too. There it is, all for us. This world is what has survived so far, after countless births and deaths. All that's possible right now is what we've got, and vice versa. So here we all are, getting ready for the next page to turn."

"The question is, how much is written on the new page that comes up," Kristi said. "Sometimes I think it's almost blank, and other times written in a profound language I can barely read but must keep trying. For the parents of baby birds, if you watch them, it says, 'We'll take turns bringing back food and looking after things.' I like keeping the book as blank as possible most of the time, so I can write it myself by living it."

"A family changes things," said Jill. "Sometimes life seems all written out, with the phrase 'or else' following every sentence. It isn't as it was when we were suddenly magically free and on our own. But I wouldn't trade Angie for anything most of the time. Any of the time. Right, Tom?"

"Right," Tom said. "I've never felt magically free and on my own. I've felt scared sometimes. Sorry, Jill. I had to find a job, right away. And now I have to keep at it for more years than I have lived, or try to find something else when it becomes possible. What happens to us next? All I can see from back there is 'or else.' Make bombs, or else."

"Or else 'Nam, a place that seems too small to worry about from here, unless you're about to pay it a visit."

"I can't watch the news. I keep thinking we'll nuke 'em," said Tom. "The old guys I work with actually hope so. They'll be ready. But then also dead, probably. What are you going to do about the draft, now, Burge?"

"My draft board rejected me back in college. 1-Y, actually, meaning 'we don't want you now but maybe later.' Football knee. I never thought I'd be glad I got damaged. Without that, I would have had a deferment at Hanford one day and been overseas the next. People are burning their draft cards, as if that would make any difference besides starting them off in life in trouble."

"I have to take Angie upstairs," Jill said. "Give me the keys, will you please, Tom?"

"I'll take her if you open the door. She's getting heavy."

Tom lifted the child, her blonde head wobbling from sleep, and took her toward the door as Jill grabbed up the small quilt and followed, the worn room key on a ring with the number '1' on a tooled leather fob in her hand. Kristi and Burgess sat back in the silence and didn't speak to one another for over a minute. Burgess rubbed his eyes and straightened out in the overstuffed chair brought from Richland.

"So HERE they are," Kristi said, and paused. "And here we are. Every time I've visited the mountains I've thought there was something I should be doing here, besides just hiking around and grooving the scenery, but I've never known what, so I left feeling the trip was incomplete. No personal fulfillment. Which always makes me want to come back, or just to not leave in the first place.

"For hundreds of years in China," she continued, "mountains and streams were places people visited to meditate, place after place, back from a thousand and more years ago. I saw scrolls of landscapes once at a museum in Seattle, and then searched out some books in the library. You look down to the scroll as if from high in the mountains and even above them, but you see multiple perspectives of place instead of just what you would actually see in nature. You end in a sort of revelation, as if what you see and what you remember and imagine are present all at once, but then you roll the scroll and the scene changes. You want to see how deep things go. How broad. Mountains like that, for generation on generation. Epiphanies, all themselves."

"I'd like to be enlightened like that for real just once," Tom said. "Now no one can travel to China, and no one knows what Mao is doing to it. I don't know, at any rate. Maybe some of it's the same, China is so vast."

"So my mountains are here," Kristi said. "With new expectations—for the unexpected."

"You're always inside books, Kristi," Burge said. "The cartoon wise man always sits on the top of a mountain peak, and the seeker struggles to get to him to ask the meaning of life. The wise man delivers a one liner, like, 'Don't ask me, I'm lost myself,' or 'Get me a ham on rye and a brew. Buy yourself some, too. I just realized what it's all about.'"

"What what's all about?" Jill asked, rounding the doorframe into the parlor and sitting back down on the sofa in front of the tall night-black window, Tom following behind her.

"Oh, you know. Life," said Burgess.

"Maybe it's ultimately only discernible in the moment and can't be abstracted much," said Kristi, "because it's so full of contradictions that even dialectic or deconstruction can't reach it. Just shred it, and you recreate it, with an array of leftover universe. Sometimes it's like that. Whatever's there to talk about, someone has to have made or seen it out of some quandary or other. Not the big Someone, just many people back and back through time.

"Then there are collisions of someones, and eventually just a collection of perspectives that let you see some things but not others. I sound as if I've grown really nihilistic, but I'm not. I never want to stop being on a pilgrimage, even though we've stopped this one here for now. And I want to see what nobody else has seen, including the other side of death. But that only when I have to."

"I'm glad just to have a home again," Burgess said, "and hope this one doesn't fall apart, too. Some things I'm happy not to know."

"Burge, you sound really old," Tom said.

"Back in high school, or even college, or even yesterday, I never knew life was like this."

KRISTI TOOK off her sandals and rubbed the inside of her bare left foot with the ball of her right.

"Life isn't like this," she said. "It's only what's happened to us so far, and our lives are taking a different shape now. Everybody else seems just fine, mostly, except in poor countries, where they aren't so fine. And there are too many people not so fine. So this is where the dice have stopped rolling."

"I'd much rather be able to see what's up ahead of me than only be static old fine," said Tom. "Better still, to create what's up ahead of me."

"Do you remember taking a dive and getting your head sliced? Some foresight," Jill said.

"You've got to have some adventure, or you do get stale," Tom replied, "especially to yourself. It's like Kristi wanting to see what nobody else has seen. You wouldn't like us any other way. Would you?"

"I like you the way you are, except when you do get hurt."

With a pause in the conversation, Burgess said, "I have an adventure if you're interested."

"What?" Jill asked.

"I found out there are a bunch of trails and half-trails here and there, and one goes by behind the lodge and runs along the hillside and back into the mountains. I haven't traveled to the end of it. It intersects some other trails. I thought it would be a good idea to do a map for our future guests. Nobody else in town has done one, so far as I know. It shouldn't be too difficult."

"I can't take Angie along. Someday we'll go."

"Someone has to mind the store," said Kristi. "We'll stay here together, Jill, and keep Angie company."

"We'll blaze the trails so you three can make the hike later on."

"Why don't we trade places?" Kristi asked. "You two look after the front desk and Angie, and we'll do the trail blazing."

"Or we can go couple by couple," Jill said. "Angie should be easy to look after now that we've spent all this time together. She should be. That's not to say she will be."

"Or we could switch partners," said Tom. "Are there enough trails to do all of that?"

"I don't know," Burgess replied. "I don't know where any of them goes, so we'll just have to explore. Maybe the first people on the trail can make a map for the next two to test out to see if it's accurate, then trade off exploring. Do you want to try this?"

*   *   *

ANGIE AWAKENED first the next morning and struggled to get free of the bedcovers, which had been tucked in tightly over the deep blue metal frame of the rollaway bed let down at the foot of Jill and Tom's tall oiled mahogany four-poster.

"I can't get out, Momma," she said, as Jill struggled awake and Tom rolled over onto his back and lifted his head to look at his daughter.

"Wouldn't you like to sleep a little bit longer, Angie?" Jill said. "It's kind of cold being up this early."

"I want to get up and I can't."

"Just a second and I'll come help you. The quilt must be caught on something."

Jill got up and tugged at the top of the quilt, made for a larger bed. Her daughter wriggled free, put her feet on the floor, then quickly lifted them back up on the bed.

"The floor freezes my feets."

"Here. Come step on the rug while I get your clothes. Let's wash you first since you're up. Do you have to go potty?"

THEY DISAPPEARED into the bathroom while Tom rolled to his stomach and dozed. The door opened and the child emerged, a shadow into the darkened room.

"Tom, I'm in the shower first. Please watch Angie."

The little girl stood on tiptoes to look at her father dozing. She reached her wet right hand up and over the edge of the bed to touch his stubbly mouth.

"Daddy's sleeping, Angie."

She waited a moment, then touched him again, and put her hand down and waited, staring. He opened his eyes.

"Okay, no sleeping for us."

He sat up on the edge of the bed, the left side of the collar of his maroon pajamas up, and scratched the sleep from his head with both hands.

"Do you like staying in the mountains with Kristi and Jim?"

"Uh-huh."

"What do you think of that big steer that came to dinner last night?"

"I was scared."

"We wouldn't have let him hurt you. Do you know that?"

222

"Uh-huh."

"He was a funny old steer. He made Mommy and Daddy laugh. Do you want to have some breakfast?"

"No."

"We'll see if we can't find you something when Daddy's out of the shower."

THE DOOR knocker sounded downstairs, brass on brass. Tom could hear Burgess in the hallway, then on the stairs. Muffled voices. Heavy eyed, he was a child himself in the morning in some other upstairs, shivering and hungry again, wondering who had come to the door, who had invaded his world of trouble. *Just something before a dream.*

Chapter 19

W ITH THE breakfast done and their husbands on the trail behind the inn, Kristi and Jill unloaded the liquor boxes carefully packed with kitchenware, washing out and filling the old knife-and-fork drawer by the sink and placing cups and plates on freshly scrubbed shelves. The kitchen had been designed for a much larger, wealthier family, and several shelves, especially higher up, remained bare behind closed doors.

"Let me get these empty moving boxes out of the way, Jill. I don't want to wait for Burge to do it. It's too cluttered in here. I'll stuff them into the basement if there's room. Just a minute."

Kristi opened a door beneath the hallway staircase and twisted the old light switch to her right. The plaster was sea-foam green with signs of soot in the corners and along the ceiling. She walked halfway down the worn stairs into the cellar, her right hand on the railing, and then returned to the kitchen.

"Cobwebs," she said to Jill. "I can see well enough to take these boxes down."

"Let me help."

"I've got them. You're busy with Angie."

"She's safe around stairways now. At least she's less of a walking disaster than she was."

Kristi took five boxes down, two at a time, the newspaper stuffed back in, and stacked them against the stone wall facing the stairway. With the last, she looked back in to the left along the floor joists and pipes and floor supports and old wooden furniture covered with dust to a big trunk of wood and cracked brown leather with a rounded top. Alongside were several dark picture frames arranged back-to-front and a tall bookcase scattered with old books and ancient dusty knickknacks—a rusty hand iron, shoe lasts, worn wooden jewelry and stationery boxes, glass figurines (seal balancing ball, ballerina, terrier with ruffle collar begging), the glass shining in bubbles where the dust recently had been rubbed off in a single streak. She went upstairs, leaving the light on and the door opened.

"Treasure hunt," she said to Jill. "The basement has some goodies for us to look at. Want to do some exploring?"

"Come here, Angie, and let's go downstairs. Kristi wants to show us something."

ANGIE BUMPED into the back of her mother's leg, swung around her at the top of the stairs, and backed down the first step, holding on to her mother's skirt. The little girl reached in front of her and grasped at the railing above her head. She stepped down each enormous step left leg first. The women slowly followed, a step at a time. At the bottom, Angie paused and looked toward the mass of antiques, her eyes stopping at the top shelf of the bookcase where an aged doll stood, dressed as an angel with a worn ceramic head. In the doll's hand was a tarnished wand tipped with a small star. It had flowing stiff silk robes, a crown slightly awry on its head, and a bent and re-bent wire halo.

"Mommy, reach her."

"She's just to look at, Angie. She's all dusty."

"I want her."

"She's yours to look at, but you can't touch."

Kristi lifted down the doll before Angie's tears started, then balanced it on the trunk for Angie to see up close. Angie stood on tiptoes and touched the doll's face.

"This angel hasn't looked after anyone for a very long time. She has the ages on her."

"I wonder what she's hiding in that trunk," said Jill.

"Careful. Pandora's box."

"What's hidden away, I wonder. I'm putting the doll back for a minute."

The trunk was lined with coral and ivory aromatic cedar. Pressed once-white bed linens with just-darker embroidered edging had been folded neatly to fit on top. Kristi looked at her hands to check for dirt, dusted them off, one against the other. She began to lift up a top layer, put it back down, stood up and brought two of her packing boxes over to form an impromptu table to keep the linens clean. She placed them on the boxes, their scent in the air. She lifted out a hand-stitched wedding-ring quilt, pale blue, and placed it on top of the sheets. A second chest was next, surrounded with bundles of old letters.

"This is somebody's box of memories," Jill said. "The littler chest looks like what my grandmother used to keep her grandmother's silver in. You may have struck the mother-lode."

"I wonder who left these here. The names on the letters don't match up with the previous owners."

"That's probably why they were left behind. Maybe every owner leaves them behind for the next, back a way. Maybe for someone who might come to claim them. Back from the dead. Aren't you going to open the chest?"

"I'm more curious about the letters. Aren't you? But I feel as if I'm violating somebody's privacy."

"I know. Hurry."

KRISTI UNDID a piece of string wrapped midway along each side of the envelopes and tied with a bow in the middle. The top letter was addressed to Daisy Savage, Sawtooth, Idaho, from Martha Greenway, 271 Noble Point, Norristown, Pennsylvania, and dated April 30, 1926. Kristi read aloud:

Since you went away so very long ago the snow has come and gone—less snow, I'm sure, than you have there in the mountains so far from home, but enough to be winter. We miss you but realize your father must follow his fortunes, even if they take him to such a far distant place.

Thank you for writing. In reply, we all continue to be in good health, despite a bout of influenza in the family and much hard work to take advantage of the spring sunshine. The farm is glorious with new life—birds of every sort and calves and lambs. Sadie had six puppies. We have no idea who the father is, since the pups look like nothing around here—more like baby wolves, though there haven't been wolves here in even my dad's lifetime. Jonathan said they were coyotes and howls at them in play. They don't pay much attention, being much more interested in Sadie and each other at this point, but Jonathan gets a thrill from doing that. You said you heard coyotes at night. Do they come close?

It sounds as if you have a nice house to stay in, and so new! Is it far from your father's mine? Do you have friends to talk to? Are you to be sent away to school or do you want to stay there next year? I wish I could just go over next door to see you.

Please write to me again soon.

Ever your cousin,

Martha

"There are so many letters here," Jill said. "She's young. Maybe sixteen? I thought we'd find torrid love letters."

"Me, too. Maybe they are later on in the bundle. Are you curious?"

"Yes. Except I feel, you know, as if we are not supposed to be looking at these. What if we were supposed to find them to keep someone from vanishing altogether? How can you do both? Let's check out the silver first."

"If it is silver."

Kristi drew the box from the surrounding bundles of letters and folded cloth. She balanced the bottom of the box on the edge of the trunk and opened the lid. Inside was not silver. Instead, two leather-bound journals had been placed side-by-side—no titles showing, just blank covers. Inside the first volume, she read, in small penned script that was almost printing.

Ruby Silver: A Story of Sawtooth.

"I guess it's at least about silver." Jill said. "I wonder if this is a history or just made up? What's 'ruby silver?'"

"Maybe it's somebody's name or a kind of silver. I've never heard of it before. What's in the second book?"

"Nothing. It's blank. The writer of the first book probably intended to write in it but didn't, for some reason."

"Perhaps he intended to come back to it. Maybe he just moved away."

"Or wrote with invisible ink. Or left it for us to write in. What's his name?"

"Charles Mann."

"Did he live here?"

"I don't know, Jill. I've never heard of him. Except for the people we bought this place from, I only know the name of one person who lived here, and that's from a name on an envelope. Maybe whoever wrote that book was a boarder."

"But this is all packed away so neatly. On a winter's evening, you'll have to do some sleuthing to put it all together. It's like a mystery."

"A part of someone's life ended, and this was left behind like a ghost. Maybe the whole of someone's life ended except this. Someone else packed this stuff away for them in hopes that a kindred spirit would one day find it and bring the memories to life again. A reach beyond. One to one."

"Listen," Jill said. "That's either the doorbell or the bell on your front desk."

"It is? I'll run up and see."

"We'll be right behind you. I'll put this stuff back for you first."

KRISTI RAN upstairs in anticipation of customers, rounding the top and stepping quickly through the unlit hallway.

Steve Bourne, much unchanged at 27, in the same Brooks Brothers casual clothes though slightly heavier and a day unshaven, was about to push on the desk bell once again. He stopped and knocked twice when he saw Kristi emerge from the shadowed hallway, his eyes still adjusting from the bright outside.

"Steve!"

"Kristi! I got your change-of-address card and had to come to see what's going on. Where's Burge?"

"He's on a trail somewhere behind us with Tom Henderson. You remember Tom, from Richland?"

"Oh, yeah, Tom. Where's 'behind us on the trail'?"

"Your guess is as good as mine where he is exactly. I'll let you find him if you'd like. They are trying to put together a map of the trails around here for our guests. So how do you like this place?"

"I like it, but I just got here. I thought you'd never leave the Atomic Paradise."

"Did Burge tell you about that? Our leaving, I mean?"

"About what? All I know is, I got this change of address postcard saying that you'd moved here. I thought Jim—Burge—was preempting me on the ski resort idea, so I thought I'd come to see if it were true. That and to welcome you to Idaho, gem of the mountains. *Esto Perpetua.* Home of the mountain bluebird, the white pine, the syringa and me. I couldn't very well call you, since you'd already moved."

"We don't have a ski resort in mind just yet, but that's a good idea. All we could afford is this old house that's been converted into a hotel of sorts, as you can see, but it fits. Do you want to go try to find Burge and Tom?"

"Where do I look?"

"All I know is, they headed south up the hill, to the left out the back way. I've never been on any of the trails, so you'll have to make your own way."

"I'll check it out. Let me check in first, though."

"You're staying? Oh, excuse me. I didn't stop to think. I'll give you a room looking up at the mountains. They all do that, but this has the best view. That okay?"

"Great. Give me the key and I'll run my bag up now."

STEVE DISAPPEARED out the back door five minutes later, down the granite double step to the ground, up the shaded trail through thick pine. Soon he was almost out of sight up the hill and into the trees. The two women watched through the rusting screen of the back porch until his blue-shirted shoulders disappeared.

"Who else will just drop in on you before you can get all unpacked?" Jill said. "We thought we'd come to help and would have you to ourselves. We've gathered in a new helper."

"Thanks," Kristi replied. "This was first-order void-leaping for us. I suppose there always is that when you start out with something new that is something. You reassure me that everything will be okay. Steve does mean well. I hope he doesn't have any trouble finding Burge and Tom. They are such different people. He seems so lost at times, even when he's in command. He's part of Burge's college days. Single people like him are alone too much. Was I like that, I wonder? Of course I was, without my realizing that it was so obvious."

"Can't he find a nice girl and settle down? Isn't that the usual line?"

"Burge says women used to chase the guy. I don't know why he didn't pick one. Maybe it was just too easy for him."

"He isn't . . . you know."

"I don't think so. Burge would have said something. Steve can't let go of the past, that's what I think. The college social scene that disappears at the end of four years. Nostalgia choking the soul. Or maybe what was once so easy for him isn't, any more, now that he's no longer BMOC, and it's hard for him to adjust. Perhaps he just doesn't want to try. Glad Burge did."

"Your situation was so unusual. Were you hard to get? I don't mean it that way. I should shut up. You don't have to answer."

"What do you want to ask?"

"Did you have difficulties after what happened to you? Like sexual. I would have."

"Of course I did. I was impossible. I'm still impossible. I couldn't respond normally. I was so hopelessly strung between wanting to see Burge and to not see him for such a long time. I hated myself. I did get through it."

"We weren't such good friends then."

"You and I had just met. I couldn't tell anyone what happened to us, anyway, not even my mother. Now everyone knows, with salt, spices, and strychnine. People lied. It made a better story. It was easy to run away from that, mostly. The idea of going back now gives me the shudders."

"Maybe one day you'll feel nostalgic yourself for home."

"I'll miss my mother and I'll miss you and Angie and Tom. How can I feel nostalgic, though? After all that happened."

"What I mean is, you wanted to come home once before, after college. Maybe you will again. Wasn't it just a blip in time?"

"Too much has happened. We're lucky to be here. We were stepped on by the Atomic Bomb. All we wanted was justice and to be let alone. I would have taken just the being let alone part. I don't understand Burge fully still. Perhaps it's just a part of his being a male. At first he wanted revenge, but he could never find the person who confronted us in the Blue Mountains. The guy was a ghost, and Burge wanted justice. How does that work out for you? He thought he had no other option than to defend himself. Against what or how, I don't know. Any possibility of what it might have been was thwarted in the end. We weren't big enough to matter."

"I'm sorry, Kristi. I didn't mean to upset you. I guess that was the end of it."

"I'm not upset, Jill. It's just that I was so long being obsessive about what happened to us in the Blue Mountains, I couldn't see what else was going on. I could forget about it for a while, until the memory would come down hard and my heart would palpitate and I couldn't sleep again. If it had only been a flat-out rape, it would have been different. But I had to perform it myself to stay alive, and mess someone else up in the process. So I thought.

"But afterward I would argue with myself wondering if that were completely true, and I would feel waves of guilt. Then I tried to force myself to feel nothing rather than have compromised emotions, but couldn't because Burge's mere being wouldn't let me. Do you understand? And I feel guilty for pitying myself when there is so much else wrong in the world. Sorry."

"I THINK I understand. But I haven't gone through what you've been through, which means I probably shouldn't even try to understand completely.

"Oh, I put the things in the trunk again that were out, and straightened the angel on the shelf after I dusted her. Angie didn't want to give her up."

"Do you want her to have it, Jill? I'll be more than happy to give it to you. Angels don't work for me."

"Angie's too young. The doll would be in tatters in no time. I don't dare have it in the house. Perhaps you could wait until she is older and will appreciate it more."

"I'll clean it up some more and put it away someplace where it won't get so dusty."

"Thanks. I was also tempted to read the last letter and the end of the journal, just to find out what happened to everybody, but I resisted. Something would always be missing. I seem even more intrusive, now."

"I should read it all, just to know more about a place where I am expected to be something of a hostess."

She looked down at her hands, folded her fingers slowly together, then put them on her knees, as if to stand.

"Kristi, you know you can talk to me whenever you want to, don't you, Kristi? I wish I could have been more of a friend back when you really needed one. I didn't know. I just needed to say that."

"You were having problems of your own. At any rate, I couldn't talk about it, and so I didn't. We did survive."

"Our problem seems like nothing now. You helped us."

"We didn't do anything."

"You helped. We can't repay you. We were numbed into inaction. You must have helped, because here we are."

"What if I couldn't shut up about what happened to me, Jill? Have you ever thought about that? I have, when my thoughts wouldn't turn off about it. That would be how to lose friends, instantly. I even lost myself in those periods. So you were lucky you didn't have to hear it. That's what made having it unhidden and twisted so difficult, one of the things. It was like having to start all over again with it. The obsession. So I was glad to leave, except for missing friends and family. Do you see?"

"Yes, I see."

"Because even one little memory was doing it to me again, doing it to my mind, and that was too much. So enough was enough."

"I understand."

"Burge and I . . . well, Burge and I. We'll make it, because I want to. He never presses me. There is no analysis to twist things up. I can say 'no' whenever I want to, and now I never do. Mostly."

"Sometimes we don't. You know. He seems not to want to be bothered. Now."

"Let's go read the last letter, just to prove that everything in that other world is as it should be."

"'Kay."

"Jill, I don't want to. Promise me you'll read it with me later."

"Your place, Kristi."

Chapter 20

*I*T WON'T *take too long to catch Jim and Tom,* Steve told himself, his eyes struggling to adjust to the quick passages from intense mountain sunlight to shade to light again, alternating as he moved up the trail through the lodgepole pines and dense brush. His hands throbbed with his heartbeat as he walked.

He rolled up the sleeves of his blue button-down shirt three neat folds each and put his hands in the pockets of his chinos. The new wide ties and lapels he saved for work. *Soon they will be all there is to buy. Everything changes. What's next?* He had to get his doctorate to keep working in higher education, where there was no money, anyway. The dean told him that in no uncertain terms.

What else can there be? Can he do that? Two-thirds of those who start study for a doctorate drop out. How can he make it? What'll he do? What'll he do?

This moment of panic brought to you by modern life, he thought. *Nothing. What else is there?*

The trail was overgrown, not traveled much, but he did see fresh heel and sole marks in the dark mountain soil. This was the way, since probably Jim or Tom's shoes have made the marks. Clark's nutcrackers shrieked like crows on low pine boughs among a scattering of sparrows; the air smelled slightly of dew on loam and pine. He couldn't tell where the trail was going because of the trees, the curves and switchbacks. The side of the mountain was unusually steep to his right, then to his left. The trail was going upward and keeping him winded. He had become out of shape since college intramurals, and he had lost some then since high school. *The flash of age. No, I'll get back into shape starting now.*

He looked down behind him at how steep the trail was and how far he had come without knowing his destination. Behind him seemed much steeper than ahead, what he could see of each. He hiked. There were no alternative pathways. Then there was one, leading steeply upward and out of sight, which he did not take, thinking Jim will choose the lower trail if he is doing first-time mapping, and kept on. Perhaps deer have made the upper trail. Mountain goats. The boulders and rocks were pale gray granite and rain-washed and stained with age, with only a little lichen in unworn crevices and no moss. At an outcrop free of tall growth he saw down below the hotel and a part of the town, quite small through the trees. He was surprised to have climbed so far. He kept on, the trail before him looking much the same as when he started out. He saw no sign of life, though he heard distinctly a few cars streaming their way around the town. They sounded much closer than he knew them to be.

He could have waited. Why didn't he wait back at the lodge? If they came off the trail somewhere else and didn't return the way they came, he was going to miss them and would just have to return to the lodge anyway. *Deer tracks. They'll come back this way. I did the right thing. I'll meet them on the trail.*

IN TIME HE was on top of a ridge and looking down into an untouched small valley on the other side, then across it and up to a much larger pine-covered mountain that the ridge had concealed completely from the viewing angle of the town. Still partially blocking the view of the town, its trunk rooted thirty yards down the hill, was an old white-bark pine, its thick branches for bearing the weight of snow spread out almost like a decid-uous tree in the absence of other pines crowding around it, its five-needle structure making the tree look out of another eon. He still couldn't see where the trail went, but it started down into the valley, angling back in the opposite direction from the trail he had just come up. It made its way around a cluster of granite boulders that reach to the top of the ridge.

He had been hiking a long time. Fifteen steps down he saw a division in the trail leading back up to and, he guessed, along the top of the ridge. Should he take it? Should he go back? Did Burgess take the other trail after all? Which of these did he take? Steve's loafers were not the best shoes for hiking and were now covered in dust. He could feel rocks through the shoe leather as he stepped. This slope of the trail put him in new territory, and it was almost as if the populated world no longer existed and the nature of time had changed somehow without the presence of other people to shape it. Minutes seemed longer, though it was the middle of the day.

Steve started down the long trail past the fork. He found himself also hiking upward over boulders and rises in the hillside in order to climb down again in keeping to the trail. He had seen no one all morning.

As he looked over the top of the third of these rises, he saw what seemed to be a piece of colored cloth disappear beneath brush covering the trail below. He kept his eyes on the spot, tripping to a forced hop over a partially buried stone.

As HE regained his balance, he saw a woman to his right against the mountain sitting half-lotus on a flattened granite slab. Her eyes, the color of honey, were fixed on him, looking through him. She stood to acknowledge him, her eyes unchanging as she watched him. She was alluring, athletic, her features northern Italian: not Botticelli's Venus, but the nymph behind Venus, there with the zephyr, commanding, unadorned, an incarnation of nature.

"Excuse me," he said to her, "I was looking for someone and think I've taken the wrong path. You didn't pass anyone on your way along the trail, did you?"

"Nobody takes these trails," she responded. "I think I have made them up myself. What are you doing here?"

"I'm looking for friends. Two men my age. One of them owns the little hotel at the foot of the hill over the ridge. You haven't seen them?"

"Perhaps they've taken the ridge trail or maybe they are behind me. I haven't seen anyone. I rarely do."

"You're from here, then. Where does this trail lead? Am I likely to reach the end of it anytime soon?

"It leads cross-canyon to other trails, some up the mountain. Nothing's marked. You have to know them. You can get lost and turned around if you don't know the way. You have to find a mountain peak as a landmark, and it will want to disappear. It's not likely your friends are behind me. I would have seen them unless they reached another path before I came along. Probably they've taken the ridge trail."

"Maybe I was on my own way to being lost. Do you mind if I go with you back up the trail?"

"I might not want to go that way. I usually don't like the way everyone else goes."

"There aren't that many options over this way that I can tell. I didn't mean to disturb you."

"I'm not disturbed. You can go with me. I'll walk down to the lodge if that's where you are going."

"I don't mean to take you off course. We can go along the ridge if you like. Where were you going?"

"Just walking." she said. "I have my places to go and like to find new ones when I can."

"Let's take the ridge path first, then. Perhaps my friends are there. I'm happy to have the company of someone who knows things as well as you seem to. My name's Steve Bourne. "

"Oh, I'm Andrea."

"Just Andrea?"

"Yes. I've always been just Andrea. My last name is rather long: Boccaccio. My initials are very easy to remember."

THEY WALKED back up over the two rises and found the footpath starting out beneath the granite boulders near the top of the ridge and walked upward again. Steve panted to keep pace. His shins burned. She looked at him and slowed her pace.

"Sorry to be so out of shape. I'll try to keep up."

"It will be easier to talk if we slow down a little, perhaps. I'm used to walking by myself."

"What do you do here?

"Wait tables in a bar. What else? I go to graduate school and am here just during the summers. My family is here. My father is a miner."

"Where do you go to graduate school?"

"Stanford. Physics. I have a fellowship. There was no other way, and I have to take a lot of shit because I am a woman in physics and have a funny name, but science I love. During the academic year it's all graduate school. Waiting tables here in the summer gives me lunch money, and I get to be in the mountains and home for a season. I do physics. What do you do?"

"I work for a college. Student affairs. I have to get my doctorate if I want to do anything in higher education, I'm told. Right now I appear to be a lost soul. My mind sort of dropped out with graduation. I'll get that back into shape, too."

"Do you like what you do?

"I like students, or I wouldn't be doing what I'm doing. I like them when they're not screwing up, anyway. I see a lot of problems. Students' options for some kind of life become really clear to you. You can help some of them."

HE TOOK a break in conversation to adjust the rhythm of his breath and steps. The sun was intense with the high altitude, the sky rich blue.

"There are the protesters," she said. "Didn't used to be like that. It spills over into everything now. Sometimes I want to protest too, but I don't like my possibilities in life without doing what I'm doing."

"Mostly I see depression and alienation and ignorance, but those words don't mean anything until you see them manifest in actual human beings trying to deal with their lives, or escape dealing with them. It's different from the high spirits of student government, where you can work and put on a dance or speaker series or some other event. I get the problem students. That's my usefulness to the course of things. Students have problems. Want to hear my latest 'I saw a kid yesterday' story?"

She turned and looked at him, as if first contact.

"Why not tell me?" she asked.

"Some students just drop out and work in the potatoes and have some kids and beers, and maybe are happy. Or maybe that doesn't happen to them at all. I never see them again unless they are townies. Do you want to do physics forever?"

"If I could be as good as Marie Curie and Lise Meitner, yes and yes! Do you want to keep helping students?"

"I don't make any money. They don't pay us anything. Every year there is a new list of student body officers who just graduated who can do the job as well or better than I can because they are closer to the age of students and can identify better. They will want the job in the worst way, the way I thought I did when I first started out. A chance to really help people, to change a piece of the world is what they want. My boss, the Dean of Students, says I should get a doctorate. So I'll get a doctorate. I can't do that particular job forever. Maybe I can't even do it next year. Things can change a lot with the next class of students."

THEY WALKED on, more intent on viewing and being with each other than talking.

"You should come to Stanford and do physics," she continued.

"I'm more of a people person. Social sciences. Humanities. Maybe education. I couldn't concentrate on physics when I took it. Life as an inclined plane."

"Don't you like finding out about the world you're walking on?"

"I guess it's a different world for us. Don't you like people?"

"Sure I do. You're really being defensive, I think."

"Where did you learn that concept?"

"I live in the world, too. I wish the social sciences could be real sciences, is all. But they're not. Not the way physics is."

"We have hypotheses to formulate and test and reformulate. Data to gather. We can determine when something is counter-intuitive."

"Testing human nature is like testing . . . well, it isn't possible, is it? People act in every which way, and who can tell why?"

"Sometimes you can if you listen to them."

"They can't even tell themselves the truth. Can they? Not much of it."

"But you can still find out things worth knowing about people. Don't you think? Like ignorance and fear, for example? Stir those two together and see what you get?"

"Wouldn't you rather study something you can actually know about? I mean, as close to the truth about something as you can get? With still more to learn later on as things get tested and new ideas are created—the whole stretch of effort to know."

"You still have controversies in science. How was the universe formed, for example—steady state expansion, big bang, or bang bang bang?"

"You took astronomy. But we can figure out ways to make discoveries that will let us answer that someday. Good old "Steady State" discovered that the universe is expanding. Now cosmic background radiation, discovered just recently. There's a 'we' I can pretend to be a part of. How do you figure out what someone will say or how they will behave, given certain circumstances? I'll never know. We can get a rocket to the moon. How do I know what you will say next? How do I know what even I will say next?"

"I'll try to defend myself," Steve said, "if I meet the needs of your hypothesis."

"Okay, so we defend ourselves when we talk. Usually. But we aren't really being scientific when we say that. I like knowing what we can come closest to knowing. Like what happens when you drop two objects together in a vacuum or how the sun works or why we have tides or what makes an earthquake or what else we can predict about physical objects. Why the sky is blue. Real world stuff, you know?"

"And I like finding out what I can about people. Like now. We've shared our first likes and dislikes. We haven't stepped on each other's napkins yet. I like that in making your acquaintance. I'd like to try to replicate it."

"Not bad, aye?" Andrea said. "I found someone who hikes in the mountains, even if he only does so to find someone he doesn't know the location of. Do you like walking in the mountains?"

"Do you want me to tell you the truth or what you want to hear?"

"What do you think I want to hear?" She asked.

"That I love walking in the mountains and could go on like this forever."

"Isn't that being a little . . . what? Blabstract?"

"Well, the walk did improve a lot when I got over the top of the ridge and found you on the other side, instead of a bear. I'll say that much. How far does this ridge trail go?"

"Not very far. It dead-ends for people at a big drop-off, then we'll have to come back."

"Will you walk down the trail to the lodge after? I'd like you to meet my friends if we don't run into the two I'm looking for first on the trail. Even if we do. They have wives and a kid waiting back at the lodge."

"You scarcely know me yourself," Andrea said, stepping ahead of him as the trail narrowed along the ridge crest. She led them along a rock face, leaning toward it to avoid the tree branches. She put her hand against the exposed rock for balance as the trail narrowed to almost nothing, then opened again.

"It's not as if I were taking you home to meet the family. I just think you might enjoy each other's company, since they're new to town and you know it so well. Burge wants to make a map of the area. For his guests. Hiking trails and the like. I'm sure you'd be more than valuable in helping him."

"Well, you're honest about your motives. I kind of like having the trails to myself. On the other hand, company sometimes would be nice. I like it right now, for example. I'd like to meet them if you don't suggest I help with the maps."

"You were the one that said people could get lost. Did you just mean me?"

"People could get lost. No maps."

SHE LOOKED back over her shoulder and slowed to catch his eye. She was serious, her eyes pale in the bright sun, her hair in waves, in sun streaks the same color as her irises, her hair blown quickly across her brow and put back in place with a quick hand. She returned her eyes to the pathway.

"I could lay out some hypotheses why not," Steve said, "but I'll drop it. We don't know each other very well."

"Thank you for dropping it. Does that mean you'd say something if you knew me better?"

"Perhaps you'd want me to say something if you knew me better?"

"I don't think so. It wouldn't make any difference to me now. Would you say something?"

"Not if you didn't want it. Perhaps you'll tell me why sometime. You don't have to right now."

"Do you think I 'walk these hills in a long black veil?' It's just that there are some places that mean enough to me that I don't want to make them a public attraction. That's all. Don't you see?"

"Will you show them to me? Sometime? Not today. We should be getting back."

"We'll see. No. Yes."

"Tell me about them, then."

"What's to tell? There are small water falls and a stream. Farther up, part of the stream runs from the mouth of an abandoned mine shaft. My grandfather died there. One day his heart stopped working, so he did, too. The same day the miners hit an aquifer. Pumping water out of the mine would cost more than the silver left there was worth at the time. So they all stopped working. Fires, too, with burnt timber supports. Some trails lead to old mines where nothing is left but occasional pieces of rusted equipment. The mines are dangerous. They've been sealed, but high school boys open them up for an adventure. Only one mine is left that still holds enough silver to work much, except even that depends on the value of silver and the cost of labor. The town needs to diversify to stay alive."

"Diversify with what?"

"People don't want it to change. I guess I sound like one of them, but I don't live here full time any more, not since high school. It can be hard to get to for skiing because of the pass, but skiing is good. Really good. Maybe one day the road will be better. Now you can usually make it with chains, except when the pass is closed. When there is no snow, there is a lake you can walk to, too, but it takes a long time."

STEVE'S FEET jammed repeatedly into the toe boxes of his shoes on the way down to the lodge. Walking fast was difficult for him by the time they arrived. He was weary, and Andrea, except for the dust on her boots and her somewhat tousled hair, looked as if she hadn't been hiking at all. Kristi and Burgess were waiting at the foot of the pathway for their descent.

Kristi had been worried, and now they understood. So like Steve to find somebody. No, somebody to find him.

Chapter 21

STEVE MADE introductions as fast as the words would come out of his mouth:

"Kristi and Jim, Andrea. Call Jim 'Burge.' Let's go inside. I've got to sit down."

He made it through the back door to the kitchen. He plopped down on a kitchen chair and gazed. He removed his dusty loafers and, with some care, his socks.

"Sorry about this," he said. "Do you have any band-aids, Kristi? I overdid it with the hiking. Andrea knows these mountains, to my exhaustion. I met her on the trail while I was searching for Burge and Tom. I thought the two of you might like each other. She's a Stanford bright star grad student when she's not working here summers. She says she's just a local kid."

"Please, let's talk, okay, Andrea?" Kristi said. "We still don't know anything about this place, and you can really help us. Steve, band-aids are in the downstairs bathroom cabinet. Let me go get them for you. You probably don't want to walk much right now."

Andrea suddenly knelt in front of Steve and picked up one foot, inspected it, set it down. She picked up the other, looked at it, then began to massage it, the balls of her thumbs against his sole. He gave a jump with the first push and slapped his sole flat on the tile floor.

"I can't stand to have anyone touch my feet."

"You can't?" Andrea laughed, sitting back on her heels, then standing up using only her legs. "You don't seem to have any blisters other than the small one on the side of your right little toe. I wish someone would massage my feet."

"Mine feel like I hiked in the rocks barefoot," he laughed back. "What did you do to me?"

"Just now? Nothing."

"On the trail. I hardly noticed my feet until it was too late."

"I tried to slow down for you."

"Wrong shoes. I should have known better. Next time I'll wear some hiking boots or at least gym shoes. I just wanted to talk to you, and hiking with you seemed the only way. You've bewitched me!"

"You were quite a way up the mountain on your own," Andrea said.

"How did we miss you, Steve? You got by us somehow. We didn't see any sign of you. We didn't know we should be looking."

"Did you make any maps?" Steve asked. "How far along the trail did you go?"

"Not to the end, Burge said. "I don't know how far it goes. We went over the top of the ridge and down in the valley until the trail forked, then forked again and headed up a mountain that you can't see from here. Honest. We ran out of time, so we came back. That gave us one angular line on the map with some cutoffs. Not much help, I'm afraid. With only that on a map, you could get lost pretty easily."

"You're right," Andrea said. "People do disappear occasionally, and have to be hunted for."

STEVE LOOKED as if he wanted to say something but was silent.

"Have you lived here long?" Jill asked Andrea.

"Just the summers now, but I was born and raised here."

"You must know the trails well."

"Since I was old enough to explore them."

"You'll have to give Burge some advice on the maps sometime," Kristi said.

"Sometime, perhaps. Be careful."

"She has her private places," Steve said.

SILENCE. Who knew what to say?

"You'll never see them," Andrea replied abruptly and started toward the back door to go.

"Sorry," Steve said. "Guess I said something wrong."

"Please sit down and stay a while, Andrea," Kristi said. *Steve struck a secret.* "You must be tired after such a long walk. Would you like something to drink?"

"Just water," Andrea said. "It's easy to dehydrate with so much sun."

"We really would like to get to know you better. We know hardly anyone here. Joy and Cos. That's it."

"I can only stay a minute or two. I have to go to work. There are old mines at the ends of some trails, that's all. Pilgrim, Ruby, Silver King, others. They can be dangerous if people don't know what they are doing."

"Thanks for telling us," Kristi said. "How can we get in touch with you?"

"She works at Mac's Place," Steve said. "Evenings, and walks during the day thinking about the earth and stars. She does physics."

"You must have gotten to know each other a little on the trail," Burgess said.

"Not well enough," Steve said, "or as much as I'd like to."

"You can reach me at my parents. The only Boccaccio in the book. There's a breed of dog with the same name—also a writer. I imagine us to be related to the writer, but maybe not. Bye."

She took a step, turned around to say, "Kristi, will you give me a quick look at this place before I go? It was a great mystery of my childhood. The past owners have all been sort of private about it, at least I thought they were, and it was off-bounds when

I was growing up. I don't want to take much of your time."

"Listen," said Kristi, "do you know anyone named Savage who might have lived here? Daisy Savage?"

"I didn't know Daisy Savage, though she used to live here. Miss Savage was really old, and all alone in this big old place. It wasn't a lodge then, just a big house. She had had borders during the war. We were told not to bother her. We were too young. But I remember her. She must have had a lonely life. Why?"

"We found her trunk in the basement with some letters and were curious if she had a family we could return them to."

"Not that I know about. Probably the trunk is all yours. Who owned it is only a wisp of memory now."

"Want to see it?" Kristi asked. "We can start the tour down in the basement, where we found it."

"Sure, but I really can't stay too long. This is the house that let us know there were rich people in the world. I thought the rich were all old and alone until I had grown enough to read about them in books. It seemed they were everybody else but the people in this town. Rich people could do so much with their lives. Then I learned about universities. Soon I'll have choices, like them. Let's see what Daisy Savage's house is like."

AFTER A look at the basement from the stairwell, Kristi led Andrea and Jill room by room through the downstairs. The dining room was now one of the rooms where she lived with Burge, with its old crystal chandelier tied up by the anchor chain to be out of the way, heavy age-darkened pine wainscot and crown molding, and built-in carved sideboard looking incongruous with Jim and Kristi's headboard-less bed alongside it. The parlor, the living room, the entryway, the staircase. Kristi left the guest rooms open, she explained, to keep them from smelling closed up and stuffy. It hadn't entirely worked. Andrea filled her eyes with each, floor to ceiling, as if to remember them for the last time, then turned to the next.

"Occupied rooms are off bounds for us, unless Jill wants to

show you hers," Kristi said. "Sorry. They're the nicest."

"I'll show you," Jill said, "if you let me check to see if Tom's decent first."

She opened the unlocked door. Tom was not in the room.

"Well, I wonder where he went. He had the same foot prob-lem as Steve, so he can't have gone too far. He's somewhere with Angie. Come in and see what's to see."

"You don't have to show me Steve's room," Andrea said when they had ended their tour in the upstairs hallway standing next to the open stairwell. "He may be a very private person. Does he have a temper?"

"No, I don't think so," Kristi said. "He was Burge's fraternity brother. He's now our good friend."

"I never get to see anybody here except bar twonks. I wonder if I'll ever see him again."

"We can drop a hint for you," Jill said. "Shall we?"

"No. Just if he wants to, that's all."

"I should go find Angie and Tom. They're probably tossing pine cones or looking at the chipmunks. It was nice meeting you, Andrea. Excuse me. Good luck with Steve, if it works out that way."

"Thanks. We'll see. Nice meeting you, Jill."

THE THREE walked downstairs, and Jill disappeared down the hallway toward the kitchen and out back. *Andrea will be here through the summer before returning to Palo Alto,* Kristi thought. *We'll get together sometime before then. Perhaps.*

"Please feel free to stop by Mac's Place some evening," Andrea said. And maybe she'd meet them somewhere. *They'll love it here, or will leave, same as the others.* Some have stayed, and she hoped they would.

Kristi closed the front door behind Andrea and walked back to the kitchen. Steve was reading an old copy of *Time* edged in red and warped with water vapor, perhaps from some past visitor's shower. His right ankle and bandaged foot were on his knee, his foot white with a sole turned shoe-dye orange.

"Everybody's out back being scolded by the chipmunks," Steve said.

"So how did you meet Andrea?"

"She was on the trail and seemed to know her way around. We said 'Hi.' Did she go? I should have seen her off."

"Yes. Do you like her?"

"She's okay."

"Just okay? That's everyone with you."

"I'll go ask if I can see her sometime. I do owe her. Right now, though, I'm a gob of lead."

"You're leaving tomorrow. Do you want something to drink? I think there are some brews left in the fridge."

"I beat you to them. Thanks. There are two left if you want them."

"I'll leave them for someone else. Don't you want one?"

"No, thanks. Thanks for showing her around. She really wanted to see this place, for some reason. I'll pass along a warning: You'll have to be careful that your guests don't fall down any mine shafts."

"That's good to know, isn't it? Are the mines close by?"

"We never made it to any. The trails must be something for her to spend as much time on them as she does. There's not much else going here unless you commune with nature. I'm sure you can make them an attraction for guests. She's used to them being hers alone, though."

"Yes, and we have to make a go of this place as best we can."

"She really knows the territory well. Maybe you can get on her good side, and she'll draw you a map you can put in a brochure. Don't ask her right now, though."

"I don't want her to feel used."

"Make the map yourselves, then. Unless you've got a lot of time to spend, you're bound to get it wrong, it would appear."

"I'll ask. We could pay her if we had any money."

"Why are we all so poor? We weren't always so poor."

"Being a student is different. We aren't poor. Just look at this place. It's only that this is where all our money is. The Sawtooth Inn has it."

"I wish I were doing something like this. I've said that before."

"It would be nice to have you as a partner, but right now we're strictly a mom and pop operation."

"Maybe I could get a job around here. Maybe I could have Andrea's bar job when she leaves."

"You need to go back to graduate school, too. I wish I could."

"She's at Stanford, which I can't get into. I mean, I can't get accepted. Too much college fun. I'll try Washington State instead. It has a good program."

"That's fairly close, isn't it? Maybe you'll meet in the summers if she comes back here again. We'll be glad to have your company."

"She will. This is her home."

WHEN THE conversation stopped for the evening and friends moved off to their rooms, Steve put on low-cut black Converse gym shoes and thick white socks, slipped out the front door and walked down to Mac's Place. They stepped over a high pine threshold, much worn from having been stepped on and tripped over repeatedly. The extra wide entry door, oiled with the ages, opened back on the sidewalk. The scent of tobacco and beer wafted into the street. The bar itself, crowded with miners, was to the right and dark wooden booths to the left, with tables in back, where Andrea traded an empty fluted glass pitcher for one full of beer, suds rocking gently back and forth, then made change. Andrea saw him and beamed her surprise. He sat in the last booth, and she followed him there quickly to take his order.

"You're here, Steve! I can't believe it!"

"I wanted to see you again before I go. It worked."

"How're your feet?"

"Fine. I wore gym shoes this time."

"You'll have to come back or stick around until my shift is through, which should be in about 45 minutes. Then I'm free. Bring you something?"

"A draft of whatever's on tap."

"First round is on the house if I pay for it. Why not?"

"Why not? Thanks."

HE WATCHED her work the booths and tables, fast. She was still on her feet after so many hours on the mountain. He looked at the foam on his beer. He picked up bits of conversation, but couldn't hear anything whole because of the noise of too many people talking at once. Happy crowd, mostly. He felt strange to be drinking alone.

The jukebox was playing, "I Walk the Line." "I Wanna Hold Your Hand." "Theme from *A Long Day's Journey into Night.*" Country songs, most with the same twang. He thought about her being in this place, a Stanford physicist, slinging beer. *She would fit,* he thought, *anywhere.* "Joe, you want that beer freshened?" he strained to hear her say. "You've been nursing it so long it's probably flat." He tried to imagine her white coated in a lab, with protective lenses. Finally time was called, and she was standing alongside him and the booth.

"How DID you come here?" Andrea asked him.

"How? Oh. I walked."

"Then let's take my car and we can sit down for a minute. It's parked across the street."

*   *   *

He SAT in the passenger seat of the '56 Ford Victoria coupe, sky blue and white beneath a flickering streetlamp and waited for her to get in the other side. The street was not well lit, but he could watch her open the door, then darken into a silhouette as she slid in and slammed the door shut. The interior light was out. She fumbled the key into the ignition but didn't start the car.

"C'mere, lover-boy. Let's try this."

The first kiss warmed up fast, until in a minute she pushed him away.

"We can't just be here on the street like this," she said. "People will see us."

"Let them."

"No. I have to live here."

"Can't we go somewhere? Maybe back to the inn? Everybody's probably asleep by now."

She waited a minute, thinking.

"Don't get too eager," she admonished. "I know where we can go. But I have to get something first."

She reached over, opened the glove box, took out a worn nickel Eveready flashlight, and flashed it on and off quickly, the light shining bright against the dashboard. She handed the flashlight to Steve.

"It still works," she said. "Just a minute."

She got out of the car and opened the trunk, closed it, opened her door and, tilting the seat forward, tossed an Army blanket in back.

253

"That's in case I get stuck some cold night going over the pass. You say your feet are okay?" she said.

"Fine. All healed. Why?"

"Because we're going to do something I've always wanted to do, but only if you're up to it."

"I'm up to it. Whatever it is."

"Talk softly. Your voice carries. Do you see those stars up there? That's where we're going."

FIVE MINUTES later, and Steve was following a moving patch of light as Andrea led him up the trail to the same ridge they had been on earlier that day, her dark form moving steadily onward behind the light.

"I've been up here a thousand times but never at night," she told him. "I heard it's unsafe for a lone woman to be out under the stars like this. You're my protection. Look at them! Doesn't the Milky Way make you soar? With no light pollution, there's so much more of it you can see up here. It can't be quite like this anywhere else on earth. And to think, it's been here all along. Now I'm seeing it with you, and I can imagine the whole galaxy around us!"

Steve looked up over her head at the sky, then from the vertigo downward quickly to the oval of light in motion ahead of him. He regained his balance. Stepping into emptiness was hard, but he grew accustomed to it. His feet bent on the rocks, and he had difficulty staying on the pathway.

She was in front of him, so close that he could touch her. If he could only just touch her. He mustn't let her know how hard he is trying to keep up, he thought. The night smells of wood loam and cool pine breeze. He thought he could smell the sea. His breathing caught the rhythm with his legs. He tossed the rough blanket over his outside shoulder so he could guide himself along the underbrush with his right hand. She was just ahead of him. And soon he could walk and see by the thinnest slice of moon and bright starlight through the hidden shadows, while the flashlight beam jiggled its way along, as if an accompaniment.

And what had she behind her? What had she come upon, she thought, just by living her life? He was following her. At last she was safe and could be free to live in the moment, and at this moment. She could climb toward the constellations she saw through and above the pines, the mountain very close beside her, and it would be the first time. And what will be on the crest in a clearing, as if waiting for her—what she thinks of in secret moments but doesn't know how it must be and what completely, she tells herself, but he might want her in the deep indigo mountain grasses and hushed and drifting pines, need her. No drunken propositions, just something like the real thing.

"There's Cassiopeia and Pegasus and Andromeda just over the eastern mountains," she says. "I am the horse with wings."

They embraced for a long time in the clearing, then stopped to spread the blanket, and go on, she looking up past him into the stars, and then they did together. They were totally alone to open themselves to each other. Deep space was above her, the cosmos, her love, and nothing reached so far.

AFTER, THEY became cold, and it became time to go.

"Did you get any bites?" she asked.

"Bites?"

"You know. Insects."

"I felt something crawling on me, I thought, a time or two, but was too lost to do anything about it. Part of the experience. Did you?"

"I got bitten. I didn't want to stop. It made me lose it even more."

"Bitten where?"

"On the backside. Never mind. It didn't even happen. Except it itches and burns at the same time. Probably just a big mosquito bite."

"Let me rub it for you. Put my fingers on it."

"Then let's dress. Where's your hand?"

"I'll always, you know," she said. "One of those moments, when so much of the rest of life is made brighter, and you remember that moment in time always. You are my first, my very first. Let's start down the mountain. Follow me again, yes? I'm not as enthusiastic about walking down as I was coming up."

The stiffness in his feet and legs came back as he tried to stand, and he grumbled.

"Tie your shoelaces tighter," she told him. "Then your feet won't slide forward and scrunch your toes when you step."

SHE SHINED the light at his feet so he could see. He looped the laces in a double bow, and placed first one foot, then the other on the steep trail. He stood and followed again as the light made its way along the mountain edge of the trail to their left. It was much slower going downward in the surrounding darkness, though she made a steady pace along the narrow pathway, around rocks and trees.

They were well past halfway down when the flashlight dimmed. Andrea shook it, and it came back on, bright.

"Don't go out on us now," she said.

"I could almost see without it in time if the trees didn't shade the sky as much as they do in spots."

The light dimmed and stayed dim, even with three quick shakes and three more.

"It's burning out," she said.

"Try turning it off when we're not in the shadows."

"Let's try going slower. Take my hand. You be the stable spot, and I'll do the advancing. We'll make it down together."

The light came on dimly, went out altogether. They started to walk down sideways, Andrea still in front, feeling their way along the brush and trees in the shadows. They had to be very careful where they placed their feet, and steadily they move down, one side step at a time. Their eyes adjusted somewhat to the darkness. She instructed him in a loud whisper as she found obstacles or when the trail turned. Their arms and legs grew weary from the muscle stress of their awkward progression. Through the trees to the right they could finally see a light from the Sawtooth Inn.

"The path widens a little down here," Andrea said.

"I remember, but it is still rocky. All the dirt is washed away in places."

"A tree root just got me," she says, trying to recover her balance.

HE TRIPPED over the root and fell against her back, knocking her to the ground, and he fell on top of her. He caught himself with his right hand as he fell and rolled to the right against a tree, away from her. A dog barked in the distance. It was still a moment, and totally quiet. Another bark. Then Steve:

"Are you all right?"

Silence.

"No, Steven. I think I've broken my arm above my wrist. I had the flashlight in my hand."

He struggled up, avoiding bumping her.

"Let me help. We're almost there. We'll get you to a doctor."

"What'll I do? I can't wait tables like this. I'll get fired! I need my job. I'll have to drop out of graduate school!"

"Don't worry. We'll get you to a doctor. Things will be okay."

"Okay? Everything comes easy to you, doesn't it? You don't have to do anything. You're a rich fraternity boy, why should you worry? You broke my arm."

"I'm sorry. I didn't mean to do that. I'll make it up to you, honest. Things will be all right. We'll get a doctor."

"Stop saying that. Things are not all right. Things are never all right. I should have known better than to hope otherwise. I'll get to Dr. Groves, and I'll pay for it. This really hurts me, Steven."

"I'll call him the minute we're back at the lodge."

"Miss Savage's house. That's fitting. I've gone over to Miss Savage's house. I should have listened to my parents."

"I'm sorry the best evening of my life had to be this way. I would never deliberately hurt you. You are so alive to me. I love you."

"You're blubbering like one of the drunks. Just let me get my arm fixed, okay? Call Dr. Groves. His number's in the book. I'll wait for you in my car."

"At least come in and get cleaned up."

"I'm not facing your friends like this. I'll wait in the car. You go call. I lost the flashlight."

"I'll go find it for you tomorrow when it's light."

"Never mind. I'll buy another one. With what?"

"You're hurt worse than a broken arm. Please let me help you."

"I'll be fine in a minute. Please go call."

HE TILTED the passenger seat forward, tossed the blanket in back, returned the seat and tried his awkward best to help her in. She suffered the attempt, and he shut the door. He went back to the hotel, where a light was on, and let himself in. He found the small phone book in the top drawer of the reception desk. He called Dr. Groves' home phone and got a slow answer.

He is a doctor, of course he will come. Please meet him at his office in half an hour. Is she hurt anywhere else? Be careful of shock; put her on her back with her feet raised if she feels faint. Things happen in a town like this. Goodbye.

Steve found her on her back on the front seat, her knees against the passenger door. He opened the driver door. She sat up.

"I was feeling nauseous for a minute and had to lie down. Is he coming?"

"Yes, in a half hour, at his office. You know where that is, I guess. Forgot to ask."

"He delivered me when I was born. He's a block over, in a storefront. He used to be upstairs, but it was too difficult for people to get up and down when they went to see him.

"We can drive over and wait for him. You'll have to do it this time. Thank God it's the left arm. I'll be able to manage once the cast is on. The cast will really help. I'm sorry you have to go home tomorrow. No, I won't let you stay because of me. I'll be just fine."

Chapter 22

ALL DAY Kristi had been concerned about Andrea but hadn't called, not wanting to disturb her. What could be said, anyway? She should say something. Kristi and Burgess' guests had gone, Steve first, with the story, or part of it, of how Andrea had broken her arm, and would they please look in on her at Mac's Place later that evening, where she was sure to be.

Steve broke Andrea's arm, that's what he said, Kristi thought. *He's obviously worried about what else broke. Her arm is broken. She must know a lot about this place. Children learn a lot of things their parents don't know about, and sometimes just because they don't. She knows where the trails are dangerous, and we have our guests. No guests yet, not real ones.*

They will come. The Hendersons have gone. They wish they could come back every weekend, it's so peaceful. So much to do. We must eat. We all must, and have a place to sleep. 'Death has no dominion' yes it does. Please don't let it be here, too. There's no proof about it, you know there's no proof. What would proof even be?

ANDREA WALKED between the tables in back of Mac's Place toward Kristi and Burgess as they entered. She gestured toward the booths with her good arm with a smile and slight bow.

"Sit wherever you like. You're early arrivers. Would you like to see menus?"

"Yes, thanks," Kristi said. "Sorry to learn about your broken arm. Steve told us before he made his guilty way out the door to the roadway. We came to see if we could do anything. Are you okay working here so soon?"

"It's only the six-weeks-to-heal variety of break. I'm tough."

"Does it hurt?" Kristi asked.

"Only when I think about it. Then it's just my imagination. It's good to keep busy."

"You're braver than I am."

"Steve headed back this morning," Burgess said. "He's really sorry it happened. You can tell with Steve."

"He asked us to come see you," Kristi added. "So here we are. You two are adventuresome souls to be hiking at night. Especially on that trail."

"It was my idea," said Andrea, "so it was probably my fault, too. We would have been fine if the flashlight hadn't given out."

"He hiked up to find the flashlight before he left and asked us to bring it to you," Kristi said. "You probably don't want to see it again if it quit working."

BURGESS GAVE the flashlight to Andrea between his two index fingers, one on the lens, the other on the end.

"It's just an inanimate object. The only flashlight I have, though. It just needs batteries. Thanks for returning it."

Andrea carefully turned it on, shook it with a muffled rustle, not the usual dull-metal sound, and it came on weakly, then went out.

"Just like our relationship," she said.

"He said he hoped to see you again some time soon," Kristi told her. "The flashlight contains a message from him, which he made us promise not to read."

"He said that? I mean to see me again? I don't know. I have to go back to graduate school soon. Do you know what you want to eat yet? I'll come back in a minute if you want."

She walked behind the bar, looked at the lens of the flashlight, screwed open the battery compartment while wedging the flashlight against her stomach with her cast. She fished out a piece of folded paper wrapped around the batteries. She glanced at the note, put it in the pocket of her apron, replaced the cap, slid the flashlight onto a shelf under the bar. She hustled to a back table where a short elderly man in a dull-gold golf jacket and Yankees baseball cap pushed back on his head was waving to catch her attention. Her wrist ached under the cast.

Too damn tight. Maybe swollen.

When she returned to the bar, her face to the mirror, she read:

Dear Andrea:

I need to see you again but have to get back to my students. Please understand how sorry I am for what happened and forgive. Something happened on the mountaintop that I've never experienced before, and I hope you felt it, too. My best view of the stars was from looking in your eyes as you watched them in the midst of our loving. Please don't let my clumsiness spoil things between us. Write to me, as I am never at home and the office phones aren't private. 205 Cincinnatti Road.

Steve

THE BARTENDER, smelling of Wildroot hair tonic with a Camel smile, leaned close to Andrea's ear and said, "No sandbagging. You got customers."

"The flashlight under the bar is mine," she replied.

She returned to the Burgesses to take their order.

"I hope you're not too disappointed with the food. The burgers are best though the cheese on the cheeseburgers is processed. The cook gets the buns greasy by putting them on the grille. The food's better elsewhere in town but we're the friendliest and have the best service. Right?"

"You're the best, Andrea," Kristi said. "I still don't know how you're doing it."

Burgess ordered hamburgers for both of them, no cheese or onions but everything else. It was a quick evening out with the "back soon" sign up again on the door of the inn.

Next morning, at the kitchen table in the miner's log cottage of her parents, Andrea wrote:

Dear Steve:

Sorry the light went out and my arm got broken. I should have known. But then what? I'm actually getting along much better with the arm than my outbreak after the point of impact warranted. Perhaps 'twas just your basic angst that buzzed together with the snap of the wrist. As you can see, I did open the flashlight to find your message. So we're not beings totally alien to one another once again. Kristi and Burge brought the flashlight over to me at Mac's and had burgers. This is all what happens when daydreams—night dreams, too—get out of alignment with reality.

Right now I want to have more dreams, and I don't care beyond that. When are you coming to town again? I'm glad I didn't scare you off in my awkward way. I keep surprising myself by my behavior. Are you like that, too? It's like growing into yourself and finding you are different from what you really thought you were. The music plays along, somehow scored from our evolutionary and living past, an immense score, and the differences play out measures of new life in a minor key never heard before. I'm meant to be someone else to you than I really am right now, I think, though I don't know who, or meant by whom. I wonder if you think that way of me.

Given what other people seem to do, though, it's almost is if we're supposed to fake each other out so we look better than we really are to one another. But I never liked faking it and am really bad at it, anyway. I'm just a miner's kid in love with science and why it exists, and besides that I sound like a teenager to myself right now. I did love you in starlight when you were a loving presence I could scarcely see at times. The stars were all around us, and you were so real, as if you were a wondrous part of me I never knew existed, and the universe was ours for the first time through newly opened eyes. Next time I'll have extra batteries, though, if there can ever be a next time.

Let's write, and then we'll meet again.

Keep freedom shining,

Andrea

She thought she had said too much, and will this scare him off? She decided not to redo the letter, written to herself as much as to him. She won't think about his reply, she told herself. But she did and nothing came back for a week, two weeks, three. One day she drove up to the Sawtooth Inn to hear something about Steve in his absence, as if to make sure she had really met him. The inn and his friends were the only trace of him she now had—save for a piece of paper and an arm cast, which had begun to smell.

Everything was going along fine, so why did this happen? *Why should I get involved with someone so far away as he's going to be? There are too many complications, but a letter would be nice, so why doesn't he write? Some people don't write letters. But why the flashlight note if he didn't intend to communicate? Maybe I'm just too impatient. Maybe I said too much. His friends might know. He said not to call him. Kristi might know if something has happened to him.*

THE DOOR buzzer startled Andrea as she entered the inn, then it was quiet as she shut the door. The room was full of deep shadows and September sunlight. No one was around. She waited. The cellar door was ajar in the hallway and a light on below. She waited, then said, "Hello?" There was no response. She walked along the creaking floor toward the light. She said "hello" louder from a step down the stairs.

"Andrea!" Kristi belted back. "The bell needs to be fixed, I guess. I didn't hear anybody come in. This stuff has me too absorbed." She put down a single small parchment letter on a closed steamer trunk, stood and stretched. "Here I come, excuse me just a minute. Come down here, second thought, and I'll give you a peak at the shining past."

"Here I come."

"Another peak, anyway, since you saw some of it last time you were here. This substance you see about me is called 'dust,' and I've been trying to remove some of it so I can stand to be down here, because it's about time I read more letters. What can we do for you?"

"Just wondering, have you heard anything from Steve?"

"Steve? Why, no. Should we have?"

"I don't know. His flashlight note asked me to write to him, and I haven't heard back. Just concerned, that's all. He sounded urgent. I don't know him very well, that's for sure. Just wondering if I should be wondering, or if I should just expect the letter when I see it.

"You know how you do. Every day I keep thinking there will be a letter, but there isn't one. I guess I should just drop it. You haven't heard from him either. He seemed rather urgent, that's all. Now I seem a little foolish for coming here and asking. Maybe he didn't get the letter and I should try again."

"Burge knows Steve better than I do, but I'm thinking Burge won't know how to advise you either. Men don't even try, you know. It's not part of their world. You should just do what you feel like doing. Don't be too concerned with the result. That's what I would do."

"I don't know anything about men other than the few I know, so I can't think much that reflects on Steve."

"I know the feeling."

"Are men all alike? I haven't a clue. I hope not. I don't think so. I thought he was different from some I know. More like me, but maybe I was only wishing. Sorry for disturbing you this way."

"Come by here anytime. You don't need an excuse. It gets lonely in a strange way when you are new, and I'll really appreciate seeing you. You know this place so well."

"What did you want to show me?"

"Just one of the letters from the trunk, since you're here. The one I've been reading is too far along in her life to get a good sense of things. But perhaps I'm not being overly sensitive. Maybe you don't want to see someone else's letter right now. Just a thought."

"Because it belongs to a dead old maid?"

"That wasn't the thought. I just had the idea that you might find some genuine common interests because you liked walking in the same mountains. I really don't know if you like such things. I'm reading with a stretch of a week or so between each letter so I get a better sense of passing time."

"But it's so far in the past."

"Sometimes it's actually like having a spirit loose in the house for a minute or two. Except the spirit is me and I never can quite imagine what I have said or done to elicit what happens next."

"Like being Daisy Savage for a flash, with no memory but what she has perceived. Right?"

"You don't have to read them all. Just try one."

Kristi opened the trunk, which had been left unlocked, its tarnished brass clasps hanging outward and down. She had aligned the envelopes, bundled on edge, on top of the trunk's contents. She thumbed through six loose ones on the left, lingered over two, then pulled out one of the last. She stood and handed it to Andrea.

July 28, 1925

Dear Daisy:

I've just been thinking about you in that place so far away from everything. I wondered about your walks in the mountains and who you saw—especially that strange boy you met going to the mine. Be careful, please, when you walk, over mountains and all.

What did he think, I wonder, to be like that? Maybe ways are different there. When you said, "Yes" when he offered to show you "secret places in the mountains," well, I wouldn't have, that's all. You always were the adventurous one who was so curious. What did 'secret places' mean, if not to do something wrong? You are just lucky that nothing happened to you. Perhaps your being the mine owner's daughter protected you. If you're not careful, something else might happen, though.

I've become too much like a preacher, but please don't make me worry. Now, what really happened with a boy like that? I imagine you still the way you were, but if you meet people who might try something, what then? You may be just fine, I know. It was as if I saw him showing you a lake and waterfall. With beautiful high cliffs like a giant throne and the bluest sky with clouds up on the mountain tops, all framed in trees with lots of song birds.

It's all been there forever. But there you were, for the first time, and it was yours to see. What did he say to you, then? Was he dashing and did he fill the air with romantic talk, or was he just quiet, letting you see for yourself? Are you going back there again with him?

My life is much less exciting, so I pretend I'm you. Time runs on slower for children than for adults. They have more pure being compacted into a moment with fewer memories and thoughts shaping what they see. An hour must seem like forever to them, when it's nothing to me, and I haven't lived so long.

Maybe everything we remember shortens our time as we age by getting in the way of just simply seeing things. Do you remember when you were little? My little Emery is having his long minutes now. I coaxed him into a nap so I could write this. He's talking to himself in his crib. He makes sounds that he thinks are words, and they will be, someday soon. He'll say the baby version of "so that's it!" when he makes the first words we understand, then there'll be no way to quiet him. That's what my mother tells me.

My Sam must work so hard and is rarely at home. He scarcely knows Emery, I think. At least not as I do. A sadness for a father, but not yet a shame.

Forever your friend,

Martha

"Daisy walked the mountains like me," said Andrea. "And she met a mysterious stranger there, as I did—'a boy.'"

"Steve? Steve isn't so mysterious. Maybe a little strange, but I think that's changing. You're right on the 'boy' part of what you said."

"Maybe I was too forward with him, but I would never have met him if I were the passive little thing that ladies are supposed to be. So I got hurt, so what?"

"I wouldn't be so eager to be hurt, if you mean more than the arm. He may just be slow at writing letters. I don't think we've ever had one from him, not even a Christmas card. He just shows up. What did you think of the letter to Daisy?"

"Fear and fantasy. Perhaps vice versa. Martha said something she thought she was supposed to say, then said something else, what she wanted to say. She seemed trapped and in need of release, which Daisy provided her."

"What about Daisy?"

"Why not walk the mountains? I do. I always have, it seems, and have only been afraid alone once when I misjudged my time toward dusk, and everything has always been safe on the trails. When there were more miners, I don't know, but it couldn't have been too different from now.

"What Martha imagined about this place is different from what it is, but not too different. Looking back on it when you've been away for a while, I mean. Its physical presence, if things are just right for it. There is no throne-like cliff, however, that I've ever seen. Rocks are not rainbows, and I never saw the actual Daisy on a trail. She stayed here in her house, so far as I've ever heard. I wonder if something had happened, or if she just took Martha's first advice to the extreme and crawled inside to stay. What do you think, Kristi?"

"She shouldn't have listened to either of Martha's voices, which were Martha reinforcing Martha, with not much balanced between two people. Whatever the sounder advice is depends wholly on the stranger on the trail, it seems. Does she avoid damage from him by not associating with him, or does she miss out by not getting to know him?"

"My plight, too, sort of. Excuse me, Steve's your friend. I do wonder what happened. With Daisy and with Steve."

"Strangers in the woods."

"Shall we look to see if the next letter is from Martha?"

268

Chapter 23

August 24, 1925

Dear Daisy:

It seems that I waited for your letter forever. I was very glad when the mailman finally brought it. I knew you hadn't forgotten me. Then I seemed hit and kicked. Any hurt that comes to you comes also to me. I understood why you took so long to write. Please, I worry when you take so long to write because I am your friend. You are so many miles away.

I know that you know I'm your friend because you wrote so many things—going on the new trail behind your very house, and walking up a long time and having to stop to catch your breath. Then you walked over the mountain and down into the valley. Meeting something so scary as a naked man with a beard who pressed himself against you must have been very shocking. Even if he ran away afterward. Where did he come from, and where did he go?

Aren't you worried all of the time about seeing him again? Other men can protect you, and the mountains are so big. I bet he was not someone you know or are likely to see again. Is he?

"I GUESS I know what happened, then," Andrea said, as she stood before Kristi in the basement of the Sawtooth Inn, the letter she had been reading aloud suspended before them momentarily.

"Something I didn't want to have happen where I'm used to walking."

Kristi paused before she spoke.

"But it was so long ago. It seems almost funny, now, doesn't it? Can't you visualize it?"

"Naked men in the abstract do seem funny, especially if they have beards and very white skin. Not that I've seen a lot of them. It's just the thought. A bump and run is even funnier."

"Would that be enough to keep someone off a trail if she really wanted to take to it?"

"You're probably not going to find that out from a letter. Are you?"

Andrea read:

I don't understand your father making you stop hiking in the mountains. I guess he knows best, though. He doesn't want anything to happen to you. You still need to be able to move around and have some adventure, too.

"I used to wonder a lot why people like the naked guy did such things," Kristi said. "Really. I took abnormal psychology in college, read books and so forth, like I was fascinated with it. Their lives were so different from mine, but I thought I still learned something about myself in an odd manner when I discovered something about them. So I'd try to learn more. Then something happened to me in the woods, once. I experienced one of those people for real. No book or clinic. Out doing weird shit for kicks."

"What happened?"

Again, Kristi waited.

"It must get easier for me to say this. I was forced into something by a voyeur. Sometimes they do more than just peep in windows. I'm mostly over it. I could say now that if I'm going exploring points unknown, it will be with my man. Sometimes even that doesn't work, however. You need to watch out."

"Sawtooth is my home, and what happened to Daisy was a long time ago."

"My experience wasn't here, but it wasn't so long ago or far away, either. It was certainly different from what you'd expect. You'll probably find out about it sooner or later, so I'll tell you now, straight from the source. It could have ruined my life, you know? Events have antecedents, and you don't always know what's going to happen to you next because you can't always see that a cause is a cause until something else happens as a result of it. What happened to me happened in the Blue Mountains in Oregon. Like here. I was forced to have sex at gunpoint. It was with Burge on our first date. Someone forced us to do it. It was our secret for a long time, but now I can talk about it.

"Only, let's keep it a secret here, okay? Nobody needs to know just yet because it could be the only thing they'll ever know or remember about us, the way some people think about things. I tried telling myself, 'Don't let it get to you.' It did anyway. So do be careful."

"Are you okay now, though?" Andrea asked. "You seem okay."

"Yes, fine. You go through changes. That's the price. Bad times."

"I won't tell. You seem to have everything, however."

"Who does?"

"To me you have everything, I mean, this place and a smart, kind, hard-working husband. I still envy you. I hope you really are okay."

Andrea's words made Kristi introspective and sent her attention adrift.

She said, "I didn't mean to keep us from the letter."

ANDREA CONTINUED but Kristi wasn't listening. She tried to listen, but there had been the forest floor and rocks and pine needles pressed into her bare knees by her own weight, kneeling closer. *Everyone watching. Dead from a bullet, found dead with the flies. Penetration, found dead, naked there. It wasn't Burge. So much has happened. Since then. Where is Skinner now, what can still happen? It's over, he's gone, and it's over. He's found out, we found him out. Never again will he yes he will.*

Kristi mentally shook herself. Here Skinner had intruded, while she was listening to a letter:

. . . had secrets from each other, have we? Of course we have. Life's too long and people are alone too much never to have had secrets. But I can't think of any, can you? All the mischief we could get into as kids and thoughts of boys, we thought things to be such secrets. What a confusing thing for you to go through! As if the woods were only for men and not put here for women at all.

Still, you seem to like the mountains so much. They must belong in part to you as well, even with what happened. You always turn things into something to talk about. I'm not very good at guessing. Are you telling me everything? Are you?

You remember when we spied on my cousin Margaret with her boyfriend? We wondered how two such people could ever like each other that way? He couldn't keep his hands off her. They thought nobody was watching. She sort of clutched him there and pushed him away here. She had him frustrated and not, like a flower yanked up and repotted again and again. I have known weeds that seemed smarter than he was. She thought he was Balthazar with shining gifts to present, if only the time were right and the moment secret enough.

And then there's how I came to be where I am, and everybody these days becomes involved in strange ways that turn out to be perfectly ordinary in the end because that's where everything ends up. Somehow you will become what you will become whatever happens if you keep trying to do what you should.

So don't be too upset if you seem now to be stuck. I know you can't have the adventures you love in the mountains. I'm sorry you can't find anyone there to be with or marry. In time you will find yourself in the mountains once again, I hope, if that's what you want. The person you meet on the trail will be someone you like, properly introduced, someone you like being with. Don't be upset, because in time it will be like that. I'm saying this to myself, too, because I have no one to tell it to me but through you. So you should write to me and don't wait until everything comes to a stop between us.

Ever your faithful friend, no matter what,

Martha

"Martha's stuck, too," Kristi said, "or she would never say stuff like that. What do you think she did about it? Do you think it could be anything?

"Events can change everything, right?"

"They changed everything for us, Burge and me. We're here rather than in Richland, where we are probably known as those really strange people who moved away. Under different circumstances, we would still be there because it was home. That was our life."

"Don't you like it here?"

"It's not that. It's for the best that we're here."

"And so?" Andrea asked.

"Some people think that things always turn out to be the best they can be on this planet. Being here's our personal best, we think."

"That's Leibniz, the old math and logic guy—binary number system, mathematical notation, "compossibility," calculators and so many other things that how could he possibly not be an optimist? He invented calculus independently of Newton."

"It's just as easy, it seems, to say they always turn out for the worst, so tend your own garden, like in *Candide*. But they haven't turned out for the ultimate worst, yet, or more atom bombs than two would have dropped on people by now. It seems so close to that happening at times, Cuban missiles and all. Sorry to bring that up. Just my own obsession."

"Nobody talks about that stuff here, Kristi."

"I know."

"No fallout shelters. We've got mountains."

"It's only from my part of the world. The memories and old worries hang around, even when you leave it."

"You must have thought about it a lot."

"We had drills in school where you ducked under your desk. As if that would help. My father worked at the Hanford plant before he died. He never talked about his work, just like everybody else who worked there, but we knew what it could do. Even if we couldn't see the operations because they were many miles away, they were still a kind of omnipresence. It seemed that way to me."

"That all seems a generation ago to me, Kristi, like something before I was born."

"SOME THINGS are forever now, when they used to be nothing, and even if they sometimes still seem like nothing. They will never go away. Until things go away utterly."

"But that's morbid. Why do you want to think about it?"

"I don't, Andrea. In part, it's as if it were a responsibility discovered with coming of age. Something you should concern yourself with because you are a good citizen. But you are supposed to be able to act, aren't you? There isn't anything to do in this bind. All of us are in it because our taxes make it possible. So that's where I stay with nothing to do. We make more bombs because the Soviets make more. The Soviets make more because we make more. Many lifetimes have gone into protecting the Free World with atoms, until atoms have become the end as well as the means to staying alive. We need to have more than they have, and then more than that, and at huge cost that few contemplate. Then everything became 'too much with us.'"

"So you left."

"So Burge and I left. We couldn't change anything. What would we change it to? It's just too big, and we must be silent, by oath. They have you inside the gate, almost at work, when you have to sign it. It's a long way back home if you don't.

"I'm sorry to lay this on you, Andrea. I intended just to keep quiet. It actually might be a place you'd really like. There are lots of scientists there."

"You'll like it here, I promise," Andrea said. "It gets cold sometimes, but I like doing what Daisy liked to do—walk in the mountains. Meditate. It is bliss."

"WHY DON'T we get out of this basement and go for a walk ourselves? You can show me where Daisy might have liked to walk."

"There are too many places to name. If you feel up to it, I'll take you to the ridge above the inn. You'll see your home from a new perspective. Your being here has given me happy memories, since we're blowing secrets."

"I still can't tell you what to do about Steve, if that's what you're referring to. Burge should be back soon. He had to drive down to Ketchum for parts for an upstairs sink and some other stuff. Things are slow and nobody's coming here today that I know of. I'll close the front door and leave a note."

ANDREA WAITED on the screened back porch while Kristi put on shoes and socks, then they left out the back door and started up the trail. Andrea tried to imagine from the rising trail the spot where she and Steve fell. The daytime revealed too much, visually—a sensory overload. They stepped over a tree root only a short way up—she knew the place. The cast on her arm had begun to itch and she had a tightening sensation under her chin.

"This is where it happened," she said. "We had almost made it back. Watch for this tree root the next time you are up here in the dark."

"I'll leave nighttime climbing to you two. All yours."

"The stars were as close as I ever expect to get to forever. You could see the soaring disc of the galaxy and let your imagination shape in motion what you know of things—the spiral and how much more there is beyond what we can see using just our eyes. I'd always wanted to experience the stars and planets from up there with nothing to obscure things. I couldn't because too much can happen to a woman alone. Then I met Steve. It warmed up the universe. I had this impulse and followed it. How strange is that?"

"Not so strange."

"Well, I think you know what I mean. I associated freedom with who knows what. Too much talk now."

"You're in far better shape than I am, Andrea. Slow down."

"Do you want to stop for a minute?"

"No."

"If you're not used to walking, this can be pretty steep."

"Let's just keep a steady pace. I'll survive."

"I'm the only person I know who walks these hills any more. I'm secretly looking for a fellow traveler to walk with me, and I don't want to scare you off just yet."

"I'm enjoying this. What do you do for burning lungs?"

"You'll get used to it pretty soon if you just walk a little more every day. Good for your figure, though you don't need it for that."

"Give me a kid or two."

"Are you planning a family?"

"Tried. No luck, obviously. We probably should wait anyway, for financial reasons."

"I want a family. Only I don't want to be married just yet."

"What about Steve?"

"Way too early for that. Maybe I'll change my mind. If I ever see him again."

"He's the strange one. For not replying to your letter, I mean."

"Stranger. Strangest. Maybe I scared him off. Too much all at once. I don't have much practice with men."

"I thought you'd be surrounded with them, being in physics."

276

"They treat me like I'm one of the guys. Or ignore me. Or talk about girl problems. Or are just plain barbaric, as bad as the worst miner."

"Seriously?"

"I don't know how it happens. In high school, I was the only girl in science and math. Same thing. I wasn't a different person in English. You do get used to it."

"Psych was a mixed bag. Male and female, everything and everybody."

"You have to do what you're good at and what grabs you. I was good at math and science, and that's where the scholarships were, besides. I had a way to make a life. Still do. If I get pushed around, I push back, which means I've survived. So far."

"You'll make it. Whatever *it* is. You'll get the job, I guess."

"It's the girl geeks who are truly happy."

"Don't give up on Steve. Maybe try again. No point in getting passive."

"I can't. Get passive. How do you do it?"

"Steve's a different sort. Everybody's golden boy, and loving it, and hating the pigeon hole and watching his old life disappear into nostalgia."

"Is he, really?"

"Burge said you should've seen Steve in his element, back in college. Very BMOC, center of attention. Then the great escapist. He could never make up his mind who he was."

"Or like it long?"

"Or like it long."

"Until what?"

"Maybe he's still going through that, and that's the problem."

"Maybe it's me. I hope not."

"I don't think it's you. It's been around too long for that."

"He left me a note in the flashlight you returned, asking me to write to him. I did. No reply. I was anxious to hear from him. Anxious. Maybe too enthusiastic is the right phrase."

"He said we should tell you to change the batteries soon. I don't think we told you, now that I think of it—or that you needed to be told."

"I must have read his mind, but also you told me about the note. The first thing I did when you brought the flashlight back was to open the battery compartment. It's like that was all there was left of us for then."

"Then I wouldn't worry. When the right person turns up in his body, he'll write. You could maybe nudge him a little with another letter. I don't think it would hurt."

"I'll write again. I'd like to call him, but he said not to."

"Why?'

"He's never near a phone where he can talk, he says. People listen in."

"He would say that."

"Should I believe him?"

"Yes. Tell him that he should call you."

"Each of us works while the other is free. Tough to connect. Unless we set a date. I'll try that. For my day off. I'd like my parents to hear. They've been thinking I'll be a spinster forever."

"If he misses you, try not to be hurt. He's probably just lost in his work. Men do that sometimes. Believe me."

"Did Burge do that?"

"Yes. So did my father, and probably his, too. You just have to let them. Because they won't do otherwise."

"Did you ever try to change Burge?"

"I have to be myself, so I have to let him be himself. Of course I tried to change him."

"How?"

"I wanted him to be more attentive. You know, in the sack."

"I'll mind my own business."

"I don't mean to embarrass you. You work things out or you get used to them."

"Were those the bad times you mentioned having?"

"No. Then I had strong feelings of attraction and repulsion at the same time. Sometimes I really wanted Burge to evaporate and the world with him for making me feel so stressed and guilty. But I had to stay alive. The repulsion slowly wore away with him around and my trying to reason my way through things."

"Yes?"

"I'm still very attracted to him. Most of the time. When I am not, I just forgive myself and have my other thoughts. So then I'm the one who's not so attentive, perhaps."

"But you'll be attentive again."

"We like trying to have kids. Except when I don't."

ON THE ridge of the mountain with trails leading both from where they had come and off down into the hidden valley on the other side, Andrea looked without speaking toward where she and Steve had lain, the boulders and pines surrounding. The grass was standing as if nothing had happened there at all. In a place or two, she imagined it bent down, as if a deer had found its bed there, an invitation to return. Perhaps all she had of Steve was gone, except this memory. Perhaps only to become just a flight of imagination.

Down the trail she stepped over where she had fallen, and Kristi stepped over behind her. They could now see down to the Sawtooth Inn through the trunks of pines and a clearing.

279

Then Kristi stopped, stiff legged, for a truck was pulling away from the front of the inn—not Burgess', but a dull-white older one. Skinner's?

Chapter 24

WHEN BURGESS returned from Ketchum, a grocery-sized brown paper bag half full of household hardware in his hands, he was surprised to find the front door locked. He opened it and called to Kristi, who came into the entryway from the parlor quietly with Andrea, like shy children. Something was wrong.

"Why was the door locked?" he asked.

"We went for a hike up to the ridge. When we were coming back, we saw Skinner's old white truck pulling away from the inn. Really. I'm sure it was. At least it looked that way. We thought he might come back. You know I'm afraid of him. He might try to get revenge on us for taking away his living."

"How can you be sure it was Skinner?"

"You know these things. It was Skinner all right."

"Did you actually see him?"

"No. Just his truck. What are we going to do?"

"Until he actually does something, there's not much we can do that I can see. He's free, remember?"

"Well, I can't take his being here."

"Keep the door locked."

"How can we run a hotel with the door locked? People have to come and go."

"Then I'll have to see what he's up to. Did you see where he was headed?"

"No. Maybe he has a gun again. I think you should leave him alone."

"I'll be back in a minute," Burge said, turning quickly toward the glass door.

"Where are you going?"

"To look for his truck."

"I don't want you to do that. Leave him alone. I need you to be alive, don't you understand?"

"I can't stand having him around like this either."

"He'll probably go away."

"Like ringworm and bed bugs. I'm going. Sorry you had to get into this, Andrea. You learned too much about us in a hurry, I'm afraid."

"This isn't her fault."

BURGESS SHUT the front door hard, leaving the sack of hardware forgotten on the small reception desk that doubled as an office. Kristi was silent.

"What happens now?" Andrea asked.

"Nothing. Burge won't be able to find him. He never can. I hope."

"Has this happened before?"

"Not like this. Burge has just never been able to find Skinner, that's all, and there's no one he can hire to look for him. At first, not finding him was fortunate because Burge had a gun himself. I didn't know it at the time. It was just a souvenir gun from the Wild West he picked up from a friend who needed school money, but it still worked. Colt .44. We didn't see each other for quite a while. I couldn't."

"So what happened to change things?"

"Burge became more rational as we started to make a life together, or maybe I just got used to him. Skinner seemed not to matter because he wasn't there, and nobody knew him so far as we could find out under the circumstances. Then there was an event at the plant, where Skinner showed up suddenly as a security officer, as if he'd been there all along. There was a confrontation, charges and countercharges, and a security revolver that went off, not Burge's. The law put distance between them. Skinner disappeared again. What happened in the Blues was just something we couldn't prove because there was a counterclaim that must have seemed more likely to some than the strange thing that actually happened. Burge won't find him. Skinner's coming here was an accident, that's all. Wasn't it? He's long gone. If it's even him."

Burgess drove the few streets of Sawtooth in his truck once, seeing nothing. He was nearly through a second search when he saw the white truck pull up and park diagonally two vehicles in front of him, the hood angled away toward Crawley's Pharmacy. Burgess pulled up behind the truck bed and stopped, double-parked. He got out on the street, his eyes on the truck door to his right. A foot in a moccasin under bell bottom denims stepped down backward out of the truck, the back of a blond head emerging last, the hair long and stringy, the pony tail hanging over the collar of a long-sleeved blue striped shirt. It wasn't at all Skinner.

"Excuse me," Burgess said to him.

A FACE OF a college sophomore, blond, peeling at reddened cheeks and without a concern, smiled back over his left arm at Burgess.

"What's hap'nun, man?"

"Mind if I ask if this is your truck?"

"Yeah, man. Just got it. Ugly, ain't it?"

"Mind if I ask whom you bought it from?"

"Off a lot in Ketchum. Charley's Cars, that's whom. He had it parked in back for some time, 'til he thought he could sell it. Then I came along. Ain't many of these left, and it's already been customized a little. Why?"

"I used to know somebody owned a truck like this, that's all. Thought you might have gotten it from him."

"If his name was Charley, then yes. Otherwise, then no. Want to buy this truck?"

"No. Just looking for its former owner, that's all."

"If I can turn a little profit, I'll sell this truck to you. Or negotiate a trade with the one you're driving. This is a good truck. Fast, and it don't rattle much."

"Thanks. Just looking for the man. You say you got it in Ketchum?"

"That's it. Gotta git now. You're new here, ain't you?"

"Yes."

"Thought so. Bye."

"Oh. Why did you stop at the Sawtooth Inn today?"

"Didn't. Might have just turned around there. Looked closed. Bye."

BURGESS WALKED back around the front of his truck, waited for the narrow street to clear of cars, got in and drove up the street and then to the right, toward the inn. Once there and up the stairs, he unlocked the glass door and opened it wide. Kristi was at the front desk with a blank expression on her face, twirling the stub of a bitten yellow pencil, and no Andrea. He picked up the hardware sack from the front desk, with the thought of fixing the upstairs sink. He put the sack back down.

"You don't have to worry about that truck, if we saw the same truck," he told her. "It's not likely there are two of them alike. Skinner sold it to somebody. The person who eventually bought it looked like a college kid but didn't sound like one. You can never tell these days."

"That's a relief."

"It looked like Skinner's truck to me, too. Pretty hard to mistake it."

"I hope you didn't scare the guy driving it. Did you?"

"No. He tried to sell the truck to me. Can you imagine owning that thing?"

"Wish you had the Corvette back?"

"No point in wishing."

"This is where we are now with our lives."

"How did Andrea take our story? I assume you told it to her."

"Had to. It was awkward explaining things to her. I don't think she's the blabbering type. I felt dissociated, telling her."

"The past shouldn't intrude on our lives so much."

"I want to forget about the Blue Mountains—everything. I had hoped moving here would help us forget."

"Try," he said. "I do."

"It wasn't Skinner in the truck."

"I hope you don't start ruminating, the way you do."

"Don't tell me that, or I will start. And you know you do, too."

"How far did you and Andrea get?"

"We hiked to the top of the ridge. Past where she was with Steve the night she broke her arm. He broke her arm. I guess she had to check it out again with someone else around to prove it was real. She broke her arm farther down the trail, she said, just up from the inn."

"Steve?"

"He's being unresponsive after having invited her to write to him. There was a message to her in the flashlight we returned, remember? Knowing Steve, she made too much of it, but I didn't say anything."

"So much for commitment."

"I need to tell Andrea not to worry about Skinner being around when she's out hiking. She left too soon. Excuse me and I'll call her now."

KRISTI REACHED Andrea on the phone at Mac's Place, though found her unconcerned. Skinner was just like any other man in a bar, she told Kristi, and she shouldn't be so upset. Some are nice guys, some monsters, most just guys. He was long gone by now. Long gone. Stop to think about it. Did you ever put yourself in his shoes? You really think he's going to show up after that? He *disappeared* himself!

"By the way, you aren't going to believe this," she told Kristi. "When I got to the bar, there was an envelope for me with no address, just with my name and the name of the bar, Sawtooth, Idaho. Steve lost my letter and didn't know how to reach me, so he thought he'd try writing here. "Sorry for the delay." What do you think of that?"

"I don't know why he didn't send it to us to forward. I'm glad he finally wrote, though, and hope you liked what he said. What did he say?"

"I liked it well enough. He's so smooth. Where does he get off, being so smooth?"

"He's Burge's friend. They were in the same fraternity."

"I know. Where do I get off, being attracted to some fraternity boy?"

"You have your rights, you know."

"I'm the little girl that couldn't go over to the rich person's house, remember?"

"Steve's not rich."

"He's an educated guy who helps to run a college. Almost the same thing."

"But you're college educated, too. And going to graduate school."

"But I'm a scholarship kid."

"So much the better. Right?"

"Right. I worked for it."

"So, are you going to tell me what he said?"

"Are you trying to pump me?"

"Of course, I am. So what did he say?"

"He just wants to see me again because we have something special. That's what he said. Special. Hmm. The problem is logistics. I thought perhaps he had sensed the futility of it all and just decided to stop writing. But he's in the thick of it, he said. At least he was when he wrote to me. He said he wanted to be with me but can't because Stanford doesn't want him. How can Stanford not want him? He's the Golden Boy."

"STANFORD WANTS you," Kristi said. "So you should stay with it and not do anything rash. He could be a will-o-the-wisp."

"But I really want to do something rash. Don't you ever want to? To be free a while?"

"I sort of did something rash. Look where it got me. But everybody's different. I'm not getting to go to graduate school, and you have so much going for you."

"Isn't he a good risk? You can tell me."

"Every woman at Cal who knew he existed was after him, but he mostly ignored them. Maybe he had too much of a good thing and is ready to settle down, now. That's a big maybe. He has a reputation of changing his mind quickly without ever saying why. Burge told me. I just don't want you to be hurt, that's all. We do like him. Who wouldn't? Jealous folk, I suppose, or someone who lost out in a play for him."

"How many times has 'I don't want you to be hurt' been said? I wonder if anyone really listens."

"Yours to decide. We'll still like you, however things work out. It's your life."

ANDREA LOOKED around the bar, checking to see if anybody needed anything. Nobody was there, but a dreary fly landed on the phone on the wall next to the cash register, disappeared into the phone's blackness in the dim light, then buzzed into the bar's daylight air, only to return nearby for a repeat performance.

"Nobody who says that really means it. What they really mean to say is, if you do that stupid thing, you're on your own."

"That's not what I meant, Andrea. I just don't believe in meddling in other people's decisions, even when they want me to, and I nearly did. It destroys part of their capacity to be themselves, and mine, too."

"How does not being hurt destroy my freedom?"

"If I color your thinking with my own, I'm keeping you from being fully you. Right?"

"What if I make the wrong decision? I either miss out on being with Steve or I am hurt by him. A diminished being. I don't have enough information to make up my own mind."

"What I might give you would only be my information, which is possibly wrong for you because I am not you. You should make your own decisions."

"But you're telling me what to do even as you say so, aren't you? Make my own decisions, I mean."

"The objective is to protect your freedom."

"You mean, don't ask."

"Ask if you will, but only listen to yourself."

"Listen if you will, but only ask for yourself. If I make the wrong decision, it might have an impact on you because you are Steve's friend. So you'll want a happy outcome. Yes?"

"But I'm your friend, too. I really don't know Steve that well.

You should ask Burge, who spent some student years with him. And I'm really not trying to put you off."

The old man who entered the bar then was a regular—faded red plaid cowboy shirt, dirty Levi's jeans, worn brown boots, the toes pointed upward from kicking against the bar getting on and off his usual stool. He kicked the bar again, getting in drinking form.

"Burge is a male," Andrea whispered loud into the handset.

"But he understands things. I'll get him on the phone."

"No. Someone just came in. I've been talking too long. I'll get fired."

*　　*　　*

W HEN ANDREA and Steve did get together in Sawtooth, it wasn't until summer's end. She had no longer thought about him except also to feel a little hurt, then not so hurt, but relieved. It had been weeks since his letter and well past her moment's eager response. He came with his office desk emptied, his home desk gone to a retired janitorial supervisor at the college who sold old furniture and appliances from a small whitewashed barn behind his house to successive generations of students, "just to keep in touch," then bought them back as the students moved on.

Time to start over again himself. This time he would work harder and get into his books. He'll have to, and forget about anything else—no more student anguish and hostility and fear about the draft and finances and the ever-present face of failure, fail now, fail forevermore. No, there was Andrea. He needed to see her, if only she wouldn't grasp. He kept thinking about them arched with the galaxy, and to think about it was to be with her almost, somewhere in the mind, until 'almost' over time wore into its nothingness and brought him to this.

Behind the inn Andrea and Steve skipped seeing Kristi and Burgess, Steve not wanting to have to explain anything just yet with no answers himself, and set forth up the trail and past the spot where they had fallen, to the crest and its white-bark pine, warming with sunlight, to see down into the valley over the ridge. They walked a long time down the overgrown autumn trail with insects floating almost motionless in patches of bright sun like dust suspended in beams of light, and the morning smells of trees and dew on undergrowth and sun on damp loamy earth. When they hushed, they heard crickets, mountain bluebirds, finches and orioles from the mountainside above and below them, and they walked on like this, Andrea in the lead, close beside the steep up-thrust of the mountain.

"Are you taking me to your secret place?" he asked.

"I never see anyone here, so every place is my secret place."

"Then to a favorite place. Yes?"

"Yes, then."

"Sorry to have been so insistent, but I had to see you again."

"Why?"

THE GROUND flattened toward a fast stream fifteen feet wide, lined and partly filled with granite boulders. She walked parallel to the stream upward to the trunk of a big pine log uprooted and fallen across to the other side to shape a natural bridge. She climbed up and walked across quickly, Steve following, eyes ahead, the log solid. She dismounted to the left where dead branches stopped her advance, jumping one foot at a time onto gray rocks flecked with black, and she was on the trail continuing upward, alongside the stream, then leaving it, hiking into the pines and nettle of the far bank. Steve walked fast to keep pace as it became more difficult to see where they were going or where they had been. Still he walked behind, for now he could see no trail or direction other than Andrea walking.

"Is this a shortcut?" Steve asked.

"No, just the regular way."

"I don't see any trail. How do you know where you are going?"

"I've been here before, lots. With you here, though, it seems new, like my first time."

"You know where we're going."

"In the broader sense, or just now? Just now I know exactly where we are going. After that, I don't know so much. Is to go where we are going enough right now, Steve?"

"I don't know so much, either."

"I shouldn't be so direct. I scare people away, it seems."

"I just don't have any answers. Where our futures point. You know, that stuff. My life just ran out where I was, and I had to see you."

"Let's just live in the present, then, shall we?"

"I'm still trying to get over the past. Not our past, Andrea. My past."

"Was your past so bad?"

"No. It was so good. But it ended at Commencement at Cal on the edge of a knife, that's all. Not all of it, of course. Just the part of it that made sense—in part it was being with my friends. I never even knew what was happening until we were all gone."

"Are you feeling nostalgic about college?"

"No. It was time to be out. Sometimes I miss it and feel damn lonely. Heck of a thing to have to admit, with people all around me."

"You are friends with Burge?"

"We were in a fraternity. Same pledge class, did all the same things together. But you grow up and things can't be the same any more. No more 2 a.m. sessions over beers where, just talking, you explore for the first time things that really matter, because now you've already explored them, and new ideas don't come the way they did in the moments you remember. It's like part of the world was scraped away."

"I think I see."

"Your differences amplify and you fade away. You try to re-capture it but the present gets in the way. Not to mention the future."

"And?"

"And it's far too big to get over. Sometimes I'm the present that's in the way, you know? The trick is on me. I'm not living up to my promise. Or maybe finally I am and was deluded back when I thought I saw things clearly."

"I had to work hard as an undergraduate myself."

"Did you have friends that way?"

"There are no sororities at Stanford and I couldn't have af-forded one if there were. I just worked. You have to do that with physics, and you want to. I had my classmates and my messy spoiled lost roommate who now teaches seventh grade in San Jose. A few of us studied together once or twice, maybe some-times more. It was enough."

"But you have good memories."

"Oh, yes. My professors and the act of discovery. I love find-ing out about things. That's what I do. Sometimes I used to pre-tend I even had you, in much the same way. Don't be shocked. I was just being presumptuous, I suppose. You gave me a night to remember. I don't ever want to change it."

"So we are making memories. Like when the inevitable sur-prise happens, and you say to yourself, 'I'll always remember this.' And you picture the way it is so you will get it right in all future recollections."

"Some things I can do without remembering."

"What do you mean?"

"You know. The arm."

"I guess I'd forgotten, given what happened before that."

"Fine. It was skinny and weak and smelly, and the skin peeled when I got the cast off. But it was only a few days until I wasn't favoring it. I don't want to remember how angry I was at you and scared that you'd messed things up for me. It doesn't make sense now, but that's the way I felt. Hopeless. End of encounter."

"I'm sorry to have lit on top of you."

"As I say, some things I can do without remembering. And now, Steven, you and I are going to forget about each other."

ANDREA SUDDENLY sprang ahead of him and ran, and was nearly out of sight up and across the steep terrain and into the brush before Steve discerned what was happening. He started after her, the thought of being left alone and lost in the mountains suddenly in his mind. This was the answer to her dilemmas and his. Soon he felt the real shock, for Andrea had disappeared.

IV. INFAMOUS PRAISE

Chapter 25

THE SNOW was gone from all but the mountain peaks surrounding Sawtooth following the late storm, and Galena Summit up from Ketchum was no longer worrisome. The good skiing was lost to the slow 'between season,' this time three years later, 1973.

Andrea, who to the Burgesses had completely disappeared without a word for all that time, walked up the front steps of the Sawtooth Inn and found the door unlocked. A bell sounded her presence. Kristi came from the kitchen, drying her hands on a white terrycloth dishtowel. *Who could be here at this time of the season?*

"Hi, Kristi, do you remember me?"

"Andrea! Where have you been? We missed you!"

"Just the usual Stanford. 'HooTow,' 'MemAud,' 'MemChu' and 'MemClaw.'"

"What?"

"Some students refer to buildings by their abbreviations. 'MemClaw,' though, is actually a memorial fountain that looks like a claw. I was just saying I felt at home there, and that's where I've been."

"Well, this is your first home, and we haven't seen you for such a long time."

Kristi stopped talking, the words missing. Andrea gave her a quick hug, which both needed, and Kristi hugged back.

"Don't remind me," Andrea continued, as if picking up yesterday's conversation. "I've been really busy, and finally I did it!

I'm now a Ph.D. I practically just stepped off the Commencement platform."

"We thought you'd gone back to Palo Alto after the last time we saw you. But then you didn't come home the following summers."

"Just briefly to see family. I had research projects to attend to. All that's completed, and now I have real work, big time. In Richland!"

"You do? Really?"

"I guess I surprised you. I did listen to your views of the place. But they were actually enthusiastic about having me work there. Me!"

"I'm so envious, maybe."

"To be here would have been better, of course, but what's a physicist to do? Government contractors do recruit and hire women scientists these days. It's a solid place to start work."

"Come sit down and tell me what's happening. I guess you've been to Richland already, at least for interviews. Where are you staying there?"

Look, do you feel like a hike? We could take on the hill again. Stimulates conversation."

KRISTI LOOKED out the glass doors behind Andrea at an empty street. She found the "back soon" sign in the top drawer of the front desk and hung it on the door.

"Let's go!" she said. "You were saying?"

Their conversation and curiosity kept them standing alongside the front desk a moment.

"Do you know where the 'rabbit hutches' are? I'm told that's what everyone calls them."

"Yes. That's where we lived," Kristi said, "just starting out, and also finishing up. You'll be saving money."

"I can't believe what I'm renting a whole apartment for compared to California. Power bills are nothing, and I have so much room!"

"Why did you choose Richland?"

"It chose me. They recruited me on campus. It's my opportunity for now, and I can drive here to be home in half a day."

"You shouldn't have any trouble meeting people there. The ratio of men to women is still greatly askew in your favor, I'm sure, not to mention you are very attractive. I guess you don't have any other problems with working there, then?"

"Problems?"

"With the defense industry, I mean. This is not a popular time to be associated with it if you happen to be our age."

"Those problems I can put up with. Nobody has them there. I am doing physics, and that's what matters to me. I'm in a lab, and they like me there, or at least seem to. Everyone's working to the same end.

"Women can't be too picky, you know, especially in physics. Who can tell where I might end up when the postdoc is through? I might actually decide to stay if they still want me. I might also teach in a college somewhere if I can get a job. None pending, by the way. It all seems like such a long freight train sometimes."

"Steve asked after you once or twice. He came back hang-dog from a walk with you before he went home. Probably served him right, whatever happened. We didn't know where to find you, though, and thought you'd forgotten us. You remember Steve?"

"Yes. Sorry. I couldn't deal with him. I'm glad he made it back okay after I . . . hmm."

"Left him howling in the pines?"

"Left him there behind me. I didn't intend him any harm, really. I just couldn't deal with him at that moment. It was an impulse I didn't know how to recover from."

"The mountains were conquered, and no apparent damage done. They do seem impossible at points the first time or so you're in them, though."

"How did he respond? I suppose I made him angry."

"Nobody had ever dumped him before—certainly not that way. He didn't want to talk, as I remember it. It was almost dark when he got back to us. He said you had run off, and he had looked for you but couldn't find you. He said he figured you knew what you were doing more than he did. So then he got in his car and drove off to Pullman, night coming or no. He promised to call from there in the morning because I was worried, which he forgot to do. I called him."

"Does he ever come back here?"

"Every summer. He's decided he likes the out-of-doors."

"Did you ever finish the map of the trails?"

"Yes. He helped, actually. Will you look at it and tell us what we have missed?"

"Sure. I was half hoping to see him again to tell him I was sorry. But then I also didn't want to see him. I don't know why. Maybe out of embarrassment. Or maybe I was right all along, or just couldn't handle the situation. Loss of face? No matter, I'm still without him. Speaking of which, let's hike!"

KRISTI OPENED the top drawer of the front desk and pulled out a piece of type paper, on which a map had been penciled in, erased, and drawn in again.

"Here's the map. I'll keep on being nonjudgmental. You both

300

seem to have managed just fine without my views, so who am I to say anything?"

"Thanks for talking with me way back when. I might be married with smelly babies by now if you hadn't."

"Would that have been so bad?"

"A knocked-up single mother?"

"Steve would have done the honorable thing."

"I wouldn't have wanted that. It all would have been my fault."

"Well, you did resolve the ambiguity, if that's what it was. Are you still unattached, then?"

KRISTI LED their way out the back door, down the steps and onto the trail, upward bound. Andrea stepped alongside her, then ahead of her as the trail narrowed.

"I don't want to be unattached any more. But there's nothing I can do about it."

"Women do have ways, you know."

"There has to be someone in sight. There isn't anyone in sight."

"Maybe Richland will be the place for you, then. That's where I found Burge."

"We'll see. At least I'm not Miss . . . what's the name of the person with the letters in the trunk who used to live here?"

"Daisy. You are richer by far."

"I'm not. How did she finally end up? Here, I'll bet, alone. But what else? Did you read all the letters?"

"Every last one. 'Finally' isn't what counts, though. I like 'what' and 'how' along the way. The letters just stopped. No conclusion. Lights out."

"Did she ever walk in the mountains again?"

"Would you like to read the letters? I shouldn't spoil it for you."

"Do you remember if she did?"

"There's only one occasion to go from."

"The mountains are a big part of what I've missed from being away. You are so lucky to be here with what you have."

"We almost didn't make it. Burge tending bar down the street and help from our parents got us through the first year. I felt like a contempo version of my great grandmother on the homestead. It's better, now, though, with more food on the table. The word's getting out that we're here."

"The map has the basic trails, but there are other places to see. We can't do them all. Wanna see some? I'd love the company."

"If you promise not to lose me, too."

"No way. You're my friend."

"I think Steve might be, too."

"After what I did?"

"In the stretch of time, you possibly only piqued his interest. But I'm butting out."

"He was screwing around with my head."

"He wasn't very attentive. His own was screwed up."

"When he was, he was. When he was, he wasn't. A real quantum man—like Shrodinger's cat."

"I don't presume to know what's best for you. I just thought if you're interested, he's at least closer than he was. In miles, I mean. Never mind."

THE HIKE ended back at base camp, the lodge parlor, on much-welcomed overstuffed chairs. Kristi rubbed her calf muscles and shins. She stood up suddenly and walked to the doorway, stopping there to listen. She called to Burge. No response. She called to anybody.

"I thought I heard something," she told Andrea. "This place isn't very lively this time of year. We have some friends you might like in Richland—Jill and Tom, and they have Angie. She's six. You said 'hello' to them the first time you were here, but possibly don't remember them. I'll give you their address."

"I'd like that. I really don't know anybody else. You know how it is when you're new."

"Matter of fact, you can do me a favor if you'd like. Say 'no' if it creates problems."

"What is it?"

"I promised this toy angel doll for Angie when she got older. It was the inn's sole resident for a while. Angie's old enough now to have her, but I forgot to take her to Richland the last time we visited Mother. I've had her under a plastic bag in the basement ever since I discovered her and cleaned her up. That was just after we moved here."

"Sure. It can ride alongside me in the front seat. The back and trunk are jammed with clothes and stuff."

"I didn't think about that. Are you sure you have enough room? I can just remember to take it the next time we go if it's a problem."

"It will be a good introduction to your friends. Of course I'll take it."

"Let me go fetch it from the basement before I forget."

KRISTI WAS gone a long time—long enough for Andrea to wonder after her:

Has something happened on the stairs? Shall I go see no I won't be nosy, I won't be. I thought something had happened to. Here I am to be here. These people I don't have to I'll just leave the doll. Maybe they'll be, maybe I'll be lonesome. Everyone married but me. I'll work hard I always do, not always. Always men are hard to find, my kind. There? I have my own self to satisfy now that I'll call at the stairs. She's coming.

"Now it's the plastic cover that's dusty," Kristi said, setting the doll on the coffee table in front of Andrea, wiping at the cover with a dust cloth. "I think I got most of it off. The doll seems to be just fine for her many years."

"I can't keep up with this big place. The cellar is hazed with dust again, and it seems as if I just cleaned it. It actually hasn't been since the last time you were here that I dusted, though. My confession. There's too much to do for just us."

"It's really a beautiful angel, though she is obviously very old. See how real its hair looks."

"It probably is real. It's looking a little faded. I can't get all the dust off the plastic because of the static electricity."

"Use a damp cloth."

"I've got another bag. I'll get it. In the meantime, I did find this letter. I remembered it tucked in with the others, unsent, I would guess."

April 16, 1928

Dear Martha:

There is something I haven't told you out of fear that it would cost me our friendship. I do hope it won't. When things are not the same, it is very difficult to pretend that they are. When I saw the naked man before me three years ago, about to run, I said to him, "Wait, don't go. I won't hurt you. I want to know you." But he ran away anyway, only pausing a second. I couldn't believe what I had said.

I did recognize him. He was the grocer's son, Brad Henning, younger than I am, just getting a beard and discovering himself alone in nature and physically changed with his age. I so wished I could be like him in the time before we met, so free. He was Rousseau's native—I hope you know who that is, because Rousseau thought we should all be that way, too, be free, that otherwise in civilization we are so in chains. The boy was my 'noble savage,' and in an instant I wanted to capture him, to have him.

When I saw him in the grocery store, though, he would look away and become red, and I would attempt to say a few words to him, to say that I understood. But he would go about his work, silent, his eyes downcast. Then he flared at me, "Leave me alone," and I didn't know what to do. I left him alone, but I still couldn't keep my eyes off him. It was more than just Rousseau. He was the first man I had ever seen before, you know, that way, and I thought he might be the last. I was so drawn to him, though his long face and black hair were so somber. I had all these feelings.

Finally he said in a tremulous half-whisper one day to meet him where we had seen each other before, if I pleased, which is a long way from where I live, over the top of a mountain-like hill. I remembered well where the spot was. Despite what I knew my father would say, I went to meet him on the day he said. I waited for him a little while. When he came, he came bursting through the brush wearing white butcher's clothes, too big for him.

He pushed me down on the ground and peed on me, holding me down with his foot on my dress, and then he kicked dirt on me, which stuck to my dress in dusty, muddy spots and streaks when I could get up. He lifted me up. He said that he was quitting the grocery to work in the mine, and that I should meet him there at the same place next week at the same time when we would be lovers. Or else. I did go to meet him, through the disgust and shame. I don't know why. I guess I just wanted to.

Nothing came of it but silence, and then he disappeared. I told my father who it was that scared me in the forest that first time, and my father had him fired almost before he had started at the mine, then run out of town. The grocer kept quiet for fear of losing his store, I think, because of what people would say. Now they're moving, too. I didn't tell my father the rest. I shouldn't be telling you, but I had to tell somebody.

Please don't think the less of me for what I did. I am in this place, after all, trying to be alive.

Should I be forgiven?

Love,

Daisy

ANDREA FANNED herself with the letter, then refolded it and slid it alongside the angel on the coffee table. Kristi sat beside her and lifted the dusty cover from the doll.

"Daisy's mother gave her the angel so they could 'look after one another' just after the boy had been sent out of town," she told Andrea. "I learned that much from Martha's letters. The halo is as it has been over the years, as you can see. Touched by a little girl."

"The doll's story is just between us."

"The doll makes a nice gift for Angie. She's just a doll now. Angie's parents have had some troubles. Angie's been a big help to them."

"You said she was only six."

"In addition to being married, they are also sister and adopted brother. He's a computer guy. You may get to know him professionally, as well."

"You mean they . . . . I see. Well, biology is biology. That aside, I know punch cards well."

"I thought I should tell you to avoid an awkward situation. You never know how or when something might come up that upsets them, but they're our friends and really worth getting to know. They've had a few family problems, like everyone else."

"He's a computer guy? I can forgive that. I don't understand what the problem is otherwise, except they might know each other too well."

"Their parents flipped. All is mostly forgiven, I think. Jill thanked us for helping, but we didn't do anything besides be there for her. She's alone too much. She'll appreciate a friend."

Andrea looked at the doll, too big to top a tree, looking out of place and time on the table before them, the edges of its robe darkened gold braided thread, the wings, too small for flying much, of stiff white embroidered silk, its beatific painted gaze forward, arms open and beckoning from one narrow direction. *To restore the past, a small inanimate protector.* Kristi shook out a new plastic bag, gathered the sides together and placed it over the toy. It was done.

"Got the map?" she asked Andrea. "Let's go exploring."

THE SNOW was gone from all but the mountain peaks surrounding Sawtooth following the late storm, and Galena Summit down toward Sawtooth could be maneuvered with greater speed. But speed picked up fast, almost imperceptibly because of the slope of the mountain. Sharp curves in the roadway brought one up short. Burgess came back along this roadway toward Kristi and Andrea and home just before dusk. He caught himself accelerating and hard braking repeatedly despite the number of times he had traveled the pass.

As he rounded a curve he recognized on the downward slope not a hundred yards ahead of him the old white Ford truck that he had seen three times or more before, this time speeding on in front of him, growing smaller, its brake lights on, then off, just making the curves that Burgess could see.

Until it slid off the left-curving road looking almost like an old toy truck, down a slight embankment, and crashed headlong into the rocky mountainside rising before it dark as a bruise. The truck rebounded back toward the roadway in a quarter-turn, and then didn't move, then drifted back, destroyed hood touching the road cut. As if abandoned there.

"That kid," Burgess thought, braking to stop and help. "In Skinner's truck." He pulled off the road behind the truck so that his lights would help him see in the dusk, feeling physically whole and lucid, heart pumping, his left leg stepping down out of the cab of his truck, his mind clear.

This accident isn't mine. Is he still alive?

With a great strain, Burgess opened the driver-side door of the white truck on the second attempt, the truck wheels stilled in the wide gravel shoulder of the road, aslant.

The driver's averted head and shoulder had wedged between the steering wheel and column and the top of the cab on impact, and then recoiled, caught by the broken wheel. The windshield was a web of cracks in the tempered glass, showing in Burgess' truck lights like bleached straw around a dark hole nearly the size of a human face. Jim pulled back gently on the man's body, which fell out suddenly onto the sharp rocks of the road's shoulder, Burgess' arms breaking the fall.

There was blood. Pumping, then stopped. It was not the kid. It was him all right, Skinner, his eyes open and staring motionless, as if in final rapture. There was no pulse.

Burgess moved like an automaton, matching the motions of a first-aid film shown at work. He repeated them. It didn't work.

He repeated them.

He realized himself to be alone. He tried again, until he couldn't any more. Then he could only kneel and look and try to recover his breath.

JOY COSGRIFF pulled behind Burgess' truck and walked to Burgess and the dead man on the tilted ground. She looked and waited for a response.

"It's him, isn't it, Burge?

"You tried to save him, Burge. You've got blood on your face, so I know that."

She looked at Burgess, still staring down, catching his breath. She was lost to him.

She paused, then said, "I don't think I would have.

"Take care of yourself, Burge. I'll go find a cop."

V. MOMENTARY VISION

Chapter 26

BURGESS STEPPED into the kitchen of the Sawtooth Inn on August 8, 1974, where Kristi had a pot of water just boiling and said to her, "Richard Nixon disappears tomorrow. It was on the radio."

"Yeh? Tomorrow's also the anniversary of the Nagasaki bomb," says Kristi. "As if it were all timed."

"Why do you remember stuff like that? Why not let things be new? Maybe now things will straighten out. Everyone's been obsessed with the news for over a year, the trial, the indictments, the tapes, so now he beats impeachment by quitting. A double bombing, given a few anniversaries. So what happens to us next?"

"It's only politics, a blip in the stretch of things. What's really happened? Mother will be upset. We should go see her. Just pretend we can afford to. We can get Joy Cosgriff to take charge of things here for a day or two. Nobody's coming here because of the gas situation. We can make a quick trip, if 55 mph is quick, and see old friends while we're at it."

"When I left, I said I never wanted to go back there. We do go back, though. Other than to visit your mother and friends, I'm not sure why. I feel sneaky driving into town."

"They're still our people. Some are, anyway."

"'Daddy, where's America?' A little kid asked his father that in a company paper cartoon from the early days. I saw the cartoon in the Science Center. Your home's not a place to escape to."

"The bomb hasn't been dropped in some time, you know," Kristi said. "Not on people. I mean right on them, not just fallout from tests or anything."

BURGESS SAT at the inn's kitchen table, stood up, and began setting it: woven import placemats, two tumblers of water, yellow paper napkins, stainless steel dinnerware in a narcissus pattern (a wedding gift from Eileen), all on bare wood.

"Yep. New finger's on the trigger. Unelected, Nixon's choice."

"Nixon did China. Even if he playacted it for history, he did it."

"Yep. To divide the Communist bloc. Kissinger told him to, I'll bet."

"Maybe there's not so much to worry about."

"Fewer jobs at Hanford, then."

"Stop teasing. We all want peace, don't we?"

"And! The best way to secure that is! More bombs!"

"You've been dreaming up clouds of Senator Magnusson again."

"Scoop Jackson."

"Both."

"I was joking. What did you expect? We were real people for a while."

"Not any more," Kristi said, dropping at an angle a shaft of dry sticks of spaghetti into boiling water.

"Not their people, at any rate."

SHE WATCHED the pasta spread against the side of the pan, then waited for it to sag and slip into the water. "I hope you're not hungry for something new to eat. This is what we've got again tonight. The sauce will be reheated in a minute to match. Got wine?"

314

"Right out of the water tap. Let's celebrate."

"Let's just have dinner. At least there's that."

RETURNING TO Richland meant a drive south and west past Boise, then across the northeast corner of Oregon and unavoidably through the Blue Mountains before crossing the Columbia and moving homeward north and west, not a comfortable truck ride except along the stretches of straight road through sagebrush and, where water was to be had, farmland.

Winding through the hills upward into the Blues, Kristi tried to think in the afternoon heat of something other than being raped there, but the feeling persisted, well along into the depths of pines.

"Burge, we really do need to come camping here."

"You want to come camping here?"

"No, I don't. I don't want to be here, period."

"I didn't think so. Don't throw out camping, though. Camping's a life experience—like being in touch with nature when we were all hunter-gatherers. Back and back for thousands of years. You get to know yourself in different ways. Why did you say we should come camping here?"

"Because I'm tired of feeling the way I do every time we drive through these mountains. I need to be jolted out of the rut."

"You're always so silent here. Why? It's like making us relive the ride back after you-know-what. For me, it's that way."

"Sorry our truck radio doesn't work here. Or much of anywhere else, for that matter. At least we could listen to something."

"What do you want to talk about?"

"I'm whining again. You aren't going to help me out of this, are you?"

"Okay. Tell me what you are feeling."

"I shouldn't feel this way."

"Tell me."

"It isn't as if I had been raped, I say to myself again. We're together, you and I. I thought we would be killed and found like that. Awful dreams. Flies laying eggs in our noses. Then when he went free, I felt he would come after us again. Skinner. What if he's still lurking in the pines? He just disappeared. Where was he? Then he pops up, dead. In your arms, on your face. Joy told me you tried to save him."

"Dead is dead. That happened to us years ago, you know. Dead. If he wants to be in your mind, you should throw him out. I did. He's gone."

"Don't you think I would have long ago if I could? Should I tell you something? In my dreams, I have been completely stripped of my will, as well as my clothes. He has sex with me, and I don't know where you are. He just takes me. I feel so ashamed when I wake up wet and throbbing. Sicko, huh?"

"It's only a dream. Nothing's real there. Right? Right."

"So why do I feel this way?"

"So why?"

"He is my Mr. Death. His is the face. Him all along. I just didn't recognize it until I dreamed it. Nothing's rational about it. Him between my legs."

"Is that what you think?"

"What does thinking have to do with anything? It's my emotions that get me. The way I feel. I can't shake them off. That's why I don't like being here. So here I am."

"I get it. Maybe."

"But I shouldn't avoid being here, right? It's one way I can dull myself to the whole situation. You want thought, that's what I just thought. Just like school. Actually doing something about it, though, is another matter. I wish I knew how. So I'll just sit here quietly and desensitize myself with thought."

"Do you want to go back to where it happened?"

"No. We couldn't find it if we tried. A trip through the Blues is quite enough for one day."

"So how do you plan to desensitize yourself?"

"I'll experience the forest as forest and me a speck in a hundred generations on a thousand planets. A pine needle. What's so different from home? Then I'll pretend we're Rousseau's monkeys, you and I. The painter Rousseau?"

"We could pull over and . . . you know, do it."

"Oh, that. Somehow I don't have the urge to do that in broad daylight again. The thought makes me shrivel."

"Sorry. Just a thought."

"Nice try."

THE HOUSE where Kristi grew up felt less secure than it once did, with the furniture newly moved, the Cutty Sark picture above the mantel replaced by a mirror with a gilt florentine-like frame from Richland Fine Furniture. It showed suddenly an older Kristi with pale skin, darker hair disheveled from travel, and much the same clothes she seemed to herself always to have worn, now rumpled and baggy.

She was surprised to have caught herself there above the fireplace, older, grown somber with care. She smiled at herself. Her face wasn't right any more. She saw Burge come along behind her, reversed image but still Burge. Kristi's mother was no longer being isolated, alone with tv newscasts, her hands washed forever of the former President and now empty.

"You've moved the furniture, Mother. What possessed you to do it?"

"Don't you like it this way? I was getting awfully tired of the other way round. I like the change."

"I'll get used to it. Your new mirror gave me a start, is all."

"It makes this room look bigger, don't you think? Please sit down, both of you. The ship was your father's pick. Always sailing somewhere, never arriving. I don't know why I was so afraid to touch anything that was his for such a long time."

"'Weel done, Cutty-sark!' That's what Miles used to say, then he'd say, 'Bobby Burns.' Remember? I never did understand. Now it's just a memory and forever an incomplete experience. The room does seem bigger, but also smaller for some reason when I stop to think that it is supposed to seem bigger. I wonder why. The reflection has things out of place. How do you get used to seeing yourself above the fireplace all the time?"

"Don't be so critical! It's like having company when the place is empty," Eileen said. "A moment's anticipation of it, anyway. Perhaps I'm just a parakeet with one of those round mirrors with a bell on the bottom. The bell keeps ringing."

Kristi said, "I guess you've been following the news, like the rest of the world."

"I wish there were something else on the television that I liked to watch besides that, which has become really only a habit to satisfy."

"Nixon, most powerful man in the world, the will-o-the-wisp, on the verge of returning to California," Burgess said.

"I still miss you both and wish you weren't gone so far away, you see. Thank goodness, I still have work and all. By the way, you can use the phone any time when you want to call your friends. You usually call them, don't you?"

"We can't stay longer than the weekend. We've really got to see Jill and Tom while we're here this time, and we haven't heard from Andrea since she moved here over a year ago."

"She did stop by to say hello to me once. I neglected to tell you. She seemed very busy."

"It's her first real job," Burgess said. "I'm sure it's pretty demanding of her time. She has a Ph.D., you know, and the job must match. They expect more of women who survive the hiring process. Really."

"I didn't know. I guess that sort of thing happens these days. She is so beautiful I didn't think she would be driven in that direction."

"Women who are dedicated can do what they want," Kristi said. "At least in some places. She's very determined and couldn't be anything else, I think, but maybe that idea chases its own tail."

"But that shuts her out of certain of life's options, doesn't it? Men get scared away by women who are too smart."

"Not the right men, Eileen. Burge remains untested. If I only had the means to accomplish what she has."

WITH EVERYONE seated, Burgess nodded toward sleep from the long drive. He rearranged himself in the wing chair off to the side and at a slight angle to the sofa, near the fireplace. There, in a series of slow nods, he closed his eyes. From where Kristi sat, the mirror showed empty space and a reverse view of her old comfortable living room.

"Darned few 'right men,'" Eileen said. "Burge qualifies."

"Andrea left Burge's friend standing with his jaw dragging in the forest, where she had led him and then vanished. Steve the Golden Wonder. So she can still do her attracting magic."

"So there's hope."

"Once I could see them getting together, but that's obviously just me with a loose wire. I miss out on people sometimes. Me the psychologist."

"Don't put yourself down, Kristi. Too many others will happily do that for you. You'll give them ideas."

"Hanford makes people such humanists."

EILEEN WAS silent, then responded in that questioning, unbelieving way: "Kristi?"

"I didn't mean it quite like that."

"Like what, then?"

"People seem misanthropic and jaded, that's all, but I didn't mean you. The people Burge worked with, others you come to know. You can see why, can't you? Not everybody's that way, I hope. I wonder if it has changed Andrea. I didn't have the heart to tell her what I really thought of her coming here. What if she didn't have any other options?"

"Is that just the way you think people here are because now you live somewhere else? People who need to accomplish things seem to behave that way sometimes. They are really trying to get things done in the best way they can. That's why they become so . . . domineering. They want the power to have things done right. To make things right."

"I didn't mean to be ungrateful, Mother. I just wish you worked elsewhere, that's all."

"Because of what happened to Burgess? I might understand that."

"Because of Hanford. Don't you think it's just the nature of the business? Bombs meaning ultimate power and all. Maybe that does things to people, even if they're only around it a little."

"I have to make a living, Kristi. This is what there is. It's what I know. You have to behave like it all means something."

"I hope Burge's whatever it was that happened hasn't had some impact on you. Has it?"

"I'm good at ignoring things," her mother explained.

"What things? Please tell me."

"How would I know that if they were ignored?"

"I would be very upset if you were mistreated because of us."

"Kristi, I will not have you worry about me. Nothing has happened."

"How can I be sure now?"

"I've been there your whole life long, Kristi."

"So had I, you know, Mother, and look what happened to us."

"Are you happy? It has been a few years since you moved away. You seem forlorn. I thought you would be happy to return to your home."

"I won't have you worrying about me, either. We came hoping to console you, and I'm being a flop at it because you seem far from needing it. So let me just be happy to see you. Mind if I make the phone calls now?"

Kristi stood up and saw herself mirrored, a flash of before, fast into the immovable present moment of just standing there, looking at an image of herself.

The way I always see myself has a way of changing.

She smoothed her hair back with both hands, held her cheeks, walked to the kitchen and called.

"So how is Kristi, and how are you, Burgess?" Eileen asked as he stretched awake in his chair.

NOW WE HAVE SECRETS

EILEEN'S KITCHEN was patched with late afternoon sunlight, a little sultry from the swamp cooler blowing evaporate through the ductwork of the household forced-air furnace. Kristi stretched the white telephone with its twisted cable from its niche in the wall and sat down at the breakfast nook to call. She was unable to reach Jill on the first dial, and so she phoned Andrea.

"Kristi, is it really you? Darn," Andrea said. "Have you talked with Jill yet?"

"No, Andrea, I tried but couldn't reach her."

"Oh."

"Is something the matter?"

"I don't know but whether you should talk to her first. We are worried about her."

"Who's 'we?'"

"Mm."

Kristi thought Andrea always had the right words, her words, without the silences. She'd wait.

"Tom and I. Such a mess. I've never felt like this and wished I didn't."

"I'm not understanding you."

"Tom and I, like, together. We got together, romantically. Why does it have to be this way?"

"You mean, you're seeing Tom?"

"I didn't want to. He was so persistent. Men usually just disappear on me, but he didn't. What should I do? I should have asked you long ago. You at least knew him."

"Well, Jill obviously already knows about it. Just how far

along are you with Tom?"

"I don't know. Tom says Jill had almost invited him to leave several times, and before this happened. Before we met, even."

"None of my business, but so how did you hook up? I hope it wasn't my fault."

"I went to their house to reintroduce myself and deliver the angel doll, just as you had asked me to do. They all three were there, family. But he wouldn't keep his eyes to himself and off me. It made me uncomfortable, as it would anybody. But he also broke through my loneliness in a new place. The lid wouldn't fit back on the bottle. I became busy with my new job and didn't see them for a while after that, though I talked with Jill on the phone out of a need to get better acquainted.

"One night he called me, he said to invite Jill and him to pay a call on me. What could I say? Well, only he showed up. He had risked doing that. I should have known, but I was too attracted to him, and curious to know what was going on. You know how it can be here. All of the sudden there was someone who cared about me enough to make contact. Everything seemed to have happened at once, and the time disappeared.

"Jill found out about it, of course. His stay was away too long. She said she knew him so well, and I'm sure she does. They did grow up together, you know. No mystery in the great mystery, you'd think.

"Anyway, she wanted him again then to herself, and said so, and insisted on it. It was 'just friends' with me, platonic. Um hum. He called me again, and every now and again he kept calling until I gave in. I didn't encourage anything, at least not anything I was aware of. I still don't know what I gave in to, being basically nuts.

"They have a child. He keeps seeing them, now that he's moved out to be alone."

"Alone?"

"That's what he said. He's never had his own life since he was adopted. I hoped you had called her so I wouldn't have had to tell you. I don't know what she would say, though. I didn't know what you would say or what I would say, and now I've gone and told you. I tried to tell him to get lost and go back to his wife, but my voice broke and I cried, I felt so alone. That isn't me. And then he wouldn't let me alone, and I didn't want him to. It's a totally thoughtless situation. What can I do? I think it's actually being done for me."

KRISTI PUT the phone down, inhaled and rubbed her eyes, trying to straighten her emotions. She picked up the phone and continued, "Then you are his lover. Tom has a mistress and you are that person. Is that how you want it?"

"Those are just words. There is something between us, something deep, even if foolish. Maybe the foolishness is what made it that way.

"It was worth having as a moment of my life. That's all I wanted to tell you in the second I wanted to tell it—that we had a relationship, that they are both alone now, and thus I am again, too. I love their child and the angel, and I love Jill. I worry about everybody because of me. Then all of that goes away and we're just a bunch of people. Why did you ever introduce us?"

"I'm sorry, Kristi said. "I didn't mean to seem to accuse you. Angie did love the angel, but it was a changeling, a witch in disguise for me and for her, too, it seems.

"I just thought you and Jill would be friends. You seemed so happy to be here after you got your doctorate, and I wanted you to stay happy. I suspected you'd be alone and lonely because that's what I was. You're a single woman, and you're not from here. This place is strictly families. Jill said she felt that way at first here, even though she was married. People can be cold. It's as if everyone knew. What had started was just a secret conversation."

"I was friends with Jill, it seemed, Kristi. Friendship was possible. And now it's all spoiled. I seem not to have anybody here now except Tom, and he's not exactly what you mean by having somebody. Sometimes he's a mutt who farts, drools and growls. So how can I even talk to Jill? Do you dislike me now, too? Maybe I'm the mutt."

"I try not to judge people, you know? Who am I, anyway? I don't want to lose you both, so I'm afraid, that's who I am. Do you love him? I didn't mean to ask that. Do you?"

"I needed him. I don't know what love is any more. Did I ever? Maybe it's just a convenience for people, a made up concept. Maybe it was just me wanting physical gratification. Love? I see him less and less, and I won't give chase."

"And he still sees Jill."

"Yes. He told me so, as if he blamed me for whatever state they're in."

"And?"

"Maybe he just used me to get free, the way he might have used Jill to free himself of their parents. Or maybe he was just getting free of me when he went back to her. Just when my work brought me to the possibility of a relationship."

"There's no one else, then?"

"Who else would there be?"

"Burge's friend Steve? You seemed to like him at first."

"I dropped through a hole in his pocket. The distances stunned him, and he couldn't remember that I existed, except in fits and starts. Three seconds on Saturday."

"He asks after you as if he didn't really want to know, but of course he does want to know, because he keeps asking. He's still in Pullman with his dissertation and job as a T.A. It's not so far away. I didn't want to bother you before, since you did ditch him."

"You'd like me to take up another option so Jill and Tom's marriage will go back together. I think it's maybe broken, anyway. I have little hard evidence, though, whatever that might be. As I say, I won't chase him."

"It's not your fault. Tom took the lead."

"Transgressors, both of us, ultimately. If that's the way you look at it. It's not the way I look at it. We both consented to it. Maybe it's too late for me. But I have to be alive, too. Don't I? Why can't I be?"

"Aren't there other men around?"

"Bar twonks. Good laughs, sometimes. I need more than that. Don't I deserve . . . . There isn't anybody, no."

ANDREA PAUSED, Kristi not knowing what to say next, not saying anything right, since life invisibly had moved her away from direct speech toward pointlessness, as if someone else were saying through her voice something like what she thought, but enough off to be entirely wrong. That's how she felt at that moment.

Andrea told her, "Maybe I should just be enough for me? I'm not, you know. Tom knew I wasn't."

Chapter 27

Empty, CONFUSED, and fearful of having nothing to say to Kristi if not now, Jill pleaded with her to visit for coffee and talk. Jill started with a confession: she and Tom were "in separation." Jill hated the word "separated," with its echoes of rumors, and didn't know how else to say it, or to whom. To speak about it perhaps was for her to accept the truth, but what truth?

Kristi, her one friend, had introduced Andrea to them. After, when Tom came home so late the first time, Jill sensed that something had happened—something to do with Andrea. His eyes said nothing. He wouldn't speak. Jill had seen his eyes follow and hold when Andrea gave the angel doll to Angie. Jill wouldn't believe it, she wouldn't, until she could no longer stay silent and protested Tom's nights away. Andrea had just stopped calling her.

"Alright, then, I'll move out," Tom had said, "and we'll be separated."

"I don't want it to be that way," she told him, but after all, that's the way it was. They seemed to live out their own imagined rumor, with its commonality almost their protection.

He would send checks for the mortgage and food (she knew he had little more to spend), and then request to see Angie, then to see them both, because he missed them, he said, which she hoped was true—hoped he would miss them. What else could she do? She didn't have other options, with the hurt Tom would feel and answer back with. He would say she didn't really love him if she didn't let him see Andrea, who enriched his life in ways Jill couldn't even understand—so she thought he would say.

That was enough. He did see them both. Jill might only ever know him again as the father of her child and nothing more, doubly lost, and then that relationship would grow thin and anguished as she gave up Angie for part of her life the way other

327

people must do when they become divorced. Therefore, it was a matter of family, no matter what, she told herself, and she feared she would never make love with another man again, for there had forever only been one to approach her. She remembered the first time, when he told her, "Now we have secrets," and they were bound together that way, each private to the other no more.

ALL THIS she told Kristi, wondering that Jill had said nothing to her before this moment, the steam from the hot coffee with cream now lingering briefly in their noses, in the bright breakfast nook, like Eileen's.

"I wish I had never seen Andrea sometimes, Kristi. Am I supposed to hate her for what she did? I still like her somehow, though she never calls and I can't call her. We have the same tastes in men, it seems. Angie likes her because Andrea brought her your doll and then talked with her as if they were best friends. It must be difficult being an only child. Is it? I only remember from early on. I wish you had brought the doll to Angie yourself. Why didn't you?"

"Jill, I thought you and Andrea would be friends, you know, that you both could use someone to talk to. You can't foresee such things. Anyway, I didn't."

"I don't know what Andrea talks about with him. It's beyond me. How can they talk about physics when there are people to be understood first? A strain of me feels as if I'm the one they must be talking about. Do you think they do? It's only a strain, I say. Do you think they laugh at me because I have given in to their relationship?"

"I'm sure they don't laugh at you. You are the mother of his child."

"And he can never undo that, right? He loved me for a long time. Only me. I knew. And he can't take that away from me. But now he's trying to."

"Andrea is sorry for your predicament, too. Like, she confessed it. You didn't really give in to anything, did you? You just endured it and were strong. I think you're strong."

"You've actually? I mean, talked to her, then? About me?"

"Only to hear she worries about you, about everything. I called her when I couldn't reach you. I didn't know about anything, you know—naive old me. Sorry. Neither of you wrote or called. No way I could know."

"I couldn't call. I kept thinking things would go back together and be normal again, then I'd just have pointless embarrassment to deal with. I never really expected Tom to move out. We were too close, too deep and too soon reaching each other growing up. Naive of us. I was only trying in a moment to get him to be more attentive. I think that was what it was. At least for now that's what I think. Let's take our coffee to the living room."

JILL UNPLUGGED the chrome coffee pot and lifted it from the counter. She warmed up both their cups—hand-made of dark clay, textured umber brown with a cream-colored glaze defining the rims, of slightly different shapes, from a farmer's market. She guided Kristi to Tom's chair.

"Then this happened," Jill continued, "and I've never been more alone. He used to be my only brother, my lover. I couldn't stand it, what he was doing. Our secrets made it possible for us to be fully alive to each other when we were so young. The kitchen drawer had been yanked out and spilled all over the floor. Pick up the knives and forks. That's all. Where do they go, now?"

Kristi said, "Andrea says she sees Tom less and less, as if it were about over."

"I don't know what that means, 'over.' It happened. He still sees her, and I know that he does. To me he will always see her, and she will be a part of him. Because he knows he can see her, and I can't stop him. If I could, he'd still have his memories of her, excluding me. And I also won't ever say anything. Memories grow brighter when they are escapes and promises. What if Burgess had done that to you? Could you divorce him?"

"I don't know what I could do, or would do. I don't even know what he would have done to me, even if he'd done that. Everyone's different, then different again. Continuous possibilities, and even the impossible. Sometimes that most of all. I'm not really trying to avoid telling you. Perhaps I should ask myself why I don't know, but I couldn't come up with an answer. I don't think I could."

KRISTI STOOD up from Tom's old brown chair and walked to the window opening on the back grass, where she had had her first long talk with Jill, Angie exploring outside, finding firebugs.

"It honestly doesn't matter so much, now," Jill said to her. "Maybe I'm getting used to the situation. I know less about Tom's needs than I once did. He outgrew them, I guess. Or wore them down, then out. I used to think I was everything to him because that's what he said I was. Before that, it was as if I'd never thought before—about anything. So now what? He commanded my love, and I'm now giving in. All I know how to do. She's exotic, like a goddess, like no one I've ever seen. I empathized with him when I wasn't being jealous and could find some distance from the situation. I became him and wanted her, too. My confession."

"Really?"

"The Tom part of me wanted her, you know?"

"I'm trying to understand."

"I wanted to see what they looked like together, even in bed. Maybe especially there. I wanted to experience her the way he did, as if I were he, like in the moments I had wanted to be him—him touching me. I wanted to touch her. When he came back to me, I wasn't ashamed. Except sometimes in the moments when we finally looked at each other again as one, and only in a slow moment that faded into something else. I was just so glad to have him back in my presence and happy, despite a knife in my heart that really wasn't there, was it?

"I had put it there, made of ice, clear, to see through. Until he'd go back to his place to be alone, I had imagined. Twisted, I'm thinking while I tell you this. Maybe he was with her then and we both were deceiving me because that's what I wanted. Maybe he'll come back here soon for good. I'm afraid to suggest it, even to myself."

"Jill, is he going to move back in with you?"

"You know, he does stay over with me sometimes now. Can't stay away from family, I say, not really believing that's all of it. Not completely, or even half way. He keeps clothes here. He went out the door with two suitcases, then came back in, set one down, and left, knowing I would put his things back in place for him, saying without words this was still his place, if I still wanted him, and he knew I did."

"So you think he will move back."

"When just Angie and I are here together, just the physical presence of his clothes seems to comfort me some, though there the suitcase is, tattered and waiting. Just like me. Am I wrong in saying any of this? Is that how I am and we are? Excuse me. I've really needed someone to know this and talk to me—someone like you. I hope you are as I imagine you."

BACK TO the room, Kristi returned to Tom's chair, sat in it with one leg under her.

"Sorry," she said. "I'm gifted for saying the wrong thing. I'm not a very good friend for judging such matters, I fear. So I'll keep my mouth shut and wish what I can for you. But I can listen, if you need that. If that's what you want, I mean. From me.

I shouldn't feel so stupid-awkward, and I'm better at friendship than judging others."

"You probably think I'm being a fool. Maybe Tom's using us both, Andrea and me. We are the only personal world outside himself he had. He's so driven, and there's nothing else here but work and books. There are times when either you stand by him, or he changes and becomes somebody else. I never know who. Sometimes someone I don't like very well, who sees me as being a parasite. Jill's a tapeworm. A succubus. He'd be thinking, 'Jill, you kept me from having a normal relationship.' It wasn't like that at all, of course. So then, the true Tom would return."

JILL'S HANDS surrounded the coffee mug, into which she stared, as if at empty palms in prayer. Kristi looked back at her, wondering what to say, her coffee untouched. *Palms are the open book.* She drank.

"What *was* it like?" Kristi said.

"It's all there was," Jill replied. "He found someone else to tempt, to bring into the mystery of his darkness. Just as I'm here in the shadows like a nocturnal creature waiting until it is darker and safe to move about. Here I am in this place, a bushbaby with a bushbaby, lost forever, with nowhere else for a world. He is my family. What I have, he gave me. There's nothing more to do or be."

"Why are you punishing yourself this way? There's always something more you can do. What do you really want to do that doesn't involve Tom?"

"Nothing."

"Jill, a woman needs herself first of all. You've given up on yourself because you feel guilty or something more I can't articulate for losing Tom, when it seems you really haven't lost him after all. Anyway, he's the one who did whatever he did, not you.

He's the one responsible. Haven't you ever thought maybe you should kick his ass on out the door?"

"There he is at the plant with his computers, night after night, watching his nuclear waste bubble, so he says, but I knew what was up when he smelled of someone else in bed rather than himself, and then somehow he didn't want to make love when I touched him, because he just had, I thought, and so couldn't. 'Tell me all your secrets.' Not hard to guess that one."

"You can tell me whatever you want to, but please remember my response problem. If I do say the wrong thing, I still want to be here for you. You know that's what I want."

"Oh."

"We all sing off key at times. That's me. I'm really good at it."

"He did it to prove I couldn't stop him, and that he could go on however he wished, that nothing had changed that way as far as he was concerned. He's free. He can't be a boss at work yet, so he had to show me who's boss, maybe. I no longer satisfy him as a human being who interacts with him, though I keep trying. How did I change?"

"He changed, then? Work sometimes takes men over."

"Isn't love supposed to be stronger, Kristi? Most men have jobs."

"That and other wishes. He's still a man. The world presses on them in different ways, and it's not your fault. It makes them something other than what you want them to be."

"What does it matter what caused it? Other families stay together here, despite work. In fact, they need the work to continue as a family."

"If you know the cause, maybe you can know what to do about it."

"It's me, that's what. We were like two plants growing together, one of which should have been thinned. He felt crowded with me around, especially when there was someone else he wanted to love."

"Do you feel crowded?"

"No, he does. But now he misses us, he says."

"So then he comes back."

"Yes. I try not to repel him, honest. Perhaps I do, anyway, even in the trying. He still goes away quietly. Nothing is said. He just stands up and walks out the front door, gets in his funny old car from someone else's dreams, and drives off. As if he said anything, he might stay. As if I said anything, he might not come back. And the fugue of his emotions goes out the door with him. Some lingers like smoke. As if it could leave me."

"You sound as if he never really left you. Not all of him, I mean. That's part of what you've been saying."

JILL DRANK from her cup, the rim imprinted with pale lipstick, matching the prints to her lips. "Did he? He could be a thousand miles away and never leave."

"That's not really completely true, though, is it?"

"Of course not. And when he comes back, he hasn't, really."

"You mean, until he actually moves back?"

"Not even then."

"Something changed?"

"Who knows? I don't seem any different, at least to me, except for the perpetual cold anxiety nested in my stomach like a half-forgotten secret. I can't say that there's anything different about him, except that he has had experiences with Andrea certainly at sometime more to his liking than doing things with me, but he won't tell me what it is, how I can be like her, what he felt and she felt. I only asked. Maybe I can't and that's the point. Or he doesn't want me to even try. I would, if I knew how to be like that. Wouldn't you? It seems like a perfect vacuum tube for the old dead radio I have for a soul."

"Whatever 'that' is, I'm the wrong one to ask such things. I'm always the wrong one. I'd rather be just like me instead. You start faking yourself out otherwise. Existential, and all that, in a sidelong way."

"If you wanted Tom, would you take him?"

"No. I have Burge. One's quite enough for me."

"But Andrea took Tom, just like that. Except I think he wanted her first. Wanted someone new. I wasn't enough for him with the temptation hanging there. He wanted a different person in his life's core. She's very bright. I didn't try to keep my education going once Angie filled all my time. It seemed that a mother was all it was possible for me to be, with meeting Tom's needs as well. I am a thinking person, but he was the one who usually taught me, you see, him being older and world wise. Even if I was a fast learner, it was still my fault."

"You shouldn't blame yourself. It never changes the past or much else the way you want it to. Usually the opposite."

"The present changes everything."

"Except when it hasn't changed anything. You went through a lot with this. I'm glad I've never had it to go through. How would I survive, now? I just have my old problem of being strange sexually sometimes, which now really concerns me. I keep discovering I don't know myself very well. Maybe that goes on until there's no longer much self to be concerned about and you totter off three-legged to the graveyard."

"I was never like that to myself. Maybe I was too eager to have all I could with Tom. Once I knew what was up with nature."

"Shouldn't you just stay yourself a little?"

"That's not enough, Kristi. I have the evidence. I don't know what that means, anyway. Jill is sometimes what Tom made her, after all. She was so young and he was this presence in her life, wherever she turned, big, bright, up there and not to be missed. Maybe Tom wanted to try having an 'up there' person, too. Do you think so? As much as a man could have one, who was also a woman? Because I think now he rarely looked up to anyone except to get something he wanted for himself. Sort of like the little crab who disguises himself and goes around in bits of camouflage found on the sea floor, always trying for a better fit."

"I WONDER if anyone is more than the things people think about them, or if that's exactly what they are not. Everything at once, including pretenses? I certainly don't know Tom at all as well as I thought I did, and less so the more you talk about him. Are you just being resentful? Not that you don't have the right to be that, so long as you're being honest with yourself. Are you?"

"Are you implying that I am not?"

"Of course not, Jill."

"You're such a funny person, sometimes. Perhaps you just don't like having your ideas about people upset. I'll be quiet, then."

"In fact you've made me intensely curious—more than I have a right to be."

"Excuse me, Kristi. I've got a load of clothes to move from the washer to the dryer. Follow me, and we can keep talking."

They walked together to the utility room—small, humid, a pale blue and bluer in fluorescent lights. Jill opened the washer top, lifted out a twisted mass of clothes in many colors, and tossed them, not gently, in the dryer to her right, against the wall.

"So you've come over here to see what you could find out?"

she continued. "Not much happening here, boss. The clothes still get wet when washed."

They returned to the living room and their old chairs, Jill in the lead.

"Yes, some of those clothes were his," she said, "as you probably noticed. I can't escape that, either."

"I came over to see if I could help somehow. I owe you that as a friend. Friends strive for honesty—ideally, they do. I really don't mean to be prying."

"'...mean to be prying, but,' is how the phrase usually goes."

"No buts, Jill. Can't I help you somehow? If I can, I want to."

"How did you think you could help me?"

"I had to do something. Were I in the same situation, I'd want a friend. You're here all alone, and I might have done something that rightfully I shouldn't have done."

"I'm alone, mostly. Tom comes back with his dork in hand. Maybe I'm more interesting now he has two of us to mess around with. Why don't we try for three? That might be really interesting."

"What?"

"Just kidding. Bad joke."

"Shall I go, Jill? I think I caught you at a bad time."

"What's a good time? When your expectations get shaken, sometimes you wonder what could possibly happen next, and you start to prepare yourself for it mentally. For anything."

"Anything?"

"I didn't mean to say that, really, you know. I know what happened to you."

"I'm getting desensitized to it after so many years. I was a boob. Once, it was such a secret, and that's how I wanted it."

"It was insensitive of me."

"If Andrea found out she were in a foursome, though, that might cure her. Was that your idea?"

"No. It was only a weak defense. Honest."

"Sorry if I made you feel threatened."

"Just being alive makes me feel threatened. My life does. Doesn't yours, Kristi?"

"What do you mean?"

"You tell me. You grew up here, Kristi."

"YOU MEAN, like, here we are, in a place to make the world end? People are just like everywhere else, except here each has a piece of the secret and a furtive individual calling for the sake of security. As if they each had a mission in a sacred society—Tom, Andrea, Eileen, and thousands of people I don't know, even Burge. It's as if I feel their aura sometimes. Really, except I know that's not something to believe in."

"For me, it's try to be like everyone else, or else not like them. Try to change, I tell myself. I knew Tom would be back. Because this is part of the world he must hold on to right now, even if he doesn't want to think about what you can't really think about anyway. Nobody does, or they couldn't go on. As I see it.

"But it's there, like a pointless thrill, like love, like death. It's who we are because we have been chosen. By something, if even just by happenstance. Maybe you and Burge have escaped. But even living in the mountains, have you?"

"It's supposed to make us feel safer," Kristi said. "Mountains for ramparts. I thought that's a small part of why we did this,

Jill, moving to the mountains. America's therapy at Hanford we mostly don't remember having. Like, the more bombs we have, the safer we feel? Everyday life makes us feel not much of anything. Tired, maybe. It's been this way for so long maybe people in the real world have all but forgotten how many there must be by now, or never knew, and so bombs keep on being made, with a smile. Don't think about it. Let Washington. We've got enough to worry about with the family and all. Still, the tallest mountain knows fallout."

"I wanted Tom to leave this place, to find something somewhere else, anything, Kristi, and maybe be like everyone else. But I offended him by saying so, and then he found someone else outside our little realm. That's what I was thinking. Except maybe now that I've said it, I might have been mistaken. He sought someone who is new and unafraid. He left me awhile. I had thought about the wrong thing. I hadn't reached the synthesis."

"I CAN'T STOP thinking it, even when he is sleeping by my side. I imagine him, his skin red and black and blistered and gone. Only his blackened bones. He had taught me something again. I learned to be quiet."

"You've never talked that way before, Jill. I guess I haven't either, or even had much thought of doing so. It's not a way to become popular."

"Do you think the way I do? Even a little? All this just slipped out. I thought I was the only one."

"It's not an easy place to reconcile, especially when it's home."

"It's my home. Look what I've done."

"And Burge and I are no longer here, and are missing you."

"We miss you."

"Then you aren't still angry with me?"

339

"I was angry with myself. For everything. Now we have secrets, too, you and I."

"Do you feel comforted by that?"

"Why? I don't think it's important to feel comforted. I prefer the nag of doubt to that kind of sleep. Nothing's really worked when I've tried doing things to feel comforted. I'd rather just keep out of people's way."

"Living in the secret," Kristi whispered.

"The safest way to be."

"The way I found you."

"Except everyone's always looking at you. Even in the midst of so much secrecy, there isn't any for anything that matters beyond defense. Sometimes it's as if people were in my mind, as if they could listen to my thoughts. I want to keep my own secrets, but it's as if people already know things about me, those very secrets, sometimes even before I think them. I felt this even when we were here in town all alone.

"It surprises me to have a friend like you who doesn't sometimes know everything and to whom it doesn't matter that I don't either. I know it isn't logical. It's just a matter of feeling, to be this way. But then, sometimes feelings are everything there is for a person.

"Silence is the secret armor beneath my clothes. It's my comfort and defense. When Tom is not here, in the absent moments. I don't look for what I already have. As if it were a kind of oblivion—a kind of lotus."

Chapter 28

THE FEATURES of the man looked familiar to Kristi: his hair ash-blond and face tan, in a light Hawaiian shirt printed with patterns of black bamboo, worn outside his khaki shorts. She couldn't place him as he walked up the stairs, into the entryway of the Sawtooth Lodge, and up to the registry desk. She was sitting there absent mindedly, looking for the fifth time over the weekly calendar with pencilled-in names of upcoming guests, wishing for more of them, wondering who they were.

He wasn't among the four with reservations, those who had already checked in and were out for the afternoon sun, not yet hot enough on this mid-May day in 1982 to be thought hot, with snow still on the peaks and in the shadows of the mountains. The face she remembered was younger, from the '60s.

"Do you have a room available for a married couple and two blooming orcs?"

"Orcs? You probably mean teenagers."

"Yes. They are that, too."

"We've got one room with a queen bed and can furnish roll-aways. It's a big room. Are they teenagers?"

"They didn't start out that way. How much will I owe you?"

"$54 plus $4 for the additional beds, linen included. Per night."

"Should I sign something?"

"You look like someone I've met before. I'm usually good remembering faces. Have you been a guest, or did I see you in a movie?"

The man wrote 'Del & Ellen Carpenter' on the registration

card with an ancient tortoiseshell Pelikan fountain pen from his stretched pocket, then turned the card around and handed it to Kristi with both hands and a bow, Asian style.

"I don't think so," he said. "We're from the California coast. Carmel. Paradise, if you can take the tourists. This is my first time in this part of the country. Everything's booked in Sun Valley and our reservation got lost, so someone suggested coming here if we were brave enough to drive up the mountain. It wasn't that hard. We're lucky to have found this place."

"Oh, we've been in California down that way. On our honeymoon. Did you ever do any hitchhiking there?"

"Hitchhiking? Did long trips a few times. To Cal and back."

"Do you remember a young couple who might have picked you up outside Carmel once a long time ago?"

DEL THOUGHT. He looked at the floor, then at the front desk. He scratched the back of his head with both hands and looked long at Kristi. He put his hands in his pockets.

"No. Blue Mustang, maybe? Midnight blue, metallic. I remember a ride with somebody once when I was stranded. It was a couple of newlyweds."

"In a Mustang, I'm sure. Thought it might be you, but you never know. It was our honeymoon, Burge's and mine. You retain such impressions."

"You took me all the way into Berkeley. Sorry I didn't recognize you. It's been a long time, different place. What are you doing here? I thought your husband made A-bomb stuff."

"He did. Now he doesn't. We left Richland years ago. My mother still lives there, so we go back. Have you ever seen it?"

"No. I think I'll wait awhile. Just a second. I left my wife and daughters in a hot car. They don't like each other."

"Here's your key. I'll have Burge roll in your extra beds when he gets back from the gas station. Burge is still my husband. You possibly met him when he was called 'Burgess' or 'Jim.' We had a flat tire he's getting fixed, like somebody shot a hole in it. Probably just a nail. Who knows? Burge will tell me. My name's Kristi. There's no reason for you to remember it after such a long time. I wouldn't."

"It was something like that, I remember. You were on your "just married" thing, right?"

Before Del could stop talking, three women were up the steps and starting through the doorway to the inn. They were obviously travel-stiff, hot, sweating in wilted summer attire, and out of patience.

"You were just going to run in to see if there was a vacancy, Bonzo, remember?" asked the dark-haired woman, large-headed, her hair in a page-boy, in front of what obviously was a pair of daughters in their teens. They were taller than her five-five height by inches.

"Yeah, Bonzo," said one.

"Yeah, Bonzo," said the taller.

"Here's where we are staying tonight. Ellen, that's Kristi, and her husband's name is Burge. Right? I met them a long time ago. Carmel guests."

"Teaching her golf." Ellen said. "He's good at something, anyway."

"My older daughter is Upanishad," said Del. "Uppy for short. She's the taller one — and her sister is Celeste. Say hello, ladies."

"This place is really old," said the taller sister. "If you weren't such hippies, I wouldn't have that name."

"And I'm like a tinkley music box," sighed the other.

"You're a true Bonzo, though," Uppy said to her father.

"The name's Del," he retorted. "Father, to you. You can manage 'Del.' One syllable. And we're not hippies."

"But you were. You went to Cal."

"Where you'll go, if you think you're smart enough to get in."

"We're not going to college," said Celeste, glaring at Kristi, then at her sister.

"Speak for yourself, Fido," said Uppy. "Wherever you're going, I'm going somewhere else."

"Upanishad is such a beautiful name," Kristi said, nervous from the fighting. "They're both beautiful names, Ellen."

"Well, mine's dirt plain," Ellen replied. "I was only doing them a favor."

"Everybody out to the car to pick up your own bag," Del said.

"Oh, Dad," Celeste said. "They're too heavy."

"I told you to pack light."

"We don't have anything to wear. Is there a laundromat around here?" said the elder sister. "I — Fido smells."

"You're too finicky," Del said. "We're on vacation."

"Oh no, Dad, she's right the first time," said the younger. "She smells."

"What is there to do around here after we're unpacked?" Ellen asked. "Keep 'em busy, they don't fight as much. Right? Do you have tennis courts?"

"No tennis," Kristi replied. "We do have nature, though, and lots of it. Many trails for walking, and we've got maps. Trees and streams. You can see where the River of No Return begins. That's

344

the Salmon. Lewis and Clark called it the 'River of No Return.' I like that better, don't you? It adds a little mystery. There are also more trails than are marked on the map. You can explore, but be careful of getting lost."

"Get lost, Celeste," her sister said.

"Small world," Del said. "Life turns things inside out, though you seem the same. I seem the same, don't I?"

"I feel as if I'd missed out on quite a whole lot, actually. There is something changeless about you. We can't get away much from this place. It has become so different from when we first discovered it and thought it was paradise. Sometimes it is, and that's the part we hope you will find. I'll get you the beds. Burge is being slow. We can make them up if you'd like, but later on while you're out. That will give you more room in the meantime. The laundromat's located east a block and down a block."

Ellen, leaning close for a sniff, said, "Upanishad, you do not smell. That's just your imagination again."

"I want to wash my hands and face."

"Let's get the stuff from the car first."

"I want to do it now, Mother."

"Fine, here are the keys. Your suitcase will be in the street waiting for you."

"Oh, never mind. I'll get it. We get shuffled along, just to satisfy you. We never get to do anything for us. All we are is what you want to do. That's where we came from."

"We're in these mountains for you," Ellen said, "so you could see them and remember them, so we could see them as a family. Memories, for when you are older. What do you want to do anyway, just watch television?"

"There's nothing to do."

345

"You mean there are no boys," said Celeste, turning to accuse Kristi. "Maybe we can find boys. Where are they?"

"I don't know that I've ever looked. Possibly there are some on the trails. There aren't any staying in the inn, that I know of, except possibly one, depending on how you are counting. Sometimes people camp, though, so you can't always tell. Young men in town, that is."

"She doesn't know," said Uppy. "We'll have to find them ourselves."

"You'll do nothing of the kind," said Del. "So long as your feet are under my table. Don't be so predatory."

"Where's the table that my feet are under?" said Uppy. "I like 'predatory.'"

"Race you up the stairs," said Celeste.

"You win."

THE POSSIBILITY of eventual diversion from ordinary existence moved the girls up the stairs to unpack and then to come back down, finding their way out the back door with Kristi's help, down the stairs and toward the trailhead behind the Sawtooth Inn, the nearest possible entry to the mystical forest in which boys would come to rescue them from certain boredom.

"So you think we'll find some boys up here, huh?" asked Uppy, shallow doubt in her voice.

"It has been known to happen," Kristi said. "You'll never know what you'll find. Aren't you going to wait for your parents?"

"They want to have a nap," said Celeste. "I hope."

"They'll catch up," said Uppy. "Dad got on the phone."

"Be extra careful, then. Mountains aren't safe if you break

346

the rules."

"Good," said Celeste. "'Safe' sucks."

"No, it doesn't," Kristi said. "It's a good thing."

Kristi turned from the girls, who were headed too fast up the trail to go very far. The long-corroded metal spring near the bottom of the screen door squawked as she went back inside. She let it bang shut behind her, and the sound reversed, until it stopped with wood slapping wood.

*W*HAT CURIOUS *creatures they are,* she thought. She tried to remember herself so young, what she'd do. She had been so kept from everything. She would never have been in the mountains alone, or even with someone she knew, except in the presence of adults.

She remembered wanting to stand next to a tall boy with perfectly combed black hair in the hallway at school, so that's what she had done, just to be close to him. She felt a rush of emotions, a start of love, until he took a step sideways, as if to get away from her, and her emotions in less than a moment became more complicated and inexplicable to her. They were still inexplicable. She didn't even want to know why she felt that way; she wanted him to step back where he was or go away.

He stepped back with a nervous chuckle, his face red, but was silent. She couldn't say anything, and he finally moved quickly down the pale green tile floor and hallway lined with lockers, then disappeared into the men's room. He avoided her eyes every time they passed in the hallway after that, his face reddening, until she didn't see him any more because his family moved away.

She thought about Burgess, their first difficulties, wanting him and not. She walked across the kitchen floor through their living quarters, past the staircase and into the front hallway. Del was still on the upstairs phone, a square button on the bottom of the front desk phone lit. The light went out, then lit up again.

347

Then it was out after a longer time, and Del and Ellen walked down the stairs looking refreshed. *Bonzo? And so she was . . . ?*

"It's so quiet around here," Del said. "Where are the girls?"

"They're on the trail that runs in back of the house. Come out the back door, and I'll show you where it goes."

"It's really pleasant to be without them for a minute," Del said, his head wobbling slightly. "You understand?"

"I don't know. We never had children."

"If you had, you'd know. But we're glad they're here. It's only *sometimes*," said Ellen. "One year we won't have them."

"Then they won't go away," said Del.

"You don't know that."

"I've heard tell."

Ellen WALKED across the floor and sat on the couch, which was frayed with the years, yet almost spotless. "What a thing to say. But sometimes I do look forward to having an empty nest. You must enjoy the freedom, Kristi."

"This place still keeps us tied down, even now with the help. We have trouble letting go."

"I wouldn't have any trouble at all," said Del. "I came from a tourist town."

"Stay off the phone then when you're on vacation," his wife said.

"Some chance, Ellen. We've got to eat. Maybe we should try to go find the girls. Do you want to go for a hike?"

"It's so beautiful and untouched here. Do you have bad winters?"

"So cold the truck won't start if we forget to plug it in at night, Ellen," said Kristi. "You wouldn't believe how high the snow can get, especially if the wind is blowing. The pass closes and we sometimes can't count much on customers, or even on getting in supplies if we did have customers. We have to stock up, like the squirrels. It seemed like such a good idea when we first came here. Then it took all our life savings and then some, so we were stuck, with nowhere else to go. We're good at taking care of stranded skiers and one-time woodsmen. But it's our home now, where we live, sort of beyond love and hate."

"Well, we love it, Kristi. Yes, Del, I'll go on a hike with you to find the girls."

"They took off pretty fast, but will slow down if they're not used to it. They could be over the top of the hill by now. The trail runs out of sight down the other side of the mountain and into a secluded valley, with stop-offs along the way. It's everybody's secret hideaway."

Ellen went first up the trail, following where it narrowed. The heat, loose dirt and dust had been scuffed off the top of the packed-down soil and piled into the grooves and runnels the rain and people's feet had made over the years from far back, for over a hundred years.

"I wonder what was here before anyone got here," she said. "Don't you wonder who else has hiked up here?"

"Just as long as the girls have."

"Where else could they have gone? They'll stick to the trails. I don't see many diversions."

"We probably should have gone back to Sun Valley or Ketchum, but I was tired of driving. A hike will do everybody good."

"They've never been easy to travel with."

Soon talk stopped as the mountain became steeper and breaths grew shorter from the altitude. The smell of sun on pine was there, thick for a breath or two then gone again, and there was no wind, only echoes from the valley below and their footsteps. And the echoes were displaced with the sound of jays as they rounded the hill heading south, then west again over the summit of the trail and down into the hidden valley.

THE TRAIL unfolded before them a small portion at a time, around rocks, embankments, and pines on the slope that ran mostly downward, but also upward in portions and along brief flat stretches, some in tall grass. They rounded a granite boulder, and there the girls were, many yards away but visible, kneeling on the ground. Celeste was facing them, kneeling and looking down intently at something. Uppy, also kneeling, had her back turned. Between them on his back and elbows was a nearly grown boy.

"It's Bonzo and Mom!" shouted Celeste, standing up quickly. "Hurry!"

The boy glanced toward the parents and jumped fast to his feet, yanking up his jeans and taking off down the trail, around an embankment and out of sight. Uppy leaned backward on her hand to see over her right shoulder, then awkwardly stood up. Del stepped quickly ahead of Ellen and ran to the girls.

"Are you two all right? What on earth was going on there?"

There was silence. Uppy looked at the ground.

"Well, what?"

"We met this boy," said Celeste, bubbling, "coming up the trail back there. He was really cute. Uppy said she saw him first. He was walking along, then he saw us and smiled at us. He scratched himself in the front of his jeans like a baseball player. Then he came next to us and stood. Upanishad asked what he had down there.

"He goes, 'Want me to show you?' So he did. She goes, 'C'n

I touch it?' So we did, and then he goes, 'Want me to show you something else?' So he showed us how to do something to it. Then he goes all, 'Come and sit on the grass.' He laid down leaning back on his elbows with his thing sticking up and . . . What's wrong? You have this awfullest look on your faces!"

"Don't you know that's wrong?" said Del. "You're not supposed to do that. Why did you?"

"Why are you always trying to make us feel so awful?" she said. "We were only having fun."

"Why did you leave us? Upanishad, say something, you're older. You both should know better."

The jays had disappeared and it was quiet except for heavy breathing around.

"It happened all of a sudden," Uppy said.

She paused, hearing the echo. She cleared her throat, then spoke.

"Sure can run fast, can't he?"

VI. SOMETHING SO NEW

Chapter 29

3 November 2004

Dear Andrea:

I badgered Kristi for your address, so blame me for this. I hoped the years might let me exist for you again somehow, so here I am, at least on paper. The promise of something new and good for me would be to communicate with you. I know little more of you than I did watching you before you vanished into the mountains. But there had been our galactic journey!

What I've been told is that you're still at Hanford and are needed to the point that you remained, even after the plant closed production. Jim Burgess says it still has thousands employed but a great many are new. I read in the newspaper that Washington passed an initiative and will accept no more out-of-state shipments of nuclear stuff until the Hanford waste is finally made safe for future generations, which may take several decades beyond never. But what's a state to do?

So you are busy, I'm sure. As for me, I'm retired from the university since July. I swore I would quit after each next student let me know about our mutual difficulties. (I came to think I would never be listened to, so what was I good for? Never would I let anyone know that, of course.)

Strangely enough, after the requisite years I realized a good retirement income—not as good as it might have been, but enough to create the inner freedom I didn't seem to have beforehand. Given that, my life has more loose ends than a broom. Since I've thought about you over the years and what you must be like now, I had to seek you out. Age leaves me with many fewer inhibitions than I once had, but also with a collection of new ones.

So here I am, single and solitary like you, my ex having thrown me out (I probably helped) a few calendars ago after our last child moved to Texas to get married and left my ex with nothing at home to love. Our firstborn has a partner of like gender, and was never to be seen. She was 'in your face' as a teenager. She left us, and in moments I felt the way I did when you left. Having friends stay overnight wasn't what we thought it was. The university makes us open-minded though does less sometimes for our hearts, where words stick. I'm not a failed father, I say now, but only one with prismatic emotions.

If I haven't switched you off completely again with all this, perhaps you'll write and tell me how life is with you, or even a moment of your life. Our meeting again is not obligatory, though I'd enjoy seeing you. I have been owing Kristi and Burge a visit, however, and can make a grand loop there on my travels if you're interested sometime. Or it can be in Sawtooth, which sometimes you must still call home. At any rate, please do write.

Sincerely,

Steven Bourne

*　　　*　　　*

November 9
Richland

Dear Steven:

What a surprise! I thought we'd forgotten each other, or at least you me. I confess I did run away from you back in your memory. The evidence is beyond doubt. I did it to regain my psychic balance, as I saw it then (or perhaps a bit later when I had to find some reason for an impulsive act).

From my perspective, things were not coming out right between us. I had thought they might, but a flash walking the trail told me they wouldn't, and that you'd ignore me, wounded again. So to my mind I cut things short before you could. The distance between us has been the only thing we shared, and the rest seemed illusions. I had wanted to be with you, but you ozoned me. I had just gotten used to the rarified air with nothing more, then you were there and I had to escape you.

In some lonely moments, I wondered what happened to you and wished I hadn't had the impulse to do what I did. I didn't think I might have hurt you, then I thought I must have, and I genuinely didn't know what to do about it. The rest is all inertia.

Kristi told me a few things about you, seemingly offhand. Just then I didn't want to know more. I hadn't wanted to upset you, but we were in different dimensions.

As of now, some of me is still where I was, trying to shape a career. It seems never to end. I did what amounts to a double doctorate in work to get myself in a position to stay here, a mere one of 700 Ph.D.s. I'm glad I'm not designing nuclear weapons, my other option. It would have been California or New Mexico for me. I also might be on the street now, without knowing what was coming next. (Who ever really does?) The political winds might also have made me the next hot commodity in bomb design, perhaps somewhere in Idaho.

As it is, I'm the most sophisticated of custodians, with my daily dalliance with the unknown, trying to keep a stretch of humanity safe from itself in the Post-Atomic Age. What I do is a secret, and I'm sure you'll understand that from what you know of Burgess' work. My own job seems to have possessed me, increasingly becoming my life and who I am, starting from a long time ago. A chunk of me will continue unknown to you, but at least you can know some of me before I disappear completely.

For over six decades, billions of dollars in equipment and chemicals have been buried here—used up, highly radioactive. Moreover, 177 huge underground tanks hold 56 million gallons of nuclear waste with millions in leaked chemicals. Yet more contaminated water down below reaches in a plume stretching toward the Columbia River. It's not there yet. Portland, Oregon, is at the river's mouth, the Pacific Ocean its destination. Portland knows about us.

You've been here and have seen the place from a distance. Well, at least you know where I am, then. The current 'big plan' is still to turn nuclear waste into vitrified logs if the politicos and beyond what we know about things will let us. Glass logs encased in stainless steel won't ever leak radioactive materials. That's the Big Idea—actually an old one as well.

Things are very complicated and difficult, not to mention expensive. A single storage tank can include the whole periodic table of chemicals and possibly some stuff we never new existed. You and I haven't been fated to be destroyed by the Bomb, at least not directly or yet, that we know of. So now we can think about terrorists. Half of me still imagines a bomb will be dropped or scattered around in some other form of terror, and that it's only a matter of time. Not now, though.

Most people don't think this way, do they? At least so far as I can tell, most are oblivious. Still, I do try to be more than my job. I've avoided turning into a man, for one thing. I mentor other women, though they're still scarce here, and they perhaps don't know I'm mentoring them. I maintain a house and pretend some nobility in that. I work up gourmet recipes for married friends in exchange for the occasional Sunday meal with a true family. You've met Jill and Tom Henderson, haven't you? They have grandkids and know my friends from back home. I read books, though am always too erratic to contribute much to a book club. I have ideas of my own most of the time and travel when I can. I run and only feel old when I don't or if I overdo it and have to hobble home to recover.

As I read this, almost all of me seems to have gotten lost in translation. That's what time can do, I guess.

So, hereby, we've started to write to one another. I also do e-mail, though it's not as private as the slower kind. I suspect the local kids of tapping in because that's what I might have done at their age, given the opportunity. You'll have my net address if you give me yours. When time's short, don't feel obliged to do a whole letter, and we can still communicate despite techy intrusions.

Let's just write for right now. And thanks. I needed your letter.

Do write to me.

Sincerely,
Andrea

*   *   *

November 16

Dear Andrea:

This time I'm writing upon receipt. My new e-mail address is *bournes@autonet.net.* I've been putting off getting it. I had my university address, but it no longer exists. If you try out my new one, I can be sure it works. I'll have your address as well that way.

I was glad to find out about your life, too. It's so different from mine, which was spent in a place supposedly antithetical to secrets.

It's not so, of course. There's always proprietary research. But try this: my colleagues and others knew about my impending divorce before I did. I was told about it quietly behind my back in a manner to which I couldn't respond. Then told again and again. That really happened, so sometimes secrets twist themselves up and flap about in higher education, too.

I can appreciate a little secrecy. What you have to deal with must make you feel very isolated at times, though. Retirement did that to me. At times it was as if some kind of neutron bomb had been dropped and everyone had disappeared. I felt relief when the mailman came, even with junk stuff.

I always wondered what would have happened if I'd been

359

more responsive to you back then. I was escaping everything by getting lost, in space or in work. You know the action—rolling up like an Asian scroll on one end of my life while rolling out the present on the other. Something disappears in the process.

You ran away from me in the woods. Disappeared. Nobody had ever dumped me before then. I'd never been in that spot in any kind of woods. There I was suddenly, quite alone and having to get back to somewhere, path to destination unclear. When I got back, I immediately blew town.

It must have done something to me. I've wondered about you at various times all these years, a ghost along the roadway in my dreams, too soon to vanish. Okay, it's a confession. In a flash you were someone I couldn't have, and I was astonished by the finality of it all. You became a hole in my life, an empty vision glimpsed on the edge of sleep while trying to escape other thoughts, or escape thinking altogether. That was me, and for a long time.

Saying this is risking making you retreat again, I know. I don't want that, but what's the point of not saying it, if it's true? There you have it, even though we don't know each other much yet. You have to do something to become more you, even when stepping outside of that would give you someone you'd really rather be.

So here I am, late and with regrets, but refusing to deny our brief, beautiful moment. In fact, I'm stuck on it. My great starscape is you, in my imagination, and so much to discover.

Please tell me more about you so I can be more responsive. I find my mind lingering over a dark night with more stars than I had ever seen, you filling my consciousness, before the light went out. The world had opened before us with so much left, like a hundred new discoveries existing as pure possibility—before me, at any rate.

It was too much beyond what I was then for me to see what I should have done for us. It was all impossible, wasn't it? Given where we were both pointed? Not that I was pointed anywhere in particular—just away from my own small past, which I couldn't keep to, anyway. You were going where women don't go, where I couldn't see, not by a small fraction. Still, I want to know what I can about you, all possible about you, and am looking forward to your next letter.

Yours,

Steve

*   *   *

Hi, Steve:

Thanks for giving me your e-mail address and wonderful message—wonderful also in the sense that it made me wonder so. I think that you were writing in maybe a personal singularity, and if you were to write it again, you might write something completely different, the wave of nostalgia having passed. I might not like it so well, even though it would be more what you are most of the time. At any rate, the time we did have was time I'm glad we had together. You really don't have to make 'back then' the thing that patterns your behavior now, though. You do make me curious to know what else you'll write.

As to my disappearance in the forest way back when, you should know that I tried to take you to a secret place I have, but on the way I realized you couldn't possibly experience it as I did. I imagined your response might spoil it for me forever, even though I wanted to be there with somebody at times who might be a lover.

I had thought it was you.

There was too much going on in my mind about everything back then. I didn't really know you, after all, and slowly I wanted to be somewhere else, where I didn't have to deal with the thought of rejection, having been taught a lesson. That is how I see it now.

361

I don't know how I saw it then or will tomorrow. I frankly had almost forgotten it—perhaps in the interest of my own defense. I'll excuse myself now for having left you there, now that you are reading this, and I hope you will forgive me, too.

It doesn't matter now, does it, having happened so long ago? The place is no secret any longer, with tourists crawling through it and so much time gone by. There's not much of life we can relive, is there?

I'm glad most of the time that I was able to break free from the stockade of societal womanhood to be able to do what I'm doing. The idea of even the male nuclear physicist keeps changing for me, though, the more physicists I meet. I can't quite fit that form and don't want to anyway, as I said. Some of them can be such bastards about females at times, as if they got together to dream up a script from boyhood, then they say, 'just kidding,' and you don't know whether they are or not. Beyond physics, they might not be capable of saying anything else to a woman, or at least to me.

You have to fight for resources to do our work, or you get left out. Everyone has to fight. What's important to me is that they accept my work, hands off, which I think most of them do—those who have a notion of what I do, at any rate.

Actually, I don't have a clue about what any of them thinks. The secret lives we keep simply make it not matter somehow, but make us co-conspirators anyway. At least, I've survived that darkness. If I had been able to get a job in a research university, I might be known for something right now.

E-mails are supposed to be short, right? So I'll avoid the chat-room abbreviations and bid you adieu until next time. Let me know a little more about you.

$$* \qquad * \qquad *$$

Hi, Andrea:

The e-mail works fine, so now I have your address. I really meant what I said, and will tomorrow, too. And of course I forgive you. That's all I can think of to say, now that you're curious.

Later. Wishing you bright lights and kindness.

*　　*　　*

Dear Andrea:

Whatever I wrote, I didn't mean it that way, if that's why you haven't written back. You are a busy person and I shouldn't have expected an immediate reply, but I did. Are we at an age when small annoyances make a difference, or when they don't?

*　　*　　*

Hi, Steve:

It depends on the source of the annoyance, I think, but mostly on what happens to be happening to you at the particular time the annoyance occurs. That can be a big, complicated field of experience or a small, simple one. What was happening with you? Do you remember that?

*　　*　　*

Hi, Andrea:

Light bulb, diode or laser answer? Diode. Steve Bourne retires early and finds himself beset with an obsession about someone he has met years before but lost. Amplify that with loneliness, matched with a momentary connection with her that fails to be a real connection—how could it be, given the distance between them—a situation that makes him slightly annoyed but willing to play it to its end, having at least made some connection and hoping the end is a real meeting between the two, after which distances don't matter.

*　　*　　*

Hi, Steve:

Not yet for a meeting. I have a project going and can't get away. Besides, I'm not feeling ready just yet. I'm a different person than the one who three times walked with you. Years different. It couldn't be otherwise. Remember what happened?

*   *   *

Dear Andrea:

Don't give up on me just yet. I promise not to be annoyed, so don't you be. We still have much to exchange that can be done from a distance. I remember. Sorry to have been so impatient.

*   *   *

Dear Steve:

You don't have to reshape your emotions to fit mine, particularly when yours are directed toward simple friendship. We all could use a little more of that, right? I do become too lost in work sometimes. It is very demanding, and it does shape who you are as you solve all the problems that need to be solved throughout the day, day by day. That is what commands your attention much more than anything else. I think I'd like to retire sometime, too. What do I do after that?

Grandchildren would be a good thing, but it is too late for me. So friendships are valuable, yes? Unless you are a teenager, they're the next best thing to family. I hope you don't have too many aches and complaints.

*   *   *

Dear Andrea:

Just call me painless Bourne, harbinger of your bright new day. Friendship it is, so long as it doesn't keep us apart. Ha ha. Do you have aches and pains? You seemed in much better shape than I was in the last time we were together.

SOMETHING SO NEW

Dear Steve:

Most of us here are in fine shape. This isn't Prypyat just yet, and I haven't developed a third eye, though there are times when one would come in handy. When was the last time you saw Kristi and Burge? I try to see them when I am home in Sawtooth but missed them last time. I first became interested in this place because I knew they came from here and Kristi was raised here. Other than that, I knew very little about it beyond legend until I had moved here myself and had a chance to tell them I had.

They tried to make me happy about my decision to work here, though I knew that they had misgivings as well. What place is perfect? It seemed as though we had swapped destinies, though of course it could never work out that way. We did share acquaintances, mostly to the better, and it was good at least to have a start at getting to know someone. I remember that you knew Burgess from college. That's a long time for a friendship. It seems that, without marital attachment or something like it, people drift apart for various reasons, or for no reason at all. Do you agree?

*   *   *

Andrea—

I still see Burge and Kristi every once a year, so I guess we're still friends. A long time ago I had the idea to go into business with them, but the tourist trade wouldn't have supported it then. Good years follow lean, sometimes. Now I'd only be an intrusion, though I do like to visit. The old pathways still have new vistas, don't they? Or do you prefer finding new ways?

Dear Steve:

New ways, mostly. Discovery does it almost every time for me. The rest wrinkles up and blows away. That's why I like research so much, even beyond any practical application of what's discovered. It's just that finding the new and true is difficult in human discourse, and discovery there never works out beyond a certain point.

At least it hasn't for me. Too many variables. But I'm just a miner's kid, and a physicist to boot. So I'll take the physical world for discovery and leave people to you, who have had to deal with them so intensely at their charging points for so long. Though maybe I'm looking to discover in people more than is really there. Am I?

I could say, 'I never cease to be amazed,' but sometimes I do cease to be amazed, when things get as old as your having to kick one more person out of school or someone telling me I must be getting special treatment because I am a woman. Maybe we can say a certain percentage will say such and such and try to avoid that group, but you can never be sure who's in it or out until you've gotten zapped.

I like research, other people's almost as much as mine when it's on something I think I really should know about. Maybe I'm just suffering from a dearth of oxytocin. But I really do like and trust most people, you see, so long as I understand them or so far as I can.

Unlike you, for instance, who saw through my behavior and wrote after all these years, knowing you might get hurt or just ignored again. How did you do it? I couldn't have done that.

So far I'm happy you did. What do you think about that?

*　　　*　　　*

Dear Andrea:

I never knew how fast to go in a relationship. Not that I've had that many. My ex said I was too fast, but she always seemed to be hurrying me along.

I remember thinking in high school when I was taking science and math, like everyone else, that I really wanted to go into something having to do with people. There was student government, which was great for the vertically inclined ego, so I followed the opportunity into what I did with my life for a few decades.

It's not that I knew anything more than anyone else about people. It was great confusion and curiosity about them that pulled me along, until I knew a little more from college and thought I might make a living if I went into student affairs. I did help some students, or rather I saw them come to help themselves. So the story for myself goes.

Then there's Justine, a student whose parents did meth until their brains started to disintegrate with their teeth, and she was there with them when the police raided their house and took them away at 4 a.m. when they were crazy awake, and Justine awakened to the door banging open and the shouts, huddled to be invisible, then when alone tried to get herself together to come to a class, where they were reading Conroy's *Stop-Time* and it was reading her, she said, until it ended. She got an emergency loan, then a regular one, and decided she would teach school, even though she would live in poverty with the loans to repay. She would help people. And she would have, by learning how to teach in the midst of losing her parents to jail. They just needed a little relief from their lives, and they are now paying for having gotten it for a few bucks, and then a little more.

I had trouble when she disappeared. You know? It got worse for me every time something like that would happen. Was I doing something wrong when I was supposed to be helping, something a younger person would perhaps get right? So then, with freedom through retirement as an option, I couldn't do my work any more. Gone in an instant.

It used to not matter so much. I'm sorry if that's too much of me all at once, but now I'm in a void were it not for a few e-mails shared with you, someone I met a long time ago when things were new, and you're my one point of contact with promise. So there it is, and maybe we should be writing about something else. There's a lot more to be said about everything.

I wish I knew more about physics. I don't know what there is to discover in people right now beyond saying, 'More than I'll ever know.' And what's the point of saying that? What would you like to discover in people? I studied and studied, and got some guidelines and a box full of matches for guideline burning.

The decision to make contact with you again was easy because of what we shared back when, before the flashlight went out. I thought it was wondrous but over too soon, and promised so much more. It did in my imagination.

I wanted something more than "I loved it, but that's enough." I thought at least we might become friends or just write because of moments we shared, or even perhaps in spite of them. It was difficult for me because I don't like rejection either, and that possibility and too much distance were all there was back then. But for us now it's very much worth the risk. Please say you agree with this much. Cheers!

*   *   *

Dear Steve:

Perhaps we could meet if you still want to. I hope you don't expect so much that I am a disappointment to you. I'll say that the world has made my face a bit craggier, but I hope not my disposition. You seem to be okay with what there is to find thus far, given the years, miles, and means of communication.

Let's have dinner together in Boise? I can arrange to get away.

Andrea

Chapter 30

ANDREA CAME first to Sawtooth Lodge to see the "Remodeled Again, 2007" preview opening, a strictly private gathering of six friends. She walked toward the new entry with Steve behind her, the fall mountain sun on her face masking an intensely thought-out silence to be broken. She darkened into angles of shadow as she stepped between the big log columns of the portico, her marathoner's body in washed indigo jeans and cardinal cable-knit cotton sweater over a tattersall shirt. She walked through newly varnished double doors carved to image the surrounding mountain forest.

That moment freshened memories of growing up here, of the aged spinster resident of the first inn, of their epistolary meeting in the basement with an angel doll, and the subsequent brief relationship with Tom, who she would see again, today.

She came with Steve, from Washington. Could she remember all the pathways, the trees now grown taller? Some trees would be gone. It seemed as if her experience might have gotten something of the place wrong, or her past perceptions of it wrong, but she was unable to stop the minutes to figure out why, or what it was. This was a time for her to celebrate with old friends, in a world apart from her times-gone-by life of seldom-violated solitude. The friends all mattered to her now—their presence here—for what they had changed in her sense of being, for accepting her, and for being so profoundly other than herself.

STEVE PULLED the suitcases along, one case stacked on top of the other, though both had wheels, and entered as Andrea held open a door. Burge greeted them, coming from behind a check-in counter, also carved, a match for the front doors. Opposite was the lodge hearth, stacked glacial boulders reaching three stories through a vaulted pine log ceiling from a flagstone floor, and surrounded with new plover-colored leather couches and easy chairs, with pillows woven in Navajo rug patterns of red, black, and cream. The outside chill intensified the lobby's warmth and stirred the scent of both newly stacked and freshly burning pine.

"Thanks for coming to help us open this place again," Burgess said, his hand out for a shake. "Let me get someone to help you with your bags. We've got you down as test pilots for the bridal suite, and you have to tell us how we can make it better. No instructions necessary. How was your drive from Richland?"

"Fast. We brought Andrea's hybrid."

"You drove, that's why it was fast," said Andrea. "Where's Kristi?"

"Looking after the lodge gods. Anything here that looks like paradise took more work than you can imagine. There are so many details. She insists on doing for herself, bless her soul, and I can't break her of the habit when I'm afflicted, too. I'll call her on her cell. I don't expect she'll emerge any time soon otherwise unless she needs something."

"She's probably really busy, then. We can see her after we get checked in."

"Our bellboys have disappeared with the season. Can you wait a minute? We're understaffed with the start-up of the universities. The student staff just one day disappears.

"Our suitcases have wheels," Steve said. "Point us in the right direction and we'll find our way. This lodge is some task to take on, so near to retirement."

"What's retirement? This is our home, what we do. It's our chance to begin again. It's the place we wish we had when we were just getting started. We designed it ourselves, and we're really glad you could come to help us celebrate again after so many years. We won't make you work this time."

IN THE HALLWAY near the second-floor elevator, Jill and Tom emerged abruptly in front of Andrea and Steve. Jill stared, caught up in thought. They rarely saw each other any more, except in passing, and then with too much to say to say anything at all. There was Steve, changer of everything, and unaware of it. She was suddenly sure that his existence had ended her husband's long-waning relationship with Andrea, returning Tom to her. Smoke from a snuffed candle. Doused wick on a firecracker. Jill turned away, eyes closed, incredulous.

"Jill and Tom, this is Steve," Andrea said. "Do you know each other?"

"No secrets in the land of secrets," Tom replied.

"We met Steve when Kristi and Burge moved here from Richland." Jill said. "We've seen you around town together. Always you seemed too busy for us to interrupt you. We used to see you more often, Andrea."

"You should have yelled at us," Andrea said. "There's always time for friends, yes? We couldn't have been so busy as not to say hello."

"I doubt you would have recognized me," said Steve. "I've grown some since the old days when I ran up the hill behind the inn. I guess it's now a lodge."

"When did you ever run up the hill?" Andrea replied. "I carried you."

"Hey. I was in good shape then."

"Actually, he's been running with me some," Andrea said. "Showing steady improvement. Gets around pretty well for a big man."

"I had to work up to it. She can still outdistance me. Faster, too, save for grace and mercy."

"Who are they? I've been at it a long time. You do have to

work up to it."

"Okay, I can make it up the hill," Steve said. "Now you can show me all your secret childhood haunts, though we probably won't do what we did back when."

"I'm curious to know what's happened to them myself, if you're up to it. Some, anyway. Regarding the other thing, try me."

"If I can trust you not to run away?"

"Oh, she'll run away," said Tom.

"No, she won't," Jill replied. "What a thing to say."

"Steve knows what happened between us, Jill," Andrea said. "I had to tell him what he should know before we came. Otherwise, he'd still be clueless, with his tongue set on untoward courses. I won't run away from him this time, but I didn't want to feel the urge to do just that."

"I didn't know you ran away in the first place," Jill said. "Did she, Tom?"

"That's something between them. I don't know."

"I disappeared from Steve's presence a long time ago so that we could live our lives the way we did live them. So here we are, both someone else and both who we are. Who we were no longer matters. A good place to be. I hope you feel the same way."

"Yes, I think so," Jill replied. "We do wish you had grandchildren like ours. We'll get settled, then see you downstairs. I love you, Steve."

Jill couldn't read Andrea's face, but was glad for her on-the-spot confession of an on-the-spot emotion. Steve seemed unperturbed, though his feet stuck to the floor. Dust roamed through shafts of window light.

"Just realized I shouldn't have said that about grandchildren. I was just trying to say we like ours, 'kay? We've always wished the best for you and are so glad that Steve found Andrea again, though it's old news that he did, I suppose. That they found each other again."

"We'll get settled," Andrea said, "then see you downstairs."

ON THE OLD trail next morning, Andrea, Burge and Steve disappeared up the mountainside with learned feet. Tom left himself behind, still dressed for the hike but having developed a cramp-like unremitting pain in his left leg. Kristi and Jill remained with him as company around the hearth of the new lodge in the quiet season.

"The pain'll go away," Tom said. "Let me give you all some oft-spoken advice. Don't get old."

"Don't you, yourself," Jill said. "Are you going to be okay?"

"I'll just will this thing not to be there. That would have been easy once upon a time. Only there's no way I'm going to make it up that mountain now, and would only hold everybody back."

"You're doing the right thing," Kristi told him. "Just sit here with your leg up in front of the fire and be with us. Or I'll get you to a doctor, if you'll let me. Burge and Steve will be competitive up the mountain until Andrea smokes them. Some people think the trails are our prime attraction. I like the hearth, myself. Lots of people have them but not like ours—big enough for a crowd."

"I'm glad we're here," said Jill. "All of us."

"I wanted to see where Andrea used to hang out," Tom replied, twisting his leg on the ottoman and wincing. "No doctor. Just an old boy's cramp."

THE BARK on the big logs cracked in the flames, which whipped in the air, quick, lifting dust motes and ash in swirls, waking the moment's calm.

"I'm glad we're here, all of us, too," Kristi said. "And you two together again. I mean, not to judge anything."

"Andrea and I, actually all of us, I hope, are still friends. I work with her. She's so good at everything, what's not to like?"

"I don't see her very often. She's busy with Steve, no doubt," said Jill, "who must sit around thinking of things to do with her to keep her interest. That's what I think, and good for them. Why not? He surely moved to Richland fast. An instant marriage, with no second thoughts, sure of every moment. I'm glad you invited us here. We might never have gotten the chance to talk to them, even though we're right there in the same town. I guess they're both just too busy."

"Our own lives attest to it," Tom said. "Things get busy."

"Would you folks have something to drink, Mrs. Burgess?" a hostess asked, dressed in gray starched cotton with a white collar and apron, prim as an Asian stewardess.

"Coffee, skim milk and sugar, please," Jill replied.

"Black with Jack Daniel's," said Tom.

"Pretty brave this early," Kristi said. "I'll just have water, thanks. Out of the tap, with a little ice."

"The drink's to make me fit for the day, or at least bearable to be around. Ow."

"He's doctoring himself again, Kristi."

"*Cogito*, Kristi. Sometimes I'm the error in the equation. *Ergo sum.*"

"You're being a sophomore, Tom."

"Let's let that be our secret, okay? I wish I could be that fresh of thought again."

"What's secret about being a sophomore?" Kristi asked.

"That's when we left our parents to become human beings," Tom said. "When I did, anyway. Beginning the existential journey one more time."

"But things had gone on a long time," said Jill. "Things don't get undone. Afterward, the ambivalence, you know, is sometimes like a cut on the foot. Sometimes it is healed, then it isn't. Sometimes when another person is around, it isn't. That used to be when thoughts of Andrea would appear in Tom. Now it's because she's walking up the trail. Right, Tom?"

"It becomes a lie when it is not a secret. It is purely a cut."

"It belongs to both of us."

"Just mine. My cut."

"Stop feeling so alone and sorry for yourself. You're a morbid grandpa. I still love you, as much as ever and for all we've been through."

"Yup. My cut."

"So you see, Kristi," Jill said, "we're stuck together. Tom can't even have a decent affair without me."

"I can't even have one with *you*, but I keep trying. We're definitely us, no doubt about that."

"Here comes your toddy. Time for bed. What if Daddy ever knew?"

"My cut."

"You two shouldn't fight in public," Kristi said. "It makes people nervous."

"Sorry. It's the only place we can fight. He just shuts up otherwise. We need the exchange."

"We're all so quiet, Kristi."

"Why fight?" she replied.

"SOMETIMES WE WANT an adventure without consequences," Tom said. "Or seem to. Or consequences without adventure. We all have some of each but not much. We only know each other when a branch breaks or a heart does. Like in Dante. Just my view from up too close. It's the only way we can find out anything about each other that we don't already know, this far along in our relationship. Isn't it important to know each other better than we do? Taking risks for insights?"

"All secrets aside. Never mind him, Kristi. I love him but you don't have to and couldn't possibly anyway, at least not the way I do. Thank you for being our friend and inviting us here. We live so far apart, yet you still keep helping us, and I'm so glad I know you."

"I fear I create new difficulties sometimes," Kristi replied, "though I never intend to, I think. I make them for me, too, without meaning to. I used to know everything."

"We have too many secrets," Tom said, "and sometimes maybe too few to always know what to say or do, even if you live one of the Christian or Buddhist modes of being or Muslim or pragmatic or existential or what the television wants. Or some other program. Usually we fumble around a lot in the drama and become puppets to our own secret monologue, or define ourselves by struggling against that, or all of the above. That's me. But you're the psychologist, Kristi. I just do two numbers: zero and one. But lots of times."

"You're a computer scientist, one of the best. I just make sure the rooms are ready at the lodge."

"Everybody wants to have a mountain lodge," Jill said. "I wish we owned one. Don't you love being able to be here all the time? You're always so busy, though."

"To be honest," Kristi replied, "I've asked myself many times why on earth we ever came here. Try bitter winters. Try no business, try nothing but being here. We came here initially because we were disgraced, you know, and this place would take us in and give us a living. This was the place to rebalance ourselves in our own eyes, at least. But it worked."

SHE STOOD up to attend to the fire in the hearth. She pulled open the fire screen by its brass knob and chain, then rearranged the logs with an oversize poker from a set with a rearing grizzly bear handle. The fire spat, flames and sparks reaching out of sight up the chimney. She returned, fluffed the pillow behind her, and sat, one leg bent, the ankle beneath the other leg.

"What a thought," she continued. "It actually was all we could find at the time—a place to stay, away from other eyes, that would provide us rest, something to eat and something to learn, the basics of a new life. We were young, and our inner lives had been gutted. We could scarcely stand each other, and scarcely stand to be apart. This is where the world stuck us and gave us back our lives."

"We all love coming here," Jill said. "Right, Tom?"

"Here I escape everything grim that has ever happened to us that darkens our memories," Tom said. "Escape into reality, as I heard it."

"The present moment here and the next demand my care," Kristi said. "My acts are my responsibility, no avoidance. And when I go back to my memories, most everything is still there, just like going back to Richland. Then I wonder if memories change, the way a town does, and how much of my memories are false memories now, or which ones are just more vivid because I somehow thought or felt they should be, or because they had kindly associations. They were something against disappearing contexts, when little else availed.

"Still, I'm glad I don't remember everything. What a lot of clutter. Imagine every dish you've ever washed, stuck there in your mind. I'll take my own sweet story line, minus a few hard times and folded sheets. Keep the hard times and add some people like you, and you still have a rich life. Even though we're not fully who we think we are or show ourselves to be."

"You mean to other people or to ourselves?" Jill asked.

"We think things matter so much," Tom interjected. "Perhaps they do, but never as we think they should. The future is usually so much the same when it arrives. But never entirely the same. Sometimes it blows apart for a moment or holds out something that changes everything else. The computer gets invented step by human step, and then in less than a lifetime makes possible the types and apps of our millions of computers, our own and comprehendable version of the universe after the Big Bang. No need to say what else because we have all seen it.

"Some of us still look after our predictions. Obsessions. That's me, it seems. We come so close to death sometimes, without a thought. A passing car, something at work. I snuggle up to it every day, a 'gaunt man.' And you?

"Like right now the pain is shifting up my leg. Let me talk. No complaints. I don't think it's the Irish coffee. I think it's something has invaded my foot or clotted itself up and is on its way to get the rest of me. Blink me out. Just happenstance. Something else with consequences. Nothing new about a world of my own making. Where's the sense in this? I'm not evil, only a mere fool. I don't bother God with prayer just because I want or need something, as do the billions. Perhaps God is everything. The first moment. The last. Hands are opening one last time for me. Us?

"You got a doctor in this town?"

*　　　*　　　*

"I WANTED to come find you but couldn't because Jill would have been left alone," Kristi said to Burge. He was following Andrea and Steve in through the front doors of the Sawtooth Lodge in an aura of fresh cold air after their long hike.

"Something bad has happened to Tom," she said.

She said, "I was going to call the doctor so Tom could go

see him about his leg, but I had to call for him to come here instead. Tom just passed out sitting in front of the fire—talking to us. We were just sitting there talking. He never finished what he was saying. He probably had a blood clot and it broke loose, the doctor said, like a runaway truck. There was nothing that could be done about it. Tom's dead. The doctor closed Tom's eyes. We tried to do what we could.

"I can't reach Jill. She won't come out of her room and locked herself in with the night latch. She pushed herself away from me and ran out of my arms. She said she hated me. Us all. I'm crushed. I can't think of anything to do."

"Someone knows what to do better than I do," Burge said. "What would you do, Andrea?"

"Leave a message on her cell phone," Andrea replied, "and slide a note under her door telling her . . . we're here for her when she feels ready to be with us. Speak with us. Or maybe that you're here for her, and want to help is better, Kristi. What would you do, Steve? I know how she meant it, but she said she loved you."

"Yes. Be accessible, not intrusive. Knock quietly, then come away. Would she hurt herself, do you think?"

"I don't know," Kristi said. "She seemed so resilient, in her own quiet way. What if she really does hate us? Shouldn't you be the one to talk to her, Steve? She scarcely knows you. She can't possibly hate you so much."

"I had to deal with suicide attempts in my work too often. But it may just be grief and her need to be alone with it. People are different and respond differently, but seem to share patterns of grief. Denial, then anger. It's death she hates, not us.

"You can imagine what a shock it must be. I'm shocked, and I didn't know Tom well at all. Andrea's right. Better not to be intrusive. Just let her know we are her friends. She has our help and love when she wants it. Needs it.

"She'll have to call the rest of her family. Perhaps we can help if she wants us to. Perhaps you should be ready to do that, Kristi."

"I will be. Her mother is very old. I can talk with Angie, though, Steve. Perhaps she'll want to be the one to tell her grandmother if Jill is unable to."

"If it has been a while," Steve said, with the passing of time and shared silence. "You can probably tap at her door again. There are also the arrangements. You should be thinking about helping her with them, but don't press them on her. I don't know what you do in these mountains when anybody dies. I suppose someone has in the past. So you'll have to find out about that. Maybe the doctor can help you."

"He tried to but Jill would hear nothing of it," Kristi said. "He said to call, as if I should understand."

"His father delivered me, Steve," Andrea said. "And fixed my arm. I don't know where our time went. It seemed so slow when I was a girl. He was younger than I was in school, and he was so right with the world, the doctor's kid with curls of red hair and freckles, laughing. I haven't seen him for so long. It's different now than I imagined it would be. The world has probably taken his smile away. He'll help you, though, Kristi."

"Why don't you be my intermediary, Andrea? You'll have a chance to say hello."

"I don't think he knows me now. I was just one of the older kids, a miner's, like the rest, with not much to say to a doctor's young boy. I'll call if you'd like. Maybe I can be of some use to Jill that way. I'll let you know what he says. You understand, don't you? I'm feeling as if I shouldn't be here.

"Now all Tom's a secret."

EPILOGUE

Epilogue

BURGESS AND KRISTI turned to get back on the aluminum and sky blue transport bus carrying people who resembled them—older folks, retirees. Alongside the bus, a tall chain-link fence surrounded an immense open trench several stories deep, dug into an ice-age lake bed plateau on the arid steppes 70 miles east of the Cascade Mountains in Washington State.

Inside the excavation were six dozen tan cylinders, each the size of a Manhattan rooftop water tank and aligned in pairs, some vertical, most horizontal. Each contained a nuclear power reactor. They occupied two-thirds of the rocky site back-to-front and side-to-side. They looked new but their contents were not. More reactors like them were to come, cut from decommissioned submarines and aircraft carriers, to be buried in this protected area. Atomland, U.S.A.

Somber people filled the bus seats. Most of them once worked in the shutdown nuclear reactors and processing plants. The visitors had been more animated at stops at the small ghost towns alongside the Columbia, where some had had ancestral homes once, the land long ago condemned for worksites for the 55,000 construction workers at peak who built the world's first production nuclear reactors and processing plants.

This was the top-secret Manhattan Project—a piece of it. Workers constructed it without knowing what they were constructing, but this was a high wartime priority.

"YOU'VE BEEN given the Hanford story, the Hanford side of things," the retired nuclear engineer tour guide said through an oval black plastic microphone from the front of the bus, riding backward, Mercury hairless and smiling. Kristi and Burge sat facing him in artificial leather bus seats three rows back.

"The shutdown was an enormous task," the guide went on. "I recall the days and months it took just to destroy the years of paperwork and data. It had filled vast rooms when the plant was running.

"You've also probably heard of the 'down-winders,' and of all their efforts to get compensation. Well, they are wrong. This has always been one of the safest places in America to work. People are safer here than in their own houses," he said, glancing at his feet.

"Sure," a voice behind the Burgesses replied, just above a whisper. "If somebody up above wanted it, by God it was going to happen. Just like closing this place."

"Just like Hanford."

WHO ARE all these people? Burgess wondered. *They spent their entire lives here. I might have. We two are long forgotten, as if nothing had happened, as if we'd never even been here. Once for us it was almost all there was.*

The local headlines after the war read, "Peace! Our Bomb Clinched It! Japs Surrender. Plant Will Not Close." It didn't close through all the Cold War years. Nine big reactors and many chemical processing plants, some with immense encased concrete canyons to contain radiation, came on line in succession and produced. They outlived their functioning and were shut down for newer technology, onward through the decades. Closing such facilities safely was an enormously complicated matter.

That's where Burgess started out, with REDOX closing, PUREX on line, when he found Kristi. Nuclear weapons worldwide were to number over 100,000, and America's intercontinental missile warheads were over 7,000, and couldn't all be maintained, with little need, and so were reduced step by step in the years following the Cold War.

A new possible use for the atom came up after the century's turn—bunker busters for going after new and deeply buried threats to America. There was the "War President." Thoughts of smaller tactical nuclear weapons than what had been stockpiled lit hopes of renewal of the plant and the recovery of disappearing expertise. Weapons had to be updated and their operation assured. Putin announced Russia's next generation of weapons, even as the breakup of the Soviet Union was freeing nuclear materials for threats from other lands. Dr. A. Q. Kahn of Pakistan sold his stolen secrets, was made a hero, and then still others had the bomb. There was the Ukraine, then the headlines, "U.S. Ramping Up Major Renewal in Nuclear Arms."

KRISTI TOLD Burgess, "At least Hanford didn't command our whole lives. Richland is such a beautiful place—like memories from my first-grade reader. And more Ph.D.s per capita than most anywhere on earth. So much here is new now. Bad as it's thought to be, it keeps getting better."

"Hanford is still the most polluted place in America," Burgess said. "It will take thousands of workers decades to clean it up, if it's even possible. It's just that it's out here, hidden, where it's easy to forget.

"We were the lucky ones to have left back then, Kristi, even with the regrets."

"My father's people lived along the stretch of river I had a chance to see for the first time today. I'll always remember what we saw across the Columbia—a land left much as it was when this was their natural home—along the river, white bluffs above many trees, living and dead but still standing as nature witnessed them, with eagles and ospreys soaring. There were salmon. My people's home, Burgess. A secret kept from us for the good of the nation is now part of our memories. At last, we've seen it, if only a glimpse. Life didn't let us stand there for all of our years on Earth."

"What if it had?" he asked, puzzled that she had been so quiet about it when they were standing on the site together.

"Would you still be you?" she replied.

"Who am I? I hopped on someone else's dream starting out and got thrown off. I didn't know the right secrets, I guess. I still don't. And all the catastrophe—Three Mile Island, Chernobyl and the USSR-classified others, Fukushima, each with its secrets and people acting or not acting, but both out of ignorance, and lives and promises gone forever. Some dream."

"What secrets would have saved us, Burge, and from what?" Kristi asked. "The dreamers must have been crazy then and even the sanest can't escape. Except for taking care, cleaning up, and managing waste, the Hanford Engineer Works is closed."

"This place will never close, will it?" he countered. "It'll be looked after far beyond our lifetimes, still local news while there still is local news, with the twisted lessons people try to make sense of from human memories.

"Then science will give us new visions beyond our eyes, with new tools, and we'll see and understand things new about the universe: first a few of us, as before, then more, and many will try to understand. If we can only make it that far, and keep on making it."

He listened to the drone of the bus. He looked at the sagebrush and thought of the cycles of ice-dammed lakes that could one day return to cover this place, and spill into great floods, and return in time to be sage and grasslands once again.

"This was only one nuclear site," he continued. "There are eight major others, each retooling, plus new bombers, subs and missiles, for over a trillion of the U.S. budget over the coming years. That was in *The Times,* along with the usual reasons. Secrets are still around for other countries to discover, buy or steal. So they can steal people's lives, or make the silent threats that possessing the secrets can mean. So more and more gets reclassi-fied that had been set free after the first Cold War."

"Sh-h. People are listening, Oldtimer," Kristi said. "You do talk on, you know."

"Okay, Kristi, I'll shut up now. I don't wear a halo, anyway. It's *our* book of secrets. The latest news from forever."

T HE BUS drove on, carrying its bearers of thousands of memories, as if spun from the hum of bus wheels passing year after year over the shrub steppes, the lakebed, the desert, the way toward home. This was continuous with the life of Kristi's par-ents for most of their years on Earth, to become with others but a half-whisper of time.

"I didn't think to tell you this, Burge. Just before I woke up this morning, I saw a lotus in a dream. Really. It was standing above the water—white petals opening to early daylight, and showing a center like its own spot of sun. As if to prove ev-erything and heal everything, its own creation. I couldn't have reached it, except that I was dreaming it into being. I wished we could have had that as an experience in common, you and I. But we're just folks in need of our individual dreams—secret minutes something in us makes that no one else can ever witness.

"The lotus filled my sight and then vanished. Nothing. I couldn't call it back.

"But I wasn't dreaming when I saw your face."

With My Thanks

Sissela Bok's quotation, p. 1, is from *Secrets: On the Ethics of Concealment and Revelation* (New York, Pantheon Books, 1982), p. 281. The quotations from the *Bhagavadgita x. 38* are two translations, by Kees W. Bolle and C. Wilkins, of the same line.

The song reference, p. 15, is to the Beatles' *Sgt. Pepper's Lonely Hearts Club Band.*

I am indebted to a government application, the Department of Energy, Richland Operations Office's *National Register of Historic Places Multiple Property Documentation,* especially for two history sections: 3."Ethnographic/Contact Period of the Hanford Site,Washington (Lewis and Clark 1805—Hanford Engineer Works 1943)" by J.C. Bard with the assistance of R. McClintock, and 4."Euro-American Resettlement of the Hanford Site,Washington (Lewis and Clark 1805—Hanford Engineer Works 1943)" by J.C. Bard and J.B. Cox with the assistance of R. McClintock. (See www.hanford.gov)

The history of the Atomic Age is considered in four books by Richard Rhodes, *Arsenals of Folly, Dark Sun, The Making of the Atomic Bomb,* and *Twilight of the Bombs: Recent Challenges, New Dangers, and the Prospects for a World Without Nuclear Weapons.* Also see Craig Nelson, *The Age of Radiance: The Epic Rise and Dramatic Fall of the Atomic Era.* Earlier works include: Kai Bird and Martin J. Sherman, *American Prometheus: The Triumph and Tragedy of J. Robert Oppenheimer;* Samuel Glasstone, ed., *The Effects of Nuclear Weapons;* Richard L. Garwin and Georges Charpak, *Megawatts and Megatons;* Hugh Gusterson, *Nuclear Rites* and *People of the Bomb;* Robert Jungk, *Brighter than a Thousand Suns,* and James Thackara, *America's Children.*

The Times, p. 386, is *The New York Times* via NYTimes.com, with a news story September 21 and editorial, "Backsliding on Nuclear Promises," September 22, 2014.

Cover photo #3: *Nagasakibomb* by Charles Levy. The picture was taken by Charles Levy from one of the B-29 Superfortresses used in the attack.—http://www.archives.gov/research/military/ww2/photos/images/ww2-163.jpg National Archives image (208-N-43888). Licensed under Public Domain via Wikimedia Commons - http://commons.wikimedia.org/wiki/File:Nagasakibomb.jpg#mediaviewer/File: Nagasakibomb.jpg

Cover Photo #5: *Milky Way Night Sky Black Rock Desert Nevada* by Steve Jurvetson—Flickr. Licensed under Creative Commons Attribution 2.0 via Wikimedia Commons - http://commons.wikimedia.org/wiki/File:Milky_Way_Night_Sky_Black_Rock_Desert_Nevada.jpg#mediaviewer/File:Milky_Way_Night_Sky_Black_Rock_Desert_ Nevada.jpg